MOB MEN
ON THE MAKE

Edited By

ERIC SUMMERS

Herndon, VA

Published in the United States by STARbooks Press

PO Box 711612, Herndon, VA 20171

Many thanks to graphic artist John Nail for the cover design. Mr. Nail may be reached at: tojonail@bellsouth.net.

Printed in the United States

Herndon, VA

STARbooks Press Titles by Eric Summers

Muscle Worshipers

Love in a Lock-Up

Unmasked – Erotic Tales of Gay Superheroes

Don't Ask, Don't Tie Me Up

Ride Me Cowboy

Service with a Smile

Never Enough – The Lost Writings of John Patrick

Unmasked II: More Erotic Tales of Gay Superheroes

Can't Get Enough – More Erotica Written by John Patrick

Unwrapped: Erotic Holiday Tales

Teammates

Big Holiday Packages

Rock & Roll Over

Who's Your Daddy?

Mob Men on the Make

Contents

LUCKY STIFF
By J.S. Cook

The phone woke him late in the afternoon, shrilling just inches from his ear and jarring him from an unsettling dream of night and endless city streets. He rolled over, a handsome, stocky young man in silk pajamas, and grabbed the phone just before the ringing stopped. "What?" Nino Armondo Bartolemeo Moretti had a flat, rather nasal voice – a New York voice, born on the Lower East Side among tenements and corner stores, cigars and street cars and laundry hanging from the fire escapes and iron balconies of innumerable overcrowded, low-rent apartment buildings.

"Hey, Nino, you up?" His brother Tony was younger by three years but infinitely simpler in temperament and disposition, the stereotypical goon of a thousand afternoon picture shows, a thing of meat and muscle. His one positive attribute was his ability to back Nino to the wall, no matter what. "It's Ma. She ain't so good."

"Whatta ya mean? She was fine the last time I seen her." He grabbed the alarm clock and held it close to his eyes; like the rest of the Moretti family, Nino was slightly near-sighted, a fact he refused to admit. At thirty-eight, he was quickly approaching the age when spectacles would be necessary for any ordinary man. Not Nino, though – not The Little Prince.

"The doctor says it won't be long. Maybe you better come home, Nino. Come and see her before it's too late."

A click and the line went dead. Nino lay back for a minute, screwing his fists into his eyes. What day was it? Yeah, Saturday ... or maybe Sunday, something like that. If he were still living at home, he'd have been up for hours, going to Mass with Tony and his mother, but Nino didn't do that anymore. He hadn't been inside a church since Louie the Goat was bumped off, and then only so the other mugs could see him and know who was supposed to get the credit. The news that The Little Prince had shown up at the funeral lit up the Lower East Side for weeks. It took a lot of guts to stand there in that church, but that was Nino.

He nudged the palooka beside him with his elbow, a compact, blue-eyed youth with a mop of ginger hair. "Hey you. Get up."

1

"Awww, Nino, come on ..." The other man winked at him. "You said last night we was for keeps."

"Ain't nothing for keeps around here, mug." Nino stuck one foot in his back and shoved. "Go on! Get out!"

The young man made a face. "You don't love me no more?"

"I never loved ya to begin with. Get your clothes on." Nino rolled onto his back and contemplated the ceiling while the palooka got dressed. "What's your name?" he asked. Somehow they'd never gotten around to names. Nino had picked him up in a club just after midnight and spent five minutes slipping him the tongue and a C-note before inviting the boy home on impulse. It wasn't something he usually did. For reasons of personal safety, Nino preferred to take his pleasures elsewhere. It wasn't good business to take somebody home. You never knew who was working for whom and what kind of heat they were packing. Marco Dinetti got it the same way, stabbed in the eye by some Village gunsel working for Lili Wacker's mob. By the time his boys found him, he'd been dead a week and blue flies had set up housekeeping in his skull.

"Don't you remember?" Nino's latest conquest pouted. "It's Charlie." He slipped into his coat. "Am I gonna see you again, Nino?"

"Don't lay no bets on it ... wait a minute." Nino reached for his wallet and gave the guy another C-note. "Here." He waved as the other man went out the door. "Go as far as that'll take ya, mug."

Nino went into the bathroom and ran the shower hot. There had been a lot of drinking the night before and a lot of whoopee, and he felt like half the Brooklyn Navy Yard was rattling around inside his head and banging on his brains in two-four time. He stripped off his pajamas and stood under the shower for twenty minutes, then soaped up good, shaved away the shadow of his dark beard, and rinsed off cold. Once the coffee got going, he swallowed a cup with two aspirins and dressed: dark suit, dark tie, black shoes. He slipped a sleek black handgun into his shoulder holster and checked the knot of his tie in the mirror.

He looked like hell.

# # # # #

Tony was waiting when Nino arrived with Danny Murphy. Danny and Nino had grown up together, stealing from freight cars and chasing each other through the streets, raising Cain wherever they could. Danny, an amateur boxer of some note, had been known to help Nino out of a scrape or two in his time. Murphy wasn't very big, but was really handy with his fists – maybe too handy. Some guys whispered that Danny Murphy was crazy, trying to get himself killed, starting fights with anybody who came near him and taking down guys twice his size, just for something to do. Danny grew up just as poor as Nino, the youngest of fifteen loud, red-headed kids in a tiny apartment on the Lower East Side, right above a fruit store. Danny even walked like a guy spoiling for a fight, balanced on the balls of his feet with his fists sorta swinging by his sides, ready to deck somebody in the kisser. Danny's big blue eyes and gentle mouth belonged on a matinee idol, but anybody who thought Danny Murphy was soft was a real dumbbell.

"How's it goin', Tony?" Danny faked a punch at Tony's jaw.

"Yeah, keep them flippers where I can see 'em, mick." Tony stepped back and crashed into the cupboard. Put one foot wrong in Nino's Ma's old place, and the whole joint shuddered like a hophead on a Saturday night.

"You wanna keep the noise down?" Nino stepped in between them. "Ma's sick, okay? Or ain't I being clear enough for you two mugs?" He looked as if he'd been run down by a milk wagon: his face was pouchy, with dark circles under his eyes and multiple small cuts in his chin where his razor had clearly missed the mark. The aspirin had hardly made a dent in the headache, which was pounding away at the back of Nino's head.

"Sorry, Nino, I didn't mean nothing." Danny shrugged his hands back down where they belonged. "No disrespect to your ma, you know me."

"Yeah, I know you." Nino found some coffee in the usual place and dug the percolator out from under the sink. It was pretty dusty, but so was everything else. "Hey, how long has Ma been under the weather?" He glared at Tony. "You don't call me; you don't get no word to me? Whatta ya think this is, huh?" The anger was there inside of him, boiling just under the surface of his skin, and the blood beat in the back of his eyes and in his fingertips.

"Don't be like that, Nino." Tony shrugged like the big gorilla he was, and searched for something meaningful to say. "You know I didn't mean nothing. I was talking to Big Jake and Arnie the Dope and nobody knew where you was."

"Big Jake?" Nino sneered at him; it did interesting things to his face. "Arnie the Dope? You know where to find me. You just didn't have the guts ..."

3

"You go on, Nino." Danny took the percolator out of his hands and ran it under the tap. "I'll make some coffee. You go on in." He nodded toward the back bedroom. "It's okay. I can handle this big mug. He gives me any trouble I'll put him out like a light bulb."

The room was dark, all the window curtains drawn. Nino's mother was a faint figure lying in her bed, pale and silent. There was a queer sort of smell in the room, like blood and vomit mixed; he tried to hold his breath and not breathe it in too much. Nino had no stomach for that sort of thing. "Ma? It's me, Nino."

"Nino?" Her voice still sounded the same as it always had: melodic and a little bit tired. "Come here, *caro*. Let me see you."

It was bad. There were bandages on her, bandages under her nightdress, pus and blood and the smell that permeated everything. "Right here, Ma. I'm right here." He sat on the side of her bed and embraced her, and tried not to cry. It was no good to cry. Ma had been sick like this for months and never told anybody; even though Nino had money for the doctor, she wouldn't go, wouldn't take anything from him.

Maybe Ma don't want your blood money. Tony's take on the whole thing was not exactly comforting.

It ain't blood money. I earned this with my own two hands, see.

Yeah, we all know how you earn your money, Nino.

You ain't never been too proud to take it.

"I want you to be good boys, okay?" She reached for him, held his wrist. "You and Tony look after each other, huh?"

"Aw, Ma, don't be talking like that. You're gonna be just fine. I'll get a different doctor. Doc Yoplanski don't know nothing. He ain't so smart." His bottom lip trembled; he struggled not to cry. It was no good to cry, not now. Now, it was too late.

She held on to his wrist. "Be good to your brother. Tony ain't got your smarts; you know that. Look after him."

His face suffused with blood, Nino stood up. "I gotta go."

He walked right out, past Tony and the coffee pot, right out into the broad daylight, right out onto Broome Street as if he was touched in the head and didn't stop until Danny's hand fell on his shoulder.

"Don't be coming down all hard on Tony," was what he said. "You know he ain't ..." He took a breath. "You know he don't like lookin' for you in them places."

"She ain't good, Danny." Nino sat down on the stoop and laid his pounding head in his hands. "She ain't so good."

"We'll get a good doctor for her, you and me. We'll get a great doctor, and he'll get her fixed up in no time, huh? That's what we'll do, me and you. We'll do that, Nino. We can do that, can't we?"

But they couldn't. Nino was in Dutch but good. And in a week or two, she was gone: cancer. He would never forget that smell, that blood-and-vomit smell that was in her room the day he went to see her. And at the funeral, carrying his mother's coffin, he thought about his old man and how he beat on her almost every day, beat on her, and beat his brother Ray, beat him till he died, and it did something to Nino, killed something inside of him. There was no point in loving anything or anybody; in the end, it didn't matter a damn. In the end, it all melted away no matter what you did to try and save it.

"Ahhhh, Sammy, how's tricks?" Nino Moretti, resplendent in a handsome cutaway coat, reached past Danny to shake Sam the Butcher's meaty hand. "Have a cigar?" Nino's thick, wavy black hair was combed back over his head, and glistened with its own cold, blue light. His dark eyes, twin pools of black water, surveyed the room and its occupants dismissively. He wore a diamond pinky ring on his left hand, while his right held fast to a thick cigar; an emerald and diamond stickpin gleamed from the depths of his silk cravat. Even the most hostile of Nino's enemies – and there were plenty – would have to concede him his sense of style; Nino was easily the best-dressed man there.

"Thanks, Nino, that's white of ya." Sam leaned in while Nino offered him a light, nodded at Danny. "Big crowd come to see Frank, huh? Everybody loves Frank." Sam was as broad as he was tall, with a huge, barrel chest and a luxuriant growth of thick, black hair on his knuckles and in his nostrils. His wide shoulders made him look as if he had no neck, which was Sam's other nickname, "No-Neck."

"Yeahhhh." Nino, contemptuous, drawled the word out to its longest possible extension. "That what he's been telling you boys lately?"

Sam bristled. "Now look here, Nino ..."

5

"Aw, stick it in your eye!" Nino puffed on his cigar, his wide mouth distorted by a sneer. "Big Frank don't frighten me! He couldn't frighten a stable full of choirboys, and you know it!"

"It ain't good business to be talking that way, Nino," Sam said. "You better watch what you're sayin'. Something might happen to ya."

"Like what?" Danny stepped sideways a little, so that he was between Nino and Sam. "Don't be getting ideas, Sammy. Your big head might burst." The Irishman grinned, a flash of white teeth. "Big Frank wouldn't like the mess."

"That ain't funny," Sam huffed.

Danny hunched up his shoulders and stuck out his head. "Dat ain't funny," he mimicked. "You're dazzling me with your wit, here."

"Yeah, well ..." Sam eyed them both. "Youse guys better watch it." He turned away and headed toward the buffet table where the caterers had laid out a diverse sampling of cold meats, cheeses, smoked fish and the like.

Danny waved him off. "Aw, watch your mother."

"You trying to get us kicked out or something?" Nino glared at Danny, who appeared to be enjoying his own joke far too much. "Don't be riding him. We're here to keep an eye on things, maybe do a little business." He looked Danny up and down. Like Nino, Danny was dressed to the nines, but where Nino favored dark clothing, Danny's outfit was a pale dove grey with a dark tie and shoes buffed to a blinding shine. His hair was combed back from his temples in waves, and he'd even had a manicure. "And keep away from Big Frank's dames. I don't want you getting dizzy with some jane, see?"

"You worry too much." Danny gazed around the room. "Here comes Big Frank. I'm so excited I think I might wet myself."

Nino stubbed out his cigar in a potted plant. "He's even fatter than he was last week," he said. "It's a wonder his heart's still beating. Hey, maybe ..."

They're writing songs of love, but not for me

A lucky star's above, but not for me ...

Nino couldn't breathe.

Eyes ... pale blue eyes ... that face ... that long-limbed angel, moving effortlessly in a too-big suit, his body drifting ... in the space between heartbeats, something slammed into Nino's chest like a freight train. Imagine making it with a guy like that ... hafta be some kind of lucky stiff ...

Danny's face swam into his vision. "You okay?" He followed Nino's gaze, trying to understand what it was his friend had seen. "You look like you seen a ghost. You sick or something?"

"Who's that?" It came out as a tortured croak. He couldn't take his eyes off the young man by Big Frank's side. If he did, he would disappear, and Nino would never find him again, not ever, and that would be ... he'd die. He'd just – no, better not to think about it. "That kid with Big Frank. Who is he?"

"Aw, that's Stan the Stupe. He's Big Frank's gunsel, you know." Danny shrugged. "So I hear. Some hick country boy. He's been with Big Frank for four, five years now. I'm surprised you ain't seen him before."

"Don't you think I'd remember?" Nino snapped. His heart was slamming into his ribcage. "If I'd seen him, I'd remember him. You think I'm stupid?"

"Yeah, I do," Danny said. "Cuz you're mouthing off to me, and you seem to forget I ain't one of these regular dopes that you can push around."

"What's his name?" Nino whispered.

"Uh ... Stanley Zadwa – something Polish, I dunno." Danny grinned. "You like him? When you take over Big Frank's territory, maybe the kid'll come over to your bed."

Nino turned on him savagely. "That ain't funny! Don't you never let me hear you say nothing like that, never no more, you hear?"

Danny held up his hands in mock-surrender. "Okay, I'm jake. Sorry I said anything."

The kid and Big Frank were standing by the buffet table, the kid staring at the food hungrily. Big Frank was talking to Rick and Blackie, two of his Brooklyn guys. They ran a backroom distillery for Frank's organization and took a little off the top for themselves. Someday they'd get caught, and Big Frank would have somebody take them for a ride, and they'd wash up on the Jersey Shore. As Nino watched, the young man edged around behind Big Frank and reached for one of the sandwich trays.

7

That did it. Big Frank whirled around and brought his fist down on the kid's arm. "What'd I tell you? Don't be eating when I'm doing business, okay? What's the matter with you?"

He was like a kicked dog, Nino thought – just like a kicked dog that nobody wanted, that nobody cared about or loved, just a poor dumb animal to be abused whenever Big Frank felt like it.

"I'm hungry." His voice was quiet, dignified, with a flat Midwestern twang. "I haven't eaten all day."

"You'll eat when I tell you to eat!" Big Frank's fist made contact with the point of Stanley's chin, throwing him backwards. The kid stumbled and cannoned into a row of chairs and slammed into the floor. He lay there stunned and raised a shaking hand to his bloodied mouth.

Nino's blood roared in his ears. "That rotten bastard!" He started forward but was momentarily stayed by Danny.

"Nino, it ain't none of your business, okay?" Danny held Nino by the upper arms, shook him gently. "He's Big Frank's punk. He ain't your problem."

Nino shrugged him off. "Let go of me!" He watched himself, as if from somewhere outside his body; he charged forward, got between Big Frank and the kid.

The crowd parted for him, re-formed a tight little circle around him and Frank. "What's your problem, little man?"

"Don't hit that kid again." Nino slipped one hand into his coat, fingers sliding comfortably into a set of brass knuckles. "Ain't none of us packing a rod in here tonight, but you touch that kid again, and I'll beat you to death."

The room was still and quiet, hushed like a wake. Nino put a hand on Stanley's shoulder and eased him around gently and walked him out to the waiting car.

# # # # #

"I just would like to know one thing," Stanley Zadwadski's pale eyes gleamed in the dark. *Goddammit*, Nino thought, *he's too goddamn beautiful. Nothing should be that beautiful ... nothing that beautiful could survive, not in this world anyway ...*

"What?" Nino deliberately sat apart from him to give the kid a little breathing room. "What is it?"

"Why me? I'm nobody. I haven't done anything to you. Why do you want to kill me?"

"Kill you?" Of course – the kid thought they were taking him for a ride! Nino laughed gently. This kid was delicate. Not yellow – he had plenty of guts. Nino could see that right away. But delicate in that God only knew what Big Frank had been doing to him for the past however many years. He'd been kicked around, had horrible things done to him ... "You got me all wrong," Nino said. "I'm taking you away from Big Frank for good. He ain't never gonna hurt you no more, see."

The gunsel – Stanley – stared at him. "But he'll kill you," he whispered. He turned around in his seat, glanced back at the club, now vanishing swiftly into darkness behind him. "You gotta let me out! Big Frank will kill you for this! I can't be part of that, I can't let you ..."

Nino laid a hand on his shoulder, pressed him back into his seat. "Let us worry about Big Frank. Okay?"

"I don't know who you are," Stanley said. He was shivering, probably from cold but more likely from fear. "I left my hat in the club. I haven't got another hat." His mouth was still bleeding, but it had slowed to a trickle. A dark bruise stained the pale skin of his face.

"I'll get you another hat. I'll get you all the hats you want, okay?" Nino had a sudden, inexplicable urge to cry. "It's okay. You can have anything you want." He forced himself to breathe; it felt like a sob. "Anything. Anything you want."

Stanley straightened his back against the seat. "Why should you want to help me?" he asked. "I'm not your problem."

"Big Frank ain't no friend of mine, see." Nino lit a cigarette, offered them to Stanley, who shook his head. "I see him beating on you; I think it's good business to step in and say something about it."

"Do a lot of that, do you?" Stanley looked him up and down – slowly, taking his time, his gaze sliding over Nino's clothes, his jewelry, his face. "Saying things about things?"

"Yeah," Nino replied. "Yeah, I guess I do. But you can relax now, kid. I rescued you." He sat back and puffed on his cigarette. He couldn't figure this one out.

9

"What makes you think I wanted to be rescued?" Stanley asked. "And I'm not a kid. I'm twenty-eight."

Nino frowned. "Say, kid, you screwy or something? Why wouldn't you want to be rescued? You like Big Frank beating on you?"

"I didn't say that." Stanley slumped back into the shadows. "I didn't say anything at all."

# # # # #

It went on that way for quite a while, until eventually Stanley settled down, began to relax around Nino a bit. Nino set him up in his apartment, gave Stanley privacy, his own bedroom, a space where he could stretch out, be himself. He never asked for anything, and Stanley never offered. If Nino's motives were purely carnal; Stanley had yet to see it demonstrated. Nino had never laid a hand on him. This depressed Stanley just a little bit and baffled him. He'd heard about The Little Prince, about his peccadilloes and his appetites, and his perverse desires. There were plenty of rumors, and Stanley had heard them all. He wondered when the thin veneer of Nino's kindness would crack, revealing what lay beneath.

When Stanley put his key in the door one evening, he was greeted with almost complete darkness, and Nino in his shirtsleeves, lighting a barrage of candles. "Hey, baby, did you have a good day?"

"What's all this?" Stanley hung up his coat and hat, slipped out of his jacket. "Somebody's birthday?" It was unusual, to say the least, to see Nino like this. Maybe this was just a prelude, and Nino was softening him up.

"No, I just felt like splashing out," Nino said. "Figured it was time we had a little treat. I called up Marcino's and got Eddie to do us up a meal in fine style. Yeah." He pulled out a chair. "Sit down – are you hungry?"

"Starving," Stanley said. The food smelled delicious. He wondered if it would be bad manners to roll up his sleeves: he wanted to dive into dinner and eat his way to the bottom. Nino was just as hungry as he was, and it was a while before their respective appetites were sated enough to allow conversation.

Nino sat back in his chair. "If I die tonight, God forbid, I'll die happy after such a meal." He picked up his wine glass and motioned to Stanley. "Come on, let's go sit in the other room and put the radio on."

They sat for a while, talking in a desultory fashion of nothing in particular, while the late spring evening closed in around them. Nino sat on the sofa listening to the radio with his eyes closed; Stanley got up and went to sit next to him. He snuggled close to Nino's side when Nino put his arm around him, laid his head on Nino's shoulder. Nino stroked his face; Stanley leaned in and kissed Nino's mouth, gently. Nino returned the caress, deepening the kiss, his eager tongue slipping between Stanley's parted lips. *Danger*, his mind whispered. *This is dangerous. Don't get too involved.*

"I want to touch you," Stanley whispered, when next his mouth was free. "Can you take off your tie?"

"Sure, kid ..." Nino did, and unbuttoned his waistcoat and the top two buttons of his shirt. "That better?" He hissed through his teeth as Stanley slipped a hand inside his shirt, stroking his bare chest. "Aw, kid, you're killing me here ..."

Time dissolved into nothing; there was nothing in the world for Stanley except this: Nino's mouth on his, the scent of Nino's cologne, the heat of Nino's body. Their kisses became deeper, more torrid, with long bouts of tongue play and periods of unendurable bliss when Nino's talented mouth licked and sucked at Stanley's slender neck. He drew back, gazed at Nino with passion-weighted eyes and took hold of Nino's hand, pressed it against the bulge in his trousers.

"Oh, baby ..." Nino kissed him, licking and sucking at his top lip before taking the soft cushion of the lower between his teeth, nibbling it gently. Stanley whimpered, pushing into his hand, and Nino cooperated, rubbing him through his clothes. A pause and Nino's hand went away; Stanley felt his fly being opened and then ...

He groaned as Nino's hand closed over him, stroking him, handling him deftly, gently. He clung to Nino, shivering when Nino's thumb slipped over the head of his cock; sparks formed and burst behind his eyelids, and he pushed himself harder into Nino's hand. Harder and faster, driving himself forward, and Nino was with him, varying the speed and rhythm of his strokes, keeping him always on the ragged edge, near enough to coming to feel the first, tantalizing shudders of his orgasm. If Nino didn't let him come, he would die. He would die of pleasure, right here; he would shudder himself to pieces, he would ...

Sudden, shattering, brilliant, it ripped into him; it tore him to pieces and pulled him over the edge. He panted against Nino's neck, spilling himself into Nino's hand, groaning. He held Nino's wrist, held Nino's hand against his body as the aftershocks rippled through him, going out and out, obliterating him. It was too much; he'd die from this kind of pleasure, he would ...

He came to rest against Nino's chest, his head on Nino's shoulder. He lay for a long time like that, held in Nino's arms, safe, protected.

Nino lay half on and half off the sofa, holding Stanley in his arms, his body taut with unspent desire. He shifted slightly, adjusting his erection in his trousers, suppressing a groan as his silk boxers slid enticingly over the head of his cock. It wouldn't take much ... his fly was already undone, thanks to Stanley's wandering hands ... he was hard and aching, and it had been ages, ages since that sandy-haired palooka had come into his bed.

He slipped his own hand inside his trousers, hardly daring to breathe for fear he'd disturb Stanley sleeping beside him, and began to touch himself. Within five or six strokes he was coming hard, panting, forcing himself silent. When it was over, he lay very still in the dark, listening to Stanley's quiet breath. His heart thundered in his chest. *Don't get involved. Don't even bother. You should stick to dumb palookas, you know that.* But it was already too late for caution. Already, it was much too late for anything like that. Nino Moretti was gone but good.

He sighed, resting his head against the back of the sofa while Stanley dozed in his arms and a distant siren split the night, wavering and ghostly.

PAY-OFF
By Landon Dixon

"Know anything about that fur heist, Lemmy? At the Hurtzig warehouse?"

I could tell Shanahan was really concerned because usually his job was the last thing on his mind when I was sucking his dick.

"Nope," I gulped, popping the harness bull's beefy dong out of my sweet kisser. I licked my blowjob lips, wet-stroking the turgid beef, looking up at the copper's hard, handsome, worried face in the dim light of the alley off Front Street.

He glanced nervously around, taking time to buck as I played my paw over the soft spot on his male hard stuff. "See, normally I wouldn't ask you, Lemmy," he stated. "But that Hurtzig warehouse was controlled by the Bristol mob. So the Captain, you know, is really putting the heat on to find out who's responsible, where the furs are … at."

"Good 'ol Captain Pay-Off," I cracked, paraphrasing Captain Payton's real name. "So, you come to the man on the street not just for your usual pay-off, huh?"

Shanahan grinned, grunted, as I yanked his chain, tapped his beanbag. "Yeah, that's it, Lemmy. You know I don't mind you plying your trade on my beat, long as I get a piece of the action. And I know you ain't normally no snitch. But the Captain's blowing hot up everyone's ass 'cause he's feeling the heat from his bosses, see."

I saw. "You gonna crack down on me, Shanny?" I teased the gaping slit of the flatfoot's rod with my flicking pink tongue.

His knees buckled. He sunk his heavy red hands into my soft red hair. "Not me, Lemmy. The Captain. All I'm askin' is that you keep your eyes and ears open, see what you can pick up."

"And my mouth open, too, huh? See what I can pick up." I vacuumed his cap and half of his club-length back into my wanton wet mouth, stroked with my lips and tongue.

13

Shanahan bobbed his head like mine, thrust his hips. He pumped my maw like he'd just been pumping the rest of me, only with even less tact. He delved deep, and fast, churning my gullet. My throat widened to accommodate the married father of eight.

A drunk urinated on the sidewalk at the mouth of the alley. Someone screamed. Fists thudded against a muffled body. A shop window shattered.

But Officer Dwight Shanahan was way off-duty, over the line even for the dirtiest police force in the country. His pay-off was coming, I could tell, by the way the big galoot was wildly ramming my gob, clutching my ears and banging his balls off my chin.

I took it, didn't mind it one bit. The throbbing, churning feel, the heated, salty taste, the frenzied, succulent sounds, feed my manly cravings. Some guys pull a cork; with me it's cock, police-issue or paying customer.

I twisted Shanny's flapping balls into a knot, gave him gritty tooth-scrape on his shunting bone. And he blew his top, and his nuts, the open-air, back alley excitement too much for the man. He yelped and jumped, his dong surging hard as his nightstick in my sucking mouth. I bit down on his shaft, and he let me have it, full-barrel.

Semen sprayed into my mouth, poured down my throat. My recessive Adam's apple bobbed like a cork on the stormy, saltwater North Atlantic. As Shanahan spurted out his massive, steaming load into my hard-drinking mouth.

"Thanks again, Lemmy," he rasped, tucking himself back in and buttoning himself back up. "Anything else you can do to help would be really appreciated."

He slipped me a sawbuck, five more than my usual pay-off. Then he grabbed a quick kiss, getting a taste of his own sticky medicine, and lumbered off onto his beat.

I swirled and swallowed a nip of club soda from the flask I keep holstered on my hip then hit the streets myself.

It was the following night, around two in the dark, deserted a.m., when a Packard limo skidded up to the curb. Two goons spilled out, grabbed onto my wings before I could fly.

14

"Where'd you think you're goin', sweetheart?" one of the head-breakers, name of Brutus, growled garlic, looking me over with evident displeasure.

I was decked out in my college boy kit – checked sweater, plus-fours, knee-highs, loafers, bow tie and poor boy cap. Usually a big hit with the older crowd. But this audience was unappreciative.

"Yeah, cuttin' class again?" the other goon slurred, Tully was his name.

They lifted me up, tossed me into the back of the limo. I landed with a rich, leathery splash. Brutus crowded inside, up against me.

"What gives?" I squawked, like I didn't know.

"Boss wants to see you."

"Beats me why," Tully added, from behind the wheel.

They drove me over to the Milton Building, dumped me onto the blood-red carpet of the big man's office on the sixth floor. I sprawled out like spilt, slightly spoiled milk, at Wayne McGuiness' well-shod feet. He waved the goons away.

McGuiness ran the second biggest mob in town, which was a first class sore point with him. He specialized in bootlegging, speakeasies, prostitution, numbers, fight and horse and judge and campaign-fixing; generalized in anything else illegal that turned a buck or a trick or a favor.

"Get up, Lemmy," he said, when his goons had given us privacy.

I climbed onto my loafers, dusted my knees off not for the first time that evening. The tall, silver-haired gent adjusted the bowtie on his tux, admired the polish on his patent leather brogues. "I've got a surprise for you," he added with his equally silver tongue.

"A cement trench coat?" I cracked wise.

He turned and took the lid off a large box that was sitting on his vastly larger desk. "Close," he said, turning back around. A fur coat was draped over his left forearm like a head waiter a bottle of champagne.

"Yowza!" I gasped, impressed.

"It's mink. Go ahead and feel it."

I reached out a trembling hand, sunk it into the soft, warm, rich fur, stroked. It was smooth as silk and ten times thicker – the real, good stuff.

"It's yours," Wayne said. "To model for me."

I looked up at the guy, down at the fur.

Then I stripped, right down to my ginger-fuzzed balls.

Wayne McGuiness had a respectable wife and family and mistress. And a raging, perverted appetite for man-sex. I was his gunsel moll, his go-to gay. Only, because of the repressive times, I wasn't stashed away in some lavish penthouse, awash in the finer things of life, like most feminine molls. I was picked up – for some tough talk, the goons thought; for some tough love, Wayne and I knew – and then deposited back into the seedier side of town, whenever Wayne so chose. The most I'd ever gotten from the guy, besides a sore spot where the sun don't shine, was a couple of hundred of bucks one time when he'd been feeling especially satiated.

But now, a mink coat!

Wayne's shrewd, grey eyes traveled over my tight, trim nakedness, paying particular attention to the rather hefty endowment I was packing between my legs for a man so small. I fondled my growing excitement under his gaze, stroking up and out and hard and pulsating, staring at that lovely mink coat.

Wayne nodded his approval, held the coat up for me. I turned around, shivered my cute mounded buttocks, and he draped the fur over my trembling shoulders.

I shuddered with sheer delight, clasping the rich robe around me, petting the luxuriant fur. Wayne gripped my shoulders and breathed, bit into my ear. "Model it for me," he said.

I danced out of his arms and paraded up and down the office, on my tip-toes, smooth-shaven shapely legs flashing under the hem of the coat, hips swishing and swaying. I was queen of the night, beau of the ball.

Wayne unbuttoned his pants and drew out his cock, stroking contemplatively as he watched me strut my stuff. I did a series of pirouettes, coat flying, cock and ass showing. I felt like a million bucks, cloaked in a thousand bucks.

Wayne grabbed my hand and pulled me over to his desk. He pressed me up against the edge, his hard cock spearing through the opening in the mink and along my belly. My heart beat like a tom-tom, my face beaming pure joy, cock hard and long as the Depression had been so far.

Wayne kissed me on the mouth, the chin, the neck. His grasping hands slid inside the coat and onto my chest, deft fingers latching onto my stiffened pink buds, rolling. The coat burst off my shoulders despite my best efforts to hold onto it, Wayne McGuiness' lustful needs overpowering mine.

The fur settled down onto the desktop. Wayne lifted me, laid me out on the coat. I squirmed higher, reveling again in the satiny texture of the lining. Wayne clamped my legs to the breast of his tux. Then gripped his dick, probed my manhole with his cap.

My eyes flew open. "Lubrication, Mr. McGuiness!" I yelped. "Please!"

He glared down at me, pressing harder against my pucker with his beefy hood, the sadistic hood. The pressure built on my bung, my cock going cold.

Wayne grinned evilly, pulled back, pulled a small bottle out of his desk. He gave his dick a rubdown, poured some slickness along my crack. Then he slotted his dong.

He slid smooth and large through my starfish and into my bung, sunk long and deep into my bowels. I moaned, he grunted, gripping my thighs, his hard rod buried in my soft, sucking rump.

I writhed around on the fur as he wanted to see, as I wanted to feel. His buffed nails bit into the taut flesh of my thighs, as he shifted his hips, shunted his cock, banged me back and forth on the desktop, on the coat.

His dick wasn't the biggest tool I'd ever had hung up my chute. But he knew how to handle a gun – in another man's holster. He fucked me fast and hard, rapping against my rippling rump, sawing searing pleasure into my anus and his cock. Then he pulled up, took it slow and sensual, stroking my bung, stoking his balls with his loving cock.

Up on that fur, on the end of the rich man's prick, I'd died and gone to kept heaven.

Wayne suddenly leaned into his lust, bending my legs back almost right over my head. He was into the homestretch now, galloping with great thrusts of his hips towards the finish line. He gripped my pecs and twisted my nipples, snaked his tongue in and out of my mouth, driving his dong into my ass with shuddering impact. The desk creaked, and the fur whispered. He hissed, I whimpered.

His stomach rubbed against my erection, as he churned my anus. I threw my arms up over my head and grasped the fur backhanded. Wayne licked my shaven armpits, lapping up the sweat.

He slammed me with machine-like power and urgency. Then he tilted his head up, neck muscles straining. Saliva spilled out of his open mouth, down into my mouth. He spasmed, violently, thumping my ass, splitting my cheeks, spurting white-hot cum inside of me.

I shuddered, shot semen up against his belly, overwhelmed and overcomed.

He helped me up off the desk afterwards. Then he carefully lifted the fur and smoothed it out and carried it over to a closet, bagged it and hung it. "My wife's going to love it," he said.

It'd just been mine to borrow, not own; for his pleasure, not mine.

I clenched my fists and fought back the tears.

Wayne McGuiness was going to learn that hell hath no fury like a womanly man scorned.

# # # # #

I pumped the mob boss for all the information about the fur heist I could get that night, as he pumped me a couple of more times. And when his goons sent me sailing out of the limo and back into the street, I landed on my feet, like a cat, flagged down Officer Shanahan at the end of his shift.

I spilled everything I'd picked up to the harness bull, less the semen, giving the copper and his Captain and the Bristol mob Wayne McGuiness for the Hurtzig fur heist on a silver platter. Vengeful pay-off for the hood pulling the fur out from under me.

# # # # #

It was Brutus and Tully again, the next night. I'd been wondering all day why I hadn't read anything in the papers about the McGuiness mob being rousted for the Hurtzig job. The goons told me why, as they took me for a ride – not to Wayne's office, but far out into the country, instead.

"That beat cop, Shanahan," Brutus explained, "is on the boss' payroll. He ran straight to us with your story, after you'd flounced to him, spilled your angry little guts."

Tully looked back from the wheel, grinned, feeding more gas to the roaring machine. "Yeah, we pay him to feed us canaries."

The night was warm, I was packaged up in a kid's cardigan and corduroy pants and a newsie cap, but I shivered.

Brutus jabbed me in the ribs with his rod, the deadly, blue-steel kind. "Time for the pay-off," he rasped.

His breath still needed work like his broken teeth. But I didn't complain, not even when Tully brought the big car to a slewing stop out on a dark, deserted country back road, and Brutus shoved me into the trees, then down to my knees.

I spun around to face the goon's groin, long years of practice making me agile at three-quarters length. Brutus pointed the rod at my mug. I had only a second to act; Tully was revving the engine out on the road.

As Brutus' blunt finger tightened on the trigger, I shot out my tongue, plugged up the muzzle. The goon gaped. I spun my slick, pink mouth-organ all around the .32 caliber gun barrel. Brutus gagged.

The heater jerking up and away on the strength of Brutus' retch was all the opening I needed. I brought my balled right hand up from the ground, slamming it straight into Brutus' balls.

The goon retched more than just garlic, doubling up, blistering pain clenching his ugly features. I leapt to my feet from a kneeling blowjob start and raced through the night forest, for dear life.

# # # # #

I took my hustle to a new city, far away from the old. And from that safe and sound distance, I mailed an anonymous note to Captain Payton, spilling all I knew about the McGuiness mob and the Hurtzig heist and a certain beat cop Shanahan who was prone to beating off on his rounds.

The pay-off came a week later, when I read a small notice in the local paper about the shoot-out at the Milton Building in that faraway city. There wasn't one member of the McGuiness mob with enough pieces left to even pack up and put in prison. Work was an especial pleasure that evening, for all parties concerned.

BANG! BANG!
By R. W. Clinger

"Good evening, Mr. Blond," Sasha Nevshlaw stared across a walnut dining room table in his Moscow castle. Again, the Russian mobster looked dashing, just as I had seen him last: thick black hair and matching eyes, reddish lips, sloped Russian nose, six-three frame, a muscular two-hundred pounds. He then told his staff of five handsome men to leave us alone, shooing them away.

"We meet again," I said, secretly hungry for his skin, or whatever I could obtain from him. Our chase was never over. History had proved that we were longtime enemies: our Prague encounter turned sour along a back street as I popped a bullet in his right shoulder; our Amsterdam occasion left me with a minor concussion and bloody lip; the New York City incident was most bloody for the both of us.

I worked for the American government as an international informant and he ... was a Russian mobster, which mostly entailed the illegal act of importing vodka into the West. My job was not as simple as it sounded. Rather, I collected classified foreign information from bad boy parties such as high-powered Mafia groups, privatized hit men, and government coos. Once my undisclosed information was gathered, I returned to my New York office and my supervisors.

It was 1958 and ... America launched its first satellite, gas was twenty-five cents a gallon, the Munich air disaster had changed all of our lives, Nikita Khrushchev was the Prime Minister of Russia, Elvis Presley was inducted into the U.S. Army, *Gigi* and *Vertigo* were at the drive-ins, and ... the Russian Mafia had invaded the country with much force, polluting New York City and Chicago.

"You very hard to find, James. My men have difficult time with you," he said in his Russian-doused English, which I found sexy as hell.

Barbed-wire felt as if it ripped along my wrists and ankles as I sat in a Nicholas II-style high back chair. My left eye was swollen, and my upper lip was split; no thanks to his Russian warlords who chased me around the castle and captured me. My response to his comments was to the point, "This is our fourth encounter ... and you didn't kill me. Tell me why?"

"I often wonder that myself each time you capture me." He poured himself three fingers of vodka in a crystal tumbler, swallowed it down, rose from his chair, walked around the table, and drew his right index finger along my left cheek. He leaned into me and whispered, "You don't kill things you tend you like, Mr. Blond." His vodka-coated tongue exited his red lips and licked my cheek, which caused something rather solid to form between my muscular legs and under my all-black tuxedo.

I wanted to turn my head to him and share an international kiss with the handsome man but found it rather unethical, since I was supposed to murder him. Instead, I turned my head away, felt his tongue on my neck, and warm kisses to the throbbing veins against my corded skin. He discovered the timber between my legs with his right hand, squeezed the beef in his palm, and whispered along my tight throat, "American men delicacy for me."

"Sasha," escaped my lips in an excited gasp as his fingers found the zipper on my tuxedo slacks and released my uncut eight inches.

"You say in American that blonds more fun, right?" His right palm worked my tool's skin in a north and south direction. His movement was swift and mind-blowing. The mobster's breath still lathered my neck and teased with unrelenting pleasure.

I couldn't answer him, caught in his sexual act. Within seconds, I fell under his hand-spell and felt a vibration of sexual desire wave throughout my core. His hand was generous on my tool, warm and comforting, and jacked me off with hungry speed. I groaned in the Nicholas II chair, attempted to buck my hips upward, but couldn't because of the barbed-wire that secured my wrists.

He fell to his knees at my right side, bent over my upright gun, and took the tip of it into his mouth as he continued to stroke its length in a feisty manner.

Lust was found as he sucked me off. My head flew backwards, and whimpers of enjoyment surfaced from my mouth. How long could I keep my load in while my international rival continued to lick, lap, and suck at my flag's length? Seven minutes ... twelve minutes ... nineteen minutes?

He took a breather from his mouth-gig and whispered up at me, "Come, American. I want to see you blow."

I listened, under his care. I jacked my weight upwards, but only once, since the barbed-wire around my narrow wrists tightened. Following my thrust, white goo gushed out of my cock's head and flowed down and over my shaft like lava on the side of a volcano. The sap was thick and creamy looking, a meal for my abductor, if he wanted it, of course.

The mobster grinned from ear to ear, obviously finding pleasure in my explosion. He whispered to me, "Good as caviar, my friend," and scooped up my spent with two fingertips. Seconds later, the goon slipped the digits into my mouth and fed me my own spill.

Truth was I wanted the bittersweet sap to be his white juice inside my mouth. I willed to get the Russian out of his expensive suit and have my way with him just for that to happen.

He stood, wiped the back of his right palm across his lips, crossed the room to a hulking mahogany and glass closet filled with liquor, retrieved a pair of heavy duty sheers, returned to my side, and said, "I let you go now, Mr. Blond."

"You're supposed to kill me," I whispered, caught in his dreamy brown eyes.

"Never," he chanted, and set me free, snipping the barbed wire around my ankles and then my wrists, avoiding my smooth skin. "You my American pet. A dog. Someone I like to pet."

"Woof," I supplied, into his sexiness, his rough gig, and winked at him.

I was spent in the chair, exhausted, and needed sleep. My stomach desired nothing less than a bowl of borsch and black bread. The last twenty-four hours was fast-paced and brutal. I stood from the chair, tucked my limp cock away, zipped up, and ...

Two mobsters entered the room and stepped up behind me. One pressed a needle to my neck and injected a fluid into my body. Instantly, I became dizzy, inebriated, and fell to the floor. In a matter of seconds my eyes closed, and I found darkness, silence, catatonic for the next day ... two days ... three days ...

I came to in one of the castle's ornate bedrooms. The room was obnoxious in size with gold-gilded baroque-style walls and crystal figurines on Russian Empire mahogany furniture. The bedroom was also decorated with two Faberge eggs and Matryoshka (nesting) dolls. One of Sasha's henchmen stood over me: hulking, handsome with iced-white hair and intoxicating blue eyes, and holding an SKS rifle.

I lay naked under a heavy goose-down comforter made in St. Petersburg. Next to the bed, on a silver tray sat a cup of dark tea, a hot cereal I knew as kasha, and crepe-like pancakes called blins. I ate in silence, devouring the food, and washed it down with the strong tea. Following my food-frenzy, the guard took the silver tray away and exited the bedroom.

Approximately two minutes later, Sasha entered the room in a white, fur robe. He held a Sobranie cigarette in his right hand, took a drag, blew smoke into the room, and found himself on the edge of the king-size bed, next to me. The goon inquired, "How was breakfast?"

"Filling. Thank you."

"No starve you. What kind of host I be if I do that?" he said in his thick accent. Another puff on his Sobranie followed, and then he dabbed the cigarette out in a crystal ashtray on a walnut table to my right.

"You like me too much to kill me," I replied and shared my dashing smile.

"This true, Mr. Blond. Unfortunately, I not say that about your sidekick, Mr. Und." He wiped a finger along my cheek, then along the length of my neck, found one of my pert nipples, gently squeezed it, and added, "We have Agent Und in basement. He not so big on torture."

Agent 301 was a hard-ass sonofabitch who could handle himself. A bunch of Russian thugs could not break him. The bald and sexy spy was not about to be captive in a torture playground and would soon escape and rescue me from under Sasha's nose. 301 wasn't a sissy and was one of our agency's best. I'm sure he was just waiting to …

Sasha took in my blond hair and piercing blue eyes. Again, he pinched my right nipple, provided it with a twist, and said, "What exactly is Iowa, Mr. Blond?"

Because he would have found out on his own, I filled him in on my history in my best Russian: Des Moines born and raised by Edna and Peter Blond, four years of college at the University of Iowa, graduated magnum cum laude in 1952 with a criminology degree, and worked for the FBI since. I was twenty-seven years old, single, and … was slowly breaking down for a taste of his skin.

"Handsome," he whispered, and pulled back the comforter from my body. The Russian gangster studied my lined torso, blond treasure trail beneath my comma-shaped navel, five inches of soft cock between my legs, blond furry balls, and my thick thighs. "What corn fed mean?"

A burst of laughter escaped me but was soon lost because he found the limp package between my legs and started to bring it to life. His right hand grappled the beef, and he began to harden it up. In doing so, he whispered, "Sexy American. I can't keep hands off you."

Although I should have feared for my life, I didn't. Had my supervisors back in the States, Agent 604 and Agent 239, learned of my heated attraction for the Russian thug, I would have been kicked out of the FBI. Truth was, it was best for such a secret not to be disclosed.

"Me fuck you, as you say in English," Sasha whispered, pulled away from me, stood at the side of the bed, and stripped out of his white robe, which dropped to the marble floor.

To my surprise, the man was already nine-inches hard between his legs. My vision consumed his erect knob with a hungry desire that was uncommon among the men in the FBI. After I licked my lips, I consumed the rest of his thirty-eight-year-old chiseled body: cut abs and pecs, chest covered in thick black fur, burly balls, meaty thighs, and hourglass-shaped hips. I said to him, "Go ahead ... rock my world."

"No understand," he confessed.

"Fuck me," I laughed, and rolled onto my stomach for his zesty action.

To my utter surprise, not even a minute later, vodka was poured down and over my rump and licked away. His tongue dabbed at each orb, fell between the two, and lapped at my tight and hairless hole. More vodka was poured along my man-crevice and licked away. Behind me, he groaned and moaned with deep satisfaction.

I had my head buried in one of his expensive pillows and mouthed silk as desire rushed throughout my core. My bottom was pulled apart by the Russian's appendages and one fingertip delved inside, up to its knuckle, twisted, and played. He then drew two more fingertips to its surface, applied vodka to the mix, and pressed the two inside with the first one. How long did they toy with my insides, readying me for his nine inches of fun? Two minutes ... four minutes ... six minutes? I murmured into the pillow, consumed silk in my mouth, and believed I was going to fall unconscious due to his engagement with my rear.

Following that fingering ordeal, the thug decided to replace his digits with his tongue. A poke was carried out ... two pokes ... three pokes, and then he lapped at its slippery tightness with an irresistible appetite. He came off for air, licked my rump another time, pulled its bulbous cheeks apart, and pressed his face to my opening again.

Bubbles of pre-leak shot out of my firm shaft and decorated the bed's expensive sheets. When the bad boy decided to spank my bottom a yelp escaped my mouth, which was muffled by the pillow against my lips. Continuous swabbing with the man's extended tongue drove me mad.

When the Russian mobster finally pulled his tongue away from my back side, he replaced it with his nine-inches of cock. There, flat on my stomach, I felt his sturdy palms on my hips. Then, the first inch of his poker slid into my bottom. A gasp mixed with an animal-like grunt escaped my lungs. I quivered beneath his touch and felt another two inches of his pole thrust into my center.

Overtop me, the Russian mumbled, "Take it, American," and pressed another three inches of his stick inside my red, white, and blue core. Again, I was spanked. Again, a yelp of gratification exited into the silk pillow against my face. Again, I was jarred by his weight as the last of his nine inches throttled my behind, became stationary, and quickly exited.

Bolts by the Russian consumed the next eighteen minutes. One hump turned into dozens as his tempo rose to a relentless flow. He became frenzied behind me and continued to bang my buttocks. Obnoxious grunts escaped his beautiful mouth with each thrust. Slaps ensued on my bulbous bottom. His action with my skin seemed to end all conflict between his illegal importing deeds and my oblique spying.

Helplessly, I couldn't keep my sticky cargo inside my joint and balls any longer. Huffs of fulfillment drifted out of my mouth, into the pillow. Ooze fired out of my erect hose and formed a puddle on the silk sheet next to my navel. As he continued to bang me, my tight belly rubbed against the gooey pool, fell away, and rubbed in it again.

Sasha kept up his in-and-out action with a steady fixation. Nine inches of his rod pulverized me, pulled out, and pulverized me again. A masculine rumble was heard in the process. Again and again, he spanked me, welting my right cheek with his right palm. His cock rode my middle with deliberate force, backed out, and took another ride, which continued for a countless amount of time.

Erotic pain skied from my shoulders to my knees. Ripples of delight flowed within my torso. The vodka smuggler built a fine cadence behind me, inside me, overtop me, and eventually confessed something loud in his thick Russian, which I knew meant, exploding.

His junk was yanked out of my man-fissure. The mobster flipped me over and onto my back, smiled down at me, stayed on his knees, and jacked himself off between my legs. Caught up in his own orgasm, he said in broken English, "Where come."

Within seconds, I was garnished in his sticky-hot cargo on my plated chest. His goo stuck to every muscle on my torso, decorated my shoulders, still-hard cock, and swinging balls.

Spent, my companion fell over me and sealed our chests together. A long and inflexible kiss was shared between us. And, after that heart-melting kiss, my captor pulled away from me, broadly smiled, and teased, "My men take you to The Metonym now. I never see you again."

I swallowed excess saliva down the back of my throat and realized he was talking about his own personal gulag in Siberia, a manual labor camp for prisoners. Before I could respond, he exited the bedroom, and three of his goons entered the bedroom. With very little struggle involved, I was hooded, injected with yet another drug, and pinned to the bed before I eventually passed out.

# # # # #

Hours later, I was east of the Ural Mountains and somewhere in Sasha's gulag, which wasn't a gulag at all. Instead, it was a winter palace with extraordinary views of the snow-capped mountains. I was guarded by six beefy men: Viktor, Alexie, Roman, Bogden, Igor, and Derik. Roman took a shine to me, and I sexually teased him. While he slept on duty, I thieved his radio, and manipulated it to reach Agent 604. Our conversation was short and to the point: "I'm inside Nevshlaw's winter palace."

Agent 604 responded, "The Polizei."

"I'm a prisoner here."

"Agent 239, and I will rescue you."

"Copy that."

Our conversation ended as quickly as it started. The radio died in my right hand.

Afterwards, I found a secret passageway under the castle and attempted to escape. Viktor and Bogden, massive men with bulky arms and powerful legs, captured me. I was taken to my private bedroom with bars on its windows and no escape. Roman, I had learned, was shipped

27

away, terminated from his position at the castle and perhaps taken to the real gulag where he would spend a few years for his inadequate duties.

A day passed. Two days. I was then visited by Sasha, who brought me a gift: a Buran watch decorated in diamonds and small emeralds; the mobster knew my favorite color was green. I accepted the gift from him, and provided his cherry red colored lips with a kiss. "You try to escape my men, Mr. Blond," he confirmed, pouring us each a shot of vodka.

"I did. I don't like to be pinned up like an animal."

"I very sorry for that. Forgive me."

We drank shots of vodka together; the same liquor that he was importing illegally into my country. He had killed men over that beverage. Murder was not beneath him, of course, since he was in the Russian Mafia. The man was powerful and dangerous and … dreamy to study.

How I coaxed him to tell me of his future importing scheme was beyond me. Perhaps he enjoyed my little striptease and lap dance. Or, maybe he liked the way I pulled his clothes off, one piece at a time, and dotted elaborate kisses to his burly chest. My Russian nemesis sat on the edge of the bed and spread his legs for my mouthy transaction to transpire. On my knees, facing his built body, I looked up into his dark eyes, and asked, "You're very hard not to like, Sasha."

He ruffled my blond hair, touched my lips with an extended finger, reached between his legs, and wrapped a palm around his swollen nine-inch staff. "Suck," exited his lips in his butchered English.

If I didn't listen to him he would have tried to kill me. Instead, I obeyed my thirst and his instruction. I leaned my head forward, outstretched my tongue to the tip of his pole, and took a lick and …

He pushed down on the back of my head, and his cock slipped into my mouth and lowered into the depths of my throat. All nine inches gagged and throttled me. I choked with satisfied bliss and continued to lather his pole with my lips and tongue.

The man groaned above me, pumped my face with his tool, and said something in Russian that I had never heard before, but knew was a compliment.

We continued that act of sexual desire for the next few minutes. The blowjob he received from me was everything he wanted: intoxicating, devilish, and persistent. He whimpered by my touch and affection, lost under my mouth-spell.

Straying fingers toyed with his hairy balls. My pets were smooth and quick, and assisted my oral gift with perfect synchronicity. He became wild underneath me and bucked his weight upwards, into my mouth. I practically suffocated from those steady thrusts, unable to breathe, and became a little dizzy.

Within seconds, he pushed me away, fell back on the massive bed, spread his legs, and insisted, "Lick ass."

I obliged with zeal, voracious for his hole. On my knees, I leaned my face into his center and rolled my tongue around his tight looking core. I swabbed the hair and hole with pacified enjoyment. And, eventually I lapped at the one-inch slit with the tip of my tongue, and drove him mad, into a spin of erotic niceness.

"More, Mr. Blond," he coached. "Do it."

Again, I obliged. My licks and laps turned into quick motion. My appetite for his ass-canal was immeasurable. At one point during our connection, my entire mouth was buried against his tight bottom, and my outstretched tongue was inside his body. There, blended with my nemesis, I pulled my tongue out of his rump, pressed it inside, and processed a rhythm between us that was euphoric for the both of us.

He almost came, I admit now. Two droplets of white cream leaked out of his stiff pole and fell into his concave navel. A murmur of excitement was released from his mouth, which entitled me to continue my dirty deed with him, and replace my mouth and tongue with my cock.

Speedily, I pulled away from the gangster and stood. I positioned myself between his legs again, collapsed his ankles with my palms, and directed myself inside his tight tunnel, ready to carry out some hearty bolts.

"Fuck me," he cried on the bed, bedazzled by my touch and experience.

I obeyed, knowing that my life was on the line, since I was his detainee. I directed half of my eight inches into his man-slip, stalled, and pushed the other half inside him. There, I twisted my cock to the right, left, and quickly yanked it out of his harbor.

"Again," he begged on the bed, needy of my post.

My pelvis thrust forward, and my shaft punctured his epicenter. All eight inches of my gun blasted his bottom, glided out, and plowed him again. My movement was steady and robust for the next twelve minutes or more. Yelps and murmurs filled the bedroom inside the castle and echoed off the walls. Bump after bump ensued, and our bodies united with a feverish longing.

At that moment, we were no longer enemies. Instead, we worked together in a steadfast and productive manner. Both of us grunted with ecstasy, lost in each other's touch. Symmetrical beauty between men of different nations and pathways was discovered. Carnal attraction between the two of us was unavoidable and …

"Shoot," he whimpered beneath me and quickly wrapped a palm around his nine inches of post. Three jacks later, and he exploded his load onto his furry chest. A guttural moan escaped the man as he pumped every drop of juice out of his meat. A glazed look of satisfaction ebbed across his face.

I came shortly afterwards. Momentarily, I backed out of his rump and cocooned my knob with both palms. Hasty thrusts were established, which were followed by a long whine. Two more final jolts to my pounder caused a vigorous explosion to circle within my torso. Fire and thunder mixed under my skin and … spirals of goop exited from my poker and splashed against his hairy torso. The mobster's tight abs, dented navel, and rounded pecs were doused in the sap. Exhausted, I huffed, puffed, and fell on top of the massive man. My mouth buried against his neck and tasted his sweet perspiration.

He whispered, "Bang … Bang. I shot you. You down."

I heaved for breath, happy against his skin, and replied, "You can bang me anytime."

In truth, I don't think Sasha understood me, but it really didn't matter, since we had joined again, limitless with our flesh.

Post-sex and spent, following our twosome, we found the extravagant bathroom connected to the private bedroom. I drew water and added bubbles in the oversized bathtub. Together, we stepped into the rising water and sat down in the warm suds. My lips met his lips, then quickly pulled away, and I admitted, "My agents are coming to save me in a few hours."

"I expected as much." He smiled at me and shared another kiss. When the kiss ended, he asked, "When I see you again, Mr. Blond?"

"Tibet. A week from today and …" I told the mobster my location, famished for his body again, unable to keep away from his skin, lust, and desire. I knew that he would follow me around the world to have me again … and again. The man was my hidden boyfriend, half of me, the reason why I stayed with the FBI.

"My game continues with you."

"And mine with you."

"I capture you myself, or have one of my men do it in Tibet?"

"You," I dotted his nose with a sudsy finger. "It's always a turn on for me. I like it when you're rough with me."

"You naughty," he shared, and opened a hidden compartment to his right. Inside sat a bottle of unopened vodka and two shot glasses. He filled both glasses and passed me one. He said, "A toast … to secret affair."

"To us, my foreign lover. May our game last a very long time," I replied and clicked my shot glass to his. Then, I downed the liquid and ended up under his skin again for the next hour … maybe even longer … or at least until the bottle of his prized vodka became empty.

BOOM, BOOM IN THE CONGO ROOM
By Rob Rosen

Place was grand. Grander than grand. Like a twenty carat diamond ring, all flashy and expensive-like, way the fuck dazzling. It was the Congo Room at the Sahara. Of course, I don't work there anymore. Don't have to. There or any place else, for that matter. I put in my time, see, and it paid off like gangbusters. Just took one fateful night, it did. Dietrich was off, the stage black as night. Meaning, her dancers had some time on the down-low for a change. Bitch usually worked us like mad, too, barking orders in her signature German drawl. Meaning, the time off came, well, just in time.

I didn't normally hang out at the club when I didn't have to. Heck, they didn't like us there anyway when they weren't paying us to be there. Only, I'd forgotten my jacket in the dressing room the night before. Vegas got downright chilly at night, so the jacket would come in handy; especially since I had me some plans with another dancer from over at the Sands. Guy was hung like a mule and was twice as ornery. Still, beggars couldn't be choosers. Wasn't like my options were like those in the casinos. The sky wasn't the limit for the likes of me, you see. Least not yet.

I recognized him as soon as he walked in, too. Well, barged in, really. Mickey "The Whip" Malone, in the flesh, glorious as it was. "Where is she?" he barked, cigar dangling from between his thick lips, puffs of smoke rising off of him like steam.

My heart iced up in my chest, sending a cold chill down my back that made my legs go weak. The blood drained from my face as I replied, "She who?"

He snickered, the sound like sandpaper over granite, coarse and rough. "She who, he asks?" He shook his head and walked inside the smallish dressing room, slamming the door behind him. "Dietrich, kid. Boss wants to see her." He raised his foot and set it on a nearby chair, bulge in his slacks bulging all the more, matching my eyes at the sight of it.

"She's, uh, she's off tonight, Mickey," I squeaked out, hand trembling as I gripped my jacket in a death lock. "What's he need her for anyway?"

He closed the gap between us, suddenly standing in front of me, gun cocked, aimed at my jugular. "What fucking business is it of yours, kid?" he asked, sapphire blue eyes squinting into my muddy browns, the smell of Aqua Velva shooting up my sinus cavity, followed by a stream of cigar smoke that he blew into my face.

I coughed, and very nearly peed myself, all while that jet black piece of steel remained pointed my way. "Sorry, Mickey," I replied, breath lodged in my throat. "Just wanted to see if there was something I could do, seeing as she's not here tonight. I didn't mean nothing by it."

He paused, bouncing his pistol off my neck, the cold metal sending my teeth on edge. "Something you could do, huh?" he growled. "What can you do, dancer boy?" The growl was replaced by a menacing laugh. "Trust me, what you can do the boss ain't interested in."

Which explained what the boss wanted with Marlene. Still, with Mickey's eyes boring a hole right on through me, I sensed I still had my own opportunities. My date at the Sands, after all, could wait. "Shame," I replied, coyly. "You don't get to be a dancer at the Sahara without quite a bit of talent."

"What the fuck you talking about, kid?" he spat. The laughter returned, the gun gliding down my neck and into my shirt, the cold steel rubbing against my nipple, making it pulse and thicken.

I gulped, my bravado all but about vanished. Almost, but not quite. In for a penny, in for a pound, I figured. Now all that was left to find out was who was gonna take the pounding. "Talent," I croaked out. "You know about dancers' talents, don't ya, Mickey?"

The pistol kept sliding back and forth, a million Goosebumps riding up both arms. "What talents are those, kid?" he asked, mouth clamped down tight around his cigar.

I forced a laugh of my own. "Let's just say you gotta be the biggest horse in the stable if you want to be a dancer, Mickey. If you get my drift." I winked at him, which could've gone either way, all things considered. Thankfully, they went mine. Go figure.

"You're shitting me, kid. Little wisp of a thing like you? This I'd like to see." He turned and locked the door, then sat on the chair in front of me, the gun still aimed my way. "Show me, kid. Or else." He mimicked shooting me, smiling all the while, teeth a gleaming white.

I shrugged. "You sure, Mickey? Bound to make you, I don't know, jealous."

He lowered the gun, laughing full throttle now, smacking his hand on his knee, his other hand grabbing at his ample crotch. "Trust me kid, they don't call me The Whip for nothin'." He eyed me long and hard. I'd seen that look before. Meaning, he might've had the gun, but I had the upper hand now. And it was grabbing for the button on the top of my pants. I popped it open, his sky blue peepers suddenly aimed at my mid-section, mouth in a slight pant as the cigar drooped.

"Suit yourself," I told him, zipper sliding down, shoes kicked off. I gave a push on the waistband and down they came, kicked off, too, leaving me in nothing but a pair of cotton boxers, tenting something fierce. I paused, fingers at the ready as I moved in an inch. "What about you, Mickey? We'll need something to compare it with, right?"

His smile faltered, however briefly. Still, he put the cigar out on the table and stood up, once again closing the gap between us. "What's the winner of this little bet get, kid?" he asked, voice suddenly raspy.

My own smile echoed his. "I'll let you know when I win it, Mickey."

He nodded and chuckled, kicking off his expensive leather shoes, unbuckling his expensive leather belt, then popping open the top button, the zipper down, material parted. No boxers for Mickey. Just a wiry, black bush, the base of his thick shaft exposed. He dropped his pants to the ground while I pushed down my boxers, both our pricks springing out at once, cocked, as it were, and ready. We both stared down, taking them in. And, honestly, it was a tough call. So I slid in, slapping mine against his. He jumped, but stood in place. "Yours is thicker, Mickey," I told him.

He grimaced. "But yours is longer, kid. Damndest thing I ever saw. Little thing like yourself. Where you pack all that meat, kid?"

Again I slapped it against his, my hand reaching down to grab a hold of both of them. He moaned upon contact. "Pack it, Mickey? Well now, since I won that bet, guess we'll find out soon enough, huh?"

His neck craned up, the grimace returned, two-fold. He lunged for me, his arm against my chest, my body thrown against the wall, his dick ramming into me as I fought to catch my breath. His forearm lifted up, pressed up tight to my Adam's apple. I choked and struggled. "You want to fuck me, kid? That what you're getting at?"

I pointed to my throat. He eased up enough for me to reply. "Fair's fair, Mickey." All things considered, it wasn't the brightest thing to come out of my mouth all week. Still, with his dick still hard as that pistol of his, it wasn't the stupidest thing either.

"You got a lot of balls, kid," he said, almost in a whisper, face up close and personal to mine.

"And they're bigger than yours, too, Mickey, sorry to say."

I locked eyes with his. He grunted and stared at me. Then he laughed and released his strangle hold. I dropped to the floor and stared up at him, his dick now pointed my way. He slapped it against my face, hard as a whip. Now I understood the moniker. He slapped me again with it. "Suck it, kid. Then we'll see about that ass fucking."

He shoved it between my lips, sending a gagging tear down my cheek. I stroked my cock as his sausage-thick prick filled my mouth. Then he grabbed the back of my head and managed most of it down my throat, pumping my face, his eyelids fluttering, his moans filling the space around us. "Yeah, kid. Like you said, you got talent alright."

You ain't seen nothing yet, I thought, reaching up to pull on his nuts. His knees buckled, his stance widened, his moan suddenly louder. Guy liked pain, fine, I'd give him pain. I yanked harder, harder still, heavy balls stretched to their limits as I sucked his tool. I let go of my prick and moved my hand up between his legs, fingers tracing his hairy ring, prodding at his chute. He stared down and grunted. "Okay, kid. You want it, it's yours. A bet's a bet."

He slid his cock out of my mouth, unbuttoning his silk shirt, top to bottom, muscle-dense chest revealed, covered in down, then his belly, same as above. Italian meat for days. Made your fucking mouth water. Naked, save for his black dress socks, he got on the floor, legs wide, bent at the knee, dick pointing to the ceiling. Then he laughed, twisting and tugging on his thick nipples. "Be gentle with me, kid."

I crouched between his tree-trunk thick thighs, raising them up, hairy hole coming into view, winking out at me. I leaned in and down, inhaling the aroma of him, garlic and musk, the smell of him making my head swim. I licked his nuts, taking one in my mouth, giving it a good swirl and a pull between my lips. He arched his back and moaned, loudly. I took the

36

other in, repeating the motion. Lick, suck, pull. Lick, suck, pull. All while he pounded his cock, occasionally slapping it on my forehead, hard, each time with a dull thwack.

But this was just the appetizer, the antipasto to his lasagna, namely his fine, Italian ass, dense with hair, firm like a ripe melon. This I dug into with gusto, licking and lapping at his hole, sucking on it while I spanked his cheeks, pounding on them until they turned beet red. I sensed this was a turn of events for good, old Mickey. Still, I wasn't hearing any complaints, just the moans, repeated over and over again.

I spit at his hole, saliva dripping through all that hair. He pointed his wide, helmeted head at me. I sucked his prick while my finger slid inside of him, then two, three. Guy was big all over, hole included. Lucky for him because my cock was about to do some heavy damage on his ass. He bucked and rocked into my pumping fist, all while shoving his tool down my throat. "Fuck, kid, I misjudged you," he panted, balls bouncing, ass grinding into my fingers.

"You don't know the half of it, Mickey," I replied, popping his prick out of my mouth.

"Kid, let me tell ya, no halves. Give me the whole fucking thing." He spread his legs wider, already with a slow, steady stoke on that fifth limb of his, face grinning like an angel. Only, we both knew better. I reached over to the dressing table and found me some makeup remover, greasing up my pole and his hole, fast as a wink.

Anyway, like he said, I let him have it. Every last fucking inch, slid inside of him in one long thrust. Never seen a body quake like that before either, like I'd set him on fire and doused it out all at the same time, his cock throbbing in his grip as he howled, all animal-like. Seemed like I found my match in this one, one big hole for one big dick, which I soon began to pummel him with. I slid it out, pop, and then slammed it home, balls banging against his ass, his hairy chest now slick with sweat.

"Make me come, kid," he grunted, torturing his nipples, the stroke picked up on his thick prick.

I pulled out, but didn't shove it back in right away. "Fair's fair, as you said, Mickey," I purred, all smiles, my own cock near ready to burst. "What did your boss want with Marlene tonight? Just curious to know. Good for me to have one up on her."

He pried open his eyes, face twisted, desperate to shoot, I could tell. "Fuck, kid. He just wanted to change their date tomorrow night. The two of them, see, they get together every Wednesday after her show, all hush-hush like. Boss just wanted to move it to Thursday this week, pick her up outside after her show." He returned my smile with his. "Now make me come, kid. I got me a week's load needs shooting."

Well now, he didn't need to ask me twice. I shoved my cock deep, deep inside his ass, ramming as far back as I could go, his fist so quick on his dick it all looked like one giant blur. I matched his speed, pumping my cock in his hole, tingles riding up my back, swirling around my belly, stars before my eyes as I filled his hungry hole with buckets of hot cum. He shot with me, that giant dick of his twitching as streams of white hot jizz shot skyward, landing on his heaving belly and chest in one splat after the next. Fucking hot to watch, let me tell you.

Though all good things had to come to an end, no pun intended. Me, I had a date waiting. Him, too, it seemed. With destiny. Panting, he watched me pull out and jump up. "You surprise me, kid," he told me, with a chuckle.

I walked to my jacket. See, I had another need for it, besides keeping me warm. "Do I, Mickey?" I asked, turning around with what I'd retrieved out of the pocket.

He chuckled again, louder this time, wiping the come across his belly, sticky globs of it dripping from his sausage-thick fingers. "Not like any dancer I've ever met before."

I laughed, too. He was right. I wasn't. And I wasn't just a dancer, either. See, he had a boss, and so did I. And, man, did those two ever hate each other. Enough to kill, if one knew where to find the other one, and what day, and what time. Now that information, it was valuable. Guy could retire if he had that sort of information to share.

Only, sorry to say, Mickey's boss couldn't find out that anybody else knew. Mickey heard the click, of course, but it was just too late. That big, bulky body of his couldn't move fast enough for my lithe, little, limber one. Not that it takes all that long to cock a gun and let it shoot, mind you. Boom, boom!

Poor Marlene, I thought, stepping over him to get my clothes. It was gonna be a bitch cleaning up the mess I'd made. Thankfully, I wouldn't be around to help, 'cause my dancing days were over and done with. And that was just grand. Grander than grand. Just like the Congo Room at the Sahara, which I never stepped foot in again.

THE GUNSEL, THE NANCE, AND THE REDHEADED ROOSTER
By Michael Bracken

The gunsel's Tommy gun burped, and two of Risotto's boys collapsed in a heap of human marinara sauce. Neither of their Roscoes had cleared leather.

The baby-faced blond smiled and rubbed the front of his gray wool trousers with his left hand, leaving his right index finger on the chopper's trigger in case the wooden door behind the dead men opened unexpectedly. The gunsel's cock was rigid as a railroad spike and just as long when fully erect. If he didn't do something to relieve the pressure soon, he would come all over the inside of his silk boxers.

The door had developed lead measles and was wet with blood. The gunsel stepped around the stiffs and tapped the chopper's muzzle against it. "Open the door, Billy."

He waited until he heard the latch being lifted. Then he threw his shoulder against the door, surprising the dark-haired nance on the other side and knocking him backward against the desk. One of two matching accounting ledgers that had been open on the desk fell to the floor.

"Where's Risotto?"

"He ain't here, Kid," the nance insisted. He was pale and sweating, and his brown eyes darted back and forth as if he couldn't focus. He wore a white shirt buttoned at the cuffs and the fingers of one hand were stained with ink. "He ain't been here all week."

"Why'd you take a powder, Billy? What'd Risotto promise you?"

"I see you got a redheaded rooster wants to crow," Billy said nervously, changing the subject before the gunsel went too far off the

39

track. "Let me take care of that for you, Kid. You know you like it when I do."

The room had no windows, no way in or out save for the door. The gunsel crossed the room and leaned against the desk, his ass atop the remaining ledger, facing the open doorway. The nance dropped to his knees and unbuttoned the gunsel's baggy trousers. He reached through the open fly, through the opening of the gunsel's blue silk boxers, and released the gunsel's erect cock.

"It's so hard, Kid," the nance said before he took the head of the gunsel's cock in his mouth. His tongue painted the swollen cockhead, and he licked away the first few drops of precum.

The nance bobbed his head forward, taking half the length into his mouth before pulling back. His teeth caught on the mushroom cap, and then he bobbed his head forward again.

The gunsel was impatient. He grabbed the back of Billy's head with his left hand and shoved the full length of his redheaded rooster into the smaller man's mouth. He still held the Tommy gun in his right hand, and he watched the door as he drew back and thrust forward again and again, face fucking the smaller man.

The nance accepted every one of the Kid's powerful thrusts, just as he'd done many times before at the rooming house where they had lived across the hall from one another until the nance lammed off, stiffing the old broad who ran the joint a week's rent.

The gunsel pounded into the nance's face harder and faster and when his redheaded rooster crowed his trigger finger twitched. Lead peppered the wall next to the open doorway at the same time he fired a thick wad of hot spunk against the back of the nance's throat.

Billy swallowed every drop of the Kid's cum and licked his slowly softening cock clean. When the gunsel's redheaded rooster finally stopped spasming in his mouth, Billy release his oral grip on it and shoved the gunsel's limp cock back into his trousers.

The Kid grabbed Billy's arm and pulled him to his feet. Then he pulled back one of the nance's shirtsleeves to reveal the needle tracks on the smaller man's arm.

"Risotto do this to you?"

"It's nothing, Kid," Billy insisted. "I can quit any time."

40

"Don't lie to me." The gunsel backhanded Billy, knocking his former lover to the floor. "It cost me a double sawbuck to find out where you'd got to, and now I wished I ain't laid out the dough. I been played for a sap."

He pointed the business end of the Thompson submachine gun at the nance but didn't squeeze the trigger. Instead, he awkwardly buttoned his trousers with his left hand and then tore apart the desk until he found Billy's sewing kit. He laid the fixings on the desktop and smashed them with the butt of his Tommy gun.

"You ain't the man you was," the Kid said. "You ain't nothing now."

After he finished, the Kid made his way out of the warehouse. When he reached the street, he jumped in his flivver and faded.

The Kid stopped at a hash house for Adam and Eve on a raft, a cuppa Joe, and a long think. He'd been able to get the drop on the two mugs at the warehouse because they hadn't been there to keep people out but to keep Billy in. What had the nance been doing for Risotto that he would require babysitters?

He ankled his way to the Ameche and dropped a dime. When Bertha, the old broad who ran the rooming house, picked up the other end of the line, the gunsel asked two questions. After he heard the answers, he left a half on the counter for the waitress and returned to his flivver. He reloaded his Tommy gun and then drove downtown.

Speakeasies littered the city, offering everything from bathtub gin to untaxed Canadian imports, but only one served men who liked men. The men inside this speakeasy weren't Capones or North Side Gang, Risotto's boys or O'Malley's boyos. They shared a secret that usually transcended their particular employment affiliations.

The baby-faced blond gunsel rapped on the steel door until a dark eye filled the peephole. After he gave the password, the door opened.

He stepped inside, and the gorilla who worked the door frisked him, spending a little too much time scrambling his eggs. The gunsel slapped the gorilla's paw aside and stared him down.

Then he made his way to the bar and ordered a straight shot of Canadian whiskey. While he waited for his drink, the gunsel lit a gasper and drew the harsh, unfiltered smoke deep into his lungs. He exhaled it through his nostrils. Then he threw back the first shot and ordered a second.

He looked around. The place was filled with a bunch of daisies, and he saw the man he wanted standing at the far end of the bar, a man with a cauliflower ear. He walked up behind Eddie the Ear and dropped a hand on his shoulder. "Buy you a drink?"

The other man turned, gave the Kid a look over and said, "Sure."

The gunsel held up two fingers, and the bartender brought two shots.

"Do you know who I am?" the Kid asked.

"I seen you around," Eddie the Ear said. He picked up his shot glass and downed his drink. "You're one of O'Malley's boyos, ain't you?"

"Yeah." The Kid downed his own drink, his third since arriving at the speakeasy. "They got rooms in the back where we can talk private. You interested?"

Eddie held up his shot glass. "Buy me another?"

The Kid bought a bottle and carried it and two clean glasses to the back.

Half a dozen private rooms lined the rear wall of the speakeasy and were accessible through a narrow hallway with a skinny shine sitting on a high stool at one end and a door leading to the alley at the other. He handed the attendant a half and received the key to room three. The room, like all the others, was sparsely furnished – a single bed covered in a thin cotton sheet, a waist-high stool, a nightstand with a lamp, hooks on the wall to hang clothing, and a partially used jar of petroleum jelly.

The gunsel had brought Eddie the Ear into the room, so they could talk privately, but Eddie had other expectations. While the gunsel poured two shots, Eddie undressed.

The Kid was still hyped up from giving two men a dirt nap earlier that evening, and his drug-addled former lover had only temporarily satisfied him. When he saw Eddie's naked body, his redheaded rooster stretched its neck, preparing to crow again.

The Kid peeled off his jacket and hung it on one of the hooks. He sat on the side of the bed to remove his shoes and socks, then stood again and pushed his braces from his shoulders so that he could remove his shirt and undershirt. He hung his baggy trousers on the hook next to his jacket and finally peeled off his boxers.

When the gunsel's redheaded rooster finally sprang free, Eddie's eyes widened in appreciation, and he said, "Well, cock-a-doodle-doo!"

Eddie reached for the Kid's cock, but the Kid wasn't interested in foreplay. He spun Eddie around and bent him over the waist-high stool. He grabbed the jar of petroleum jelly, pried it open, and two-fingered out a glob of the lubricant.

He slathered some of it on his cock and worked the rest into Eddie's bum hole. He massaged his companion's tight sphincter until he could slip in one slick finger. A moment later, he slipped in a second finger.

After he pulled his fingers away, he pressed his redheaded rooster between the other man's cheeks. Then he thrust his hips forward and drove his cock deep into Eddie's keister.

He grabbed Eddie's hips as he drew back and drove forward again and again. By then, Eddie the Ear's cock had grown just as hard as the Kid's. The gunsel reached around and grabbed Eddie's nail-pounder with his petroleum jelly-slicked hand and jerked off his partner while he pounded into him from behind.

Eddie came first, spitting spunk all over the stool.

Then the Kid's redheaded rooster crowed for the second time that night as the gunsel slammed into Eddie one last time and fired hot spunk into the other man's keister.

They remained connected for more than a minute as they waited for the gunsel's rooster to stop crowing and withdraw.

After they finished, the gunsel dressed and lit another gasper. He drew in a deep breath of unfiltered cigarette smoke and asked, "You know Billy Hansen?"

Eddie shook his head. He sat on the edge of the bed, his nail-pounder having deflated into a limp noodle that hung between his thighs. He seemed in no hurry to dress.

"You convinced Billy to vacate his room at Bertha's, take up residence in one of Risotto's back rooms."

Eddie the Ear shook his head. "You're tooting the wrong ringer."

"I don't think so," the gunsel told him. "Bertha saw you visit Billy one afternoon. That night, he made like a ghost and faded."

"Wasn't me."

The gunsel's hand snapped out and clapped Eddie's cauliflower ear. Once. Twice. Three times before Eddie winced. "Don't lie to me. That ear's a giveaway, Eddie."

Eddie cupped one hand over his deformed ear and turned his good ear toward the gunsel.

"How'd you convince him to go to Risotto?"

"I told him the coppers were planning to raid the rooming house. I said a pretty boy like him wouldn't stand a chance in the big house and that you wouldn't stand up for him. I convinced him that Risotto would."

The Kid crushed the butt of the gasper under the toe of his shoe. "Why would Billy think Risotto would protect him from the coppers?"

"Because Risotto knew his daddy, Big Jim Hansen."

Big Jim Hansen had run Central Illinois with an iron fist until Johnny Torrio, two years before he turned the Chicago Outfit over to Al Capone, had a pair of torpedoes give Hansen a fatal case of lead poisoning.

"Big Jim Hansen was his daddy?" The Kid hesitated. "He never said."

"I don't think he wanted anybody to know."

"Why did Risotto send you?"

"Because I knew Billy from when he was in diapers." Eddie turned his deformed ear toward the gunsel and pointed at it. "His daddy done this to me."

"So why'd Risotto want him?"

"Billy does the books at The Diamond Exchange, and Risotto has a truckload of liquor money he needs to launder."

The Kid remembered the matching accounting ledgers that had been on the desk when he'd burst into the office where he found Billy. "I saw Billy's arm. He's stitched up. Risotto put him on the needle?"

"He did that to himself. Risotto just keeps him threaded."

The chatter of a pair of Thompson submachine guns interrupted their conversation, startling both men. The background noise of a busy speakeasy – idle conversation, bottles clinking against glasses, chairs scraping across the floor – turned to dead silence when the choppers quit spewing lead.

Through the door, they heard someone shout, "Where's the Kid?"

The gunsel recognized Risotto's voice. When no one responded to the question, he opened the door a crack and looked up and down the hallway. The man at the far end saw him but didn't react.

The Kid slipped out of the room and had just made it to the exit when he heard someone say, "The Kid's in back."

He pushed through the door and headed down the alley. Another one of Risotto's torpedoes was standing guard in front of his flivver, but facing the entrance to the speakeasy, not the alley. The Kid was on him in a flash. He snapped the mug's neck and tore the chopper from the dead man's hand. Then he reached under the front seat of his flivver for his Tommy gun and turned to face the alley with the butt of a chopper resting on each hip.

The first of the three torpedoes with Risotto rounded the corner and the gunsel cut him in half with bursts from both guns. As if he had a death wish, the gunsel ankled his way toward the alley entrance.

The muzzle of a Tommy gun rounded the corner. The gunsel sent a burst from one of his, shattering brick all around the muzzle, and the other gun drew back.

The gunsel stepped into the mouth of the alley. He filled it with lead mosquitoes that ricocheted from one wall to the other. Another of Risotto's torpedoes dropped dead.

"You want me, Risotto?" the Kid shouted. "Here I am!"

From behind a garbage bin, Risotto shouted back. "Does O'Malley know you've gone off the rails, Kid?"

"This is between you and me, Risotto."

"We didn't find Billy until it was too late," Risotto shouted. "He killed himself. He left a note, said it was your fault."

"I didn't stitch him up," the gunsel shouted. "That was your doing."

Risotto's remaining torpedo stepped out from a doorway and unloaded his chopper in the Kid's direction. Brick chips peppered the gunsel's face and ricocheting lead imbedded in his left bicep. He winced.

The Kid's Tommy guns burped in return, halving the torpedo.

"You stitched him up, Kid," Risotto continued. "I just gave him the sewing kit. He loved you, but you just used him, and he knew it. You don't love anybody but yourself, and he needed a way to escape from the pain."

"Why dope?"

"It's the future, Kid, and you're the past."

The gunsel felt the cold circle of a revolver barrel against the base of his skull and heard a hammer being cocked into place. Risotto'd had another torpedo the gunsel hadn't accounted for. The Kid was about to die, and all because of some nance he'd been banging.

He squeezed the triggers of both Tommy guns, filling the alley with ricocheting lead, and never heard the bullet that bought him a wooden kimono.

THE TRUTH THAT WE'LL MISS
By Robert Saldarini

"We can live with the lies,

It's the truth that we'll miss"

– "Rumors Are Flying," Les Paul, 1946

Boxing Day 1947 brings about 27 inches of snow to New York City. New Year's Eve offers a cold but clear forecast. As many make their way to claim shoveled space in Times Square, Tony and Mary Grace Marchetti exit the L.I.E. toward Roslyn Harbor. Tony turns through the front gate of the DeLuca estate. He salutes the man in the gatehouse who returns a quick nod.

"Oh, Tony, I always love going to these parties. They are so grand. It would be wonderful someday if we could have a Long Island home like this one."

"Ah ... yeah."

At the front entrance, the sedan's doors are quickly opened by what looks like a pair of English gentlemen in long wool coats and white gloves. Both men murmur, "Good Evening." Mary Grace responds in kind. Tony rolls his shoulders naturally adjusting the holster of his gun before buttoning his tuxedo jacket. He grabs his wife's mink sheltered arm escorting her up the white marble steps.

In the foyer, the Marchittis are greeted by women offering to take hats and coats. Beyond a lavish centerpiece, the great room hosts a huge fireplace ablaze with radiance second only to the dazzle of the women's jewels. The sound of an orchestra playing "Near You" can be heard mingling with conversation and laughter. Mary Grace leans toward Tony's ear, "I'll meet you inside. I must go to the powder room and check my face."

Tony walks toward an adjacent sitting room. Many of the boys are assembled in here looking like penguins taking shelter from a storm. His arrival makes the younger men jump to their feet while the older ones continue in conversation smoking cigars. The new *picciotti* are in awe of Tony, and the rest either respect or secretly fear him. He stands six-foot-two; a man of unadulterated Eros and adrenaline. His chiseled features would make Ann Rand beg Vidor to cast him in the upcoming film, *The Fountainhead*. Tony is DeLuca's number one hit man and with good reason. He was trained as a sniper by Special Forces during WWII. He can control either a Tommy gun or Remington 1903A4 rifle with near perfect precision.

Vito Ricci navigates the crowd vying for his attention. He calls out, "Tony!"

Tony turns, grabbing Vito's right hand with a firm grasp pulling him forward while delivering a hard slap to his shoulder. Vito can smell the mingling of Tony's male scent and Pinaud-Clubman. "Happy New Year, Vito, may '48 be your year."

"And may it be a good one for you, too."

"Vito, do me a favor. See if you can find my little woman and keep her occupied for a few minutes while I talk to these guys."

"You got it." Vito grabs a cigar and tucks it into his jacket. Unlike many of the men in the room, Vito doesn't carry; firearms make him nervous. "I'll gather the girls."

"Girls?"

"Yea, I brought a baby-doll I've been dating. Her name is Ellie. She's the daughter of my mother's butcher on Arthur Avenue. Maybe she's the one." Vito winks as he departs.

Tony walks up to a small mahogany bar and orders two-fingers of Jack Daniels. Frankie Dianopli, a *caporegime* from Jersey, approaches asking the bartender for a dry martini. "So, Tony, what's Vito's story? Why does the Boss bless this guy?"

"Well, it's like this. DeLuca has always been big into the dough made off of boxing. So anyway, the Boss 'acquires' this gym in Brooklyn ..."

"Acquires?"

"Yea, the gym was Vito's old man's place. One of Ciccino's men pops Vito's father and then dumps the body under the Bridge. I'm not really sure on the specifics. I think it was something about one of the boxers not taking a dive when he should have. Anyway, the hit was done without protocol. A little push, a little shove, a call to the Boss from

Ciccino, all is quiet, and the Boss owns the place. When the Boss goes out to Brooklyn, there's a scrapping fourteen-year-old who thinks his *i coglioni* are the size of cannonballs. I mean you can't blame the kid for being full of piss and vinegar after what happened to his father," Tony said.

"Vito didn't see the hit, did he?"

"No, he didn't see a thing. So, the Boss takes a liking to the boy. He assigns one of his men to fill his father's shoes. He lets Vito work and train at the gym and throws him a few bucks for keeping the place clean. I understood that Vito just about lived in the gym. He became quite a good boxer," Tony answered.

"He doesn't talk about it. But, I've seen him duck or weave in a way that looks like there's been some kind of training."

"Yea, he boxed for a while. Business took us to Atlantic City in October of last year. Vito had us make a little side trip into the locker room. The minute he saw Gink Belloise they were punchin' each other and smiling like two brothers back from different summer camps."

"So why did he give up the ring?"

"When the day was through, Vito didn't make the grade. He could never grab a belt. The Boss called him in, the father-figure disappeared, and Vito's been working directly for DeLuca ever since," Tony continued.

"Got 'ya."

Tony never cared much for Dianopli. He plans his escape, "Listen, I better get out there, or Mary Grace will give me the silent treatment all the way home."

"Don't forget, meeting at eleven o'clock in the Boss's office."

"Yep, see you then."

Tony surveys the great room. Vito and the gals established residence at a small cocktail table. Mary Grace waves him to her. The sight of his stunning wife gives Tony a stir in his shorts. Vito, too, is stirring; nevertheless, it's not the ladies driving his libido.

Mary Grace is already feeling her Dom Pérignon, "Ellie, this is my handsome husband, Tony. Isn't he dreamy? I fell madly in love with him when he flashed me those baby-blues."

A bit shy by his wife's comment, Tony extends his hand, "It's nice to meet you."

49

Ellie accepts the gesture, "And it's nice to meet you, too. Oh my stars, Mary Grace you are so right! His eyes are beautiful. Vito, aren't Tony's eyes absolutely dreamy?"

"Yea, kid, they're dreamy." Vito stares into his almost-empty glass.

"Vito, don't be like that. You have beautiful eyes also. It's just not every day you see such blue eyes on an Italian."

"Yes, I guess that's true. Listen, I need a drink. Does anyone else want one?" Vito asks.

Ellie pats Vito's arm, "I think we are fine."

On his way to the bar, Vito is stopped by a young waiter with a tray of prosciutto and melon. "Sir, may I serve you?"

"No, thank ..." Vito stops speaking when he notices the waiter's face. This man could pass for Marlon Brando's twin. "Wow, has anyone ever told you buddy that you look exactly like ..."

"Marlon Brando, the Broadway actor? Yes, all the time. But, if I were Brando, I wouldn't be working this party on New Year's Eve for two-bucks an hour."

"Very true ... very true. Anyway, I'm not a melon fan. Also, I don't think you can serve me in the way I need to be served right now."

"You'd be surprised." There is a moment of silent tension between the two men.

"Ah ... I need to get a drink." Vito orders a Dewar's and water. With fresh drink in hand, he returns to his date.

Ellie snuggles up to Vito. "We were just talking about how posh this party is. Wow, I had no idea that there were would be so many magnificent people here. I almost died. I met Fanny Brice. Can you believe I met Baby Snooks herself? Who would think there is so much money to be made in the insurance business? Thank you for bringing me with you tonight."

"No sweat, sweet pea." Vito sighs because he finds himself once again alone with the dames. The drone of their conversation slowly converts all words to sounds. He notices the Brando look-alike is no longer working the crowd. The waiter stands in military at-ease position near a service door leading to the kitchen.

"Excuse me, ladies; I have to see a man about a horse."

The ladies giggle. Vito walks by the waiter. Both men exchange glances at the instant of the pass. With not the slightest change in stride, Vito pushes through the door and advances half-way down the corridor and stops. The sounds of the catering staff drown out any trace of the orchestra's rendition of "Take the A-Train." The door soon opens. A swell of good-hearted laughter spills into the hall when the waiter steps over the threshold. Without acknowledgement, Vito makes a sharp left and exits the building through a small mudroom. He leans on the railing of the cement porch. The cold night air is stimulating. Vito lights up a cigarette while studying a snow-cleared path to a back alley gate. Beyond that gate is a trash dumpster.

Vito hears the door open and shut. He trots down the steps following the path into the alley. The dumpster area provides the needed seclusion. The gate slowly swings open, and the waiter steps out. The men are face-to-face in the night air.

The waiter shivers from a chill, "Shit, it's cold out here. We should get to it. What do you want to do?"

"We can do an Uncle Francis special or something like that?"

"A what? What is an Uncle Francis special?"

"Ah ..." Vito fidgets, "ah ... it's ... mmm ... it's *un pompano*."

The waiter tilts his head back in surprise, "You are telling me an Uncle Francis special is fellatio?"

"Ah, well, it's only that when guys do it ... ya' know?"

"Man, I get the drift. Why in the world would sucking on another guy's meat be called that?"

Vito becomes defensive. He clears his throat. He pauses uncomfortably in light of the fact that the waiter spoke the words. "My father owned a gym and called it the Uncle Francis special whenever guys did the deed. He told me that my mother's Uncle Francis got caught by the cops doin' it in a passageway. That's where the name came from I guess. But, listen, I should be getting back inside; my date must be wondering where I am."

"No wait, an Uncle Frank's special it is."

"Francis."

"What?"

"It's an Uncle Francis special."

"Fine. Get it out."

Vito opens his pants and pulls his skivvies' side ties. With his thumbs, he grabs the cotton tucking it under his scrotum.

"Very nice." The waiter squats and slips Vito into his mouth and begins rigorously stroking his shaft. Vito grimaces due to his sensitivity and knuckles the edge of the dumpster in response. Shortly, Vito can no longer hold back and ejaculates heavily. The waiter turns, clears his throat, and spits.

Vito tucking his shirt back into his pants is infuriated. The waiter stands anticipating the switch, but, reciprocity is never given. "You spit! You didn't swallow, you son-of-a-bitch."

"What?"

"You never spit – it's an insult. That's a lack of respect you stupid fuck." With this said, Vito delivers a sucker punch hitting the waiter squarely in the face causing him to stumble and fall backward into the snow. Vito fixes his jacket. Walking along the path, Vito thinks now the guy looks like Brando with a broken nose.

The meeting is underway when Vito cautiously enters the large office. He takes his place in the back of the room behind the *picciotti*. He always finds a sense of comfort in this pack of soldiers.

Tony's eyes shift from Vito to the Boss. For some, arriving after DeLuca starts speaking could throw him into a rage. In this case, there is not even a hint of dissatisfaction. Dianopli is right; Vito is blessed by the Boss. Tony then notices Vito trying to unobtrusively expand and flex his right hand. He thinks, "Jesus, who did he hit?"

Andy Diorlini is sitting in a club chair next to the Boss's desk. Rumors have been circulating that Andy is getting out. Getting out is a hard thing to do because you know too much. Such an action must be sanctioned by the Boss. And from the tone of DeLuca's introduction, it sounds as if this is going to happen.

"Gentlemen, my family, my boys, you know I love all of you as if we were my blood. So I have a sad announcement to make. Andy is leaving the family. He goes with my blessing. He has proved himself loyal and worthy. Andy, we all send you off with Godspeed." DeLuca pauses, "Okay, that's it. Now this is a party. Go out there and make those bitches' moist. With the exception of Andy, Tony and Vito, you are all dismissed."

The senior men leave first. Low and respectful whispers fill the room in the same way they fill a church after Sunday mass. Vito stands as doorman, securing the large wooden doors after the last men leave.

DeLuca stands, which in turns brings both Tony and Andy to their feet. The Boss leans against his desk, "Sit boys … sit. Gentlemen, Andy has made me exceptionally proud. He brought hard evidence that someone in our organization is a rat."

Surprised by the news, Tony asks, "One of our boys, sir?"

DeLuca slams his fist on the desk. "I have every reason to believe so. The fuckin' rat was right here in this room."

"Do we have any idea who he is?" Tony asks.

"No, that's what so damn frustrating. Andy found out that shit has been leaking to the Feds, and in return, we now need to make Andy disappear. Should the Feds make any connection that we know something, the rat will escape before we kill the son-of-a-bitch."

"I understand," Tony says.

"So this is what we are going to do. I have one of our cabbies all set up to pick up Andy and his wife and take them to Grand Central tomorrow morning. Vito, you tail the cab at a safe and unassuming distance. Got that?"

Vito shakes his head, "Yes, Boss."

"Tony, you be on the platform when the train pulls into the station. You watch every person who gets on that train. If even one person boards her looking suspicious, get on in the same car as Andy and take the ride."

"Got it," Tony acknowledges.

DeLuca takes a manila envelope off the desk. He hands it to Andy. "Okay, in here is everything you need. You got two train tickets out of the city to Indianapolis. Importantly, you have all your paperwork for you and your wife. I mean, you got birth certificates, baptismal certificates, a new marriage and driver's license – everything you need to start your life as Andrew and Marian Adsee. And as my gift for what you done for this family, I wired fifty-grand to the Lake City Bank in that name. That should keep you comfortable until you find work."

"I don't know how to thank you, sir." Andy postures to kiss the Boss's ring.

DeLuca pulls his hand back. He brings his middle and index finger to his cheek, "No, here, you are my brother, and you are leaving our house." Andy obeys. "Vito open that door. My wife must be having kittens fretting that I won't be with her when the New Year rolls-in. Let's go downstairs."

The men enter the party taking places by their women while the band leader is coordinating the count, "29-28-27." The place is alive with voices joining in chant. Vito scans the room. He visually sorts through the waiters now holding trays of champagne glasses. "18-17-16." There is no sign of Brando. He breaks-out into a shit-eating grin thinking, "Uncle Frank special, what a stupid ass."

"4-3-2-1, Happy New Year!" The crowd roars, and confetti flies. Noisemakers and blow-ticklers whistle, clank, ring and whir to almost a deafening level. The orchestra immediately begins playing "Auld Lang Syne." Kisses fly everywhere.

Tony taps Vito on the shoulder, "I'm going to take Mary Grace home."

Hearing his voice, Ellie spins on her heel. She pulls Tony down by the neck and kisses him, "Happy New Year, blue eyes!"

As he raises his head, Vito gives him a kiss on his cheek. In response, Tony darts his eyes in his direction.

"What? Can't I give 'blue eyes' a New Year's kiss, too!"

Ellie bursts into laughter.

"Okay, I'm out of this joint," Tony says.

# # # # #

As Tony anticipated, there is little traffic on the roads. He looks at Mary Grace, "Did you have a good time?"

"Yes, I did. I wish we could have stayed longer and danced."

"Sorry, Babe, I have to work tomorrow for a little while."

"Tomorrow? What about la Nonna's New Year's Day dinner?"

"I'll join you there. You take the boys. I'll have Vito drop me off."

"Okay, but I think you work too hard."

"Not your worry."

Mary Grace realizes this is not the time to resurrect the ongoing battle of family versus work. She changes the subject. "Ellie is divine. I hope so much that this relationship sticks. I cannot understand for the life of me why Vito is so picky when it comes to the girls he dates."

Tony drives on.

# # # # #

At the apartment door, Vito slips off his shoes and gathers them under his arm. He slowly inserts his key gently turning the lock. He opens the door as quietly as possible and steps inside; yet, he is not quiet enough. From his mother's room, he hears, "Vito, is that you? It's after three o'clock. I was worried."

"No reason to worry, *Momma Mia*. I'm fine. Happy New Year."

She replies, "Happy New Year to you, too, my one and only son."

In his room, Vito tosses his shoes next to the dresser. Stripping to his underwear, he pitches each item in the same general direction. After a visit to the bathroom, Vito pulls back the linens and jumps into bed. An overtired body and active mind provide no formula for sleep. In the dark, he flexes his right hand a few times. There is still a dull throb in his knuckles.

As Vito tosses, he revisits the dumpster situation. Beginning as nothing more than working the edge off his sexual desire, the event turned into a complete disaster. He wonders how the waiter explained what went down. The guy would never tell his boss the truth and whatever he told would never make its way to DeLuca. The catering company probably gave the waiter the bum's rush. He whispers aloud, "Who the fuck trained him about the guy thing? It certainly wasn't Whip, that's for sure."

Louie the Whip, known to his friends simply as Whip, stepped in for Vito's old man after the situation, which took his father's life. Whip pressed Vito about making it big as a boxer. He also taught him that real men needed to have power, not the power of guns and blades, but of their hands.

Vito remembers as if it were yesterday the many times he and Whip would sit in the locker room talking about pure power. Whip explained the most powerful thing in the world is a man's private parts. He would declare, "Yes, my boy, men say this all the time 'I had the fucker by the balls.' And, when you can possess them – you own him." At some level this all made sense to Vito.

Vito was around nineteen years old when he was showing exceptional talent. One night after a long and exhausting session in the ring, Whip undid his boxing trucks and took out his mighty erection. Vito looked at him in confusion. Whip decided the time had come to train young Vito on how to hold a man by his balls. He pushed Vito to the mat. He then dragged him to a seating position against one of the four-inch corner poles. With his right foot on the lower rope and his left leg extended for purchase, Whip pried open Vito's mouth. He slipped his fat cock into the young man's throat and began thrusting. Vito felt the back of his head bang against the metal pole, but he hung onto Whip's balls and did not resist the force-feeding. Whip went ridged, and Vito started to gag on the spray of semen. Within seconds, the men were nose-to-nose. Whip clamped Vito's mouth shut with his powerful hand. With fire in his eyes he commanded, "Swallow! Swallow every drop. In your mouth is the supremacy of being a male and never insult the man who gave you his power."

As a result of this experience, Vito vicariously learned what his father meant about Uncle Francis 'doing it' in the alley. From that moment on, the expression 'Uncle Francis special' was as good enough as any. But, Vito wasn't queer like some of the other guys. He and Whip were certain of that. During the years that followed, Vito did these deeds in the manliest sense. The thought of dressing in women's clothing and swishing when he walked was queer; he never wanted to be or act like a woman. In fact, Vito often concerned himself that women were more to his disliking with their little slit that oftentimes stunk. But, he'd find the right one and make her have his babies.

Vito flips his body flat on his back. His exhaustion brings him down to face the demon; the one he works so hard to keep chained. He thinks, 'Why is it all so fucked up with Tony?'

Everything was right until that night in Boston. Vito and Tony were sent to make a very important drop; so important, even they didn't know what was in the briefcase. They stayed over one night at the Pieroni's Hotel at Park Square. Once the drop was completed, the boys stopped in the Hotel bar for a few drinks. Sitting at the bar was this hot broad; she was all alone; her name, well, she said her name was Lily.

It didn't take Lily long to make her approach on Tony. She quickly joined them. Tony was intoxicated by this woman. Vito found her quite true to form; a bar bitch wanting some schmuck to pick up her tab. The flirting between the two edged Vito out of conversation. By the swell in

Tony's trousers, neither of them cared about the ring on his finger. Vito excused himself wanting only to go to bed. Tony on the other hand yelled to the bartender to hit him and his "little lady" with another drink.

It was about 2:30 when Tony came staggering into the room. He was as quiet as a horse trying to kick out the stall door. Vito got out of bed to help his buddy who in turn insisted he was alright. The way Tony was put together furnished no doubt that he scored with Lily. Vito helped him out of his shirt, unbuckled his pants and pulled them down. This caused Tony to fall backward onto the bed. Vito removed Tony's unlaced Wingtips. When Vito raised his head he was eye-level with Tony's crotch. Luck was on his side. Tony never re-buttoned his boxers and they were wide open giving Vito a look at what he longingly desired. Good sense overcame him. Vito simply fixed the button at the waistline and put Tony to bed.

It didn't take long for Tony to roll onto his side. The sour smell of cigarettes and Jack Daniels was strong. The heavy breathing in his ear provided every indication that Tony was down for the count. However, his virility was wide awake. His cock found the wide opening that remained in the boxers and was thumping against Vito's ass.

Vito could no longer resist. He slipped under the sheet and took Tony into his mouth. He could smell the sex that Tony and Lily shared only hours before. Tony stirred. Vito backed off and waited. Vito continued when Tony's course breathing returned. Following a cough, Tony mumbled, "Come on baby, put me back inside you."

Overwhelmed in the situation, Vito crossed the line. He slipped out of his skivvies and straddled Tony. When Vito bore down on Tony's girth, he was put on the edge of pure pleasure and excruciating pain; not knowing if he should dismount or continue. The pain diminished somewhat when Tony started working his pelvis. For a second, Tony's eyes fluttered open yielding a befuddled expression; nonetheless, he didn't slow his momentum. Then a deep moan came from Tony, and the act was done. Vito returned to his side of the bed. He worked hard not to let Tony's power seep out of his no-longer virgin ass.

While reliving his memory of passion, Vito leisurely strokes himself to completion. He is too tired to get up and change. The orgasm serves as a sedative. Drifting to sleep, he fights back the nagging thought, one which of course cannot possibly be true: He is not hopelessly in love with Tony Marchetti.

# # # # #

At the start of July, DeLuca's men begin making decent headway toward flushing out the rat. It's going slow because the Boss is exceptionally articulate that the process arouses no suspicion. Yet, even DeLuca is nervous about how hard this nut is to crack. He calls for Tony Marchetti and Marcus DelVeccio. It is time to close in and get the rat's identity. As the boys enter the office, the Boss tells Marcus to close the doors.

"Listen hard boys, I think we finally got our break on this rat business. I found out for sure that Bruno Cacini knows the name of the guy who's yappin' to the Feds. I just got a call telling me that Cacini is at the Italian American Club in Chelsea. Get Vito to bring you guys down there and wait for him to leave; no shots, no noise, no nothing. Convince Cacini to take a ride. Bring him to my warehouse on the pier. I don't care what you do to him. Get the name of the fuckin' son-of-a-bitch who is ratting me out!"

"Yes, sir. We're on this."

Vito has the car ready to roll and is waiting by the gatehouse. The two men jump into the back seat. The sedan flies out of the driveway. Tony asks, "Vito, you know where you're going?"

"Yep, I know exactly where the Club is."

The ride is uneventful. Vito finds a parking spot on West 23rd Street offering a good view. Shortly, an old man leaves the Club. He passes the sedan and taps twice with his knuckle never acknowledging his action. The men are satisfied. Bruno Cacini is still inside. All they need to do now is wait.

Marcus sits up nudging Tony, "There he is."

Vito starts the engine and slowly pulls away from the curb. Marcus rolls down the window and says, "Bruno, come here a minute."

Cacini nervously looks around realizing he has no cover. The muzzle of Marcus' gun is a visual cue not to flee. A shoot-out in this neighborhood would be certain death. Acquiescing to the situation, Cacini walks over to the Ford. "What's going on? Why you drawn here during the day? Why do you need hardware to talk to me?"

"Get in Bruno, up front with Vito. We're going for a little ride."

Cacini gets in the car, "Where we going?"

"Never mind."

Vito drives to the Chelsea piers. Two men open the warehouse doors, and the vehicle slips out of view. The car doors are opened simultaneously by four guys. Cacini steps out, "Is anyone going to tell me why I'm here?"

"I'll tell you," Marcus replies. "Who is the rat that's working with the Feds?"

"What? I don't know what the hell you're talking about. I don't get involved with that shit."

Tony comes at him from his other side. "We have it from good authority that you know exactly who is spilling his guts."

"Listen, you got the wrong guy. I don't know jack shit man."

Marcus lights up a thick cigar. He takes some hard puffs and blows the smoke into Cacini's face. "Tell us."

Cacini clears his throat, "Come on; you think I would take on the Boss? Do I look like a mental case? I'm nothing in this outfit."

"We can make you talk," Marcus says.

"I have nothing to say. I'm leaving"

Tony motions to the boys. The men quickly surround Cacini. He shakes his head, "What are you going to do, kill me?"

"No, killing you would shut you up. Gentlemen, take him over to the packing table."

Cacini tries to push his way free, but it's a rabbit's attempt in a snare. "Let me go!"

Marcus commands, "Boys, put him over the edge of the table."

Two men hold Cacini across his back. His right ear is pressed up against the table's cool steel. Tony walks over and squats down, "So are you going to talk? Or, do we have to get it out of you?"

Cacini's voice starts to quiver, "Tony, listen, this has got to be bad if you're leading this pack. I don't know nothin'."

"Go ahead, make him talk."

Marcus kicks Cacini's legs apart. "Giorgio, strip him down."

The young solider undoes Cacini's trousers and pulls everything to his ankles. Bruno Cacini starts to tremble, "Please, I don't know shit. I'd tell you if I did."

"You'll remember quickly enough. Giorgio, pull his fat ass cheeks apart."

Cacini attempts to break free, but there is no way with now three men holding him down. Marcus takes the tip of his lit cigar and presses it on the rim of his asshole. He grinds the cigar deeper. Cacini roar of pain echoes throughout the warehouse. Marcus turns to Tony, "Buddy, light up another cigar!"

After the second cigar, Cacini is drenched in perspiration. Tony squats down again, "Did that jog your memory, or do we have to heat up the end of a poker?"

"Will you let me go or kill me anyway?"

"We'll let you go," Tony says.

"You have always been a man of honor, Marchetti; don't go rotten and ruin your word."

"Tell us who it is, and you're out of here," Tony says.

"It's Dianopli."

"Dianopli? I always hated that guy. My word is only as good as your silence. Cacini, you open that fuckin' yap of yours, and the next time you'll be going feet first into the East River. Boys, get him out of here. Dump him at the door of Saint Vincent's Hospital. Where's the phone? Break it up boys, the show is over."

Vito pushes through the men's room door. He gets busy doing target practice with a urinal cake. Giorgio walks in. Vito stands upright. He looks straight at the wall. He notices Giorgio is having a bit of difficulty with his zipper, which finally frustrates the guy so much he just undoes his pants. To Vito's surprise, the young recruit of five-foot-six has major meat, and he is at full salute. Giorgio arches his back trying to piss and not take a shower in the process. Vito chuckles at the sight.

Giorgio shoots him a look, "What?"

"Your first one? Am I right?"

"Yea, how'd you know?"

"You're hard as hell. I've learned for a guy there is not much difference between sex and violence. You need some help with that?" Vito nods in the direction of the stall.

# # # # #

Within the warehouse office, Tony finishes his call with DeLuca. He says to Marcus, "The Boss wants us back right away."

"Okay, let's go."

Tony looks through the manager's window and sees some of the boys talking and carrying-on as they always do. "Where's Vito?"

Marcus shrugs, "I have no idea."

They walk toward the sedan finding it empty. Tony calls to the boys, "Any of you see Vito?" Before someone could respond, a male cry of pleasure resonates from down the hall.

Marcus shakes his head, "Looks like your puppy is off his leash again?"

"My puppy? What the fuck does that mean?" Tony asks.

"No offense. After all, aren't you his master?"

Tony is startled by the comment almost to the point of wanting to punch Marcus in the face. Instead, he says, "I'll go get him."

# # # # #

Initially, having no momentum at all, ferreting out the rat goes from zero-to-sixty in what seems like thirty seconds. There is an around-the-clock search for Frank Dianopli. The Boss wants to be the executioner on this one; therefore, there is a capture him alive decree. Everyone in the family is on alert and assigned to task.

Tony doesn't mind taking the third-shift watch. The afternoon's heavy downpour finally broke the stifling heat of the past few days. A summer wind followed the storm leaving a clear night; one perfect for a stakeout. From his vantage point, Tony can easily see the front portico of Dianopli's house. A large carriage lamp spills light everywhere; yet the residence seems vacant. This is no surprise. Once Cacini was nabbed, there was little Dianopli could do other than bolt. Without doubt, he sent his wife and kids away somewhere safe. The park's five-foot stone wall provides substantial privacy. A group of large maple trees with their low hanging branches allow Tony to almost completely disappear.

Time slips by slowly and steadily. Patience is no stranger to Tony. He taps his fingers on the stones thinking he'd really like a smoke but can't risk anyone seeing the burning tip of his Chesterfield. His thoughts are cut short by the '47 black Ford sedan, which pulls to the curb about a block south of Dianopli's place. The engine is turned off. No one steps out.

Tony rests his hand on his holster, barely moving his thumb as he opens the snap, which secures it. The street is silent. Tony watches the Ford like a cat concentrating on a bird within pouncing range. The headlights quickly flash twice. The job is aborted.

Tony hunkers down and quickly follows the wall. When he approaches a park entrance, he removes his fedora and places it on a stick slowly guiding the hat beyond the wall's edge. If this isn't a trap, the Ford should swing around. The sedan fires-up followed by the squeal of a quick turn. Tony advances into the light seeing the open passenger door. Within seconds, he is safely inside.

Tony uses his fingers to comb through his hair before repositioning his fedora. Following the exhale of a long desired cigarette, he asks, "So Vito, what's the story?"

"Well, Marcus nabbed Dianopli. Frankie-boy was getting some stowed cash out of the warehouse office in Weehawken, you know, his place on the Hudson River. So anyways, Marcus kicked through the office door with five of our men drawn at his back."

"So, you weren't there?" Tony asks.

"Nah, I was in Long Island. When they nabbed Dianopli, the Boss told me to come out to Jersey and bring you back. But, I hung out a bit to hear what DeLuca was going to do. Man he was in his typical form – brutal. The Boss says that Marcus was to bring Dianopli into the warehouse, yank off the guy's trousers and underwear forcing him to sit spread-eagle on the floor. Meanwhile the boys were to douse the place with gasoline. Marcus, himself, was to move Dianopli's *il cazzo* to the side, separate *i coglioni*, and then badda bing, with a hammer, nail his bag to the floor. And on the way out, one of the boys was to toss a match. Mary, Mother of God, the Boss is creative, I'll tell you that my friend."

Tony's bright smile dazzles through his late day's scruff. He closes his eyes thinking of Frank Dianopli with his scrotum nailed to the warehouse floor while his business burns around him. The violence of his job always makes his cock flex. He moves his hand to cup his swelling member. It never takes much to kick him into gear. With Mary Grace now eight months pregnant, Tony gets nothing at home. When she told him the rabbit-died, her pussy shut down for business – doctor's orders. After they were first married, he merely suggested some oral action. Mary Grace went wild, screaming in Italian, demanding to know if Tony thought he married a *puttana*. His aggression and lack of sex turns what started to be nothing more than a tingle into a raging hard-on.

The movement in Tony's pants is not unnoticed. While Vito cruises up Route 4, he manages to keep one eye on the highway and the other on Tony's growing excitement. He clears his throat, "It's not getting any easier at home with your wife's delicate condition? When is she due?"

Tony knew the intent of Vito's question. "Late September; but it took me almost six weeks to get in again after Joey was born."

"You know, Tony, I always got you covered. Ahh, do you need a release? I mean, I have no problem helping you out with an Uncle Francis special."

"Vito, I can certainly use it. I mean with the pregnancy and all ..."

"No need to explain." Vito exits the highway and finds a deserted spot. He pulls the sedan off the road and behind some thick brush. Both men exit the car. Once the engine is cut, the silence of the night is disturbed only by the sound of two car doors being carefully shut. Vito advances to the trunk of the vehicle and stops. Tony leans against the passenger door slowly surveying the terrain in a way unique to a hit man. Vito waits for the silhouette to move. The tip of a hat provides the signal for action.

Vito squats in front of Tony finding the brass zipper pull. He guides the pull down slowly because the erection is pressing firmly against the fabric. Once open, he unbuttons and positions the cotton boxers to protect against any irritation that might be caused by the zipper's teeth. Vito reaches in and gently removes all of Tony's manhood. Tony is true to his Italian heritage and always proves to be a challenge for Vito. His thick eight-inch uncut baby-maker is rock hard; a large feeder-vein along its side causes his cock to pulse. With skin drawn back, the mushroom head glistens in the night's light. A pearl of fluid puddles in its slit.

Vito cradles Tony's sac in the palm of his left hand and takes a deep breath. He slips Tony into his mouth going slowly down the length of the shaft producing what sounds like a gurgle when he nears its base. By instinctual response, Tony locks his fingers together grabbing Vito by the bottom of the skull forcing the remaining few inches down his throat. Vito's nose is pressed deep into Tony's dense pubic hair where his desire for air brings only the rich scent of man-sweat and testosterone. Within seconds, Tony begins plunging deep and hard. With his head locked in a powerful grip, Vito does what he can to breathe. Then with one extraordinarily head slam, Tony produces a low guttural grown. Vito feels the discharge of five heavy jets of semen finding their way directly into his gut.

Silently, they slip back into the sedan. Tony lights up a Chesterfield and tosses his driver the pack. Vito starts the car and makes his way back onto the highway. When the men get to the George Washington Bridge, Tony asks, "You think that Frankie Dianopli ripped up his balls and ran or do you think he went down in flames?"

Vito replies, "Don't know."

# # # # #

The following day, Vito stands at the Marchetti front door. He rings the bell. He hears the boys yelling they will answer the door; however, it is Mary Grace who peeks through the small window and greets him. "Vito, what are you doing here so early on a Sunday morning?"

"I have to speak to Tony."

"I'm sorry, come in." Mary Grace places her hand over her well shrouded belly giving Vito room to pass by. Closing the door she asks, "What's this all about?"

"I know it's unusual for me not to call, but Mr. DeLuca said there is little time for formality. Tony must be at an inspection by 11:30."

"What happened? Did a building burn down or something? I don't understand ..."

"Babe, let me handle this, okay?" Tony is dressed only in a pair of U.S. Army issue gym trunks. Vito fights hard to keep his attention focused.

Mary Grace sighs and returns to the kitchen. Once she is out of earshot, Tony asks, "What's going on?"

"The Boss said to tell you that Dianopli is alive. He got a call from Dianopli's brother-in-law who said that Frankie-boy had been framed and that he has proof. The Boss doesn't believe it ..."

"Neither do I. Vito, why the fuck would he try to run?"

"Who knows, but anyway, the Boss wants to know what the brother-in-law has. So he needs you to call him ..."

Tony is running on less than two hours of sleep, "The Boss wants me to call this guy we don't know?"

"*Merda*! No, the Boss wants you to call him, not the fuckin' brother-in-law. He wants you to go to a meeting with the brother-in-law this morning. I'm to take you to Vincent's Restaurant on Mott Street to meet the guy at 11:30."

"Okay, let me call the Boss. Go out into the kitchen and keep Mary Grace occupied. Tell her you're hungry or something. Work up the boys; that will keep her busy."

"You got it."

Roughly a half-hour later, Tony enters the kitchen. Vito and Mary Grace sit at the table having coffee. His sons are outside playing. He is dressed and ready. "Okay, Vito, let's go." Tony bends and kisses his wife.

"I'll say a prayer for you at Mass," she says.

"Do that Babe. I can take all the prayers I can get."

Vito gives Mary Grace a peck on her cheek. As the men exit the back door, she can hear her husband yelling to their boys about going into the house to get ready for church. There is the start of an engine. Once again, Mary Grace is alone.

The streets of Manhattan are easily negotiated. Vito quickly finds a parking spot near the restaurant. Being a bit early, the men sit and talk about how busy Little Italy is on Sunday mornings as it ramps up for a day of worship and eating. Vito rolls down his window because he's waiting this one out in the car. Across the street, a vehicle pulls up and parks. Vito says, "There are the guys."

"Yep, right on time. The Boss said he'd send me four men who are fully loaded. Not that I think I'll need them."

A large man approaches the restaurant's front door. Under the guy's arm, he is carrying a legal folder. He looks nervously around and then goes inside.

Tony checks his gun and says, "That must be the brother-in-law." He opens the car door and steps out.

Vito watches Tony. To pass time, he taps and fiddles with the side view mirror. By chance, the mirror tips upward causing Vito to bolt back in his seat. Hanging out on the ledge of a second story window is a man with a rifle. Vito traces the line-of-sight to Tony's back. He immediately flings open the car door, leans out and yells through the open window frame, "Tony…. DROP!"

There is a loud snapping sound. All four men scurry from their vehicle. Vito is getting a bit dizzy and sits back into his seat. Three of DeLuca's soldiers take the building by storm. He can hear gun shots. The passenger door opens, and Tony crawls in keeping low.

"Thank you buddy, you saved my life out there. Who the fuck would think this is a trap? Vito, are you okay?"

There is a small trail of blood leaking from the corner of Vito's mouth. "Yea, I'm okay, but it's hot in here; I'm sweating like a pig."

Tony realizes that Vito has been hit. "Lean up buddy." Vito's white shirt is drenched scarlet with his blood. "Oh, shit, *essere fottuto*!

Vito no longer able to sit up slips sideways. His head lands in Tony's lap. Tears start to puddle in the corner of Vito's eyes. He chokes, spraying blood all over the dashboard. He swallows hard, "Hold me." Tony puts his hand under Vito's head. In a few moments, Vito goes limp.

From below the passenger door one of the guys ask, "Tony is everything okay in there?"

"I'm fine, but Vito took it direct; we lost him."

"Vito? Is he the guy who's a little queer?"

Tony replies, "I have no idea what you're talking about."

THE GRANDFATHER
By Logan Zachary

"Welcome to the Wabasha Street Caves. These caves were built into the sandstone located here on the south shore of the Mississippi River in downtown Saint Paul. Once a speakeasy, the caves were a home to mobsters in the 1930s, but now they can be rented out for weddings and special events."

"Maybe we can have our wedding here," I whispered to my partner, Ken, as we approached the front door. "That is if our state ever gives us permission."

Lush green vines covered the brick entrance to the caves. The front looked like a castle as we entered, and a chill came over me as we walked through the thick wooden doors. Inside, I pulled my long sleeves down over my hairy arms as we went deeper into the caves. The interior temperature was cooler than the Minnesota summer's heat outside. "Ken, this was such a great idea."

The ramp led up to the dance floor complete with a mirrored disco ball, and the stage sat in the corner, where the bands played.

"I'm glad you're excited, Ryan. My grandfather suggested we take a tour here." His azure eyes twinkled with enthusiasm.

Our female tour guide continued, "Throughout the 12,000 square feet of these caves, one can see the 'tastefully finished' old decor with the newer additions, which helps create an enhancing atmosphere with a mysterious aura."

I watched the aura of Ken's ass with each step he took. His denim jeans hugged his body like a second skin. The seam rode up between the cheeks of his perfect bubble butt.

Our guide pointed to the wall. "One can notice the nicely done brick walls, stucco ceilings, and ample, carpeted dining space. In the lounge area, there are beautiful tiled floors. The original 1930s sixty-foot bar is still in great shape, as is the 1,600 square foot hardwood dance floor, located in front of the performance stage."

As I stepped onto the dance floor and stared into the mirrored ball, the lights swirled and danced around the room, and my head started to spin with it. My legs felt as if I was going to lose my balance, as a dizziness descended on me.

I widened my stance as my arms shot out to the side to stabilize my feet. I closed my eyes to stop the room from spinning …

… and suddenly, I heard big band music start up. When I opened my eyes, the eco-friendly light bulbs had changed into old fashioned ones, dimming and turning the light yellow. Cigar and cigarette smoke hung heavy in the air.

Tommy Dorsey and his Big Band played the "Lindy Hop" on the stage, and a dancing couple fox-trotted by me, almost knocking me over. The whole dance floor filled up around me. Men in suits and women in long dresses twirled and spun in each other's arms.

I looked around and saw Ken was gone. Our whole tour group, guide and all, were gone. I stepped out of the way as another wild couple almost danced into me.

A waiter standing in the corner said, "They like to show off." He smiled and handed me a martini glass. He wore a finely tailored formal black suit. His black hair was long, slicked down, and pulled back away from his handsome face. A deep dimple formed when he smiled.

"But I didn't order …" I started.

"The Boss wanted you to have fun tonight. That's my job, enjoy." He winked his blue eyes at me and headed back to the bar.

What was going on? Had I stepped into a costume party? Where was Ken?

A sharp looking man in a zoot suit strolled over to me. He slid his fingers along the brim of his felt hat with a feather and looked at me. "Are you the one making the drop tonight?" He looked me over and around my feet. "Where is it?"

"Where's what?"

He pulled on the wide lapel, shifting the shoulder pads on his muscular arms. "You're a sly one. I can see why Ma Barker and John Dillinger use you."

"What are you talking about?"

He brought his hand to his mouth and covered his lips. "Mum's the word. Now, I see why you are so good, one cool customer."

My palms started to sweat, and I wiped them on my pants. I looked down, amazed at my tailored trousers, no longer the faded jeans I had on earlier.

"Lefty was taken into the back caves, and he hasn't come back yet. I hope that doesn't mean, what I think it does." He elbowed me and moved closer. "So did you deposit the gold in the spot or not? I need to know." He pulled the gold chain that dangled from his front pocket and pulled out a golden pocket watch. Flipping it open, he sighed, "We only have ten minutes." He wiped the beads of sweat from his forehead with a handkerchief and stuffed it back into his pants.

I swallowed hard. Deposit? Gold? Ten minutes? Lefty? Why was he so nervous?

He grabbed my arm and pulled me across the dance floor. The dancers avoided us as he guided me around the corner hallway to the fireplace. We paused for a moment to warm up and then headed to the mahogany bar. He pushed me forward.

My martini spilled a little as he thrust me against the bar's rail. I set the glass down on the bar, and the bartender took it and replaced it with a new one. An olive bounced inside, slowly coming to settle on the bottom.

"Loose lips sink ships, but this is ..."

The front doors burst open, and someone ran up the ramp to the dance floor. A man in a pin-striped suit and a Panama hat started shooting into the room with a Tommy gun. Men and women screamed and scattered in every direction as they tried to escape in blind panic. The man fired into the ceiling as dust and debris fell down onto the hardwood floor.

As the bullet sprayed near me, a hand grabbed my arm and pulled. I fell down to my knees and felt something whiz over my head.

"Stay down," his voice commanded.

I looked into the waiter's deep blue eyes and felt my heart stop.

"I'm here to protect you," he said. Another line of bullets sailed overhead, and we crawled to the hallway leading into the caves.

"What's happening?" I shouted, over the gunfire and chaos.

"Follow me and stay low." His hand held mine, and I knew I was safe. We pushed through the men's room door just as a man crawled across the floor behind us. His head hit the door with a hollow thump, but we didn't look back.

Wood panels lined one wall in the bathroom, and Blue Eyes headed for the third one. His fingers pushed on a spot on the trim, and a click echoed down the hall. The panel pushed in on one side, and he shoved it open. He pulled me through and spun around to slam it shut. There wasn't much room in the space, as the panel clicked back into place.

I pressed my back against one wall as his arms wrapped around me. He held me close as my shaking started. "We're safe, we're fine," he repeated to me. His mouth was next to my ear, and I could feel the warmth of his breath on me. His body was firm and muscular. He stepped forward, and I felt his pelvis brush against mine.

I could feel an erection starting to grow in my trousers. As I shifted onto my other foot, my cock rubbed against his.

His dick was already hard.

My arms clung to him as my breathing returned to normal. "What's happening? Who's doing that? What's going on?" My mind raced in so many directions I could feel the terror start to rise in me.

Blue Eyes moved closer and kissed me. His lips found mine and stopped my panic. He turned his head, so our noses weren't in the way and deepened our kiss.

My cock swelled to its full eight inches and ground into him.

His body matched mine, movement for movement. The close quarters started to warm up with our body heat. I could feel my body relax as passion took over. I opened my mouth and let my tongue slip out to taste him. As it brushed his lips, they opened, and our tongues met. I grabbed his ass and squeezed. His butt was tight and firm, each cheek fit perfectly into my hand as I caressed and massaged them.

He pressed his body harder against mine, his heat radiated into me, and all the horror outside slipped away. His hand reached up and found a pull string. A small naked bulb slowly came to life and lit the closet we stood in. He opened his eyes, and the deep blue stared into my hazel ones.

He began unbuttoning my shirt, and as it opened, he slipped his hand across my hairy chest. His fingers combed and kneaded me. As they worked lower, I felt him start to unbuckle my belt and work my fly. As the fasteners opened, my trousers slid to the floor with a bang. My pocket watch weighted them down.

I started to open his shirt and felt his sculpted muscles underneath the fine linen. He had a small patch of hair between his pecs with a thin line running down the center to washboard abs. I opened his pants, and they pooled around his ankles on the floor.

I could feel a warm wet spot on my boxers. His fingers ran down the length of my cock, and I felt more precum ooze out and soak into the cotton. My cock sprang through the fly and brushed his hand.

His fingers curled around my shaft and squeezed.

I felt my balls rise up as I thought I was going to shoot my load.

He brought his mouth down onto mine and kissed me deeply. His hand just held my cock and didn't move. He held an even pressure on my inflamed flesh and kissed me.

My hands slipped under his waistband and worked his ass. My fingers pulled the shorts down over his bubble butt and explored the crease. Sweat made them slip inside easily. The scent of male sweat, semen, and sex filled the humid space.

How I longed to run my tongue down his body and suck his nine-inch dick into my mouth, but the space was too small to kneel.

His shorts slipped lower, and his dick popped out of them. His cock rubbed against mine leaving a wet line of thick ooze along my shaft. He pushed it against me and our hard-ons lined up together, side by side. My hairy balls brushed against his low hanging ones, and I felt them swing back and forth between our legs.

The precum lubed our dicks, so they slid along each other easily and stimulated more to ooze out of my cock. My thick pubic bush tangled with his and tickled our torsos.

I could feel the hair on his ass and felt it funnel my fingers into his crack, drawing me down to that tender spot. My fingertip circled it, and he moaned with pleasure. I pressed down on it, and the sweat made it slide around and around. My finger entered slightly, and I felt his cheeks tighten around my tip.

His ass pushed back on my hand, relaxed, and swallowed more of me.

Our cocks rubbed together harder, and more fluid leaked out.

He reached up and combed his fingers through my blond hair. "You look like you're made out of 24 carat gold."

My hair crackled with static as his hand moved along my neck and down my hairy chest. "Spun gold, just like what you brought us."

I didn't understand what he was talking about. I didn't bring anything, but his hand sent flames across my skin, and then I didn't care.

He pushed me into a corner and positioned himself in the opposite one. He reached between my legs and motioned for me to open my stance. He kissed down my neck and across my furry chest. His lips found one nipple and licked it. As it rose into a sharp point, his teeth rolled it back and forth.

I let my head fall back and savored his attention. I opened my legs wider as I pressed my back against the walls.

He must have taken my motion as a request, and he continued down my torso. His tongue cut through my pelt and washed over my abs. He circled my bellybutton and dove inside.

My erection leapt and brushed underneath his chin. The stubble sent all my nerve endings ablaze. More precum oozed out.

He felt the reaction of my cock and shifted his chin from side-to-side, sending more waves along my shaft. "You like that?"

All I could do was moan in pleasure.

He inhaled deeply and held my scent in his lungs. As he exhaled, his hot breath washed over my arousal. He stuck out his tongue and licked down my shaft. He explored the opening of my fat mushroom head with his tip. Precum and saliva mixed down my cock. He opened his mouth and swallowed me whole.

My hands grabbed onto the walls, and I tried to hold back the explosion that threatened to erupt.

Slowly, he pulled his head back, along my cock and drew down hard on it. A long string of saliva and precum stretched from his tongue to my dick. It snapped. Half swung from my cock, and the other half he sucked into his mouth, the tail snapping against his lips. He licked them and smiled.

He stood and pressed against me, his moist lips found mine, and I could taste my juices on his tongue. I opened my mouth wider as we kissed.

Blue Eyes held my face in his hands and looked into my eyes. He knew what I wanted.

He turned his back to me and spread his legs. He licked his hand and grabbed my cock, guiding it to his furry ass.

I stepped behind him and hugged him around his narrow waist. My cock slipped between his cheeks, and my hands grabbed his thick cock and stroked him.

His balls swung back and forth as my cock slipped deeper between his cheeks. As I jacked his dick, his butt muscles relaxed and opened for me. Our sweat and precum made me slide in easily. My thick shaft filled his tight opening, and my balls bounced off his ass as I entered him to the hilt.

He pushed back on me and tightened his cheeks around me.

I pulled back and slowly, keeping only my fat mushroom head inside. I plowed back into him and pulled out. My speed increased with every thrust. My hand worked his cock as I humped him.

Blue Eyes' balls swung faster and higher as he joined with my rhythm. His cock slammed into my hand, and his butt swallowed my dick.

The small space heated up with our body heat and the scent of male sweat and sex filled the area. I inhaled deeply the wonderful male smell and felt a sheen of sweat break out over his body, making our bodies slide even easier.

I increased my speed, drilling my cock into him harder and harder. My balls slammed against his cheeks and tingled with excitement. I tightened my grasp on his dick, as my hand squeezed his cock and hot, thick cream exploded out of his dick and flowed between my fingers.

As his load shot out of him, he bore down on my cock, and I felt my balls release. Pure pleasure shot out of my cock and filled his ass. I humped him a few more times, milking out the built up joy from my dick as more cum flowed out of his. White hot cream filled my hand and flowed between my fingers.

I clung to him as wonderful spasms washed over my body. My cock stayed buried deep inside him as the sensitivity was too high to be able to be pulled out.

Blue Eyes flexed his butt and another wave shot out of me. My breath came out of me in gasps.

Slowly, I pulled out of him and allowed my body to relax.

Blue Eyes turned to me and kissed me, long, hard and deep. "The gold is ..."

A pounding sounded on the bathroom wall.

"Remember where this panel is because ..." but Blue Eyes didn't finish ...

... The door flew open, and I fell out onto the floor, my bare ass exposed for all to see. I covered my quickly shrinking erection and looked around the bathroom. Luckily, the tour had moved on to the next exhibit. I pulled up my underwear and adjusted myself. Struggling to my feet, I yanked my pants over my ass.

The bathroom door opened. "Ryan, what are you doing there?" Ken asked. "I've been looking for you."

"I ... I took a wrong turn." The trap door had swung shut before Ken found me.

"You have to see this." He grabbed my hand and pulled me down the hall. "I found a picture of my grandfather. He was a waiter at the speakeasy, so many years ago. He used to tell me stories about mobsters, gang wars, and missing gold." He paused in front of a framed photo, blown up to almost life size.

Blue Eyes smiled at me from the black and white picture. The graininess blurred the photo, but there was no mistaking his handsome face and body.

Ken pointed to him. "That's my Grandpa Blue."

I swallowed hard. Turning to face him, I saw the same eyes staring back at me. No wonder they were so familiar. "I can see the resemblance."

"He's the one that told me to take you here."

"What?"

"I visited him in the nursing home, and he said I should take you here."

"The gold!"

"What? What gold?"

It was my turn to show him something. I led him back to the bathroom and the secret panel. I pushed the lever, the wood clicked, and the door swung open. The space smelled of male sweat and sex.

Ken inhaled. "Were you jacking off in here?"

My face burned as I searched the walls. One seam looked different. I felt around the wall and my fingers brushed a button in the wood. A small panel opened up.

"How did you do that? Did you know about this secret hiding spot before?"

"You wouldn't believe me if I told you." I looked into the space and saw a black leather case that looked like an old fashion doctor's bag. Reaching inside, I felt how heavy it was and metallic clicks rattled inside.

"What's in there? Could that be the gangster's gold?"

I swallowed hard as I pulled the bag free. Setting the bag on the floor, the trap doors swung shut and clicked closed. "I don't know." I worked the latch and peered inside, gold ingots lined the bag and glowed in the light. "We're rich."

"Finders keepers?"

"Exactly, and on our way home, I'd like to thank your grandfather in person."

"Grandpa Blue?"

"We owe this to him, in more ways than one." And I kissed Ken, deeply and longingly, swimming in his deep blue eyes, into his grandfather's eyes.

THE GETAWAY
By Rob Rosen

Tony parked the car just off to the side of the bank. It was safer out front, he supposed, but in terms of the getaway, easier to speed off. A calculated risk. Not that he was doing any of the calculating, mind you, but still. See, the getaway driver just had to listen to orders. Listen and drive. Fast. Now those were two things that Tony was good at. Listening and driving. Fast was a foregone conclusion.

"Keep it runnin', Tony," Guillermo, better known as Gil the Gun, told him, patting him on the shoulder as he got out of the passenger side door. "Keep it runnin'."

Tony nodded as Sal the Scar and Shorty LaRusa got out the back. He watched them through the rearview mirror, straightening their jackets as they turned the corner and into the bank. A loan bead of sweat trickled down his face, his index finger twitching as he held on tight to the wheel. Beneath him, the car vibrated, shaking his body some, letting him know that he was alive.

The minutes ticked by, slow as molasses. It was hot outside, the streets thankfully empty. Tony kept his eyes on the rearview mirror, watching, waiting. Always with the waiting. Had to be patient to be a getaway driver. Had to be cool. He breathed in; he breathed out. And then he heard the pop, sending a jolt through his body that made him jump in his seat. Pop, pop. Pop, pop, pop.

Tony revved the engine and threw open the passenger side door. In the mirror, he saw Sal go down, hard, the bag he was carrying go flying out, bills swirling around like a sandstorm of cash. Pop, pop. Shorty was next. It was the turn at the corner that got him. Shoulda parked out front, Tony thought to himself. He heard the groan next, then another pop. Gil came last, two bags in his hand, running faster than a guy his size had a right to. "Go!" he shouted, slamming the door as he tossed the satchels in the back seat.

Tony slammed his foot on the gas, and the car took off, fast as lightning, the engine loud, tires squealing. He rounded the first curve, as planned, clipping an old jalopy as he went by. This was why they parked on the side. Could disappear easier. Make a few turns and be gone. He fought to catch his breath as the flood of sweat came pouring down, the sirens now blaring in the distance.

"Turn!" shouted Gil, his fist pounding on the dashboard.

The car veered, burning rubber. Two more turns, and they were home free. The sirens were going in the wrong direction, parallel now, but on the wrong road. Tony turned again, heading west, putting more distance between them, his heart speeding so fast he thought his chest would crack open.

"What happened?" he finally asked, car in a straightaway, engine roaring like a mountain lion.

"Must've been a tip-off. Too many of them," Gil replied, fighting hard to catch his breath. "We got most of 'em, but not before they done hit Sal and Shorty." He made the sign of the cross over his wide expanse of chest. "Faster, Tony, please."

Only, the driver's foot was already down as far as it would go. Still, he nodded, the car like a bullet, racing behind a factory and out of sight of the neighborhood. "Who you think tipped 'em off, Gil?" he eventually asked.

"Good question," came the reply as Gil wiped his face with his hanky. It came away as wet as a dishrag.

"One you got an answer for?" Tony glanced over and didn't like what he saw. See, Gil looked scared. And Gil never looked scared. In fact, Tony didn't even know his friend had it in him. Which is why he'd been around so long, now.

Gil shrugged. "Either the Gambonis got wind of the heist or …"

Tony gulped at the *or*. "No fuckin' way, Gil," he said. "No fuckin' way."

"The boss and Shorty been goin' at it lately. More so than usual."

"But they's related," Tony reminded his friend.

"By marriage only, Tony," said Gil, his breathing almost back to normal. "Maybe Shorty pushed him too far this time, and we was just not-so-innocent bystanders. Shit happens like that."

Tony knew better than to argue. Still, it pained him to hear it. He'd been with them for five years now, working his way up, from runner to enforcer to driver. The money was good, the job easy. Less dangerous, anyway. Until now. "Fuck," he cursed.

Gil chuckled, then sighed. "You got that right, kid." He rolled down the window and pointed. "Head over there. Then we'll figure out what's next." He was pointing to a warehouse, the rust and broken out windows a sign that the place was deserted. Tony did as he was told, at last running the engine at its normal pace. The car bumped and shook over the loose gravel as he pulled in behind a dumpster, out of sight, safe for the time being.

It was then that he noticed it, the red on the seat, the red spreading through Gil's pants. "You been shot," Tony said, almost in a whimper.

Gil looked down. "Doesn't hurt too much. Guards must've grazed me."

They got out of the car and found a side entrance. A chain hung from the door, padlocked. Gil laughed and raised his pistol. Tony covered his ears and watched it get blown to smithereens. The chain dropped, and the pair made their way inside. Light filtered in through the broken upper windows. The place smelled like dust, like mold, like metal. A thick amber beam shot down into the center like a floodlight. Gil grabbed a metal chair as they headed toward it. That was where they could assess the damage, both to Gil and to their careers.

"Looks pretty bad," said Tony, the material a deep purple where once it had been a dark blue.

"Feels fine," Gil told him, kicking off his Italian leather shoes. "It's us I'm worried about."

Tony nodded. "If it was the Gambonis, then we're fine."

Gil, too, nodded, unbuckling his belt. "But if it was a set-up, the boss ain't gonna be too happy to see us." He dropped his pants to the cement. "Asshole hates loose ends."

Tony gulped, and not only because of what Gil had said. See, he'd never seen his friend in anything but tailored suits before, and certainly not standing there in his boxers and knee-high black socks. "Wound don't look to deep," Tony made note of, trying to keep his eyes on the gash and not Gil's tree-trunk-thick thighs, covered as they were in all that wiry, black hair, a fucking forest of it.

Gil sat in the chair and had himself a look. Again Tony gulped when the cotton parted and one of Gil's hefty balls came into view. "Still bleeding though," Gil said, moving his thigh this way and that, the light catching the wound, all that red glistening like ripe tomatoes. "Better find me something to dress it with."

Tony's head went from side to side. Place was empty. Just a lot of scrap metal, torn boxes, broken glass. "Nothin' we could use," he said. "And even if there was, you'd sure to get infected with something right quick."

Gil sighed. "You wearing an undershirt, kid?"

Tony nodded, already popping open the buttons and pulling the material out of his slacks. He folded the silk and set his shirt down over Gil's shoes. "Fucker cost me a small fortune," he said, with a smirk. "Imported."

"Goody for you," said Gil. "Now hurry before we need to import us some blood, too."

The undershirt came off next. Thankfully, the place wasn't all that cold. In fact, inside the light, it was kind of toasty. Tony glanced down at his friend, their eyes catching for a moment, Gil's so blue you could practically swim in them. "Here you go," the driver said, his voice suddenly uneven.

Gil grabbed for the material, grunted, and tore it down the center, then tore it again, until he had one long strip of it, which he gently wrapped around his thigh. He winced when he knotted it. Immediately, the blood soaked through, but it would do. For now. "Any ideas, kid?"

Tony crouched down and scratched his head. "Take the money and get it back to Geno," he said. "Or take the money and run." He looked up, his eyes darting from Gil's crotch to his stunning eyes. Both were equally as unnerving. "One way we're heroes, the other we're dead."

"Yeah," said Gil, leaning back into the chair, head tilted up. "And that last part don't sit to well with me."

"Either way," added Tony, "we stay here until it gets dark. Cops know what our car looks like by now."

Gil chuckled, then winced again. "Fine by me. Let Geno stew for a while." He wiped the sweat off his face with his hands, then unbuttoned his shirt, revealing muscle-dense pecs, a thick middle, all of it coated with jet-black hair. "And speaking of stewing, it's hotter'n hell in this place." The shirt came off, leaving him in nothing but his boxers and socks.

Tony's cock went hard at the sight of him. All things considered, it was probably a good idea to stop looking. Only, it wasn't that easy. "You ain't married, are you, Gil?" he asked.

His friend laughed. "Not a good profession we's in, kid. Best to stay unattached." He stared down at the driver, eyes locking again. "You neither, right?"

The temperature suddenly spiked. Tony gulped, shook his head. "Nah, not me."

"Smart kid," said Gil, with a nod, legs wider now, a ball dangling out, big as a lemon, brushed with wiry hair. "Girlfriend?"

Tony didn't like this line of questioning. He preferred to keep his personal life personal. In their line of work, the less said the better. "Nah," he replied. "You?" He tossed the volley back, hoping the game would soon be over.

Gil shook his head. "Nope. Just a lot of beating off." The laughter grew, the sound echoing out, swirling around them, making Tony's head go light. Then Gil grabbed for his crotch. "Only way to keep the beast happy," he said, with a lusty sneer on his handsome, well-tanned face.

Try as he might not to look, he looked anyway. "The beast, huh?" he said, trying to make it sound funny; only it came off sounding like something else. Something needy, wanting.

Gil nodded, eyeing his friend again. "Yeah," he said, almost in a whisper. "Why you think they call me Gil the Gun?"

Tony shrugged, uneasily. "On account of, well, cause you shoot people."

The laughter returned, though with an edge to it now. "Yeah, kid. That I do. Only, they call me Gil the Gun because I'm always packing heat." Again he grabbed for his crotch, giving it a lewd squeeze. And the bulge beneath grew noticeably larger in his mitt of a hand.

Tony laughed, too, nervously. "Better watch it don't go off, then."

The material was now noticeably tenting as Gil pulled his hand away. He stood and turned his waist from side to side, his cock swaying within. "Bang, bang, kid."

Tony grabbed for his chest and mock-keeled over. "Ah, you got me, copper."

When he looked back up, Gil was standing over him, the boxers near ready to burst. "Where'd I get you, kid?" he asked, crouching down, their eyes again locking, neither of them blinking. Gil rested his hand on his friend's chest, which was rapidly expanding and contracting. "Here, kid?" His thumb brushed against Tony's rigid nipple, causing the downed man to squirm. The hand moved further south, the fingers trailing through a dense matting of hair. "Here?" Tony didn't reply, just kept staring, breathing. The hand kept going, the fingers sliding beneath the belt, inside the slacks, grabbing onto the steely rod inside. "This where I got you, kid?" Gil got on his knees. "I better have a look then."

Tony stared down, afraid to move, to speak, as his friend unhooked his belt, unbuttoned his slacks, and yanked down the material, briefs included. Until they were both eyeing his erect cock, already leaking, the jizz spilling over the wide head. "Sorry, Gil," was all Tony could think to say.

Gil gave it a squeeze, precum trickling from the slit again. Then he leaned in, until their faces were up close, until Tony could feel the hot breath on him. "Why you sorry, kid?" Another squeeze, a stroke, another breath. "Dick this nice, nothing to be sorry about." He closed the gap, shocking Tony to the quick. Still, he returned the kiss in kind, their lips pressed up tight, swapping some heavy spit.

When he finally pulled away, Tony managed, "How ... how did you ..."

Gil stood up, the boxers falling to the floor, massive cock set free, swinging like a baseball bat. "Takes one to know one, kid." He gave it a thwack and sent it reeling. "Now why don't you give it a suck, see how far we can get this baby down that throat of yours."

Tony pushed himself up off the cement and knelt before the giant cock, which now jutted straight out, nestled in a thick, black bush, balls hanging low. He gave the head a lick, the salty jizz hitting his tongue like a bullet. Gil coaxed it in, moaning as Tony gave it a suck and a slurp, letting it go further in, further still. He gagged as Gil gave it a final push, a tear streaming down his scruffy cheek. The prick pulsed in his mouth, his own prick pulsing in sync. He stared up, past all that fur and muscle, and watched his friend's head tilt back, mouth in a pant. He popped the prick out of his mouth, spit dribbling down his chin. "I wanna fuck you, Gil."

Gil chuckled, belly rising and falling as he stared down and ran his hands through Tony's thick, black mane. "You do, huh?"

The getaway driver stood up, face to face, dick to dick. "If you think you can take it."

Again Gil laughed, glancing down at his friend's impressive fifth limb. "Questionable, kid," he said, giving it a tug. "But worth a shot." He winked, and added, "Provided ..." And then he turned and started rummaging around the large enclosure. Tony stared on, curious at what he was up to, hungrily eying all that muscle and flesh and fur, like a giant, horny bear, grunting as he overturned this and that. "Ah," Gil finally said, returning with a can of grease. "Looks like we're good to go." Again the wink, a kiss, lips soft as a cloud.

Then it was down to business. Gil grabbed his shirt and used it as a pillow, stretching himself out on the cold, hard ground, the bandage holding in place, the blood now brown, clotted at last. He pried open the lid and slathered some grease on his pole, then spread his legs and ran his fingers around his hole, lubing himself up.

Tony got on his knees, in between his friend's legs, bending down to run his hands through all that hair, across acres of flesh, pounding his fists against two pecs as solid as granite, all while he inched in, his cock head butting up against the greasy chute. "Anyone ever tell you that you're a nice looking man, Gil?" he asked.

The mobster laughed. "Are you telling me that, kid?"

Tony nodded. "Guess so."

"Then yes, someone has." He smiled and shot the driver a wink, yet again. "Now fuck me, kid. Nice and slow and easy."

Tony's cock slid in, just the head, every nerve ending in his body suddenly shooting off like the Fourth of July. Gil clenched, sucked in his breath, his hole grabbing on for a second before he relaxed it. Gently, Tony slid further inside, pumping his friends prick all the while with one hand, twisting and yanking his balls with the other. Gil squirmed beneath him, pinching his thick nipples as he moaned and groaned and rocked his ass into that giant cock. "God, you feel good in there, Gil," Tony rasped, almost there now, just an inch more to go.

"Ditto, kid," Gil replied, shoving his rump forward, until Tony's balls were lapping up against rock-solid flesh.

The driver dropped down, hungry lips meeting hungry lips, tongues thrashing, cock pumping in and out, in and out. "Fuuuck," he moaned, slamming his dick home.

"Yeah, kid," whispered Gil. "Now make me come."

Again Tony mashed his mouth into his partner's, ramming and cramming his cock deep inside his tight, greased up hole, both of them moaning and groaning, the sound loud as it echoed off the metal walls. His body spasmed, head suddenly tilted up, back arched, howling as he shot and shot and shot, filling Gil's ass with ounce after ounce of molten hot cum.

Gil came a split second later. It took about two strokes, his body trembling as his swollen prick erupted, shooting thick bands of pungent spunk up and out, dousing Tony's chest with it before it dripped back down in thick, gooey wads. They both fought to catch their breaths as Tony collapsed, his still spurting cock popping out, mouths again united, pressed up so close it was impossible to tell where one of them ended and the other began.

Eventually, Tony pulled an inch away, locking eyes once again, drilling down deep. "How much money did you get, Gil?"

Gil smirked. "Enough, kid," he replied. "How much gas you got?"

"Full tank," he told him. "Why, you feelin' like a ride?"

Gil chuckled. "I think I just got one, kid. But yeah, I think we should go someplace. Someplace nice and warm," he said, wistfully. "I need a little getaway."

Tony rested his head in the crook of Gil's neck. "Then you're in luck. You got the best getaway driver this side of the Hudson."

"Don't I know it, kid." Gil sighed, holding on good and tight. "Don't I fucking know it."

SAINT ALDO OF THE
SACRED HEART
By DesertMac

Hailing from a small town in Pennsylvania just four months prior, I was sitting butt-naked in the tenement apartment I shared with my mostly absent roommate Robert one sultry summer night in Brooklyn. Writing paper was scarce and expensive, so I was excitedly writing out the things I liked about his body and what nasty things I wanted to do with it on the inverted back panel of a macaroni box. I was nineteen and had just recently admitted to myself that I was totally infatuated with my truck-driving roommate. Admitting this was a big deal that also meant I could no longer deny to myself that I liked guys. Robert excited me even more than the guys my age I used to think about back in school. He was in his late twenties, big strong and handsome, and though he was rough around the edges and a take charge kind of guy who intimidated me at first – and truth be told, those were some of the things that turned me on about him – he was a really nice guy once I had gotten to know him.

I'd left home for the bright lights of New York City and gotten a scarce and precious job with President Roosevelt's Public Works Program digging subway tunnels. I was very grateful for the job, since young single guys my age were not given priority in the job lines. Finding Robert's bulletin board notice for a roommate to take care of the apartment while he was gone so much was the clincher that set me up to be my own man finally, and I thought life was going pretty great, considering the Great Depression was still going strong in 1937.

Our neighborhood was pretty rough, mixed Italian, Dutch and Irish, so there were constant turf battles going on between warring factions of Italian mafia and Irish gangs for control of the bars, gambling and prostitution trades. It was scary to see fights and shootings in broad daylight and at night, but it was exciting, too. I can't deny that the rough men who played Tommy guns like violins turned me on. Their cocky, dangerous attitudes and the way they carried themselves just caused tingles in my groin and fired all kinds of fantasies in my mind. I had always been drawn to big powerful men, even before I had realized it was sexual.

But I was sitting there rhapsodizing about Robert's sexy dark green eyes and his stout muscular body, wishing he would let me share his bed when he was here, when I heard the sound of rapid gunfire somewhere down the hallway of our third floor walkup. I bounced around startled in my seat for about two seconds then hit the floor and crawled behind the sofa to ride out the gun bursts just like I had three times before. There was yelling and banging along with the gunfire, and it sounded at times as if it was getting closer to my door then moving away then back. My heart skipped a beat when I realized that I had not locked the apartment door when I came back from the bathroom at the end of the hall a while ago! But there had been gunfights in the halls before, and no one had ever even tried the door.

As soon as that thought cleared my head someone tried the door! I heard it open and close then latch as the sound of heavy footsteps clanked on the bare hardwood on this side of it. The sounds of others yelling and running down the stairs faded and deafening silence filled the room. My heart was racing, and I tried to get my breath under control. *'Stay calm, stay calm; don't look up and maybe he'll leave quickly. He doesn't even have to know you're in here.'*

A deep and menacing voice called out, "Who's there?! Stand up real slow with your hands up, or I'll shoot right through the fuckin' sofa!"

I about peed myself. I slowly raised my head with my hands going up first. I was shaking so bad I fell off my knees and had to scramble to stand up on rubbery legs. "I-I-I-I'm sorry! I j-j-just …"

His eyes narrowed, and he leveled the mean black sub-machine gun at me as he assessed my naked form. To say I felt vulnerable, terrified, naked and … naked, is an understatement. I think my balls jumped up inside to hide. We heard men yelling again in the hall and clearly heard the sounds of them carrying a wounded man away while a woman wailed and cried. The gangster stood silent and alert, machine gun at the ready while holding his finger over his lips to tell me to remain silent as well.

When it got quiet again, his eyes softened and a bemused smirk cocked his lips up at one corner as he turned his attention back to me. He said with a chuckle, "Well I can see you ain't packin' anything." He lowered his gun and motioned for me to step around the sofa. I was too petrified to actually move, though. He waved his gun impatiently, and I jerked into motion, stumbling around to stand trembling in front of the big gangster. He looked me over more thoroughly, scanning my body in a way that just didn't seem usual – not that I knew what usual would be in a situation like this. He leaned around to get a better view of my ass, for some reason, and seeing him do it sent shivers down my spine while Goosebumps broke out over my body. He noticed that, too.

He went to the window to look out and assess the situation on the street as we heard sirens approaching, then turned to me and said, "You live alone? Expectin' anyone else?" I shook my head yes then no, and he came back to stand in front of me. His expensive looking suit was ripped on the left sleeve and dirty from the action he'd been through.

"Be real quiet, kid. Don't do nothin' stupid and you'll be just fine. Unnerstand me? Have a seat. Now look," he used his gun to emphasize his words like some people use their hands. "What just went down out there … It was bad. I just lost two of my buddies and the O'Brien goons got … Well, that's no business of yours. What is your business is that I'm gonna have to lay low for tonight. They're gonna have their goons guarding this dump real close, and the cops in this precinct are in their pockets. I'm gonna have to stay here with you at least through the night. You *sure* nobody else is comin' here?"

"My, my, my r-r-roommate is a-a-a long haul trucker. He won't be back from Chicago for three more days," I said to the barrel of his gun.

"Good, then we don't gotta worry 'bout it." He laid his gun on the table next to my pencil and macaroni box notepad. My breath caught as I saw him glance at the writing. He did a kind of double take and turned the cardboard to better read it. Once again I about peed all over myself as he read my ramblings about what a good looking man Robert was and how I had seen his huge morning hard-on and wanted to see it out of his underwear just once and maybe get to suck on it. I had *never* written anything like all that before! I had let myself indulge my fantasies in writing *this one time*, intending to shred or burn the cardboard as soon as I finished writing. I wanted to die of shame and embarrassment as he read my pathetic and twisted words.

He would probably go ahead and shoot me now. That's what they did to queers. Well, I didn't really know because I had never known or seen a queer in real life, but I had heard …

His head turned slowly my way with his finger still holding the cardboard down on the table, so the fan wouldn't move it. He had that smirk on his lips and some kind of glint in his eyes as he looked me over again. He could easily see how mortified and terrified I was as I tried to make myself small and invisible with my hands folded around my cock and balls trying to not feel quite so damn naked.

"Cocksucker, eh? You don't look like a nancy boy. I guess ya can't always tell." He grinned and asked, "Were you jerkin' off when I came in?"

"No! I-I-I-I'm not really … I mean, I was just … I've never done … I'm not a s-s-sodo …" I trailed off in despair, shaking my head in shame. It was no use trying to deny it after he'd read my self-incriminating words. I waited for a beating and then a gunshot. Maybe he'd just shoot me and get it over with quickly.

He turned to fully face me and just stared for a long tense minute. I glanced up and back down quickly several times, dreading what he was going to do to me. Finally, he stepped over in front of me and reached down to grab my chin and make me look up at him. He was a big man. He looked as if he was probably twenty-nine or thirty, at least six feet tall, broad shouldered and well built. His face was not all that classically handsome, but I found him handsome and manly as hell. His olive skin, big nose and bushy black eyebrows were very Italian, and his strong square jaw and high cheek bones set off his obsidian eyes spectacularly. He had a five o'clock shadow that made him look even more dangerous than he obviously was.

I looked up into his eyes with tears starting to well in my utter humiliation and shame. He studied my eyes for a long moment then said, "We're stuck together for the night at least. I'm not gonna hurt you. I don't care what you do with guys. You work? You gotta go to work tomorrow?" The next day was Sunday. I shook my head yes then no in his grip. "Good. Now you're gonna stay calm and just act like you always do. You ain't goin' nowhere or talking to anyone. Soon as this blows over, I can get outta here," he said in his thick Brooklyn accent. He let go of my chin and straightened up.

That's when I noticed the outline of his cock running down his leg. I tried like hell not to look. I was determined not to look. But I did, and he saw me do it. His cock was obviously at least somewhat aroused, unless it was just huge and always showed this big in his black slacks. I deliberately looked away, but saw in my peripheral vision that he was staring intently at me. I glanced up guiltily and saw he had an evil grin on his face.

I jumped when his deep baritone voice split the air. "Ya like that? Like what ya see?"

I wanted to sink into the crease between the cushions and the back of the sofa. This was one of those things I had worried so much about if anyone ever found out I liked guys, that someone would ridicule me and make fun of me, before they beat me up or worse. I wasn't real small. I was five-ten and in good shape from hard work, but I wasn't much of a fighter, and of course I didn't have a gun. I tried to act like I didn't hear his questions and was not staring at his impressive display, but my eyes were inexorably drawn back to it. I cursed my lack of will power even as I kept glancing back at the irresistible bulge.

His left hand slinked over, and his fingers smoothed the fleshy tube down his inner left thigh, accenting the outline of it. Since that was an invitation to look, I couldn't tear my eyes away from the awesome, huge shaft that had my entire body tingling. He kind of hunkered his pelvis forward and said, "Since we're stuck here all night, well ... nobody's ever gonna know what we get up to, right? So what the hell." He grabbed the zipper tab and slid it down, sounding like a chainsaw in the room. My eyes were transfixed on his big hand as he dug inside and soon pulled his very impressive cock out to flop around in the warm night air. Just seeing it so alive and twitching around had me all but levitating. My body was humming and vibrating with a desire stronger than anything I'd ever felt, by far.

I glanced up into his eyes with a million questions in mine, but he didn't seem to have any questions for me. He just looked as if he knew what he wanted and I was the one who was going to give it to him, as soon as he finished taking off his suit coat. My god, what a cock he had on him! It was fat and really wide, twitching and jerking as it thickened and lengthened, swaying around with his movements. Even before it got hard, it completely dwarfed mine at its hardest. The scent of his sweaty sex wafted to my nostrils on the soupy Brooklyn air and made me shudder, and made my own cock finish stabbing up through my hands and peeking out.

He humped his hips forward and made his cock swing menacingly side to side a couple of feet from my wide eyes and slack jaw. "Go for it, kid. Don't be shy; we both already know ya like dick, so ..."

He wanted me to suck his dick. I wanted to suck it. It was amazing, getting harder as I watched, already looking like eight or nine inches and very thick. Like mine, it was uncut, and the foreskin was slowly peeling back from the tip as it hefted itself up perpendicular to sniff out some wet warmth and eager tongue. I was too petrified and scared to move even though I was being offered my first chance to do anything sexual with a man, and that part was as exciting as the rest was scary. He grabbed it at the base, waved it around and said, "Well? Don't ya want this? Don't be scared. I ain't gonna hurt ya. Come on kid, get to suckin' it; you know ya want to."

I looked up into his eyes, and he nodded with a smile to reassure me. So I leaned forward and took possession of the base from his hand. Electric thrills shot all through me as I felt a cock other than my own for the first time. It was hot and hard, but the skin was silky soft. The big veins snaking up and down its length were bloated, and pulsing and there was already a little precum issuing from the deep slit as my grip pulled the thick rubbery foreskin back a little more. I was trembling and shaking like a toy poodle as I leaned forward and met the scorching hot tip with my lips. I used the wide and blunt head as a wedge to spread my jaw, sinking to just behind the corona, pushing the foreskin back with my lips. I sighed as he moaned and jerked around in place in front of me.

This was it! This was the confirmation for me that what I had been thinking all along was indeed true. I wanted to suck cock. I wanted to suck cock more than anything else I'd ever wanted, and now I was actually doing it – and doing it to a big dangerous gangster with a big dangerous cock, and he wanted it, so he wasn't disgusted by me, and that was good enough for me to lose my fears and build enthusiasm very quickly.

I pulled his body closer with my grip around the girth of his base and let more sink in. He liked that. He grunted as he put his hand on top of my head and started pushing more of his huge cock into my mouth. I whimpered and moaned with pleasure like I never thought I'd get. Using his hand to guide me, he got a steady in and out rhythm going while he used his other hand to undo his belt and slacks, which promptly slid down his legs, pulling his boxers with them to puddle around his ankles and expose a snub-nosed .38 in his ankle holster. Seeing his groin and balls and those incredibly muscular hairy thighs come into view sent new jolts of lust through me, and I redoubled my suction, so he sped up his thrusting. He was jabbing his cockhead at the back of my throat but not shoving it in, while I wondered what it would feel like going all the way into my throat – there was a lot more to go, which I studied intently as the shaft slid in and out of my mouth.

He fought getting loud, whisper-shouting, "Yeah, suck it! Like that. Yeah, that's good. Watch the teeth, kid. There ya go, yeeeeah, like thaaaaat."

His deep, resonant voice of approval and encouragement, as well as his firm grip on my head while thrusting in and out of my mouth were ramping up my lust and need to a fever pitch. I was moaning continuously, and my excitement was as obvious as neon as I reached up and started fondling his big hairy balls, which thrilled me even more.

"Ohhhh, slow down, kid, you're gonna make me blast ya too soon!" He pulled his cock out of my mouth and held it up against his hard flat belly over his shirt tail. "Suck my balls."

Instead of verbally thanking him for offering, I came off the edge of the sofa onto my knees as he stepped back and removed his shirt, tossing it over his sub-machine gun. I jammed my face into his nuts and moaned with pleasure as I licked around and sucked the first one into my mouth. I inhaled his groin scent and hummed into his massive balls. This was too good, like coming home. This was what I had always wanted so badly, dreamed of, prayed for long before I even admitted it to myself.

"Oh fuck yeah, fuck yeah! My wife don't like givin' head, and she's only sucked my balls a couple of times, when I made her do it. This is good."

My erection was standing at forty-five degrees and throbbing, pumping out precum like an overheated radiator. He only got faster and more forceful with his thrusting as he clamped my head with both hands and fucked my face. I had to admit that I really, really loved him controlling things like that. It just seemed natural for a big man like him to fuck my mouth and make me take it. And make me take it he did. He slowed down and began forcing his cock gradually into my throat as he thrust in and out, trying to slow it down, so he could last a bit longer.

As he got the head all the way into my throat, I began to panic as my air was cut off, but he would pull out and let me gasp in a new breath before pushing it back in, and eventually he got my nose jammed into his pubes, and all I could see and smell was his groin – I thought I had died and gone to Heaven, with that massive cock stuffed down my throat, unconcerned with the uncomfortableness of it stretching my gullet wider than I thought it could be stretched. It was a milestone accomplishment for me to feel it in there, and I would have kept it buried until I passed out from lack of oxygen had he not been pistoning in and out so forcefully but slowly.

His voice was silky dominance as he crooned, "Yeah, all the way down to the bone. That's what we both want, all the way down. Thaaaat's

it, good cocksucker. Choke on it. Yeah, it feels good when ya choke on it."
I gagged and coughed and retched a few times until my throat realized it
was helpless against a battering ram of this bulk and power and was able to
relax enough to let me revel in the wonder of what this man was making
me feel. "Oh man, kid, I'm gonna blast ya! Here it ...!" He began firing
down my throat, and I jerked my head back, so I could taste it. His was a
little more spicy and bitter than mine, but still tasted wonderful to me. The
thrill of it firing at the back of my mouth and pooling until I had to
swallow or drool – and waste his precious seed – had me on the edge of a
hands-free orgasm. He pulled all the way out to swamp my cheek and nose
with the last two jets, then he used the head to smear the remaining pulsing
dribbles of cum all around my face while he moaned and heaved for
breath, jerking the sensitive head away and jabbing it back every couple of
seconds.

Naked on my knees in front of this gangster after just sucking him off
as he smeared his cum around my face with his dribbling cock sent me
over the edge. I wasn't even touching myself. I erupted and coated his
slacks and shins with probably the biggest load I had ever shot in my life.
As soon as I started shooting, I snatched his cock head with my lips and
clamped down to suck like crazy and siphon any last bit of cum out while I
convulsed and bounced around on my knees.

When I stopped bouncing around, he chuckled and said, "Whew! I
guess ya liked that, huh?" I moaned loudly and nodded yes as I bit down
with lip covered teeth on his softening shaft. He watched me nurse
hungrily on his cock for a minute then said, "Got anything to eat? I'm
starving!"

I got a wet towel from the sink in the kitchenette and cleaned his
shins and slacks as best I could, which meant he had to take them off. So
he got as naked as I was, and I silently thanked him with hungry stares for
letting me look at his incredible muscular body. He even had a couple of
tattoos that he let me inspect on his arms; so exotic to this farm boy from
Pennsylvania. I assumed he liked Italian food, but I had nothing on hand
that could qualify, so I fixed him a bland rural cuisine spread. I wasn't all
that skilled at cooking, but I could make an edible meal. He apparently
liked what I made, and he sat sprawled on the sofa afterwards
contemplating me. I shyly went to put on some clothes, and he snapped his
fingers. "No! Stay naked. Come over here 'n sit by me."

I sat down next to him and about melted when he put his big arm
around me, pulling my shoulder up into his steamy armpit. I had never felt

so close and wanted by anyone as I did at that moment. He liked me, even though I was 'like that' and in fact he liked that I was like that. He certainly had liked my blowjob, and now he was being really nice.

"Yeah, kid, you did that real good. You done that before?" I shook my head no. "Really? Virgin mouth? Geez, I guess you've just got a natural talent for that." He leaned his head down and nuzzled into the side of my head as he said in a low and gravelly voice, "I'm gonna tell ya 'bout somethin' I never told no one before. When I was in school, I used to fuck my cousin Luigi in the ass all the time. He loved it. Well, I kinda forced him the first couple of times, but even the first time, he got to lovin' it after we got goin'. I fucked him all that year until his folks moved to Jersey. I really liked doin' it with him, and him suckin' my dick. Boy, he would chow down on my pole like a starvin' dog!" He laughed and I tingled.

He licked the middle finger of his free hand, reached over and stuck it down between my legs to work it back toward my ass. My legs spread wider automatically because his hand was big, and it just seemed as if he had the right to do whatever he wanted with me. I stared down in awe at his big masculine hand working its way under my nuts. The feelings he was causing were making me shiver and tingle. When his fingertip made contact with my asshole, I jumped in surprise at the wonderful feeling. He chuckled and said, "Like that, huh? Feel good with my fingers down there?"

I nodded cautiously. He was talking about fucking me in the ass with that really big cock, and though I had been fantasizing about this for a long time, I wasn't really sure about it, and his cock was scary big, though it *had* gone down my throat.

I felt his thick finger burrow its way into my opening to the first knuckle and shivered again as he whispered in my ear, "Ahhhhh yeah, hot 'n tight. You're a virgin there, too, yeah?" I nodded as I sucked in a much needed breath, realizing I had held my breath for too long. My left hand wandered over and plopped itself down on his cock. I wrapped it in my hand and just kneaded it as he fingered my ass. "Relax, baby, you're gonna love this so much you'll be screamin' how good it feels. You like my dick, don't ya?" I glanced up at his handsome face inches away from mine and nodded yes. I couldn't deny that I *loved* his cock, a whole lot, as I looked back down at it twitching and filling out rapidly in my hand. It was the most wondrous thing I had ever seen or tasted. "Well I like your tight little cherry ass. Just think how good it's gonna feel goin' up inside you. The way you go crazy for dick, you're damn sure a bent boy, and it's just your nature to need a dick inside you. Every virgin is scared at first, but I guarantee you're gonna be lovin' it as soon as we get going."

I nodded yes because I did believe him. He knew what he was doing, and I knew he was right about me wanting it. I had been fantasizing about this for a couple of years at least. I just knew I wanted a man to fuck my ass, and I also knew he was going to no matter what I said or did – which in a way relaxed me about it all. His thick finger felt so good inside me, but then he pulled it out.

"Here, sit in my lap for a minute." He lifted me from the side like I weighed nothing and sat me in his very hot lap. His cock was already semi hard, and it felt scorching hot against my nearly hairless ass, indescribably good. His arms came around and hugged me back into his hairy, taut and muscular chest. The contrast between my pasty white torso and his dark hairy guns clamped around my stomach and chest was at that moment the most erotic visual ever for me. He alternated kissing and licking around the back and side of my neck and ear, which sent more thrills coursing through me. He whispered, "Yeah, sit in my lap and tell me what you want; confess your dirty little thoughts to me like I was a priest. Confession is good for the soul, right? You've been fantasizin' 'bout this for a long time, ain't ya? Go ahead 'n tell me what you really want."

He worked my butt back and forth on his steely erection, and I had to keep reminding myself to breathe. His strong arms manipulating me around on top of his cock and squishy balls with his chest hairs scouring my tender back was sending me over the moon! Nothing had ever felt like this before. I thought his confession thing was rhetorical until he said, "Well? Tell me what you want, baby! Ya gotta confess to Saint Aldo what ya want."

I giggled nervously. I was turned on like crazy, but I was still scared as hell. He was making me feel like a little kid with this confession talk, but I didn't really mind. I wasn't sure what he wanted me to say, but I ventured, "Ummmm, I want … I want … your thing in, you know, in …"

"It's my dick, baby, my dick. Say it. Dick, big fat dick."

"Dick, big fat dick." I giggled and wriggled on top of said dick. "I want your big fat dick in my butt."

He brushed his hand over my drooling cock and chuckled. "Yeah? That what you want? Tell Saint Aldo all about it." He lifted me up enough to aim his cock between my thighs before setting me back down. The big angry plum colored head jutted arrogantly up between my legs, pushing my nuts further up into my body. "Like feelin' that big dick between your legs, baby? Like how Saint Aldo brought you the answer to your prayers tonight?"

"Y-y-yeah." And it *was* wonderful, feeling the steely hard shaft scorching my tender inner thighs and prying them apart like that, so I added, "It feels really good there. Geez, it's so big." I reached down and caressed the head, sliding my thumb around in the precum. "I'm kinda ... kinda scared of it ... goin' in my butt ..."

"It'll hurt a little at first, but once ya get used to it, it's gonna feel wonderful, I promise. Always trust the saints, kid. What's your name, anyway?"

"Tommy Williams."

"Nice ta meet ya, Tommy. My name is Aldo Giancini. Now that we've been properly introduced, get down on your knees 'n suck my dick like a good boy."

I climbed out of his lap and instantly missed the sweaty heat of his groin against my super sensitive ass, but I forgot all about that as I got on my knees between his hairy corded thighs and grabbed the majestic pole with one hand and his heavy sagging nuts with the other. As I engulfed the head, he growled, "Aaaaahhhh yeah, you love suckin' my big dick, and you do it good, baby, real good."

I sucked hungrily and gratefully for a couple of minutes then he went to the kitchenette and scooped a gob of shortening out of the tin and smeared it around his cock. He strutted back over to me with his cock leading the way and my eyes glued to the vision of the Gangster Saint of Brooklyn. "Get up on your knees on the edge of the sofa with your hands on the back." I cautiously got in place, and he moved in between my dangling feet to run his slickened hand up my crack and send more shivers up and down my spine. He inserted one finger, and I jumped forward with a yelp, even though he'd had this much in minutes ago, and with less lubricant then. "Relax, baby, relaaaax. I know it's your first time 'n I'm gonna go real slow. Trust me." He leaned down over my back and aimed his cock at my hole, wedging it at the opening as he clamped his other hand around my ribs to hold me in place while he breathed heavily on the back of my neck.

As the pressure increased, I whimpered in fear. He held me tighter and said in my ear, "This is happening, no matter what, baby, so just relax and go with it. You can't stop it, so just enjoy feeling a dick go up in you for the first time. You'll always remember this moment." About then, he broke through my sphincter, and the pain was like white lightning shooting through my body. He got his greasy hand up and over my mouth just in time to muffle my scream. He just held there for a while, slightly twisting his hips and letting me get used to it. I knew he was not going to stop, and I felt powerless and completely at his mercy, but I also felt that the invasion of my ass was just 'right' somehow, and the pain began receding as he rocked his hips gently back and forth without sinking much deeper. As he felt my body relaxing a little, he rocked more of the extremely thick shaft into my guts a little at a time in very slow thrusts. Each new bit of my ass he claimed hurt, but it also felt kind of amazing. This was what I had fantasized about for so long I couldn't help but moan and work my muscles around the fat pole.

"That's it, relax and enjoy feeling that dick work its way up inside you. This is what you need, Tommy. This is what you've been dreamin' about 'n writing about."

Somehow, him using my name made a big difference for me. I moaned and nodded my head as I squeaked out, "Y-y-yeah. Yeah," since he had let his hand slide down onto my chin. Then he slid his finger in between my lips, so I sucked on the greasy thick digit as I clamped my ass muscles down on his cock, making him moan with pleasure. So this was what it felt like to be taken by a man. It was the most natural thing in the world to me, but I could hardly believe it was happening. It felt like a dream, except in my ass; that felt very real and impossibly big.

I whimpered and moaned as he bottomed out and held there, swiveling his hips and stirring me up inside while my muscles began to accept the massive invasion. As he started his first withdrawal I felt as if I had to take a dump, then I just felt empty and as if I wanted it back in as he withdrew all but the head. He forged back in slowly, and I moaned with pleasure and pain. As he got a slow rhythm going, I found the pain got less and less. By the time his hips were slapping against my butt cheeks and he was driving it home, I had given myself over to the bliss of getting fucked in the ass and thrilling to his big hairy balls banging against my perineum.

"Your ass was made for my dick, baby. I'm gonna fuck you now." I thought that was what he had been doing, but no, he had been making slow leisurely love. He gripped around my chest and down at my hip firmly and started pounding my ass unmercifully. Damn, his cock was so big, and this was my first time, and I didn't think I could take this pounding! I was grunting and crying out and begging him to slow down but trying to not be too loud so no one would hear us. He was going to town on my ass and saying, "Yeah, take it! Take that dick, baby! Ooohhhh, you're so tight and hot! This is how you take a dick!"

After a while, it just felt like the best thing ever as he pounded my ass relentlessly, taking a long time to come since he had already dumped a load in my mouth earlier. At some point, he reached down and squeezed my dripping cock, and that was all it took to send me over the edge. I sprayed the back and seat of the sofa while he pounded harder and faster, saying, "Yeah! Come for me! Fucked that cum right outta you, bitch! Yeah! Now you've been fucked by a man! Like that? Like that dick fillin' your guts?"

"Yeah! Yeah! Oh god!" I cried and bit my forearm as he reamed my little ass with that huge member. Finally, he came with a howl that he muffled between my neck and shoulder, biting my tender skin and marking me in the process. Then he collapsed on me, and I could barely hold us up while he caught his breath. He flipped us around and fell back into the seat beside my cum with his cock still planted deep in my gut. He ran his hands all over my stomach and chest as he breathlessly said things like, "Fuck, baby, that was … That was amazing. Goddamn, your ass is … amazing. Fuck!"

I was like a bowl of warm gelatin. I just lay back in his lap against his furry chest and sighed with a happiness and contentment like I'd never known I could possibly have. I wriggled my ass around on his slowly deflating cock and whined when it slipped out. He said with a chuckle, "I think I created a monster! You gonna wear me out tonight, baby? Huh? Gonna ride this big Italian dick again, in a little while?"

I turned and kissed his cheek and said, "Oh yeah." Then he shocked me by kissing me deeply with lots of tongue. I had not expected anything tender and loving like that from this big dangerous gangster, and I had to hold back tears of happiness as I clung to him and melted into his passionate and very dominant kiss.

# # # # #

I sucked his dick all through the night except during the three subsequent times he fucked my raw ass. But sore as my ass was, I still wanted more as daylight filled the sparsely furnished tenement. I showed Aldo the somewhat secret way out the back window onto the neighboring fire escape and that became his entrance and exit when he came to fuck me into a coma every couple of days, always announcing himself with "Saint

Aldo of the Sacred Heart is here for confession!" So I started calling him Saint Aldo because he liked it. We didn't get together when Robert was home for a couple of days at a time, but once when he was stuck home for a week, we met over at a fleabag hotel in Queens, and Aldo fucked me all night long.

I was happy, but I knew he was married and had a little daughter, and he could never live with me, no way. In his gangster culture, the only thing worse than a queer was a snitch, and both labels were death sentences for gangsters. But he did love me, and he told me so and showed me often. Our lovemaking was passionate, tender but often rough and animalistic; we both liked that mix. When he would slap my ass and tell me to get down on my knees and suck his big ol' Italian dick, I instantly fell down in front of him and loved on that big pole and those low hanging nuts. His cum was my absolution. When he would shove me over the back of a chair, I would arch my ass back at him and hold my breath until his cock was going in.

Then one night, Robert came home early while Aldo was fucking me over the kitchen table. We all three froze in shock.

"What the …?" was all that made it out of Robert's mouth.

Aldo casually said as he slowly pulled his cock from my ass, "Close the door, guy. Now go sit on the sofa and keep your mouth shut while we get dressed." Aldo and Robert were about the same size, but Aldo had a gun in his ankle holster, so Robert didn't argue with him. Robert knew who Aldo was, and he was afraid enough of him to stay silent and sit down as he had been told.

We got dressed, and Aldo calmly told Robert that what he and I did was nobody's business, or 'bidness' as he always said in his Brooklynese. His attitude, the defiance and lack of any trace of shame floored me and made me love him even more. He told Robert that he had better never hear even a whisper that any of this got out, or he'd calmly walk in here and shoot him dead, *capiche*? He also told Robert that he had better not even *think* of giving me any attitude or grief over what we did, and in no uncertain terms we were going to keep doing it. Then he left.

Robert was stunned. He couldn't even look at me for hours. I fixed him dinner, but he didn't eat. He left around ten and went to his favorite bar to get drunk. He came back and went to bed. We didn't talk after I got home from work the next day, but later that night, he thanked me for dinner and started talking.

"How long have you been doing that kind of thing with him?"

As worried as I had been about his attitude toward me now, I really didn't want to talk about *that*. "Ummmm, well, about three months now, I guess."

"I didn't know you went for that type of thing." He didn't sound accusatory or disgusted, just surprised, or so it seemed.

I didn't know what to say to that, but I made myself mumble, "Well ... Yeah, I mean, he's pretty persuasive. He started it, and I just ... Well ..."

He asked me how we started, and I told him about that night, leaving out the written ode to his body, making it sound a lot more as if it was Aldo's idea to have sex, but not trying to make it sound as if I didn't want to as well. I guess I was feeling kind of brave after what Aldo had said to him.

After a long silence, Robert looked over at me with a crooked grin and asked, "So you mean I could've been gettin' some of that all this time when I'm home, and you've been holdin' out on me?"

I was shocked. I was too stunned to react for a long moment. Then we both burst out laughing. I managed to say, "I didn't know you wanted any! I damn sure wanted it from you! But you never even gave me a *hint* that you wanted to do anything!"

He shook his head and kept chuckling as he said, "Well you never hinted that you were offering! What about now? You offering?"

I considered Aldo, whom I had pretty much fallen in love with over these months. But I knew he was unobtainable, too, so I had only to weigh his jealousy. He looked at me as 'his,' and when he took me uptown to dine at nice restaurants, he subtly treated me like his baby, which always made me feel extremely special and loved, but I knew we could never live in connubial bliss as they say. Then I thought about how I had been so into Robert well before I even met Aldo, and he was a very, very sexy man to me. As satisfied as I was with all the cock I got from Aldo – and it was so damn good – I still looked at big hot men, including Robert, and fantasized about them all the time.

Instead of verbally answering him, I got down on my knees in between his legs as he sat back on the sofa, and I undid his jeans. I pulled his cock out and proceeded to give him the best head he'd ever had – at least that's what he told me afterwards. Then he fucked me all over the dingy apartment, and from that night on, whenever he was home, he fucked me royally. His cock was actually a little bigger than Aldo's, and between my two men, I had all the cock I wanted or needed. I admitted my sex with Robert to Aldo after a month, and he told me that he was aware of it going on. I was shocked, thinking he would be jealous, but he explained to me that he thought I deserved someone to be with and that we both knew he could never be that for me. He was just glad that Robert wasn't jealous of him. I loved him more for that. I also fell in love with Robert, and he fell in love with me.

This three-way relationship went on for three blissful years. I'm sure everybody wonders if we all three got together. We never did, although I would have loved it; neither of them ever brought anything like that up, and I never felt brave enough to broach that subject. I didn't want to risk messing with the two of them being totally okay with the other.

# # # # #

Then one night in 1940, I was sitting and listening to President Roosevelt give a Fireside Chat on the quartz crystal radio Robert bought the year before, and I heard a noise at the back window. I knew it would be Aldo, and my face split with a big smile. I got up to go greet him and yelped when he fell through the window and stayed on the floor by the bed. I ran over to him and saw that he was clutching his chest and blood was running over his fingers.

I cried out and fell to my knees beside him. I saw the bullet hole in his chest and just lost it. I didn't know much about gunshot wounds and the body, but even I could see this was a fatal wound. He was gasping for breath and could hardly speak. It hit me that instead of going home to his wife, he had come here to me when he knew he was dying. I cried and frantically ran around getting wet towels and cloth for bandages, knowing it was futile. Calling an ambulance would involve the cops, and there was nothing they could do to save him, if they even got here before he died. He called me over to him, and I dropped all the stuff.

I got down and kissed my handsome man on the cheek and asked him what could I do for him.

"Nothin' baby, nothin' now. It's over. I just had to see your face one last time." He coughed and wheezed, wincing in pain, but resumed talking in a hoarse gurgly whisper, "You know I love you, right?" I nodded and sobbed uncontrollably. I kissed around softly on his chest and face as he talked. He grabbed my hand and squeezed. "No, I mean, only you. I only ever loved you, Tommy. I never loved my wife. I love my little girl, but the love of my life has been you. I just wanted you to know that." He reached up and ran his fingers across my cheek and brushed some of the tears away. He smiled, well, grimaced, and said, "I mean it, baby. You're the only one I ever loved. You make me feel whole when I'm with you. Be good to Robert. I know he loves you, too. He's a good man, and he can give you all that I never could. If only we could've ..."

He coughed then the light went out in his eyes. I wailed into the night and just sat there, sometimes lying over his chest and crying. All night. Sometime in the morning, I got up and washed the blood off my hands and changed clothes. I had no idea what to do with his body. I couldn't bear to look at him. The pain was just so deep, even though we both knew all along this could happen. Live by the sword, die by the sword. I had loved him so hard. I was numb, but I realized I needed to find his associates and make up some story as to possibly why he had ended up in my apartment. I found a guy who I had seen with Aldo a few times and told him where his body was.

The guy was very business-like about it and had a couple of guys remove his body quickly. He sternly told me to forget I'd ever seen Aldo Giancini, dead or alive. I turned and walked away before he could see my tears. That night was hell, but Robert got home the next evening, and he consoled me. He was so good to me. He changed jobs to work in a munitions factory when the war started, so he was no longer gone for days at a time. He joined, and I was drafted into the Army. He went to the Pacific and I ended up in the south of England for three years, a lot easier duty than most guys got.

After the war, Robert and I went to college on the GI Bill and got degrees in engineering. We worked at different firms but only a mile apart in Alexandria, Virginia. We bought a house together, and there we've lived a charmed life ever since. I don't know how often he crosses Robert's mind, but I'm surprised at how often I think of my Saint Aldo of the Sacred Heart. I still miss him. My love for Robert has only grown stronger over the years, but that doesn't mean I loved Aldo any less. He was my first, my own real Italian Stallion, my secret gangster love, and I will always have a very warm place in my heart for him.

DONNIE AND CLYDE
By Logan Zachary

"Donnie, Donnie, Donnie. What are we gonna do about you?"
Detective Clyde Banister asked. He walked around the table in the small
room and slammed his hand down on it.

Donnie jumped, but said nothing. He noticed how tight the detective's
pants were as he circled around him.

"It's a cold night in the Windy City, and no one knows you're here.
We can keep that under wraps, or we can let the news slip out … *The
Chicago Daily News* is always looking for a new headline."

Donnie stared straight ahead. The bare light bulb's glare hurt his eyes.
He closed them and fisted his hands under the table.

"We know Al Capone was outta town in Florida, but we need
someone to let us know he ordered the St. Valentine's Day Massacre. If
you let us know, we can protect you."

Donnie eyed him and said, "I heard it was two Crestview police
officers in long trench coats that shot the seven men in the back alley of
that garage on North Clark Street." He looked Clyde up one side and down
the other. "You coulda been one of them."

Clyde shook his head and smiled. "Wait until you see what I do." He
left the room.

Donnie rested his head in his hands and waited. He felt a stirring in
his pants. This wasn't the right time for that, and he knew it was going to
be a long night. He knew he'd never get Detective Clyde Banister to
believe he knew nothing about the shooting. He was a small time
bootlegger that was true, but all he did was supply Al Capone and the
North Side Gang.

John May had warned him not to play both sides, but as long as he
had enough whiskey to supply both mobster's gangs, what did it matter?
He didn't play favorites, and both sides knew that.

Donnie missed John May; he was a mechanic and was working on a car at the time of the massacre. Highball, John's German shepherd was the only survivor of the day.

Clyde returned with two officers and a glass of water. He walked behind Donnie, uncuffed him and handed him the glass of water. Stepping back he said, "Donnie, I want you to strip. And if you don't do it willingly …" he motioned toward the two men.

Donnie took a drink and swallowed hard as he started to rub the circulation back into his wrists and hands. He had heard rumors of how the gangsters got people to talk. Did the police use the same techniques? He started to unbutton his shirt and stopped. He glanced at the officers and Clyde.

"Why are you stopping?" Clyde demanded.

"Do I get any privacy?" Donnie looked at the two men and focused on the one with black hair. He looked familiar for some reason, but he couldn't figure out from where.

Clyde shook his head.

The other blond officer stepped forward, but Clyde held up his hand and held him back.

As Donnie pulled his shirt tails out of his pants, he felt the fabric run along his semi-aroused flesh. He closed his eyes, took a deep breath and continued unbuttoning. He pulled the shirt off his back and placed it on the table. He kicked his shoes off and unbuckled his belt.

"Keep going," Clyde said. He pointed down to Donnie's pants.

As he unzipped his fly, he felt his cock swell even bigger. His face flushed red and sweat broke out over his body. His hands grew damp, and his fingers fumbled with his waistband causing his pants to drop to the floor.

His cock jumped in his boxers and strained against the cotton.

Clyde noticed the tenting and motioned to step out of his pants.

Donnie's balls swung free as he bent to pick them up. He pulled on his boxers, trying to keep his erection inside. As he moved, the fly opened up and a cool breeze blew through his thick bush of pubic hair.

Clyde moved over to the table and pat it, letting him know that he wanted him to sit down.

The two officers stood by the door staring straight ahead and waited. Donnie shuffled to the table and sat down gently on the edge.

"Scoot back. Make yourself comfortable. This will take a while." Clyde rubbed his hands together and moved closer.

Donnie swallowed hard and adjusted his boxers. The fly had spread wide open, revealing more than he had hoped.

"Take off our undershirt." Clyde stepped back and waited.

Slowly, Donnie crossed his arms in front of him and pulled the shirt up and over. As his hairy chest came into view, he felt Clyde's eyes caress his torso. After he set the shirt down, he folded his arms across his chest, trying to cover as much as he could.

"Are you cold? With all that hair, you should be nice and warm." Clyde's hand rose up, and Donnie pulled back, afraid he'd comb his fingers across his chest.

Donnie felt his nipples harden into sharp peaks. He pressed his hairy arms against his chest and felt the tickles all over, adding to his arousal. His cock leapt and threatened to escape out the fly.

As Clyde moved, his hand brushed along one of Donnie's hairy legs, and he felt warmth spread over his body. Clyde turned to the two officers and said, "You may leave. I think I can handle it from here."

Both men nodded and left.

Donnie swallowed hard as the door closed. He felt a rivulet of sweat run down his back and soak into his boxers. Another one ran down his spine, but this one slipped under his waistband and continued down the crease of his butt. It trickled through his hair and pooled under one cheek.

"Why so nervous? Do you have something to hide?"

Donnie crossed his legs. His dick shifted and the tip popped out of the fly. Donnie covered his groin and pulled the boxers over his erection.

"Am I getting you excited?" Clyde moved closer, his hot breath warmed Donnie's neck. "Are you ready to answer my questions, now?" He extended his finger and touched his upper chest. He drew it down to his nipple and circled the sensitive spike. He pinched and twisted it slightly.

Donnie felt wetness at the tip of his dick. His hard-on strained against the cotton and ... "I don't know anything."

Clyde pushed on Donnie's chest. "Lie back." He pressed harder.

Donnie relaxed his stomach muscles and slowly lowered to the table. His bare back cold against the wood as it touched. His cock sprang out of the opening, and he covered it with his hands.

"Impressive," Clyde said. He ran his finger down his chest, between his pecs, along his sternum and down his tight abs. His finger swirling the hair as it went lower and lower. It circled his belly button a few times.

Donnie closed his eyes and clamped down harder on his groin. He felt precum ooze out of his dick and flow into the palm of his hand. He tried to rub it away, but it only stimulated it more and made his cock grow harder.

Clyde stepped between his legs and ran his fingers up his thigh as he moved closer. He pressed his pelvis against the table and felt his arousal grow. His fingers slipped up the leg opening and explored.

Donnie tried to pull his legs together and found a warm body between them. A fingertip touched one of his balls and jolted him back into a sitting position. Sitting eye to eye, his baby blues looked deep into the detective's dark browns.

"Are you ready to sing?" Clyde asked. His fingers grasped a ball in each hand and rolled it. "We can do this the easy way or the hard way." One of his fingers trailed along his shaft. "Looks like it is hard already."

Donnie felt more precum ooze out of him. "I … I …"

Clyde leaned forward and brought his mouth down on Donnie's. His tongue explored, as his hands grasped his erection. He worked the aroused flesh.

Donnie's dick slipped out of the fly, and Clyde changed his hold. He pulled Donnie's low hanging testicles out and squeezed them with his other hand. Clyde broke their kiss and bent to lick the tip of Donnie's dick. A pearl of precum crowned the uncut end. He used the foreskin like a straw. His tongue entered the chamber and rolled around the fat mushroom. He retracted the foreskin and swallowed the cock inch by inch.

"Still just a bootlegger." Clyde picked up one of Donnie's legs and brought his foot to his mouth. "Or a boot licker?" He licked along the hairy ankle.

"I can't tell you something if there isn't anything to say …"

Clyde grabbed Donnie's waistband and pulled the boxers off.

Donnie's dick flipped out and slapped back on his abs. A wet splat appeared above his navel. A few glistening drops clung to the wiry hair on his torso.

"What an amazing view, but I need to be a bit more persistent." Clyde tossed the boxers to the floor and reached between Donnie's legs. He lifted the low hanging balls out of the way and found a tight pink opening. "If I probe you, will that get you to confess?" He stuck out his tongue and lowered his head.

Donnie lay back down.

Clyde grasped his narrow hips, pulled his bubble butt, and spread his cheeks. He inhaled deeply, smelling musky male sweat and savored it. He licked the pink circle and swirled it around. His tongue darted out and sought entry.

Donnie rolled his head from side to side.

Clyde's hot, wet tongue dove in deeper and deeper.

A low moan escaped from Donnie. His whole body tingled, and he dug his fingers into the wood. If he had anything to confess, he would have spilled his guts, but his balls were threatening to spill something more.

Clyde worked up from the tight pucker and drew a low hanger into his mouth. He rolled it across his tongue and tried to swallow it whole. He hummed deep in his throat, and Donnie's body tensed up. Clyde moved to the other ball. His hand inserted the first testicle back into his mouth, and he closed his mouth. He pulled his head back and sucked.

The pressure increased, and Donnie reached down to grasp his dick. He stroked it a few times as Clyde worked on the plump orbs.

Clyde let his balls slip from his lips and traced his tongue along the sensitive shaft. His mouth encircled the foreskin, and his lips pulled it back as they slid down to the balls. As he pulled back, his tongue played down the underside.

Donnie felt his orgasm follow Clyde's tongue to the end. The load filled his mouth and ran down Donnie's shaft.

Clyde tried to swallow all of it but only caused another wave to explode.

Donnie clamped his hands on the edge of the table and thrust his pelvis into the wanting mouth. More hot cum shot out, and he pushed back inside to the hilt.

Clyde swallowed him whole and drew down hard and drained anything left in the shaft. He let the cock flop back on his belly and wiped the back of his mouth with his hand.

Donnie inhaled deeply and waited for his breathing to return to normal. As he looked up, he watched as Clyde started to unzip his fly.

"It's time to turn the big guns on you now." He fished out his throbbing cock and stroked it to full length.

Donnie gasped at the size and thickness of it. "What are you doing?"

"I'm using the rubber hose on you." He smacked his dick on the palm of his hand. He reached forward and scooped up the overflow from the table and Donnie's abs and smeared it along his cut cock.

"That's not going to ..."

"Yes it will." Clyde stepped to the table and pulled Donnie's ass to the edge of the table. He picked up Donnie's legs and hooked his ankles over his shoulders. He slapped his dick against the pink pucker. He watched as the hole clamped down. "I can see you're gonna to be tight."

Donnie's body jumped as Clyde's hand finger the opening. He poured water into his hand and sprinkled the liquid over the hairy halo. He circled the loop and tapped the spot. He pressed the bull's eye and drilled in. The moisture helped the entry, but he needed brute force to slip the muscle ring on his finger.

Donnie's head fell back, and he spread his legs wider. This was going to hurt like hell. He felt two fingers explore and enter. They pulled and loosened. Pain turned to warmth and sent a relaxing shudder over his being.

A third digit pushed in, and Clyde knew it was time. He pulled out and grabbed his ten inches and placed it into the chamber. His hips rocked back and forth as it tried to enter.

Donnie's body tensed up and refused to allow him in.

Clyde grabbed his uncut cock and started to stroke it. With each tug, he pushed forward. As the rhythm smoothed out into an even beat, Donnie's body relaxed and hardened. Clyde felt his girth enter a little at a time. His hand worked over Donnie's dick, which grew back to its full length and started to ooze.

Donnie moaned and arched his back as his body relaxed. He felt a warmth flow through his body as Clyde entered deeper. He grabbed onto the edge of the wooden table and started to match Donnie's rhythm. He felt the pleasure rise again in his bottom and lift up through his balls and up his abdomen. His ass spasmed over Clyde's cock and milked him as he thrust deeper.

Clyde increased his speed. He couldn't control the intense tickle that grew and grew. His balls pulled up and more precum oozed out of his foreskin. The added lube allowed for the speed to double, triple. A low moaned came from his throat and vibrated throughout him. He felt the orgasm build and build until he couldn't control it anymore. He thrust inside one more time and emptied his balls.

As the cum flowed out and hit Donnie's prostate, another climax shot out of his shaft. The thick cream flowed over Clyde's hand and down his shaft. Another spurt sprayed across his chest and coated him with white heat.

Clyde pulled out and sent a stream over Donnie's body. He rubbed his cock against Donnie's. He rolled their shafts along each other and stroked down them. More cum poured out and mixed together.

Pearls of pleasure splattered the table and their bodies. Both men breathed heavily and gasped for air as they waited for their bodies to return to normal.

Clyde opened a hidden drawer in the table and pulled out two cloths. He handed one to Donnie and started to wipe the sweat and semen off his cock and then the table.

Donnie cleaned up with the rag Clyde gave him. Both men quickly dressed and straightened out their appearances.

"Let me take you home," Clyde said.

"I'll be fine."

Clyde shrugged and walked Donnie out of the interrogation room and to the booking desk. "Did you want to go out the front door or slip out the back?"

"I don't have anything to hide …"

"Are you sure you don't want one of my men to see you home safe?" Clyde snapped his fingers, and the officer with black hair pulled his hat down lower and followed them. The three approached the front door. "Go out and see if the coast is clear."

The officer nodded and stepped out into the night.

"Are you sure you'll be alright?" Clyde asked.

Before Donnie could say anything, the officer returned. "No one's out there."

"We'll follow you out," Clyde said.

The officer opened the door and exited.

As he turned to exit, Donnie got a flash of him, and remembered where he had seen him.

Clyde followed him outside.

"Wait!" Donnie rushed after him. Just as the three stepped onto the sideway, a car sped around the corner, its headlights blinding them. Donnie grabbed Clyde and pushed him to the ground, covering him with his body.

A Tommy gun fired out the car window as it drove past, red flames shot out of the barrel with each bullet. The black haired officer grabbed his chest as a row of red spots traversed his body.

The front door burst open as the blond policemen rushed out, weapon firing at the escaping car. He shot out the back window of the car and ran after it into the street. A taillight winked out with another bullet, as the car disappeared into the night.

The blond officer rushed back to Donnie and Clyde. He helped them to their feet. "Are you okay? Were you hit?" He patted over their bodies, searching for bullet holes. Finding none, he moved over to his fallen partner, but saw he was too late.

"How did you know?" Clyde asked.

Donnie pointed down to the ground at the dead officer. "I remembered him from the garage. He's one of Al Capone's men."

"You saved my life." Clyde touched Donnie's arm and held it.

"I saved mine, too."

"Well, maybe this time you'll let me take you home, personally." He squeezed Donnie's arm and waited.

Donnie smiled, "I may need that bodyguard for the night."

"I think I can arrange that, and more. There are a lot of mobsters out there in the Windy City." Clyde stepped back.

"Then maybe I'll need more protection, even nightly."

"I can arrange that," Clyde said, as they walked back into the police station.

"I was hoping you'd say that."

THE TENDERIZER
By Landon Dixon

"You tell your boss he can stick his offer up his ass! You tell him that from Joseph P. Killarney! None of my stockmen are going to be unionized – ever!"

Binns sighed, latched his briefcase, rose from the leather chair in Killarney's office overlooking the sprawling Kansas City stockyards. "I'll tell Mr. Tomaso," he said softly, but authoritatively. "But he's not going to like it."

Killarney got up from behind his huge, cherry wood expanse of desk, walked over to Binns. "Look here, Mr. Binns, I get excited sometimes." He ran a slender, tanned hand through his thick, silver hair, formed his full, red lips into a smile. "I've got no beef with the Urban Cattlemen's Association, you know that. I hear good things in Chicago. But here it's different, there's still a depression going on, we can't afford those second city wages and benefits. You understand?"

Binns didn't reply, regarding the bronze sculpture of two nude boys embracing one another that sat on a table against the far wall of the expansive office; the collection of Oscar Wilde first editions displayed in an antique glass-fronted cabinet; the original Wyndham Lewis painting, portraying an innocence scene of young men skinny-dipping. "Very impressive, Mr. Killarney," he commented, nodding at the works of art.

Killarney's smile broadened. He rubbed his hands together, plucked at the lavender puff that adorned the breast pocket of his pinstriped suit. "Thank you." He sniffed at the air, which was laden with the odor of manure, full of the dulcet lowing of cattle out in the stockyards. "I try to give this dirty business a little ... culture, you see."

Binns shook the man's soft hand, as Killarney squeezed with both of his. "I do see," Binns said.

#

"He asked for you, specifically," the deskman stated.

The bellboy looked apprehensive. "Really? Me?"

"Yeah, really, you." The deskman unplugged the cigar from his mouth, jabbed it at the stairs to the left. "So get your ass in gear."

Chester Cole was eighteen, small and wiry, with short-cropped hair, large brown eyes, a delicately-featured face and pitch-black skin. He moved uneasily up the stairs to the second floor of the hotel, down the corridor to Room 219. He stopped at the door, nervously adjusted his cap, fiddled with the brass buttons on his red serge uniform. Then he knocked.

"Mr. Tenn?" he called out.

"Yeah, come in," came the answer from within the room.

Chester turned the doorknob and pushed the door inward, froze, his mouth hanging open.

The occupant of the room was sitting on the bed, stark naked. His nude body was broad and muscular, smooth-shaven all over, even his balls. His cock hung over the edge of the bed, huge in between his legs.

"Come in," he repeated. "I got something for you to do for me."

Chester swallowed, hard, staring at the man's cock, massive even soft. He glanced up into the man's ice-blue eyes, at the sheaf of ten dollar bills he was gripping in his big left fist. Chester licked his lips and slipped inside the room, closed the door.

"I thought I had you pegged," Tenn said, voice deep and thick. "I need you to polish my gun. I got a job to do tonight and need to be ready."

"Polish your ..."

The man gripped his cock with his right hand and hefted the flaccid tool, fanning out the tens with his left hand.

"Oh, your ... gun," Chester gulped.

He walked over on shaking legs, dropped down to his trembling knees. All he knew about Tenn was that he'd arrived two hours earlier at the hotel, had listed his home as Chicago, exuded a deadly toughness incongruous with his rich blond hair and tailored camel's hair coat.

Chester gazed at the bloated purple cap of the man's cock, the wrist-thick, veined, stretched shaft. He tested his jaw muscles, his mouth gone dry. "Mr. Tenn, I'm not sure ..."

"You can handle the job, Chester. For fifty bucks."

The man dropped his dick and Chester caught it. He sucked air into his lungs, feeling the weight of the slab in his hand, the beat of the meat between his fingers. He dipped his head closer, stuck out his bright pink tongue and introduced the tip to Tenn's yawning slit.

"Yeah, now you got it, Chester." Tenn tossed the money on the bed and planted his hands on either side of him, leaned back, thrusting his loins out at the kneeling bellboy.

Chester tentatively pumped with his hand, marveling at the width and length of the shaft. He grasped the bulging sack that dangled below, hefted and squeezed the individual plum-sized balls within. Then he stuck his wet tongue out further, spun it around the man's swollen hood.

Tenn grunted, his cock surging with blood, engorging still larger in the younger man's hand, on the end of Chester's rotating tongue.

Chester looked up into Tenn's eyes. There was coldness in those eyes, deeper than the depths of the Depression. But the man's cock was as hot as any Kansas sun, pulsating in Chester's hand, straining, expanding. He opened wide and sucked the knob into his mouth while he still could, sealed his lips and sucked.

"That's the stuff," Tenn rasped, bucking his hips slightly.

Chester had never seen, felt, tasted cock so huge. His body and brain burned with the erotic knowledge, the veiny texture of the meat, the musky scent of the man's clean-shaven balls. He grasped Tenn's pouch in the palm of his hand and kneaded, as he pumped shaft with his other hand, bobbed his head, tugging on hood with his lips.

"Don't be shy," Tenn growled. He placed a big hand on the back of Chester's head and pulled the lad closer with a powerful strength.

It stretched the limits of the teenager's mind, and mouth. But his lips widened obscenely, beyond his wildest wet dreams, turgid cock flowing inside, more inches than he ever imagined. Until he gagged, and panicked, tried to pull back.

Tenn's dong had stiffened to almost three-quarters of its fully-inflated size, half of it stuffing Chester's mouth, hood pushing against the back of the teen's throat. He held Chester's head tight, not letting him back away.

And the lust for meat overwhelmed Chester's fear. Tenn's cock ballooned his cheeks and plugged his throat, balls overflowing his one hand, shaft thundering between the slippery, gripping fingers of his other hand.

Tenn pumped his hips, slow and easy. And Chester felt the wedged meat slide back and forth in his mouth, along his tongue. It felt wonderful, wicked, and he moved his head in rhythm, actually sucking on the man's tremendous dong.

The bed creaked, breath steamed out of Chester's grotesquely flared nostrils. The cock packing his mouth grew larger still, pulsed more violently. But Chester accommodated it, welcomed more of it. He bobbed his head faster, sucking harder and deeper, growing in confidence and excitement like the meat was growing.

Tenn grunted and ran a hand up onto his muscle-cleaved chest, squeezed a mounded pec, pinched a jutting nipple, twisted it. Watching the young man between his legs suck enthusiastically on his full-blown prick, taking almost a third of it in and out, the kid's dark face and lips and hands forming an erotic contrast with the pink shade of Tenn's beef.

Chester kneed into a better position, really enjoying things. He juggled Tenn's balls with his dexterous fingers, feeling with satisfaction the sack tighten. He moved his head to and fro even more rapidly, drawing wet and tight on Tenn's pipe, reveling in the sensation of its seizing hardness. The big man was going to blow his load in Chester's mouth, flood his throat with hot, spurting cream. He was ready, eager to swallow.

But Tenn shoved him backwards. His cock sprang out of Chester's mouth, an incredible slathered snake of twelve inches or more. "Good job, kid," the man snarled, tossing the sawbucks at the stunned, bitterly disappointed teenager. "Now get lost, I got a job to do."

For a man of Joseph P. Killarney's wealth and prominence, the security around his property was laughable. Tenn only had to crack the head of one solitary guard out by the wrought iron fence perimeter, to get by and up to the side of the red brick mansion. He circumscribed a first floor window with his glasscutter, reached in and unlatched the window, and climbed inside the home.

It was past 2:00 am. The house was dark and quiet and hot. Tenn mounted the winding staircase to the second floor with a stealth that belied his bulk and the huge bulge in his pants.

He found Killarney's bedroom, last door at the end of the hall, and slipped inside. The scent of lavender assailed Tenn's nostrils. He grinned, looking at the man's sleeping form.

Killarney was sprawled out on his stomach on the massive four-poster bed, buck naked, silk sheet drawn all the way down past his ass. His buttocks swelled ghostly white in the gloom, thin body rising and falling with his breath.

Tenn didn't waste any time. He unzipped his pants and drew out his rod, still wet from Chester's mouth play, and crawled onto the bed, straddling the sleeping man's buttocks. He pushed the sledge in between the soft pair of cheeks, gently frotted the smooth stretch of crack.

"Mmm, yes, Harold," Killarney murmured into his satin pillowcase, shunting his bum upwards.

Tenn grinned, coldly. He piled Killarney's downy cheeks up against the sides of his mammoth erection. The older man's flesh didn't come close to enveloping the younger man's shaft.

"Not Harold," Tenn growled, frotting harder, pumping his hips. "They call me The Tenderizer – 'cause of the work I done in the Chi-town stockyard offices."

Killarney's eyes popped open. He jerked his head around, gaped at the big man looming up behind him, the huge organ gliding back and forth in between his butt cheeks. "What!? W-who are you!? What do you want!?"

"Mr. Tomaso sent me. Seems you got a beef with him he wants settled."

Killarney gulped, licked his lips, gazing at that heavy log cruising in between his buttocks, caressing his crack, making him tingle all over. "I …I …"

"You're going to let your men unionize, Killarney," Tenn stated. "And I'm going to inject this slab of meat into your ass, tenderize your hole, so you can't take anything but big dicks from here on out – mine, twice a month, is the deal."

Killarney's pucker dilated, shimmering warmth spreading through his bum and body, the sawing slab surging his own pressed-down cock with rich, red blood. "And-and if I don't?"

Tenn stopped frotting, hauled his cock out of Killarney's butt cleavage. Leaving the man gaspingly, achingly empty where he felt it most. "Then I'm gone." Tenn stroked his erection. "And I'm taking your final offer with me." He rose up on his knees, turned to the side.

117

"Okay! Okay!" Killarney yelped. His shaking hands scrabbled at the headboard, slid a panel aside, pulled out a tube. He handed it back to Tenn. "Please, use this! And, for God's sake, please fuck my ass with that monster!"

Tenn grinned, a little more kindly this time. He set the tube of lube down on the bed and sunk his sledge back in between Killarney's cheeks, piled the pillowy masses back up, frotted again, pumping strong.

Killarney bit into the pillow, his body sliding back and forth on the slick sheets under the pressure of Tenn's piston. His own cock boiled, fucking the bed, his ass on fire with desire.

Tenn stroked Killarney's bum cleavage for a couple of minutes or so, his own cock at the same time. The man really did have a smooth crack, he discovered; the craving for big dicks driven deep up his ass that they'd researched, now confirmed. Tenn pulled his pipe out from between Killarney's buttocks and greased it with the lube the man had supplied.

Killarney's breath came in gasps. He stared back at Tenn, the man's member gleaming with lube, and hissed, "Prod my ass! Brand my anus with that big, hot poker of yours!"

Tenn shifted his hand up and down his dong, slow and sure and sensual. Then he let go, dug his fingers into Killarney's overripe buttocks and pulled them apart, letting his hood droop down to rest heavily on Killarney's pucker.

"Yes, stick me!" the man cried, thrusting his ass upwards, pushing against Tenn's cockhead.

Tenn straightened his prick to its full, awesome rigidity, pushed his bloated hood down hard against Killarney's asshole. Mushroomed cap poked inside Killarney, bulged, ballooned his ass ring, Tenn pressing powerfully forward.

"Oh, God, yes!" Killarney wailed, chute gone electric, plugged by hood.

Tenn plowed into Killarney's anus, brutally stretching ass walls, stuffing butt tunnel. He sunk inch after inch after inch of his dong inside the man, delving depravingly deep, blowing Killarney's mind and ass wide-open.

He embedded three-quarters of his cock in Killarney's gripping pink sleeve. Then he stopped, catching his breath, the man gone utterly rigid beneath him. Before he regripped his balls and the base of his cock and poured the last quarter of hot beef into Killarney's ass.

"Oh, God! Fuck!" the stockman cried, pounding the bed with his fists, impaled on Tenn's stake. "I'm yours! I'll give you anything you want! Just fuck my ass!"

Tenn planted his hands on either side of Killarney and leaned down over top of him, covering him with his massive body, massive bone buried full-length. He pumped his hips, shifting his cock slowly back and forth in Killarney's anus, rutting. "You'll get what's coming to you, Mr. Killarney," he assured the man, as he torqued up his movements to reaming speed.

Killarney stuffed his mouth full of pillow, the big man bearing down on him body and soul and hole. His brain blurred, his body ablaze, his churned chute screaming with savage sexual joy, seared deep as his bowels and beyond.

Tenn pile-drove Killarney, busting cheeks to non-stop vibrating with his banging thighs, blasting ass with his ramming cock. The bed shook and the man bounced beneath him, his pounding cock seizing up cum-hard like it had in Chester's mouth earlier, his spanking balls tightening like they had in Chester's hand. His job was done, mission accomplished. Pay-off in pure, harsh sexual terms at hand.

"Oh, sweet God!" Killarney wailed, his voice breaking along the edges like his mind. He jerked with more than Tenn's thundering body, soiling his silk sheets with hot, agonizing spurts of sperm. His ass was a raw meat mass of wicked sensation, Tenn hammering him and it into sexual oblivion.

The big man thrust, speared, grunted. His pistoning cock spasmed deep in Killarney's blown anus, blasting ruptured chute with seething semen. Tenn jerked again and again, in rhythm to his spouts of gouting orgasm. Sperm backed up from the unconscious man's crushed bowels and flooded Tenn's thumping groin.

The monetary pay-off came later. Five g's from Tony Tomaso; a solid gold cock-ring from Joseph P. Killarney. The Tenderizer became the stockman's prize bull, only it was the man who was getting ruthlessly inseminated; Tenn who was willed the stockyard operations when a heart attack claimed his benefactor one torrid, ass-punishing night.

Too much red meat in his diet, the doctor had to conclude.

JOHNNY CLUB
By Landon Dixon

"Hey, kid, watcha lookin' at?" Johnny Club laughed, idly stroking the salami dangling down between his legs, looking over at the pretty boy he'd picked up at the downtown martini bar.

"I ... I ..." the young man gulped, staring at Johnny's enormous cock, the gliding movement of the man's big, hairy hand on the thick, veined shaft.

"What'd you say your name was, kid?"

"M-Myron. Myron Dalgliesh."

Johnny laughed again, rising from the edge of the bed and walking over to the blond in the shiny blue suit and purple shirt, his dong bobbing long from his open fly. "Yeah? I thought you said it was 'cocksucker'?" He grasped the back of Myron's neck, massaged the smooth nape with his fingers, then snapped the man's head forward and mashed his thick lips against Myron's plush, red lips.

Myron gasped, trembled, Johnny working over his mouth with a sensual roughness. The big man stuck a hand down Myron's shirt, popping buttons, palming smooth suntanned skin, latching a pair of fingers onto a puffy brown nipple and pinching.

Myron moaned into Johnny's mouth. He was no match for the tall, powerful, curly-haired man, in strength or cock. So he surrendered, willingly. Let himself be mauled, kissed.

Johnny thrust his heavy tongue into Myron's open mouth and explored the moist, red cavern and sparkling white teeth, rolling Myron's nipples so hard the young man's sea-green eyes brimmed with tears. But the pretty boy moved his tongue against Johnny's demanding tongue, and the men entwined their slippery stickers in almost equal partnership. Room 17 of the Starlight Motel, on the dilapidated outskirts of East LA.

Johnny pulled his tongue out of Myron's mouth and licked the man's lips, rasped, "Well, come on, kid, live up to your name." He laid his hands on Myron's shoulder, pushed him down to his knees on the thin grey carpet, so that the blond was facing Johnny's meat.

Myron stared at the massive tool. It'd engorged even longer, thicker, the huge club head rising up into the air right in front of Myron. He swallowed, licked his lips, reached out a tentative hand.

"Yeah," Johnny growled, feeling the man's soft, warm, manicured fingers encircle his turgid slab.

He stripped off his sports coat, his checked silk shirt. His broad, muscled chest was swarthy with dark hair, skin olive. He slid a hand up onto a mounded pec and gripped and twisted his own stiffened tan nipple; other hand dropping down to Myron's blond head, fingers sinking into glossy hair. "Give it a pull, kid. See what happens."

Myron looked up at the bare-chested giant looming over top of him, back down at the giant organ overfilling his hand. Johnny's dong pulsed hard against his damp palm, shaft hot and heavy. Myron moved his hand, stroking the big man's cock.

"That's it," Johnny grunted. "Harder. Faster."

Myron tugged, pulling on the huge appendage from fur-covered balls to boiled-up cap, marveling at how the member grew larger still, seizing up to an absolutely awesome length in his quick-stroking hand. He gripped dick with both hands, jacked.

Johnny yanked Myron's head closer. "Cocksucker!" he hissed.

Myron opened his mouth up as wide as it would go and slid his lips over the hood of Johnny's dong. The big man jerked at the wet velvet warmth, speared deeper into Myron's mouth.

The blond grabbed onto Johnny's hairy nut sack, hefted and squeezed. As Johnny's cock surged into his mouth, curved down his throat. Johnny grinned, calling it, sinking his mammoth erection almost right down to the balls in Myron's face.

Myron looked up at him, cheeks and throat bulging with meat. His nostrils flared in rhythm to Johnny's heavy breathing, his hand tugging on Johnny's nuts in rhythm to the man fucking his face with his cock.

Johnny grasped Myron's head with both hands, churning his hips, shunting his dong back and forth in the young man's mouth. He plunged down his throat, his shaft squeezed tight as any ass it'd fucked. He felt the hot, humid gust of Myron's breath against his groin, against the gleaming, pumping shaft of his cock.

He fucked faster and faster, driving pretty face, his balls tightening in Myron's milking fingers, with imminent release.

"Suck my sack, kid!" Johnny snarled, suddenly jerking his shining snake all the way out of Myron's overstretched mouth and raw throat.

Myron gasped for air, fingering his jaw for dislocation. Johnny thrust his pouch into the man's face. Myron dipped lower, swallowed the furry sack in one gulp.

"Balls to the walls, kid!" Johnny blurted. "The only way to live in the swingin' '50s, huh?"

Myron glanced up at the towering man but couldn't see past the cock overhanging his reddened face. He cradled Johnny's sack in his mouth, sucked on it, inhaling the musky, cologned scent of the big man through his gasping nostrils. He wormed his tongue around Johnny's testicles.

Johnny jerked, smacked Myron's forehead with his dong, feeling the hot pull on his balls all through his body. "You got a real dirty mouth, kid," he rasped. "And it's gonna get even dirtier."

He unbuckled his gabardine slacks and shoved them down to his ankles, Myron's mouth attached to his balls. Then he whacked the young man's face one more time, hitched his groin back so that his sack popped out of Myron's mouth, dripping and matted. He swiveled around on his heels and stuck out his ass. "Eat it, kid."

Myron didn't hesitate, craven in his desire. He grabbed onto Johnny's thick butt cheeks and squeezed the rounded masses, dug his fingers in and spread the pair, stuck his tongue against Johnny's asshole.

"Fuck! Yeah!" the big man yelled, jolted by the impact.

Myron ringed his tongue around Johnny's wrinkled pucker, rimming. Then he licked the hairy crack, sliding his tongue down deep in between Johnny's legs, right down to the dangling balls, then dragging up and along the man's butt cleavage to the tip of his tailbone. He did it again and again, lapping Johnny's crack with his budded tongue, making the man shiver.

"Stick it inside!" Johnny shouted. "Fuck my chute with your tongue!" He reached back and brushed Myron's hands aside, gripped his buttocks, tore them wide open.

Myron formed his tongue into a glistening pink blade and jabbed it deep into Johnny's exposed anus. Johnny shuddered, the young man's tongue staking three inches into his ass, shooting his sensitive manhole full of shimmering feeling. Myron moved his head back and forth, plugging Johnny's chute with his tongue.

Johnny pulled a hand off a cheek and grasped his stretched-iron cock, fisted. Myron was clutching his nuts again, squeezing, pouring wet-velvet tongue down his anus.

"Open your mouth! Get your reward!" Johnny grated, spinning around, knuckles clenching his dong burning white, hand shifting to blur.

Myron threw his mouth open, shot his tongue out as far as it would go. Johnny plunged his raging appendage into the young man's face. Just in time.

"Fuck!" he howled, jerking, jetting. He blasted wad after heavy, heated wad of cum straight down Myron's throat, bucking with the savage intensity of his orgasm.

Myron's Adam's apple bobbed as fast as his head had just earlier, swallowing the hot, salty gouts of sperm.

Until Johnny staggered backwards, his spent shooter stringing a pure white line of semen from his slit to Myron's lips, connecting the two men more intimately than Johnny even realized at the time.

# # # # #

The shakedown came a day later. As Johnny was sipping a Rob Roy in Hy's on Figueroa. A man slid into the red leather booth across from him, dropped a manila envelope down on the walnut tabletop.

"Name's Shuster," the guy said. "FBI." He tapped the envelope. "Got something for your boss here."

Johnny swallowed a slug of his drink, set the glass down. He gazed sourly at the little man. "What boss?"

The guy grinned, ran a pale, puffy hand through his thinning brown hair. "Don't play cute with me, Johnny boy. You ain't got the looks for it. I'm talkin' about Izzy Green, the Big G. You're one of his bodyguards, ain't ya?"

Johnny casually glanced around the cool, dark interior of the nearly empty bar. "Beat it, half-pint."

Shuster's round face tightened. He grabbed up the envelope and ripped it open, spilled 8x10 black and white pictures out in front of Johnny.

The glossies portrayed young Myron sucking on Johnny's cock, the big man's balls, eating out Johnny's spread-open ass. The last three captured the orgasmic bliss on Johnny's face, at the moment his face-buried prick coated Myron's throat and stomach.

"So?"

Shuster laughed, nervously. He pulled a handkerchief out of the breast pocket of his white flannel suit and mopped his face, despite the cool. "I doubt if Izzy's gonna be too happy to find he's got a real ... man's man on his payroll. Big, tough, he-man Johnny Club," he added with a sneer.

"You hire that kid?"

"He's one of our ... operatives."

Johnny drained the rest of his drink. "What do you want, Shuster?"

"We want the Big G – wrapped up with a bow and ready for delivery to a federal prison, where he belongs."

Johnny laughed. "So I'm as good as dead either way, huh?"

"Not at all. We know there's a shipment of H coming in from Mexico soon. All you gotta do is tip us off to the date and location. We'll handle the rest. We know Izzy likes to attend the big transfers personally, and this is a real big one. You can be there and get busted like all the others." The little man shrugged. "Then we'll see about gettin' ya sprung – early."

Johnny regarded Shuster with a shrewdness that belied his reputation for violent crudeness. "And what do you want out of the deal, sweetness?"

Shuster licked his thin lips. "I wanna fuck you up the ass, big boy. Payback for all the times you and your boss wriggled out of our beefs."

Johnny grunted, thumbing through the explicit snapshots. "These got you hot, huh?"

Shuster didn't reply, just mopped his sweaty face with his scented handkerchief.

Johnny shrugged, pushed up. "Let's go."

Shuster watched the man's big, rounded buttocks clench and jostle in the back of his slacks. Then he shot a quick glance around the bar, shoved out of the booth, chased after Johnny into the washroom down the hall.

"Blow," Johnny told the attendant. He turned to Shuster. "How we gonna do this?"

The man's eyes darted around the black and white tiled restroom. "I'm doing it to you this time, big boy. On that couch over there." He pointed at the red leather couch parked against the far wall of the spacious washroom. "Take off your pants and get your legs up in the air."

Johnny complied, slowly stepping out of his slacks and drawers. His cock dangled heavy from his loins, hanging low.

Shuster tongued his lips, watching Johnny walk over to the couch, sit down, spread and raise his legs. The big man's hairy pucker winked at Shuster.

"Jesus!" he muttered, staring at the length of beef stretched out on Johnny's stomach. Then he flipped the lock on the restroom door and hustled over, fumbling his own belt open and zipper down as he did so. His dick was pink-shafted and purple- capped, paled in comparison to Johnny's semi-erection.

"You're not gonna do a dry run, I hope?" Johnny cracked, gripping his thighs.

Shuster fumbled a tube out of his pocket, squeezed lube onto his hard-on. He shuffled forward, poked Johnny's manhole with the swollen tip of his cock. Then he gritted his teeth and slotted his dick right into Johnny's anus.

He went in hot and tight and easy, gliding deep; until all that showed were his shaven balls. He left his dick lodged motionless in Johnny's ass, his face blazing red, as he gripped one of the man's knees, grabbed up the man's cock with his other hand.

"You're big capture, huh, Shuster?" Johnny said, his massive cock engorging still more in the smaller man's little hand, ass muscles gripping Shuster's prick in a vise.

Shuster's grey eyes went glassy. He pumped his hand up and down the length of Johnny's tremendous dong. Then remembered to pump his hips, pistoning his dick back and forth in Johnny's heated chute.

Johnny regarded the huffing and puffing man through hooded eyes, feeling the urgent tug of his hand, the eager thrust of his prick. He grinned coolly at Shuster, calmly taking the man's stroking and stuffing.

Drool dribbled out of the corner of Shuster's mouth, snot leaking out of a nostril. His face flamed, his body burning with the sexual effort of fucking the big man's ass, fisting his dong. He pumped faster and faster, gasping for breath. Johnny's cock surged massive in his flying hand, the man's anus sucking hard on his plunging dick.

Johnny grinned, as the little man yelped and quivered, spurted hot seed into his chute. He felt the guy spray over and over, jerking inside and outside his ass, gripping Johnny's cock in a death grip. And Johnny played ball all the way. He grunted, semen leaping out of the tip of his cock and splashing up into Shuster's face.

Shuster tried to control the trajectory of the gushing hose, but it, and his own orgasm were too powerful. His face and suit were striped with Johnny's sticky, heated cum, marked. As he blew out his own balls in Johnny's anus.

An abandoned airstrip in the San Fernando Valley was the setting for the second part of the transaction. Izzy Green showed up with a satchel. A plane buzzed and landed, and three men got out, one of them carrying a suitcase.

The Big G, Johnny Club and the three men met by the plane. They were exchanging luggage, when two cars suddenly roared out of the bushes one side of the airfield and up to the group.

Eight guys leapt out of the vehicles, guns drawn.

"We'll take the H and the dough, Izzy," Shuster said to the mob boss, grinning at the man's bodyguard. "See, the only G-Men I know are some of the Feds back in Cleveland, who booked me that one time."

"These bums are part of the Rizzo mob!" Izzy snarled. "Looking to expand operations outside of Ohio, huh?"

Johnny smiled at Shuster, nice and cool-like. "I thought you were a little too dirty, even for a Fed." He shook a cigarette out of a deck he pulled from his breast pocket, set it ablaze.

That was the signal. Izzy, Johnny and the men from the plane ducked around to the other side of the aircraft, opened fire. As more members of the Green mob waded out of the brush and established a second front of lead, catching the Rizzo boys in the deadly crossfire.

It was over in minutes.

Johnny didn't find the X-rated pictures, didn't really expect to. Their secret died with Shuster. But he did find Myron Dalgliesh back at the Starlight Motel. The kid was impatiently waiting, for his reward; after spilling his guts over the phone about the mob entrapment deal to Johnny shortly after Shuster had made his move. The pretty boy had a hunger for more of what Johnny had given him the first time, couldn't bear the thought of that dong being put on ice, instead of in mouth, or ass, where it belonged.

It wasn't the first time Johnny Club had gotten what he'd wanted with his oversized cock. Wouldn't be the last time, either.

He fed Myron his meat. The young man eagerly gobbled it up.

Only this time, Johnny'd packed another rod along with him. Not as large, but just as hard, and effective; to be used after the cock sucking.

The big-hearted and dicked lug just couldn't refuse a last meal for the condemned.

GOOD TO BE FAMIGLIA
By Derrick Della Giorgia

When he pushed back his chair to abandon the dinner table, the scene Antonio left behind wasn't much different than the one at Gino's a little earlier. Except here, the red stains on the impeccable white collar shirts were Nero D'Avola, not blood. The screaming, the pasta, the cigarette smoke, even the tailor that had confectioned the suits everyone was wearing, were the same. That night Don Antonio Ammazzaleoni, – back at Gino's house he was still "Don" to me – closed one chapter of his life and opened a new one. He increased his business volume by eliminating the Carusos, and added a member to the family. Me. But let me go back to our dinner, before I tell you what becoming part of the *famiglia* meant to him.

The dark room was at the point of implosion under the pressure of the Sicilian accent bouncing from one side to the other of the linen tablecloth. Don Antonio's nephew John, my cousin Vito, the faithful Pasquale, Silvio, Nick, Carmelo, and I put the silverware down to provide full attention to our Boss. When something is completely destroyed like with the Carusos, chances are something else is created right away to fill the gap. Don Antonio's *famiglia* needed another man to keep up with the new business. And that's where I came in.

"Giuseppe, you are *famiglia* now. Call me Antonio!" He kissed me on my cheek not far from my lips and raised his glass after announcing I was going to marry his daughter Nancy – to whom I had been faithfully engaged since the age of seventeen.

"Don Antonio, I am honored to be part of the *famiglia* Ammazzaleoni." I stepped towards him and put my arms around his chest. Don Antonio was about an inch taller than I – I realized when his moustache scratched me under my right eye. His words of celebration thundered in his bull neck, bringing to me the cologne Nancy and I'd given him for his name day, mixed with the tobacco he was inhaling. It felt good to be *famiglia*. It felt splendid to be under his wing.

The dinner turned into a discussion about how the business needed to be reorganized now that the Carusos were out of the picture and I was Don Antonio's soon-to-be son in law and only heir.

Only one face wasn't light and festive – John's. Don Antonio Ammazaleoni's nephew had spent the last ten years trying to make the Boss see he was the perfect heir. That he was the only mind capable of directing the Ammazzaleoni family's interests, now and after the Don's death. John would marry Nancy without any problem. She was just part of the job. He didn't need to be in love with her, nor she with him.

John cleared his throat but did not say anything. His eyes fixed on the last piece of meat in his plate. His pursed lips separated only to let the cigarette slide in.

"Grazie, Don Antonio. To the *famiglia!*" I squeezed in another toast before the Boss left. His strong hands landed on the table, and his black pin striped suite motioned to the door. Before disappearing, he called me with a traditional Sicilian contraction of his facial muscles.

"Get rid of John and then come see me." He patted my back and left the room, blocking my digestion process. I wasn't ready to be the main actor. But he needed to trust me.

"Good." I mumbled without being able to face the table again. John was a friend; only more decisive than I and definitely more power-thirsty than I could ever be. He'd been taking care of business long before my first gun shot. Remorseless, with a precise plan in his head. It wasn't a secret John wanted to inherit Don Antonio's business.

Foreseeing the attrition my marriage to Nancy would cause, Don Antonio had decided there wasn't enough room for the both of us in his family and had appointed me to eliminate the problem.

"Come in, son." Don Antonio looked even more imposing in his armchair. Exactly like King Henry the VIII in many portraits of the time: hands on the armrest, legs at a forty-five degree angle, torso perfectly adherent to the burgundy silk behind him. The room was dimly lit and wiped out of my mind the frenetic chain reaction that my bullet into John's chest had activated. The guys needed to fix the living room as fast as their full stomachs allowed them. Don Antonio didn't like a mess in his house.

"I did wha …" I tried to inform him, but his arm frozen in midair abruptly blocked me.

"I don't need to know that. You are *famiglia* now, no need to waste words." He gestured for me to move and sit on the twin armchair in front of him. "Giuseppe, we are one thing now, me and you. Like father and son, like brothers, like husband and wife. Not many people are worth this special bond. I know you are." He pulled me by the elbow. "You see this?"

"The Ammazzaleoni family ring." The gold lion head on his finger could give you power, like it had just done with me, or strip you off of everything, life included.

"The force hides in here, not in the guns we carry. A special force we need to share now, to make sure the Ammazzaleoni family stays strong and unite." He cleared his throat and paused.

"You know I would do anything for the *famiglia*." The prolonged silence obliged me to make that statement. The sweating of my palms confirmed to me I still had a lot to learn from the Boss. Control is the only important thing during situations like those the guys of our kind often found themselves in. The wrong twitching could mean the difference between life and death. The extra unnecessary word could make you lose the respect that keeps the family together.

"I know." He took my hand. My wrist hung from his for what seemed to me an infinite amount of time. As my limb travelled closer to his body, my mind machine churned all the oxygen left in my blood. But instead of fainting, I welcomed a completely unexpected scene.

Under the thin fabric of his suit, his balls felt full of energy, ready to pump orders to the Ammazzaleoni men. I got on my knees. I knew what he was asking now. We were *famiglia*, no need to waste words. In the attempt of massaging the hard shaft now reaching his belt, I took off the jacket that limited the degree of freedom of my arms. Don Antonio closed his eyes and rested his head. Wondering whether I was the only one to be granted this kind of privilege, I gave in to an unknown sensation of empowerment, together with a sense of excitement that I honestly had not before experienced. All the men downstairs couldn't even start to imagine the kind of intimacy that I was sharing with the Boss. It was clear that entering the *famiglia* was a ritual more than a simple legal act. Lifeless John himself would have probably enjoyed this more than deflowering the Boss's daughter's virgin body. My palms wrapped his cock, allowing my fingers to find the base of the head where the pleasure forced the vibrant man in front of me to emit guttural noises of lost control.

"Giuseppe." The sentence wasn't finished with words, but with a gesture of his hand that directed me further. The metal band of the lion ring landed in the middle of my skull, producing an internal thump that pierced my heart and went all the way down into my guts and my groin. His fingers navigated through my short gelled hair, without ever pushing my head down. It was an undefined desire that was eating me alive that forced me to bend on his crotch and venture into his pants.

I was afraid to comment anything. How do you communicate with the Boss when your mouth is in front of his precum-dripping uncut cock? It was probably my imagination, but it tasted just like him. Authoritative and unique. I dove on it and let it reach the base of my throat, where Don Antonio Ammazzaleoni repeatedly returned every time I re-emerged to avoid choking. His balls hit my lips when I swallowed a couple of sweet drops. It was coming. I sensed the full force avalanche of cum that was about to fill my mouth. But once again, the scene changed.

"It's time to give you some of your love and devotion back." The Boss stood up, leaving me kneeled on the floor. Without ever touching himself, he repositioned me in a way he could fuck my ass.

The first surprise was feeling his oily hand brushing my crack as if he was painting it. While I'd undone my belt and pulled down my pants, he must have applied lube on his right hand to sweeten the pain he was willing to cause me. I could still feel the ring. In fact, that was the finger he decided to tease me with. Slowly forcing my yet untouched insides, he managed to bury half his hand by time he deemed me ready for more.

"Don't move now." Don Antonio warned me before doing it. At first, the tension he created in my hole was so severe I stopped breathing. I thought the pain was going to grow and make me cry. But contrary to my expectations, the moment his cock was abundantly immersed in my ass, I recognize the pain subsiding and the pleasure increasing exponentially. The expanding waves of stimulation reproduced the effects of orgasm. Instead of hoping that ritual would finish soon, I found myself craving for more.

"I wa …" I want more, please fuck me harder. That was what I was about to tell the Boss, but I stopped myself immediately frightened of his possible reaction. Would he have liked the fact that I was enjoying being fucked up the ass by him? How would that memory work in front of the guys, when tomorrow he'd be giving orders or holding a gun? He never asked me whether there was something I wanted to say and that gave me the idea there were no comments to make.

Like in the perfect dream, he picked up a speed and rode me with more impetus fulfilling my wish. The friction in my hole was such that it started to burn with every new thrust. Don Antonio Ammazzaleoni's class didn't disappoint me in that occasion either. My father in law provoked my first anal orgasm. The same way he taught me how to hold a gun or kill somebody who could be dangerous for the *famiglia*. As he was still trying to reach his, I felt my orgasm invading me in every direction. Juice started oozing out of me, staining the armchair silk and the pants that kept my ankles together. I couldn't help but moaning.

"Hmm…" The guttural sign that followed my moaning informed me Don Antonio had come, too. Directly inside of me. He emptied his balls in my ass and concluded: "Giuseppe, it's good to be *famiglia*!"

THE FIFTH COMMANDMENT
By N. A. Hayes

Chicago is sultry and silent in the late July heat. Occasionally, a coy, tentative breeze rustles through the open window. The ratty lace curtains sway, but the breeze offers no relief to Dorian and Pawel as they play a second hand of poker and wait for Mr. Pazzo. A thick, red curtain that has been drawn across the bedroom doorframe does not move. The heavy barrier exudes a theatricality that Theresa, Dorian's mother, adores.

On the other side of the red curtain, Pazzo growls, "*Caro Mio.*"

Dorian's mother moans.

Dorian ignores the sounds as he has always done. "The heat ..." he says without finishing his thought. Pearls of sweat bead his smooth forehead. His coarse black hair falls around his face. It is shaggier than it is decent. However, outside of his mother's apartment, he keeps it tucked in his porkpie hat. His clear brown eyes glare at his friend Pawel across from him.

The glare breaks into a gentle smile. Tow-headed Pawel has no regular home. A few years ago, a drunk driving a Packard roadster killed his parents. The word in the street was that the drunk spent more money fixing the car than he was fined for the accident. Mr. Pazzo makes sure that Pawel has work; however, since Pawel is Polish, Pazzo won't extend the Organization's extra-legal justice.

Dorian asked if there was more that could be done.

Pazzo replied, "Let the Poles take care of themselves."

Dorian nodded. But he could not see how Pawel was different than himself. When they wrestled, the heat from their bodies was more intense than any summer day. They seemed to be one strength, one force. Dorian could not help sliding his hand up his friend's lean stomach or grabbing his powerful forearms. Pawel's body is as hairy as Dorian's, but the blond fur makes his skin seem smooth like a girl.

Pawel is better than any girl.

Dorian's musky essence streams from his black furred arm pits, drenching the soft fabric of his under shirt. He stretches, raising his shoulders over the back of his wooden chair. As his stretching pulls his undershirt from his pants, a dense but narrow paradise trail is revealed. At nineteen, Dorian has the cocksure swagger of a welterweight fighter.

He has never seen the inside of a ring, but he has a reputation for being a tough. A gash under his left eye still weeps.

Last week, he threw a dead beat out of Antonio's apartment. Antonio, the fairy who lives upstairs, services Theresa's overflow and gives blow jobs, which Theresa refuses to do. The drunk sat on the edge of the bed. Antonio was choking on the man's turgid member. The brute's hands were crushing Antonio's bird-like neck. His face was turning blue.

Dorian put the sweaty lush in a headlock. The man struggled, elbowing Dorian in the face but was no match for the young man. Antonio fought to catch his breath as Dorian dragged the belligerent drunk down two flights of stairs.

Antonio and Theresa are the only two girls working in the house. But at least for the moment, they were able to keep it profitable. To help Theresa make ends meet, Pazzo has been letting Dorian share Pawel's odd jobs. Initially this had been an act of charity, but Dorian's years of experience protecting his mother and her associates from overzealous clients have made him very effective muscle. Some of Pazzo's soldiers even talk of bringing the boy into the Organization.

Dorian lays down his hand of cards. He smirks proudly of the three aces before he lights a cigarette and takes a long drag.

Pawel slams down a jack high straight on the battered trunk they use as a table.

Pazzo's groans are punctuated by a rapid panting. With a final anguished moan, the boys hear their boss come. He starts to cry.

Pawel chortles.

Dorian leans forward and smacks him on the back of his head. Dorian has never had a father, but Mr. Pazzo has stepped in to teach him how to be a man. Since Dorian was a kid, the Organization's Ten Commandments have been central to these lessons. Dorian felt awed when Pazzo missed his wife's funeral in Kenosha to make sure the black market booze smuggled from Canada made it to the Organization's clubs in Chicago.

The fifth commandment made it clear a member always had to be available to the Organization.

The Organization's needs were more important than an individual's desire.

Still the guilt weighs down on the middle-aged man who now turns to Theresa as much for support as pleasure.

Theresa coos, "It's alright, Baby. What do priests know? Your wife's in Heaven. It's ok, Baby."

The sobbing trails off.

Pazzo walks out of the room. The curtain stays open. Drenched in sweat, he adjusts his black silk tie. His dark jacket is draped over his arm. His brown eyes are blood shot. He places a few bills on the trunk. "Boys, stop by the club tomorrow morning. I've got some work for you." Pazzo tussles Dorian's hair.

Exhausted, Teresa remains reclining on her feather bed for a few minutes. She wears only a negligee an old suitor gave her. A pair of old stockings slips down her long smooth thighs. Her lacy garter belt presses into her soft belly. Her long black hair pours onto her pillow. She is only in her thirties and looks like Dorian's sister. Only softness in her mouth from her missing teeth makes her seem significantly older than her son.

When Pawel started spending time with Dorian, he had been infatuated with her. Dorian tried to ignore the lust in his friend's eyes. He felt jealous of his friend's interest in his mother. One night, he lifted a bottle of gin from a truck they were watching for the Organization.

When they got back and showed Theresa their illicit gain, she scolded them as she retrieved three glasses. The three of them downed the first glass quickly. Dorian nursed the second. Theresa and Pawel kept drinking at a quick pace. As they emptied half the bottle, the young blond man pulled out a wad of bills. It was the money he had earned to pay his rent, but he shoved it at the lusty woman.

Dorian stood. He squeezed his knuckles until they turned white.

Seeing his frustration, Theresa kissed him on his cheek.

"Mama," he whispered. The word was a desperate plea not to take his friend.

She kissed his cheek again oblivious to her son's ache. She slinked into the bedroom. The curtain fell closed. The sound seemed like a dove plummeting to the earth.

Pawel scampered after her.

The sounds of falling clothing and kissing were faint, but they tortured Dorian. He crawled out onto the fire escape and let the darkness cover him. His eyes burned. But he would not let himself cry.

After the longest few minutes of his life, Dorian heard a glass shatter against a wall. Pawel yelled, storming from the apartment.

Theresa joined her son. She lit two cigarettes and handed one to her son. "Baby," she said, her eyes were soft and comforting. "Pawel couldn't make it with me. He doesn't want your old mama." She gripped his leg to emphasize this point. They smoked their cigarettes in silence.

From that night, Dorian knew he and Pawel had a special connection. They had a friendship that went deeper than friendship.

Almost an hour after Pazzo left, Theresa joins the boys in the living room. She pours some water from the pitcher into the washbowl on the windowsill. She uses a sliver of soap to wash her face, arms and cunt. Turning to the her son, she says, "Dorian, go get Antonio. He said he'd help make dinner tonight."

Dorian slips his wool hat on before he bounds up the stairs with Pawel in tow.

Antonio sits in the window, gargling Lysol. He smiles and motions them in. He is dressed in a smart pair of trousers with a white shirt. The top three buttons are undone. He wears thick eyeliner, and his hair has been pulled back with some bobby pins. His body is lean and his lips are rouged. "Oh, Dorian you just missed the fattest guy. He shot buckets," he laughs. The waif leans out the third floor window and spits cum into the street. "I suppose your Mama wants me to come down." The delicate man touches Dorian's face. His fingers glide lightly over the boy's bruised cut. He sighs longingly. "Maybe you and your friend want a French job on the house before I head down."

Antonio slides to the floor. He kneels before the boys who fumble to open their pants. His fingers scampered up their thighs between their legs. He cups a single cheek of each of their asses.

Dorian's thick, deep red cock stands from his dense nest of pubes. Pawel's velvety pink cock arches elegantly from his pants. It bows like an obedient servant.

Dorian is entranced by how his friend's length of meat disappears down Antonio's throat. Antonio swallows the full length with the skill of a sword swallower. It, however, is not Antonio's skill that enthralls the young enforcer. It is Pawel's pleasure. It is the tensing of his friend's taut ass.

Antonio squeezes Dorian's ass to let him know that he has not been forgotten.

Pawel's mouth gapes open. He whimpers as he slams his groin into the sissy's face.

Dorian leans forward and places his open mouth on his friends. Their tongues wrestle. Pawel knocks off Dorian's cap and then grips his friend's shaggy hair, pulling them closer together.

Switching his attention, Antonio grips Dorian's cock with both of his hands. Despite his skills, the prostitute struggles to accommodate the boy's width. The consummate professional, Antonio keeps working, keeps bobbing his head until the anxiety, the overriding urgency of orgasm, aches throughout Dorian's entire core. Pawel's kisses become gentle as the fury of pleasure charges out of his friend's burning cock.

Antonio gulps enthusiastically. When he releases Dorian's cock, he says, "I suppose Theresa needs me to get down to help."

After picking up his hat, Dorian leads Antonio downstairs as Pawel slips out onto the fire escape. Pawel knows he is welcome but doesn't want to burden another family.

After dinner and a game of black jack, Antonio returns to his apartment and Theresa to her room. Dorian falls into an uneasy sleep. His body is exhausted, but the weather does not allow him to fully rest. In the stifling darkness, rain-like taping rattles the open window. Not waking, Dorian anticipates cool air to trickle in. But the steady heat does not abide.

The tapping continues.

Dorian opens his eyes.

Pawel stands outside the window. The moon silhouettes his lean frame. "It's too hot to sleep inside. Let's go to the beach."

Bleary eyed, Dorian bundles his pallet and joins his friend in the night. A lot of people will be sleeping outdoors, he thinks. But they will be able to find someplace to be alone. Walking for only a few minutes brings them within earshot of the gentle rolling waves of Lake Michigan. The air seems fresher.

The boys feel their lungs. Each can barely make the other one out, but their feet lead them to a thicket of trees in a park that borders the beach. Dorian spreads his blanket onto the ground.

Pawel seizes his waist and kneels behind him. The gentle pressure of lips on the small of his friend's back brings Dorian to his knees. Both boys tumble to the ground. Pawel rests his head on Dorian's hard stomach.

"What do you think about what Antonio did?" Pawel asks. His voice cracks.

Dorian strokes his friend's hair. "He enjoyed it. I enjoyed it. Didn't you?"

"Yeah," each word struggles to escape his bee-stung lips. "But … I think I'd enjoy doing it to you." His fingers unbutton Dorian's trousers.

The boy's warm mouth engulfs Dorian's manhood while it is still soft. As the tongue slides down the shaft, the shaft lengthens. The hardness and heat quickly become unbearable.

Dorian rolls Pawel over. He begins to fuck his friend's mouth. Each thrust is slow and long.

Pawel gags.

Dorian starts to withdraw, but Pawel clamps his hands on Dorian's solid ass and forces him to do deep into the mouth. The blond no longer gags, and his tongue becomes more agile. It coaxes and circles Dorian foreskin. Saliva and precum lube the warm mouth.

In the warm night, Dorian and Pawel race against each other. Pleasure creates an ache deep in the boy's gut. He presses it onward driving himself into his friend. The electric urge charges from the rough young man.

Pawel guzzles the warm cum. He sucks the cock until Dorian forces him away. Dorian's cock remains rock hard. He drags his friend face to his. Their soft lips move slowly against each other until Dorian is ready to offer his pleasure to Pawel again. Eventually, they succumb to the exhaustion of night.

In the morning, they straighten their clothes and fold up their pallet. They, then, quickly stroll down several alleys that lead to the basement club where Pazzo and the neighborhood soldiers hangout.

Pazzo sits alone at the table in the back. A tumbler of Canadian whisky sweats in his hand. He watches some of the other men play a game of pool. Out of respect, the boys wait by the door until Pazzo notices them. He motions for the boys to come over with one of his thick hands. "You fellows know Donald Greenberg down the street?"

"Yeah, he owns the market," Pawel says.

"He's late on his protection payment. We need you to remind him to pay." Pazzo sips his whisky. "But he's been talking to the coppers, so don't let it become a scene. The Organization doesn't want any attention on this. If anything happens, get back here pronto."

The store is only a block away, so they tie handkerchiefs around their faces as they stroll. The old man sweeps the floor. His broom clatters to the floor as the boys walk in and lock the door behind them.

"You need to pay your bills, Old Man," Dorian growls.

He punches the old man a couple of times before he turns to Pawel and says, "I think he's got the message." The man cowers behind the counters as Pawel kicks him. Mr. Greenberg's nose bleeds, and he pukes.

They take the money from the till. Pawel touches the back of Dorian's neck as Dorian unlocks the door.

The battered shopkeeper clambers to his feet. He has pulled a shotgun from beneath the counter. The silence after the deafening explosion disorients. The bullet rips through Pawel's face. He kneels and touches his friend's still, warm chest.

The old man clumsily tries to reload.

Dorian wants to stay with the body, but Pazzo would want the scene mitigated as much as possible. The Organization's needs must outweigh his own.

BLACK MARKETEER
By Landon Dixon

"I just need a coupla truck tires, Ben. The front ones on my rig are shot. I can't go on the road – earn money for my wife and kids – if I don't have the tires. Can you help me out?"

Ben Jardin slowly extracted the four-bit cigar from his mouth, blew smoke rings. As the biggest black marketeer in southern Arizona, with a warehouse full of illicit goods to back him up, he could help people out, all right – for the right price. "War's on, Jace," he stated. "Rubber's awful scarce – in tires or condoms or anything else."

"Yeah, I know that, Ben."

Jace ran a thin, shaking hand through his wispy blond hair. The little guy with the big worries looked more like an accountant than a truck driver, with his delicate little hands and feet, smooth, sensitive, creamy-white complexion and pale blue eyes. He looked weak and weak-willed, too. But his family of six proved his potency, his steel in taking on Ben Jardin's terms his strength of character.

"You know I support the war effort," he pleaded. "I bought liberty bonds just last year when I had the dough, sent used paperbacks over to the GIs in Europe. But I gotta look after my wife and kids. That's why I'm not fighting with the boys – kicking Hitler's ass overseas."

Ben crossed his legs up on top of his desk, took another long, deep drag on his big cigar. "Sure, sure. I know Jace. We all got our priorities. Mine is selling goods to needing customers, maybe turning a small profit for myself." He grinned at the man, teeth uniformly straight and blazing white, as well cared for as his slick black hair and slender, manicured fingers, dark-blue suit and crimson tie and polished black shoes. Ben Jardin was a smooth operator, physically and functionally.

"I can let you have a couple of brand-new tires for that rig of yours, sure. Two hundred bucks for the pair."

Jace gasped, fingers fluttering up to his chin. "I ain't got that kind of dough, Ben."

Jardin leaned further back in his leather executive chair. "Then what are you wasting my time for? If you're hauling essential goods, get the government to pony up the tires. If not … try rolling it like those Filipino allies of ours do: rickshaw style."

He swung his legs off the mahogany desk, planted his feet on the red, white and blue carpet of the small office fronting the large warehouse, picked up a Montblanc fountain pen and began to scribble on a piece of bond paper. "I've got work to do."

Jace Williams stared desperately at the man, his entire body trembling now. "I ain't hauling essential stuff, Ben, that's the problem. My goods ain't even really legal, you know that. I …"

He broke off. Ben wasn't listening.

The only sound in the sun-warmed office was the business-like scratching of Ben's pen on the rationed paper.

Then a snicking sound, the rustle of cloth.

"How 'bout you take it out in trade?" Jace's soft voice had a quiver to it, a dose of throatiness.

Ben looked up at Jace's bare ass in profile.

The man's threadbare pants were down at his scuffed shoes. His butt cheeks were curved, mounded, glowing with a fine down of blond hair. They looked soft and lush, small enough to fit into a bigger man's two hands, big enough to envelope a man's cock, cushion the thump of a man's thighs. Jace's cock was rising up in between his legs, in the heated, breathless air.

Ben set his pen down, pushed back in his chair, spread his legs. "Well, now," he said, smiling slightly. "I'm always willing to trade."

Jace's cock speared out, smooth hood bloating, smooth shaft expanding longer and thicker, as the man looked into Ben's twinkling brown eyes.

But Ben's eyes only flicked over Jace's cock. They focused on the man's ass. So Jace turned, showing off his butt, bending forward and thrusting back and spreading his cheeks with his hands, giving the black marketeer a good look at his remarkably pink pucker. He'd come to do business, all right, one way or the other.

The growing bulge in the front of Ben's suit pants attested to his interest. He stared at Jace's cute starfish, the way the man's fingertips sunk into the plush flesh of his buttocks. As he slowly drew his own zipper down, he drew his own inflating erection out of his pants.

Ben's cock swelled huge, bulb-headed and thick-shafted, corded with veins. He gave it a tug, looking into the deep pink of Jace's spread sex. "Sure you can handle the terms?" he said.

Jace looked around, at the mammoth dong Ben was cradling, stroking. His eyes widened, misted, his mouth breaking open. He licked his lips and nodded. "We got a deal, then?"

"Two front truck tires for one man's rear box. We got a deal. Provided you can live up to your ... end of the bargain."

"Seal the deal!" Jace hissed.

Ben climbed to his feet, leisurely carried his club around the desk and in behind the shaking little bent-over blond. He pulled a bottle out of his desk, poured some greasy substance into his right hand, oiled the tremendous length of his cock with it. Jace jumped when Ben's slickened fingers shot in between his butt cheeks and scrubbed his crack.

"Nice," Ben commented, rubbing the smooth, tender skin of Jace's butt cleavage. He swirled a fingertip around the man's puckered asshole, pressed it inside.

"Oh, God!" Jace yelped, bung squeezing Ben's finger tight.

"Not God, Jace. Just me – and my staff."

Ben withdrew his finger, filled the void with his giant cockhead.

Jace jerked, feeling the huge hood-meat press against his tiny opening. Ben gripped gleaming shaft and shoved, squishing his cap up against Jace's asshole. The hole resisted, flowered, was filled with cockhead, swallowed up cap.

"That's the way," Ben grunted, driving the bulbous head of his cock through Jace's ring and into the man's anus. Followed ruggedly and relentlessly by inch after inch after inch of throbbing, vein-ribboned shaft.

The laws of physics were all against it. But the laws of physical, sexual attraction were all for it – plugging nine inches of beating, bloated male cock meat into the small anal cavity of one little man's ass.

Ben sunk in to the balls, stretching Jace, stuffing him, filling the both of them with the warm, wonderful sensations of two men meeting at the ass and dick. Ben gripped Jace's narrow hips and plowed his cock back and forth in the man's hot, hugging anus, pumping them both full of even more exquisite sensation.

"Yeah, Ben! Fuck me, Ben!" Jace squealed, rocking to and fro on his heels on the end of Ben's shunting cock. He grabbed up his own cock, numbed now by the anal assault, but still shimmering like the rest of his body, and stroked in rhythm to Ben's pounding dong.

Ben gritted his teeth and thrust his hips, watching his gleaming shaft dive in and out of Jace's obscenely stretched hole. He felt the blowtorch heat, the gasping suck of Jace's anus all through his cock and body and brain; heard the heavy slap of his clenched thighs against Jace's soft cheeks, the pair rippling before him. Ben torqued it up, ramming, reaming the man's beautiful ass, sweat prickling his furrowed brow and dousing the palms of his flesh-gripping hands, giving in to the frenzy.

"Oh, Ben!" Jace cried, cock going off in his small, shifting hand. He jerked, shuddered, buttocks jumping all on their own, as he jacked burst after burst of pure white joy out of his ruptured cock.

Ben grunted, jolted up on his toes, hammering his cock into Jace's spasming anus. Orgasm exploded his balls and blasted out his chute-churning dong, flooding the other man's bowels. Ben was ablaze, spraying Jace's ass full of fire.

It was a good deal for both men.

# # # # #

"We need gasoline, lots of it."

Ben shelved a file folder in a metal cabinet and turned around. Two men stood in his office, big, broad men.

Ben grinned. "For Mr. Moncito, huh?"

The men looked at each other. The taller of the two nodded.

They were both wearing snap-brim hats and trench coats, the taller showing brown hair under his hat, the shorter, black. Their faces looked to be carved out of stone from the same quarry, like their bodies, their eyes dark and wary.

"Yeah, for Mr. Moncito. You got gasoline?"

"Got lots," Ben replied. "For the right price."

"Name's Rocco," the spokesman said. He lifted his lantern jaw in his companion's direction. "Stone."

"Pleased to know you, fellows. Gasoline's going for a dollar a gallon on the underground exchange. Big shortage right now, big demand. But for Mr. Moncito, I might be persuaded to lower it to ninety cents or so – bulk prices."

Rocco glanced at Stone, back at the black marketeer. "Mr. Moncito wants it on credit, see. He'll pay you in a week or so."

Ben frowned. "How much?"

"All you got," Stone growled.

"All I got? Hey, I've regular customers to look after – cash-paying regular customers. I give away all my inventory on ..."

"We got some nylons you might be interested in," Rocco interrupted. "To show our good faith, sort of."

Ben cocked his head. "Nylons? Have to be a whole ..."

He stopped talking when Rocco and Stone unhooked their belts, pulled down their zippers, pushed down their pants. Both men were wearing nylons under their trousers, the sheer brown material bulging with their hard, hairy thighs – with the pair of heaters they were packing down below. The men's cocks were huge, even semi-erect, and neither was wearing underwear – just garters to hold up their nylons.

Stone rasped, "You interested in this pair?"

Ben licked his lips, staring at the slabs of meat. "Two pairs of nylons aren't going to pay for a whole lot of gasoline, guys," he croaked. "No matter how well filled they are."

Rocco's thick lips curled into a cold grin. "Go ahead, feel the merchandise, see what you think."

Ben walked closer on shaking legs, drawn by the awesome sight of those man-sausages, which were swelling up even larger. He could almost feel the hot, pumping pulse of the corded dongs, smell the musky scent of the hairy, sacked balls, taste the beefy thickness and richness, the salty extrusion from the gaping slits. He was on his knees in between the two men, facing their burgeoning dicks, before he even realized what he was doing.

"Maybe some gas," he murmured, reaching up and out, grasping the pair of turgid erections.

The men grunted, parting their trench coats with fists on their hips, as Ben's smooth, warm palms covered their cocks, his slender, supple fingers encircling shafts. Ben thrilled at the heavy, pulsating feel of the engorged snakes, at the way they surged and stiffened even further under his hands. He gripped the pair and pumped, tugging on them.

The men's cocks fully uncoiled, shooting upwards, expanding to their full erection under Ben's stroking hands.

Then Ben darted his head to the right, let go of Stone's cock and licked up the man's shaft from balls to hood. Stone grunted and quivered. Ben darted his head over to the left, tongued up the entire length of Rocco's rigid dong. That man responded with a groan and a shudder of his own. The pair crowded closer to one another, so that their cocks were within easy stroking and licking range of Ben's eager hands and mouth.

He looked up at the men, pulling their cocks, pumping the dicks quick and tight and hot. Then slower, more sensually, stretching the meat out even further, using a twist of the wrist to smother the hoods in his palms. Rocco and Stone thrust out their hips, filling Ben's hands with their cocks.

Ben let go. Ben licked up Rocco's dick, then Stone's. He covered every square inch of bloated beef, over and over, mouth-painting shaft and hood. Then he dropped his head lower, opened his mouth wider, and sucked up Stone's balls, tugged on them; did the same to Rocco's.

"Fuck!" Rocco gasped, Ben mouthing his sack, tongue-juggling his nuts. "Let's give this guy some of what he's dishing out," he said to Stone.

The men pulled Ben to his feet. He protested, wanting to lick more cock, suck cock, jack cock. He canned the whining, though, when Stone pulled his pants down and off, and Rocco hefted him by the waist, spun him around like a sexual ragdoll.

Ben ended up upside down, suspended from the men's shoulders, his thighs hooked around each of the men's necks. His face was in line with the glistening pair of erections again, his own hard, needful cock bare, in Rocco and Stone's faces.

Ben grabbed onto the men's dongs and pumped; was jolted by a mouth seizing up his cock, and sucking. Wet heat flooded his prick, his groin, his body. The mouth enveloped his dong to the balls, sucked back up, then let go. The other mouth closed over his thundering cock, sucked up and down. Ben's head spun, the blood rushing there diverted to his blown dick.

He pumped cock, licked cock; and got cock sucked, passed back and forth between the two hungry men holding him up. He pulled Rocco's dong away from the man's body and mouthed the cap. He sucked on Stone's hood and some of that man's shaft. As he, himself, got deliciously devoured by the big men's mouths.

It went on like that for a blistering few minutes or so. Until Ben tasted precum, Rocco's yawning slit bubbling semen under the oral onslaught. Then, suddenly, spurting it.

Ben yelped, Rocco jerking. Ben anxiously sucked hood, vacuuming up as much shooting sperm as he could, the big cock geysering it out. He pulled on Stone's cock with one hand, milking Rocco's shaft with the other, drinking jizz.

Stone groaned, and erupted. Hot semen burned against Ben's shifting hand. He pulled his head away from Rocco's spewing cock and sealed his lips over Stone's hood, sucking up that man's gushing sperm.

It was too much even for Ben to handle. He stiffened, his legs shooting straight up into the air, his cock spearing come-hard in a sucking, gasping mouth. Then blasting. He spouted white-hot ecstasy out of his dick, into one man's mouth, the other. Sucking up and swallowing down the two men's own spurting, salty joy.

"So, how much gasoline does Mr. Moncito get, on credit?" Rocco asked, as Stone lowered Ben back down onto his knees.

The black marketeer looked up at the pair of hoods, letting his head clear, sizing things up. "I can spare a couple of barrels," he said at last.

Stone shook his head. "We're gonna have a long ride ahead of us. We need more than that."

Ben shrugged, staring at the spent cocks, hanging below the garters. "Sorry, boys. Like I said, I've got other, cash-paying customers who ..."

His ears pricked, as hammers clicked back. He looked away from the softened dongs and into the steel-hard rods pointed down at his face.

"We're taking it all," Rocco said.

"And your chocolate besides," Stone added.

# # # # #

The G-men smashed down the door and boiled into Ben's office. They slammed the black marketeer up against a wall, roughly spread his arms and legs.

"Special Agent Drake," a tall, thin man in a straw hat and funereal suit hissed in Ben's ear. "Phoenix office. We know about your black market operations, Jardin, know you're working with the Moncito mob."

He punched the back of Ben's neck with a stiffened forefinger. "What we don't know is what they're planning – heist, bank job, kidnapping. But you're going to tell us."

Ben twisted his head around and exclaimed, "I'm not working with them! They stole gasoline … and chocolate from me last night. Stole it!"

Drake grunted, licked his plush, red lips. "So, you don't know what they're up to, huh? Well, if you can't help us, we'll just have to take this place apart."

He waved an arm, and the other straw-hatted men jimmied the door to the warehouse open, poured inside.

Ben heard bottles smashing, crates splintering. He winced, then sighed. "Wait a minute, Mr. … Agent Drake," he spluttered. "M-maybe we can make a deal?"

The Special Agent's bright blue eyes regarded Jardin's pleading face, coldly. "What sort of deal?"

Ben grinned. "I'll help you. I don't know what the Moncito mob had planned. But I do know they won't get far."

Drake shook Ben, crowding up even closer behind the man. His big hand hooked around to search for concealed weapons, closed around Ben's rapidly erecting cock. "Uh-huh. And just how do you know that?"

Ben throbbed in the handsome G-Man's authoritative grasp. "Because I sugared the gasoline, laced the chocolate with laxatives, before they stole it. They're going to run after pulling their job, get the runs, but they aren't going to get far. You can just wait and pick them up."

Drake looked into Ben's twinkling brown eyes, squeezing the man's boned-out member. "Okay, then, maybe we'll wait together, huh?"

"Deal," the black marketeer exhaled.

BLOOD IS THICKER
by Mark Apoapsis

Part 1

Water sheeted over Gio's lean, muscular chest, smoothing down the curly hairs that sparsely covered his pectoral muscles, and carrying soap lather down his belly to linger briefly in his pubic hair. Raising an arm, he soaped up his armpit then twisted his trunk toward the tiles to let the spray hit it. It was while he was rinsing the other one that he turned toward the frosted glass and was startled to see a blurred, dark, hulking figure looming there.

"Jeez, Vanni, if you have to piss that bad, you could at least knock."

There was no answer. "Is something wrong? We're not under attack, are we?" The family had been expanding its book-running business into new territory lately, so there was always a danger of trouble from the other families, and everyone was on alert.

Gio shut off the water and glanced through the glass again. Now there were two hulking figures. This was bad. One hulking figure would be fine. Vanni had never walked in on him in the shower before, but if he did, he'd have a perfectly good reason. But he'd never bring someone else in with him, not under any imaginable circumstances. And he'd never voluntarily let someone get past him, nor would he have deserted his post. He was absolutely loyal and couldn't be bought. There was a real possibility that his bodyguard was dead, which was such a horrible though that it almost took Gio's mind off his own predicament.

The lump of soap remaining in his hand weighed maybe an ounce, and was as mushy as a half-eaten serving of ice cream. Not a very useful weapon. The shower back in his family home would have had a scrub brush with a wooden handle, but he rarely used it and had never bothered getting one for his downtown apartment. Maybe he could break the bottle of shampoo over one guy's head, then use it to slash at the second guy.

The door slid open before he could do anything. Sure enough, there were two goons there, their expensive suits not hiding their broad shoulders and massive arms.

"Our boss would like to have a business meeting with you," the nearer goon said, looking him up and down. "He says that he's sorry if he picked an inconvenient time."

Gio stepped out of the shower. He couldn't think of anything to say and didn't trust his voice anyway. The second goon handed him a towel, and he hastily wrapped it around his waist, making no attempt to use it to dry his chest or his freshly washed, thick black hair.

He followed them into the living room, where they had Vanni tied to a chair. That was a relief, anyway. Maybe they'd both get out of this alive. Still, it was unnerving to see his bodyguard rendered completely helpless. He'd been gagged, and his jacket was hanging open, revealing the empty holster strapped to his chest. Vanni had been his unofficial bodyguard since they'd been in third grade, and they actually went back further than that. Gio had always counted on him being there to protect him when he couldn't protect himself. Like now, standing here wearing nothing but a towel.

A third man, smaller and a little older than his goons, was waiting for him. He made no direct comment on his host's attire, or lack of it. "Sorry to trouble you at this hour. We couldn't reach your father, so we thought we'd send him a message through you."

That was pretty ambiguous, but Gio understood what he was really saying: His father was too well-guarded for them to get at, so they were going to put pressure on him by threatening his only son.

"I'll be glad to carry a message to him," he said, trying to sound calm and innocent. They might not know how heavily involved the twenty-year-old Americanized son was in the family business. "What should I tell him?"

"Oh, you'll be carrying it in writing. But I'll tell you anyway: Your father has recently expanded his business into an area we control. I know they say competition is healthy, but we'd like to persuade him that it could be very unhealthy in this case."

"Oh, are you in the ice cream business, too?"

152

"Don't play dumb with me, kid. You know as well as I do that we're not talking about gelato distribution." He turned to one of his goons. "OK, do it."

The goon took out a knife and told the other one, "Hold him."

"What are you doing?" Gio yelled, unable to hide his terror any longer.

His arms were seized from behind, and the guy with the knife stepped closer and said with relish, "We're gonna carve the message into your chest. That's the kind of message we're talking about." Stroking Gio's chest with the flat of the cold blade, he added, "You know, all the way here we were talking about how we were going to have to take off your – uh!" There was a meaty thunk, and his taunt ended with a grunt. Across the room, Gio saw that Vanni had leaned forward in his chair and still had his arm extended, following through. Somehow he'd gotten loose. Gio knew that he usually carried a knife strapped to his ankle. Apparently they hadn't frisked him thoroughly enough.

The man behind Gio released his arms. Gio whipped his towel off and threw it over the face of the boss, who had started to turn his back on him and draw a weapon. By this time the first goon had dropped his knife and fallen to his hands and knees with the hilt of Vanni's knife protruding from his back.

A shot rang out from behind Gio, and Vanni toppled over backward with his chair and lay still. "No!" Gio cried out. He whirled and swung at the thug who had been holding him, not caring that the bigger man was holding a gun. With all his weight behind it, his fist connected solidly with his jaw with a satisfying crunch, and the huge man went down, dropping the gun. Gio dove for it and aimed it up at the boss, who immediately dropped the gun he'd been taking out and raised his hands.

He got up and circled warily around the boss to get all three enemies in his line of sight. The goon on his hands and knees was choking on his own blood and didn't look like he was any threat. "Tie him up with your belt," he told the boss, gesturing at the unconscious man whose gun he was holding. "I may decide to shoot him anyway, if my bodyguard dies."

"I'm OK," said a voice just behind him.

Gio whirled around and saw Vanni standing there, alive and free and with no sign of a wound. He was so relieved to see that handsome face grinning at him that he flung himself into his friend's strong arms, tucking his head against his muscular shoulder. His aftershave smelled good.

Only then did he remember he was stark naked. His friend's suit felt odd against his bare skin, especially his cock, which was pressed tightly against his buddy's pant leg.

"Don't try anything funny!" Vanni snapped. "Down on the ground, hands behind your head!"

Startled, Gio said, "Sorry. I just ..."

"Not you, *paisan*," Vanni laughed, patting his back. "I was talking to him." The guy Gio had turned his back on. "If I suddenly need to grab your gun, let me, OK? Now get off. You're getting my pants wet."

Gio guiltily disengaged and turned his attention back to the boss, who was obeying Vanni's instructions. The unconscious man seemed to be safely tied up, but he moved closer to them, knowing he wasn't so great a shot. He stopped when his toes touched the towel on the floor. He wanted to put it back on, but he'd need both hands free to do that.

"Here, let me," Vanni said, kneeling down in front of him to retrieve the towel. Gio was acutely aware that his bodyguard's eyes were now level with his crotch.

Apparently Vanni was, too, because he blushed and said, "I'm not lookin'." Making a point of craning his neck over his shoulder to keep his eyes on their enemies, he blindly wrapped the towel around Gio's loins and knotted it securely at his belly.

# # # # #

"Sorry I let them jump me," Vanni said afterward as they shared a badly needed drink, their ties loosened and collars unbuttoned. "I was careless."

"I'm just glad you were careful enough to wear your bulletproof vest."

"How do you know I was? Maybe the bullet just missed."

"When I hugged you, I felt something hard."

Vanni laughed nervously and looked away, not meeting his eyes. Gio didn't understand why he'd be so embarrassed about having his bulletproof vest discovered.

"How'd you get untied?"

"Trade secret," Vanni said kiddingly.

"Come on, you don't trust your old buddy? How long have we been sharing secrets?"

"Over fifteen years," Vanni said. "I guess I owe you that trust, after you were so forthcoming about your bedwetting problem."

"And a few other things since." Their fathers were longtime business partners, and the boys had been inseparable companions for as long as either could remember. Some of the people in their old neighborhood had called them "the Giovanni brothers" as kids, since they shared the same given name.

"The secret is I keep a small blade hidden in the waistband of my pants. In back, near where you'd tie a guy's wrists behind him." He grinned. "Anything else you want to know about my pants?"

"Matter of fact, yeah, since you mention it. Have you done the job on Adriana yet?"

Vanni looked embarrassed. "Why would I admit something like that to her brother?"

"Because I'm your best friend. And I'm sure you wouldn't deflower her unless you intended to marry her."

"Uh, that's just it, buddy. I don't think things are gonna work out between us. So, no, I haven't touched her."

"Why not? Is my sister not good enough for you? She really had a great time last Saturday, you know. She especially likes how patient you are. She said it was nice to go to a movie without being pawed. So I was kidding about doing the job on her. I know you haven't. But it might be time to start thinking about heading toward first base, buddy."

"I just don't think that's gonna happen."

"I know she's two years older than you. That isn't a problem, is it?"

"Uh, yeah. You guessed it. I mean, most guys prefer dating girls who are a little younger, right?"

"Well, what about Bonnie, then?"

"Not that much younger! She's still in high school!"

"She graduates next year. She likes you, you know. I think she's hoping you'll ask her out. And she's not old-fashioned, if you know what I mean."

"I'm amazed you don't mind talking about your sisters this way."

"Better someone I can trust than whatever scumbags they'd find for themselves. Just as long as you use protection. You always wear protection, right?" He playfully unbuttoned two buttons of his friend's shirt so that the bulletproof vest he was wearing over his undershirt peeked out. "That must be heavy. We're safe now, with Luigi's men posted outside. You can relax."

"I just haven't had a chance to change."

"You do now. It's just you and me. Let's get this thing off you." He undid more buttons.

"Are you drunk already?" Vanni asked, laughing.

"What's the big deal? Let's both relax in our undershirts. After all, you saw me naked."

"I wasn't lookin'," Vanni laughed, and allowed his friend to teasingly strip him of his jacket, tie, and shirt, completely exposing the black nylon of his bulletproof vest and the skin of his arms and shoulders.

"Look at these muscles," Gio said, squeezing Vanni's biceps fondly. "I'd never have to worry about my sister, with a big guy like you around to protect her."

"Except that I spend most of my time protecting you," Vanni pointed out.

Gio's curious hands encountered a hard and unyielding surface woven into the fabric of the vest. "Well, you're off duty now, and we're both still single, so we can spend the rest of the night drinking." He unfastened the vest's straps and pulled it over his friend's head. He wanted him vulnerable.

Part 2

"I'm not lookin'," Vanni Lombardo said jokingly as he carefully kept his eyes on the locked door and his back to Gio as Gio turned the dial and opened the small safe. It had been a running joke between them for five years now, ever since that awkward moment with the towel. Five years, and Vanni still remembered the smell of soap from that freshly scrubbed body, overlain with the dissipating stink of fear and a hint of other more pleasant masculine scents.

He could hear the small bags clinking as Gio rearranged the contents to make room for this week's delivery of diamonds. It must have been getting full. He resisted the temptation to glance over his shoulder. He had no business knowing the contents of the safe, any more than he needed to know the combination.

"Let's just say that we're going to need either a bigger safe or a new investment opportunity pretty soon," Gio said. "I'm betting it'll be a new investment. Your dad has been bringing people to meet my dad, and then they have loud arguments after they leave. That's always been a sign he's about to convince him to start a new business. That's probably what he's saving up all this dough for." He slammed the safe shut and smiled at Vanni as he turned around. "But we both know where the real riches are stashed, right?"

"In the freezer," Vanni agreed. That was a much older private joke. Growing up, they'd both believed Gio's father was the richest man in the world because he owned more ice cream than even two little boys could imagine eating. They hadn't understood that the gelato distribution business was a front for his much more lucrative businesses, and that, even then, his whole organization was considered small potatoes by the major families.

"If they start spilling out, we might have to get rid of some," Gio joked. "Maybe make one into an engagement ring for Carina."

"Give up! I'm not going to ask her out. I told you, she's way too young for me."

"She's old enough to get married. And you're only twenty-five, not exactly an old man! Yet. In case you haven't noticed, I'm running short on sisters. You really gonna stick me with another loser like Rocco or Vince when I could have you for a brother-in-law?"

"Give them a break. They're swell guys. Rocco and Adriana have worked out great, and they have those adorable kids."

"Only half Sicilian. Rocco's parents are from Naples."

"And Bonnie adores Vince. He even helps with the baby sometimes."

"Rocco and Vince are all right, I guess, but it breaks my heart to think that it could have been you I was welcoming into my family. Just remember, Carina is a looker, and you may not have much time to make your move. She's your last chance, *paisan*." He replaced the painting that concealed the safe.

As Gio sat back down at his desk, Vanni unlocked the door and peered out cautiously, his hand on his gun, but no unmarried sisters were lined up outside clutching wilted bridal bouquets. Nor any hit men or goons sent by an enemy. There was only Leo waiting outside. He was probably safe on both counts, having been in Gio's employ for three years on the one hand and already married on the other. As always, Gio had sent him down to escort the diamond guy, with the suitcase full of cash and his own bodyguard, to his car. Gio was always uncomfortable having the safe open unless he was alone with Vanni.

# # # # #

For an hour or so, Vanni played cards with Leo in the office while their boss did paperwork and made a few routine phone calls and received a couple of calls himself. Vanni paid no attention until he heard Gio suddenly say "What?" in a shocked tone to one caller. Vanni turned around and saw that his friend had turned pale and looked stunned.

Gio looked their way and say, "Wait outside." Leo got up to go. Then, to Vanni's surprise, Gio added, "Both of you."

Gio stayed in his office a long time, then came out and handed half a dozen sealed envelopes to Leo. "I want you to hand-deliver these personally. Don't let anyone tell you otherwise. Then wait at home, so I can reach you. Don't come back here until I call you." He turned to Vanni. "Lock all the doors and stand guard. Don't let anyone in – anyone – except Rocco, Vince, and Luigi, and whoever they bring with them."

"Got it," Vanni said. He knew better than to ask questions.

Rocco, the Neapolitan brother-in-law, gave Vanni a cold look when he let him in. Vanni wondered what he'd done this time. Rocco had never forgotten that Vanni had dated his wife briefly. He'd never touched her and had stopped seeing her a year before the couple had met, but even after years of marriage and two children, the burly, handsome man must have felt insecure because he still treated him like a rival. Vanni doubted Rocco knew just how ridiculous that was. Sometimes he wished he could get the guy alone, just once, and have it out, man to man, so afterward they could be friends.

Vince, younger and much more friendly, had never blamed Vanni for having dated the middle sister once or twice before he'd worked up the courage to ask her out himself. He was a smaller man, but made up for it in the looks department, in Vanni's opinion. Today, he looked shaken and wary, and skipped the usual pleasantries when Vanni greeted him. Something was definitely up.

Gio's tough-looking cousin Luigi was several years older than he and had been involved in the family business while Gio and Vanni were still in high school. He was in charge of the organization's enforcement and security. He'd brought only two of his men with him, which was unusual if something big was up. He seemed a little on edge, but then, he usually did.

Luigi left one of his men to guard the front door and asked Vanni to accompany him to his cousin's office. Gio seemed relieved that Luigi had arrived. He thanked Luigi politely, without a trace of his usual warmth. Rocco and Vince were standing, looking on edge.

After an unnaturally long silence, Gio asked, "How are your brothers, Vanni?"

"Huh?" That was an oddly formal question. "Fine, I guess, last time I saw them. Thanks."

"When was that?"

"What?"

"When was the last time you saw one of your brothers? Or your father? Or talked to them on the phone?"

"Well, I talked to Sergio last week, I think. Did something happen to them?"

"You 'think'? You don't remember whether you talked to your brother?"

"What day of the week was it?" Luigi asked.

"I'm not – Tuesday, maybe," Vanni said, looking over his shoulder at him. "No, Wednesday."

Luigi stared meaningfully at his cousin, who sighed. "All right," Gio said, hanging his head for a moment before taking a deep breath and looking up. "Grab him."

Instantly, Luigi and his goon grabbed Vanni's arms. Rocco and Vince moved up to help.

"Gio? What the fuck, buddy?"

Rocco unbuttoned his jacket and removed his gun. Gio said, "He'll have another weapon or two hidden on him somewhere, and he sometimes wears a bulletproof vest under his shirt."

"Not here where it's supposed to be safe," Vanni said. "Why are you doing this?"

"I'd like to believe you don't know," Gio said sadly.

"I haven't got a clue. Look, pal, if you're going to have me manhandled, you at least owe me an explanation."

"Don't tell him," his cousin advised. "Wait until ..."

"My dad's dead," Gio blurted.

"Oh my God! What happened? Was it a hit?"

"Yes. Your father killed him."

"That's impossible," Vanni whispered, stunned. "They've been business partners forever."

"Only for twenty-two years," Luigi said. "They used to be bitter competitors when I was little. They practically destroyed each other's businesses and killed a lot of each other's men before they realized they were both better off with an alliance. But I guess your father was just biding his time. I wouldn't have believed it if I hadn't been there. I lost three of my men and barely escaped myself."

"Biding his time. For twenty-two years," Vanni said numbly.

"Yeah," Luigi said, "your father's a patient man, and he put up a good act. Even letting you kids play together."

"I don't believe it."

"Are you saying they didn't tell you this was coming?" Luigi asked. "You were in a perfect position to finish destroying this family."

"You ... you don't mean Gio?"

"The longer you stand there talking," Gio said, "the more chance he has to break loose and go for one of his hidden weapons."

"Frisk him," Luigi told his man.

"Don't bother," Gio said. "I've seen him beat that. You'd better strip him."

So Luigi's man held a gun to his head while Rocco roughly tugged off his jacket and Luigi removed his holster, then his belt. Vince apologetically unknotted and removed his tie, then began gently unbuttoning his shirt. Rocco pushed him out of the way and ripped his shirt open, letting the buttons fly in all directions as if he didn't think Vanni would be needing the shirt ever again.

"No bulletproof vest," the Neapolitan reported, running his hands over Vanni's undershirt to make sure it wasn't hidden beneath that, but encountering nothing harder than pectoral muscles and nipples. He tugged the opened shirt free of his pants, then unbuttoned the pants and pushed them down to his knees, revealing striped boxer shorts and hairy legs. Also the knife Vanni kept strapped around his ankle, which he was promptly relieved of. Then, after moving behind him and peeling the shirt over his arms, Rocco wrapped his own arms around him and lifted him off the ground while Vince and Luigi each grabbed a foot and began untying his shoes.

Once they had him down to his underwear, they tied him to a chair. He'd never been so completely helpless, stripped of all his hidden weapons and tools, with his ankles tied to the wooden legs, his wrists roped to the chair's arms, and surrounded by men who were convinced he'd been involved in a plot against the head of their family.

"Gio! I had nothing to do with what happened, I swear! Are you really stupid enough to think I'd ever do anything to hurt you?" If he got mad enough, maybe no one would notice the tears he was blinking back. His lifelong friend didn't trust him.

"We can't take any chances," Gio said sadly.

"I've got a guy who's very reliable at telling when a man's lying," Luigi told Gio. "I'll call him."

"Even if he wasn't involved, we should kill him anyway," Rocco said. "The Lombardos will think we're weak if ours doesn't strike back against one of their own."

Gio ignored his brother-in-law. "Are you sure we can trust your guy?" he asked his cousin. "Half our organization was recruited by Lombardo. I'm nervous about letting anyone in but family, at least until we know who we can trust."

"He's worked for me for almost ten years. Since he graduated high school. And he's never wrong. We can use him to tell us who's trustworthy and who's working for the Lombardos."

"Call him. We have to find out what my own personal Lombardo here knows."

"I told you, I don't know anything," Vanni said wearily.

"Let's put him in the freezer while we're waiting," Rocco suggested. "Maybe that'll soften him up."

161

Gio looked at his cousin, who nodded. "OK," Gio said. "But don't hurt him, just in case he's innocent."

With five guys to grab his arms, shoulders, legs, and the chair, it didn't take long to carry him down the hall to the room with the freezer, chair and all. Appealing to Gio's friendship did no good. Left shivering in the dark in his boxer shorts and undershirt, between the stacked tubs of rock-hard gelato, he finally let the tears flow freely.

It seemed like forever before they took him out again, but it couldn't have been too long, because he could still feel his fingers and toes. They hurt. Gio's and Vince's hands felt incredibly warm on his bare shoulders. Shivering uncontrollably, and not thinking very clearly, he wished Gio would hold him tightly in his arms, preferably unbuttoning his own jacket and shirt first, and let him soak up more of that wonderful heat. Surely that would be natural enough, under the circumstances. But they set him down all too soon, just outside the freezer door.

"Bring that light over here," an unfamiliar voice said. "I need a lot of light." Vanni was already squinting against the brightness as it was, but his eyes quickly adjusted.

The guy Luigi had brought in was a little younger than Vanni, and too light to be a full-blooded Sicilian, although he looked like he might have some Greek heritage. He pulled up a chair facing him, so close that the knees of his expensive pants pressed against Vanni's bare knees. He placed a hand over Vanni's, grasping his bound wrist firmly just above the ropes, and studied him intently, his green eyes boring into Vanni's. He placed his other hand behind Vanni's neck, with the thumb resting on the hollow of his throat. Gently, he said, "I can tell you're upset – who wouldn't be? – but I need you to calm down. Gio told me that if you're innocent, you'll have nothing to worry about. So just relax. There, that's more like it. I don't think we've ever met."

"We haven't."

"My name's Alicio. What's yours?"

"Vanni."

"Your skin is cold, Vanni. Why is that?"

"They locked me in the freezer."

Alicio glanced at Gio. "OK, ready."

"This isn't fair! I've worked for Gio for years. We grew up together. I saved his skin more than once."

"He's telling the truth," Alicio said without taking his eyes off Vanni's or letting go of his wrist and neck.

"Of course he is. I didn't need you to tell me that. But that's the past. Ask him what he knew about the plot to kill my father."

"I didn't know your father was dead until you told me," Vanni said.

"True," Alicio said.

"And your family didn't tell you they were planning to do it someday?" Gio asked. "No one gave you a hint?"

"No, they didn't." Vanni had been taken completely by surprise. Of course, in hindsight, a lot of odd remarks his brothers had been making about plans for the future now made sense. The past few months had replayed unbidden in his head while he'd been shivering in the freezer, wondering if he was about to die, and the pieces of an unpleasant picture had begun to fall together.

"That's a lie," Alicio reported quietly.

"What? Gio! Are you going to take this guy's word over mine?"

"Shut up. My cousin says he's absolutely reliable. Now, were you supposed to kill me?"

"No!"

"That's true, but he's very upset about something."

"You didn't have any plans for me?"

"Plans? What do you mean?"

"He's uncomfortable with you asking that."

"It must be tough, working for me when we used to be equals, friends. It would be natural if you wanted to grab some power of your own."

"Of course not. I like things just the way they are with you and me."

"He's lying. He wants more."

"I knew it! You'd love grabbing all the power for yourself, wouldn't you? Maybe you wouldn't kill me, but you'd love to be in charge, to be able to make me do whatever you want."

"No, I swear!"

"That's a lie. In fact, he's excited at that idea."

"It's the truth! I'd never do anything to hurt you," Vanni pleaded.

"I can't tell if that's true or not. There's a lot of suppressed emotion behind that claim. I think he's covering something up."

"No, I'm not! I can't believe you're doing this to me."

"I had to."

His bare arms and legs strained uselessly against the bonds. "I'd never even think about doing this to you."

"Now, that's definitely a lie," Alicio reported.

"Interesting. So if you'd gotten the jump on me, it might have been me sitting tied to a chair in my underwear instead of you."

Vanni said nothing.

"He actually likes that idea."

Gio leaned in close. "Tell the truth, you backstabbing bastard! Suppose I was tied this chair right now, completely at your mercy, and you were standing there with a knife in your hand. No one else around to witness. No one to stop you. No one would ever find out. What would you do, if you could do anything you wanted?"

"I would cut the ropes and help you up, the way any real friend would."

"He's lying."

"Thank you, Alicio. Very helpful. I've used enough of your time. I think Luigi is holding some guys across town that he wants you to question."

"Yes, I have a busy day ahead of me, apparently."

"On your way out, please send Rocco in."

Rocco came in and said, "I knew it. Back in the freezer?"

"No. I want you to interrogate him. He wasn't directly involved in the murder, but he may know something about his family's plans and which of our men are going to turn on us. Alicio also says he had plans for me. See what you can get out of him."

"My pleasure," Rocco said, removing his jacket and rolling up his sleeves to reveal hairy, muscular forearms. Vanni didn't need Alicio's special skills to tell that Rocco wasn't just saying that to be polite.

"Don't bust him up, if there's any other way. Even now, I'm not sure I could stand to see him beaten to a bloody pulp."

"In that case, I'll have to get creative. Mind helping me move him onto the table?"

"He's pretty strong. Let's get some help."

With the aid of Vince and Luigi's goon, they untied him from the chair. Rocco pulled off Vanni's undershirt, and he found himself being carried across the room clad only in his boxer shorts, with hot sweaty hands wandering all over his body as they maneuvered him over to the table and stretched him out, spread-eagle, on the cold metal table. Then they secured his outstretched limbs with ropes anchored to the table legs. They were going to leave him alone with Rocco.

"Aren't you gonna stay and watch, Gio?" Rocco asked.

Gio turned and looked at his brother-in-law coldly. "Watch you torture a man I thought was my best friend? Just tell me what you learn, if anything. And try to leave him in one piece."

When the door was shut, Vanni asked, "What are you gonna do to me?"

"You think you're such a stud, with all this chest hair," Rocco said, running his hands over his helpless prisoner's chest. "I'll bet my wife liked it."

"It wasn't like that. We never got that far when we were dating."

"How far did you get?"

"You didn't even meet her until after we broke up! Why do you have it in for me?"

"Just curious. She never talks about those days, except to say you were a perfect gentleman. Which I guess means you kept this in your pants." He pulled down the waistband of Vanni's shorts and reached in, his warm fingers fishing out the flaccid cock. Vanni turned his head away and groaned miserably.

Rocco stared at the cock lying limply in his hand for a full minute, as if deciding what to do with it. Then he said in a quieter tone, "OK, enough personal stuff. My brother-in-law gave me a job to do." He put Vanni's cock away and snapped the elastic waistband back over his belly.

"I don't know anything! They didn't tell me nothing!" he called as Rocco walked out of his line of sight. He heard the freezer door open and felt tendrils of cold air drifting over to caress his bare skin as if the freezer missed him. Then the door shut again.

Rocco set a tub of gelato on the table, right next to him. He flinched as it touched his naked flank.

"You think the container's cold? You haven't felt nothing yet. I'm just gonna leave it here to soften while I look for a scoop."

The break room did have a scoop, Vanni knew, and it didn't take long for Rocco to find it. The gelato proved to be chocolate, his favorite, and it seared like cold fire when Rocco pressed it against his chest. It was unfair that something that would usually cause him such delight, something he yearned for and rarely indulged in, could cause him such agony in the wrong hands.

"I don't know nothing! They didn't tell me! Please, I swear!"

Rocco lazily smeared the melting ice cream around his chest, slicking down the hairs. "I'll stop when you've given me the names of some of our guys who are in league with your family."

"I'd tell you if I knew."

"Let's try another question. Who are they hitting next?"

"They don't tell me nothing. They know I'm loyal to Gio."

This earned him a fresh scoop, ground into his belly. He cursed loudly in Sicilian. His knowledge of Sicilian was pretty much limited to curses, since his parents had spoken English around him – except when his father hit himself on the thumb with a hammer. Then the Sicilian came out. It was the same with the other men of his father's generation, when Vanni had been growing up. He'd overheard a lot of colorful Sicilian words coming from them, too, whenever their thumbs were hit with a hammer by his father.

"We already know you were lying when you said you didn't know your father was going to kill the head of our family. So who else is he planning to kill?"

"I was telling the truth, no matter what Alicio said."

Rocco positioned the scoop right over a nipple. Vanni twisted and arched his back, trying to get away, but Rocco was as strong as he was, and slammed him back against the table, holding him there with one meaty hand flat on his chest while the other pressed the scoop against its sensitive target. Vanni howled.

"Alicio is never wrong."

"OK, they did say some things I can see now should have been clues, looking back. But it never occurred to me at the time."

The next one went right into his defenseless armpit. "And what were you supposed to do with Gio? Kill him, too?"

"Fuck you! I would never ..." He switched back to Sicilian curses as the scoop was ground deeper into his armpit. "I wasn't told to do anything," he finally sobbed. "They knew I'd never hurt him."

"But you helped set him up, didn't you? Or his father? By passing information on where they'd be?"

"No. I'd never do that."

"Liar. You expect me to believe you never mentioned where you'd be to your own father? Or your brothers?"

"Maybe casually. I had no reason to suspect ..."

"So you admit it. You know what goes good with gelato? Italian sausage."

"You bastard! You wouldn't – No. No, please," Vanni whimpered, but Rocco was already pulling his boxer shorts down. They wouldn't go down very far onto his thighs with his legs spread like that, but they went down far enough to leave his cock exposed and quivering, and his balls dangling unprotected.

"Always did like nuts in my ice cream," Rocco said.

His scrotum was already starting to contract in an automatic attempt to pull them tight against his body, but Rocco was faster. Vanni screamed.

"What did you 'casually' tell them?" he asked, taking Vanni's cock in one hand and holding the scoop very close to it with the other.

"Nothing important."

Rocco rolled his foreskin down, leaving the sensitive head completely exposed.

"Please, Rocco ..."

"Talk fast."

"The only thing I remember for sure is that they know Gio would be working here today, and I'd be here with him. Even if they're not after Gio, they may try to rescue me."

"They're a little late, then. And why would they think you need rescuing, if you're so loyal to Gio?"

"Maybe they figured out you're such an – Argh!"

Rocco was ruthless, swirling gelato all around the head of his cock, and then stretching the flaccid organ out along his belly, so he could apply it to the even more sensitive underside.

After he was finally done with Vanni's cock, he started all over again on his upper body. Vanni was too tired to curse anymore, and just lay there limply, submitting to whatever Rocco wanted to do with him, sobbing quietly and gasping whenever a fresh scoop contacted particularly sensitive flesh.

Rocco was grinding a scoop into Vanni's other armpit when he was interrupted by a gunshot elsewhere in the building. He dropped the scoop and went to investigate, leaving Vanni a quivering, gelato-coated mess. The hair on his chest, crotch, and armpits was thoroughly caked with the sticky stuff, and he was once again chilled to the bone.

As he waited miserably, he didn't know whether to hope that Rocco returned for more fun, or Gio looked in on him and put a stop to it. He wanted it to stop, but he didn't want his friend to see him this way. Not that he had any choice about who came in next.

The door opened again, and it was neither of them. It was Vince. He was saying to someone behind him, "He's right in here. He's OK, you'll see."

The person behind him was Vanni's middle brother Sergio, holding a gun. Both men stopped in their tracks, stunned at seeing what had been done to him.

"Hey, at least I'm in one piece," Vanni said weakly.

"I didn't do this to him, I swear!" Vince said. "All I did was help tie him up."

"Well, now you can untie him. And then you can clean him up. On second thought, untying him can wait. The poor guy's shivering. Let's go find a towel and soak it in hot water."

Vanni moaned involuntarily as Vince applied the warm towel to his chest.

"Too hot?"

"No. Feels great, after all that cold."

"He really did a number on you. But I think poor Luigi is in for some old-fashioned torture in there. And your brothers shot both of his men." Nevertheless, his hands were gentle as he worked his way slowly down Vanni's naked torso.

"My God! Poor Luigi. But you have to believe me; I had nothing to do with any of this." Despite the horrible situation, he felt his body relaxing into Vince's strokes as the hot towel melted away the tension in his chilled, cramped muscles as fast. "How's Gio? They haven't hurt him, have they?"

"So you were telling the truth after all?" Vince asked as he gently scrubbed out Vanni's armpits. "I guess you have no reason to lie now, when you brother is holding a gun on me."

"I wanted you to know that I was on the level. We've always been friends, haven't we, Vince?"

"I'd like to think so," he said, wiping away a streak that ran from his lower belly down into his pubic hair. He stopped, embarrassed, when he got to the wispy edge of those curly hairs. "Uh, maybe you can do the rest yourself."

"Yeah." Although given the choice, if he had to have one of Gio's brothers-in-law handling his genitals, he'd much rather it have been the friendly touch of Vince than the cruel and humiliating handling by Rocco.

Vince struggled with the knots, got his arms untied, and handed him the towel. Vanni scrubbed at his crotch until his scrotum, shriveled down like a walnut, was revealed. His shaft had gotten thoroughly coated, and was smeared under his foreskin, sticking it to the head.

As he was concentrating on his cock, a gun went off, practically in his ear, and Vince staggered back against the table. "Vince!" Vanni shouted, catching his shoulder. Since his legs were still tied, all he could do is lie back down on his side and wrap his arm around Vince's chest, under the wounded man's armpits, to keep him from slipping away. He glared at his brother. "What'd you have to do that for?"

"Tell the baby ..." Vince whispered, struggling to draw breath, "... I was a good guy." There was blood trickling down his chin, and a stain spreading over the right side of his shirt.

Vanni pressed his cheek against the dying man's. "I'll make sure someone provides for your family," he sobbed.

Sergio stepped forward and placed the gun against Vince's chest to finish him off. "No!" Vanni shouted, but the gun went off in his ear and Vince jerked in his arms as the bullet ripped apart his heart.

"Where are your clothes?" Sergio asked briskly, shoving the body out of Vanni's arms and untying his legs in a businesslike manner.

"My clothes? I don't know. In the office, I guess." He wanted to pull his boxer shorts up, at least, but they were gooey with gelato, and he'd just finished getting the stuff out of his pubic hair. Finally he slid them down his legs and off. They left a streak down his legs, which he wiped off with the towel Vince had given him, weeping as he remembered Vince's tender touch.

"I'll go get them," Sergio said.

He came back pushing Rocco ahead of him with the muzzle of his gun. "I couldn't find them. They claim they threw them down the garbage chute. But this guy looks about your size."

Seeing Rocco, Vanni instinctively drew his knees up to protect his chest and his balls, and hugged his arms to his sides.

"You killed Vince," Rocco said, turning pale.

"He wouldn't cooperate," Sergio lied. "But you're gonna do exactly as I say, right?"

"What choice do I have?"

"I knew you'd be reasonable. Now, strip. Now! Good. T-shirt, too."

Rocco's muscular chest turned out to be utterly smooth, although his legs were fairly hairy, especially the upper thighs. Despite himself, Vanni found he enjoyed seeing his tormentor stripped to his tight white briefs, humiliated.

"He'll need your shorts, too. His got ice cream all over them."

Rocco bashfully hid his crotch with his hands as soon as he'd straightened up, but not before Vanni noticed that he had a surprisingly dinky little dick for such a big guy.

"Now kick everything over this way, and step back. Good. Vanni, pick up his clothes."

Vanni got off the table, knelt in front of Rocco and scooped everything up, then tossed them on the table and took the briefs from the top of the pile. They were clean, but the unfamiliar sensation of cotton tight against his balls was made even stranger by the knowledge that, moments before, they had been in contact with his tormentor's hairy scrotum. The T-shirt was damp and smelled of Old Spice, with a half-familiar scent underneath that Vanni suspected was a mix of fear and male aggression, or even arousal. He tossed that aside, deciding to wear the button-down shirt directly over his bare skin. The clothes did fit him very well, although the shoes were slightly loose.

After making him watch Vanni get dressed in his clothes, Sergio ordered Rocco to back up against the wall.

"No, Sergio!" Vanni pleaded. "There's no need to kill him."

"Don't be naive, Vanni. We can't leave witnesses. And it's important to wipe out the whole family, so they can't get back at us."

The naked man fell to his knees and begged for his life. "Please, I swear I won't try to get back at any of you. I'll take my family and move out West and never bother you."

"You can believe him. I've never known him to go back on his word," Vanni said, exaggerating.

"He was the one who tortured you, right?"

That was true, but he was after all the husband of his best friend's sister. Vanni had played with Rocco's children at family gatherings. And the poor guy looked so pathetic now, his muscles on display but useless, his hands raised in supplication, his little dick dangling there forgotten. "So give him to me and let me deal with him," Vanni suggested.

"Sure. Your birthday is coming up anyway."

For an instant, his hopes soared. It had been a long shot, a desperate ploy to save the guy's life. Not that he would let him off easy; he definitely would take the chance to utterly humiliate him. He saw Rocco turn his attention to him, with a strange mix of hope and dread in his eyes. He decided he would start by laying their dicks side by side, pumping them both up to their full size, and then literally rubbing Rocco's nose in the result. His own cock would grow to at least three times the length Rocco had already seen when it lay limp and helpless across his palm. And then the real payback would begin ...

Sergio – oblivious to his thoughts and too busy keeping an eye on Rocco to notice that his brother's cock was straining against the borrowed pants, already beginning to rehearse its part in this scene without even being touched – dashed his hopes by adding, "Do you promise to kill him when you're done?"

"I can't do that," Vanni said. "But, look ..."

Without further warning, Sergio shot the kneeling man. A red hole appeared in his bare chest, and he toppled onto his face.

After a shocked silence, Vanni asked numbly, "Are you going to kill Gio, too?"

"We're keeping him alive until he tells us the combination to his safe. Maybe he'll be smart and tell us before we hurt him. He likes his cousin a lot, right?"

His brother led him back to the office, with Vanni glaring at the back of his head. When they got close, Vanni could hear a man screaming. It didn't sound like Gio, at least.

Gio was trussed up in his own office chair, apparently unharmed, but his cousin was being tortured before his eyes. Vanni's youngest brother, Nick, was seated facing Luigi, and had the tough guy's bare foot imprisoned on his lap. With a shock, Vanni realized his brother was holding a pair of pliers, and that all of the fingers on Luigi's bound hands on the armrests looked crooked and were starting to swell. Luigi screamed again as the toe was cruelly twisted. He didn't seem so tough now.

Aldo, his oldest brother, was watching the whole thing coldly. He nodded at Vanni in greeting. "Your former boss is next, if he doesn't tell us the combination before we run out of toes."

"I'd tell you," Gio said, his voice heavy with suppressed emotion, "if I didn't know you're going to kill us anyway."

"Yeah, but isn't a quick clean death better than this?" He jerked a thumb at Luigi, who whimpered as Nick clamped the pliers around a fresh toe. Vanni had always looked up to his best friend's cousin; as a teenager he'd given the boys rides on his strong shoulders. It twisted his heart to see him reduced to this. He'd have given anything to have his brother borrow Rocco's interrogation method to use on Luigi.

"So far he won't even tell us where the safe is, but maybe that will change when it's his own fingers being broken."

Vanni opened his mouth to suggest that Gio instead be stripped naked and a new tub of gelato fetched from the freezer. But what came out was, "He has you convinced there's a safe?"

All three of his brothers looked at him. "Leo once mentioned a safe to a buddy who's on our payroll," Aldo said.

Vanni was relieved to verify that he hadn't blabbed this information himself despite his habit of keeping quiet about such things. "You should have asked me. I know where the hiding place is." He managed not to even glance at the painting. Knowing that a lie is more believable mixed with a fact that they might already be aware of, he added, "He's got a huge stash of diamonds hidden there."

"Where?"

"I'll show you."

Aldo and Sergio followed him out of the room, leaving their youngest brother to guard the prisoners, with instructions to hold off on any further torture. Nick slid his chair back away from Luigi, eliciting one more cry of pain as he cruelly let the foot slide off his lap and hit the floor.

When Vanni returned alone, Nick asked him, "Did you find it?"

"Leo and I were both right. There was a hiding place in the freezer just like I thought, but it turns out, it's a safe. It was buried under the gelato. Aldo and Sergio are carrying it out now and trying to crack it. But you know, it occurs to me that Gio has a terrible memory. I'll bet he has the combination written down somewhere. Probably on him. Did you check his inside jacket pocket?"

Nick leaned over the trussed-up prisoner, unbuttoned his jacket, reached in and began feeling around. Vanni, standing right behind his brother, whipped Rocco's T-shirt out of his back pocket and stretched between his hands like a garrote. He'd previously twisted it into sort of a loose cord and knotted the ends. In a split second, he had it around his brother's throat. He pulled it as tight as he could, until his struggling brother collapsed, face turning purple. He held it there until he was sure he was unconscious, then for as much longer as he dared. Then he used it to tie his brother's wrists together in front of him, and bound his feet with his belt – Rocco's belt.

"What about your other brothers?" Gio asked.

"Locked in the freezer."

"What made you change your mind?"

Angrily, Vanni whirled on him and grabbed him by his shirtfront, cocking a fist. "You ungrateful bastard! You still don't believe I never turned on you in the first place?"

Luigi said hoarsely, "Alicio is never wrong."

"Besides," Gio said, "nobody turns on his own brothers. Even if you didn't know in advance, you've got to be on their side now. This is some kind of trick. Where are they really?"

Furious at being doubted, Vanni released his friend's shirt and dragged his younger brother's limp body over to the filing cabinet by his feet, bound wrists dragging. Vanni opened the bottom drawer and placed Nick's shins over it. He went back and turned Gio's chair, so he could see. Nick was starting to regain consciousness, which was a damn shame. Vanni took an empty chair over to the filing cabinet and raised it over his head. "I'm sorry, Nicky," he whispered. Nick's eyes, now open, grew wide in the second before Vanni brought the chair crashing down on his brother's legs, producing a sickening cracking noise and a strangled cry.

# # # # #

"I'm sorry for doubting you," Gio said that night, after the two had come back from visiting Luigi and Nick in the hospital, both immobilized in casts. Vanni felt better once he had showered off the stickiness that had remained despite poor Vince's efforts with the warm towel, and dressed in a fresh set of his own clothes. Now, safe in a locked windowless room deep inside the well-guarded family estate, both men had removed their jackets and loosened their ties, and proceeded to get drunker than they'd allowed themselves to get in years.

"Did you really believe that 'blood is thicker than water' crap so much that you wouldn't trust even me? We've been pals as long as I can remember."

"It wasn't just that. Luigi was so sure Alicio was completely reliable at detecting lies. I'm sorry. Will you ever forgive me for how we treated you?"

"Will you ever trust me again, completely?" Vanni shot back.

"If I didn't trust you, I wouldn't be sitting here alone with you."

"You know I left my gun at home before we went to the hospital."

"You're stronger than I."

"You're pretty strong yourself," he said, squeezing Gio's biceps through his shirt sleeve. "You'd put up a good fight."

"You probably have a knife hidden on you somewhere."

"I do, as a matter of fact. I always carry one. But you know that, and if you saw me bending down to get it you'd have a chance to kick me in the chin or hit me over the head."

"Look, I trust you, OK? Can't you just take my word for it?"

"Not anymore. I no longer trust you to trust me. We have to fix that. I don't want to go through the rest of my life like this, with no one I can relax around. And you're all I've got left. My family sure as hell will never trust me again."

"What does it take? I let you into my private rooms, and there's no one else even in earshot. What else can I do to prove it? I'd do anything to get back what we had."

"Really?"

"Really."

"Anything?"

"Yeah, anything, damn it."

"Then let me tie you to that chair." When Gio laughed, Vanni said, "I'm serious. You can show me you trust me, and I can settle once and for all what'll happen if I have you at my mercy. That's one of the questions you asked me."

"I already know what'll happen. I saw it. First you break the legs of your nearest brother, and then you let me go."

"That isn't funny. Do you know how hard that was for me, breaking my little brother's legs to prove I was on your side?"

"I know. I don't think I've ever seen you cry before today, not since we were little kids. I shouldn't joke about it. But the point is you did let me go."

"That was in front of Luigi. You asked what I'd do with no witnesses." Vanni spoke in a quiet, serious tone.

"You're scaring me, buddy."

"Which only proves you don't really trust me."

"But ... OK. If that's what it takes."

The wooden chair Gio was already seated in would do fine. Vanni stood up to remove his belt, then knelt and rolled up Gio's pants leg and secured his leg so tightly that the wood pressed into his bared calf and the leather bug into his shin. Then he reached for Gio's belt buckle.

"Hey!" Gio objected, grabbing his wrist.

"Are you letting me do this or not?"

Gio let go of his wrist and submitted to his belt being unbuckled and removed. When both legs were bound tightly to the chair at mid-shin level, Vanni got up and rummaged through Gio's dresser and came back with a two more belts, which he used to bind each wrist to a chair post behind his back.

"Helpless enough?" Vanni asked, patting his friend's unshaven cheek.

"What's the point of this?"

Vanni bent down and drew his knife. "You asked me what I'd do if we were alone and you were tied up helpless, and I had a knife in my hand. Actually, you asked what I would want to do."

"That won't cut through our belts," Gio said nervously.

"But I was lying when I said I'd cut you free. Alicio is never wrong, remember?" He held it near Gio's chest, which was now heaving with suddenly rapid breathing.

"Quit kidding around. It's not funny."

"Either you trust me with your life, or you're keeping me close to you for some other reason than to be your bodyguard. Like to have me killed. If I'm going to wind up sleeping with Rocco and Vince at the bottom of the river, there's one thing I want to do first, just once in my life."

Gio had unbuttoned his collar when he'd loosened his tie; they both had. Vanni moved the knife point close to his friend's exposed throat.

"This isn't happening." Gio squeezed his eyes shut.

Vanni slid the knife blade carefully past his friend's collar and inside his shirt. With the sharp edge turned outward, he drew it toward himself and downward, slicing through the strings of the buttons, one by one.

Gio opened his eyes, looking down in astonishment. He was just in time to watch Vanni reach into his undershirt with the knife and carefully slice through the thin cotton to expose the skin underneath.

"This is what I really wanted to do," Vanni said, flinging the shirt wide open to expose Gio's chest. He leaned down and kissed the helpless man's unshaven throat. His dangling tie dragged silkily over a nipple. Gio's own tie had flopped limply over his pectoral muscle, clinging to the moist skin. It was in the way, so Vanni slipped his knife under the tie where it looped around Gio's neck, and sliced through it. He dangled it triumphantly before his captive's eyes and threw it on the floor.

He kissed the hollow of Gio's throat and worked his way down his chest, lightly kissing all the exposed flesh, brushing the sparse curly chest hairs with his lips, and made his way slowly over to a nipple, where his lips lingered.

Drawing back a few inches, he said, "This is the dark secret I've been hiding. Even if you were telling the truth about trusting me with your life, it's not your life you ever needed to worry about with me. Our friendship would be a lie if I kept on hiding this, knowing you'd probably hate me if you knew." Gio, still breathing hard, was speechless. When Vanni saw that his friend was too stunned to reply, he continued working his way down his torso, until his lips reached the waistband.

Then he began attacking the shirt itself. The material yielded easily to the knife blade. A few slashes bared one muscular shoulder, which he stopped to knead with his free hand, almost painfully. He then slit Gio's sleeve all the way down, laying bare his entire arm. A few more minutes of this, and the shirt was sliced to ribbons, which Vanni then ripped away completely. Then he slit his undershirt along the tops of his shoulders and down one flank, careful not to let the blade quite touch his skin, and pulled the remains of it out from behind him.

He drew back to admire his work for a moment. His captive was now completely bare to the waist. He was lean, with not a trace of fat, and had a respectable amount of muscle on his chest and arms, a reflection of the fact that he'd long been more interested in the physical side of his father's small empire than the creamy wares that were his supposed business. Not quite as muscular as Vanni himself: They both had known Gio would lose in a fair fight, but they'd both be badly damaged by the end.

This wasn't a fair fight. Gio wasn't going anywhere, and neither of them was going to get hurt, not as long as Vanni kept him tied up. He attacked Gio's navel with his tongue, then licked his way up his belly and chest, this time teasing the other nipple, the one that he had not touched with his lips before. Finally, he tilted his captive's head back and stuck his tongue into his mouth. Gio didn't clench his jaw, but he fought back with his own tongue for a moment before letting that be pushed aside, as defeated as its owner was.

His expensive pants were the next thing to be cut up. Vanni sliced them just above the knees, and knelt to massage his bare calves and play with the hair on his shins, just above the straps. The next to go were the buttons that held his pants closed. Once the pants were cut to shreds and ripped away completely, there was nothing to hide the fact that the underside of his penis was pressing urgently at the cotton of his briefs, the head trying to crawl under the waistband. Then he had to hold absolutely still as Vanni carefully ran the point of the knife in parallel to his cock, cutting through the tent of taut fabric that Gio's cock was holding clear of his skin. The cotton parted easily, and the elastic parted with a snap.

"You know," Vanni said, kneeling between his bare legs, "close up, I can usually tell when a guy is scared of me, even if he's trying to hide it. I can smell it on him. You don't smell very scared."

"I'm not scared of you. Maybe just for a minute, but not anymore."

"You don't look scared, from down here," Vanni agreed dryly. He began using his knife to trim the curly ends of Gio's pubic hair away from the base of his erect cock, and away from his balls. "A lot of guys would be terrified in this situation."

"I told you I trust you."

Vanni stood up with the hairs he'd collected pinched between his thumb and forefinger. He bent close to Gio's chest and tickled Gio's nipple with his own pubic hairs. "Every minute you smell less scared and more ... musky. Let's see how you taste." He began licking Gio's chest again. After a moment, he moved behind him and unbelted one wrist. He forced it behind Gio's head and began licking his armpit. Gio struggled half-heartedly.

"You definitely taste anything but scared," he murmured into Gio's ear. The very tip of his tie brushed lightly against his denuded captive's erect cock. He might not smell or taste scared, but Vanni felt him trembling in his arms, which had to mean something. "You're probably furious at me, but it was worth it, just for once in my life. At least now if you kill me, it's for something I actually did, not because of something I would never do to you."

He released Gio's arm and knelt at his feet, the only parts of him not bare now, and released his legs from the belts, massaging them to help restore circulation. "You're letting me go?" Gio asked incredulously, but he sounded almost disappointed, and made no move to free his other wrist from the remaining belt.

"I had to sooner or later. What are you going to do with me?" Vanni asked, still kneeling between his hairy legs. "Are you going to turn me over to Luigi's men, or do it yourself? I know there are a lot of things worse than what you let Rocco do to me. Here." He handed Gio the knife, and bowed his head down between his knees, gripping his bare thighs to brace himself. "If you're gonna kill me for this, do me one last favor as an old pal, and finish me off quick."

"Don't be an idiot," Gio said. Vanni heard the knife skitter away across the floor. He felt Gio's hand grasping his own and interlacing their fingers. With his naked legs now free, Gio spread them even wider and slid forward on the rags of clothing he was sitting on, until the arm still bound behind his back stopped him. He pinned the stronger man's hand against his bare thigh, immobilizing him one free hand. "Finish me off," he begged. "Quick."

# # # # #

Two hours later, they were lying in Gio's bed, their naked bodies pressed warmly together, with Gio playing with Vanni's thick chest hair and still occasionally tormenting the smooth tender skin below his shoulder by rubbing his cheek against it.

"Have we both proved our trust in each other now?" Vanni asked teasingly.

"Definitely."

"Then how about untying me?" Vanni asked.

"Not until you agree to marry Carina."

Vanni groaned. "I thought we were past that."

"You and I are way past that now. But what about the rest of the family? If only you'd married one of my sisters in the first place, none of this would have happened. My father and Rocco and Vince would still be alive, Nick wouldn't be in traction, and Luigi wouldn't have to wonder if he'll ever be able to hold a fork again. Your father wouldn't have killed the father of his daughter-in-law, would he? Not when they might share the same grandchildren someday."

"I'm sorry. I just couldn't. If I'd known what would happen, then maybe I would have, but it's too late."

"You're too late to save my father, but you can do it for me. Otherwise the war between our families won't end without more bloodshed." Vanni had begged Gio not to kill his two trapped brothers or his crippled younger brother. He'd made it clear it was a request and not a demand, even as he cut his friend loose in the office, but Gio had chosen to honor it, even though it left the Lombardo family in a strong position to strike again.

"It wouldn't be fair to Carina. She deserves better. I'd be depriving her of the chance to meet someone like ... like Vince. God, I miss him. As he was dying in my arms, I promised him I would ..."

"Would what?" Gio asked when Vince didn't continue.

"Wait a minute. Does it have to be Carina?"

"She's the only sister – Oh."

"Right. We have to take care of Adriana and Bonnie, and I mean more than just sending them money. We really should find them husbands and stepfathers for their kids. I could be one of those husbands. Now the only problem is deciding which one. I want to be there for Vince's baby, but I already get along so well with Rocco's kids. I guess, either way, I'd be a stepfather and an uncle."

"Do you really expect either Adriana or Bonnie to let the brother of her husband's killer ever touch her in bed?"

"That's just it. I don't. And neither will anyone else! They'll understand when no more kids arrive. It's perfect. There won't be whispers questioning my manhood."

"Adriana is a great cook. You've tasted her homemade pasta, right? Bonnie is very thrifty, and keeps a neat house. But she's a little clingy; Adriana was more understanding about letting her husband spend time carousing with his buddies. Yeah. Pick Adriana."

"Whatever you say, *paisan*. Now will you untie me?"

"Never. I've got you just where I want you, you big lug." He reached up to tickle an exposed armpit. "Bound for life, as my brother-in-law."

THE BANKER BOYS
By Landon Dixon

"Hold it right there, mister."

The weather-beaten farmer froze, gripping the razor-sharp scythe. He'd seen the car come storming up the dirt road that led to his dirt farm, and he'd high tailed it into the barn to arm himself. Unannounced visitors out here usually carried guns.

This one carried a gun, Jerry Jenkins, Texas Ranger. He pointed it at the farmer, said, "Okay, drop the head-lopper and turn around. I'm only gonna ask you a few questions."

The farmer dropped the scythe, slowly turned around to face the Law. He was a tall, lean, sun browned man of about thirty-five, the Depression years taking a toll on his prematurely grey hair, his tattered blue overalls and torn white T-shirt. His pale blue eyes regarded the Ranger with contempt. He didn't have much, but he had that.

"You're Len Banker, ain't ya?" Jenkins growled.

The farmer nodded.

"Your nephews, Pete and Roy, are part of the Banker Boys." Jenkins slicked a finger down both sides of his drooping brown mustache. "I've traced down here from their last bank job in Omaha, figured you might know where they're hiding out."

Len sneered, "Even if I did, I wouldn't tell no copper."

Jenkins grunted, holstered his gun. He was wearing a tan shirt and pants, brown leather boots and belt. His tall, rangy body filled out the thin cloth of the uniform, bulged at the crotch. He grinned bright white teeth, brown eyes shining, as he pulled his belt loose.

"Figured you'd say that." The belt flopped open. Jenkins unbuttoned his fly. "Figured no normal pistol-whipping's gonna get it out of you, either."

He reached into his drawers and drew out his cock, a huge wedge of an appendage, as wide at the tip as all along the smooth, swollen shaft.

"That's why I come with a back-up plan." He glided a big, tanned hand up and down the tremendous length of the organ, making it stretch, hardened even further. "Think I can draw a bead on you with this rod?"

Len's pink tongue shot out of his half-open mouth and bathed his trembling lips, his hungry eyes fixed on the lawman's huge dick. Food and work weren't the only things scarce in the Dust Bowl – men were, too.

"Come on, don't be bashful," Jenkins said, gesturing with his immense member. "I ain't got all day."

Len staggered forward, dropped to his knees in the loose straw, grabbed onto Jenkins' cock and stuffed the head and half of the shaft into his mouth. He eagerly bobbed his head, sucking greedily on the pipe.

Jenkins sifted his fingers into the man's soft hair, rasping, "That's the way. Get your fill. Then you can fill me in, huh?"

Len was too busy sucking on the man's prick to even hear what he said. The warm dong throbbed in his mouth, stiffening, incredibly, even further as he slid his lips up and down the slick shaft. He crowded as much cock into his mouth as he could, which was less than two-thirds of the thunder stick. He tugged on it with his mouth like he was trying to tear it out by the roots, his six months of man-famish coming to an end. He wagged his tongue back and forth across the pulsating underside, lips stretched obscenely wide to accommodate.

Jenkins looked down at the kneeling man blowing his cock. He grinned, tightened his grip on the farmer's hair, as Len took an especially deep suck, pulled back up along shaft with a wet, air-tight seal. And when the man cupped Jenkins' balls, squeezed them, the big law officer knew that his gun was fully cocked and ready to go off.

He yanked his dong out of Len's mouth, wielded it over the man, jerking Len's head back. "You wanna taste what this dick's got to offer, don't ya?"

Len desperately nodded, his eyes frantic, red lips straining to reach the dripping cockhead just beyond the reach of his mouth. Hot protein injected down deep into a man's soul was a luxury hard to come by during hard times, with most able-bodied men off riding the rails or the dusty road west.

Jenkins tipped his cock back down, resting the gleaming knob on Len's writhing lips. "Well, before I spill, you gotta spill, mister. Tell me where the Banker Boys mighta gone to ground."

Len stared up at the lawman's impassive face, down at the lawman's gaping slit. There was a pearl of precum glistening there. He leapt out his tongue, lapping up the drop of semen, taking the bait. "There-there's an old quarry about ten miles south of here. The boys used to … play there when they were young 'uns."

Jenkins nodded, let go of Len's head. Len engulfed the man's cock again and sucked with a fearsome intensity.

Jenkins bucked, and grunted. Hot, salty, rubbery semen blasted out of his mouth-embedded dong and down the farmer's throat. Len gulped, shuddering, creaming his own overalls, clutching Jenkins' hips and milking the jumping cock with his mouth, swallowing and swallowing and swallowing the spouting sperm.

# # # # #

It appeared to be just a copse of trees from the road. But as Jenkins walked through the woods, the thick growth shut him off completely from the outside world, the area cloaked in forest far larger than it looked from a distance. The hot sun was barely visible up in the blue sky, hidden by the treetops, cut into stripes that fought to penetrate the foliage. The big lawman almost became lost, no discernible trail to follow. Until, at last, he heard yelling and splashing, and a satisfied grin split his sweating face.

It took him five more minutes before he finally fought his way free of the scraping tree branches and strode out onto a rocky plateau overlooking the old abandoned quarry. Blue-green water filled the limestone pit at the bottom. There was a strip of sand on the east shelf of the long, wide, rectangular hole in the ground. Three boys were swimming in the cool-looking water, doing laps, racing one another.

Jenkins thumbed back his Stetson, ignoring the blazing sun, as he stared at the shimmering brown bodies of the young men in the swimming hole – Pete and Roy Banker, and their third partner in crime, Tom 'Tommy' Herman – the Banker Boys.

The gang was so-named not only because two of the members shared the common last name, but also because it so suited their chosen vocation – robbing banks. They'd knocked off nine financial institutions in a sixteen-month stretch on their crime spree, one of those banks located down in Amarillo, Texas.

Pete was nineteen, Roy eighteen, Tom twenty. Plowing dirt with their sweat and tears wasn't anything they wanted to do. So they'd taken the easy road to riches, the last stop: hard time or hot death.

Pete and Roy shared blond hair and blue eyes, small, agile, compact bodies. Their faces were almost delicately featured, smooth skin burnished by the sun. 'Tommy Gun' Herman was taller, lankier, with a mop of black hair and wide-set grey eyes, built along girlish lines without so much as a trace of muscle. Jenkins studied their forms in the water, watching the flashing, pumping, dripping limbs, the upturned, floating, rippling buttocks. The boys were stark-naked, without a stitch, or a care in the world.

Jenkins spotted a trail that led down to the sandy shore, took it.

"Okay, boys, playtime is over!" he yelled, emerging on the edge of the water. He was drenched in sweat, and it wasn't just due to his exertion and the weather.

The three young men stopped swimming and swiveled their heads and stared at the big Ranger and his drawn gun. They treaded water, their brown faces gone a shade of pale.

"Dang it all!" Tom yelped, slapping the surface of the water. Pete and Roy swallowed, hard.

"Come on out, boys," Jenkins said. "Hands high where I can see 'em."

The trio swum closer to the man, then stood, waded towards him through the water, the swimming hole canting from deep to shallow in a hurry. They held their hands up over their heads.

Jenkins got a good look at their bare, smooth chests and taut stomachs, as the water receded and they came closer; at their young, dangling cocks and dripping wisps of pubic hair decorating their balls. He stepped back a couple of paces when they reached the shoreline. He held the gun steady, eyes jumping from one glistening young body to the next, around their puffy tan nipples, along the lengths of their pink, clean-cut cocks and slender, sun kissed legs.

When he'd made absolute positive identification, right down to the mole on Pete Banker's right thigh and the leftward slant of Tom Herman's cock, he said, "Okay, boys, turn around and drop to your knees, then your hands."

The young men looked at each other. But there was nothing they could do. The Ranger had the drop on them, their clothes and guns hidden away another six feet behind the man, in the bushes. They turned, dropped to their knees in the sand, down onto all-fours.

Jenkins holstered his Colt, licked his cracked lips, rubbed his jutting jaw with a shaking hand. Three tight, trim asses lined up right in front of him, butt cheeks round and fine and firm-looking, cracks splitting the three pairs smoothly. The lawman ambled forward, unfastening his belt, unbuttoning his pants, drawing his heavy rod out into the open and oiling it with the special grease he kept tucked away in a pocket.

Tom Herman gasped, quivered, when he felt the Ranger's long, strong fingers slide into his bum cleavage and scrub slickness up and down. Then he groaned, when the pair of fingers was replaced with one big cock, Jenkins splitting the trembling cheeks with his cap, busting inside the young man's anus.

The Ranger bulged pink pucker with his cockhead, let it grip there, gazing along the curved length of Tom's slender back. "Eyes front," he growled at the two brothers. Then, when he felt Tom's ring suck on his planted hood, he gripped the boy's narrow waist and sank shaft into chute, swollen, searing inch after inch after inch.

Jenkins and Tom both groaned, the lawman's entire rod plunging the depths of the boy's anus, until hairy, hanging balls pressed up against damp, cushioning buttocks. The heat of the sun glaring down was nothing compared to the oven-heat of Tom's chute gripping Jenkins' lodged cock. The big man reveled, rutted in the anal steam bath, the pulsing of his chute-buried cock thundering through his body and Tom's.

Then Jenkins drew his hips back, slowly, gliding his cock almost right out of the gasping hole, to the stretching rim. Then he drove back in, impaling the young man's ass all over again. He did it again and again and again, fingernails biting into burning flesh, hips pumping, fucking Tom's bum with a heavy, heated, thumping stroke that shook man and boy.

He moved onto the next ass, Roy's. Jenkins repeated the dirty anal cavity search, greasing Roy's young hole, penetrating it, pumping it. He reached a hand over and hooked two fingers back into Tom's anus, finger-fucking that young man as he banged Roy. He had to pull out after only a couple of minutes of torrid screwing, even his iron discipline wilting under the pressure of the reaming.

He gulped air, shifted over, stuck Pete's ass. Jenkins plowed his dong into the boy's backdoor, taking up every inch of superheated chute with his enormous cock. He tilted his head back and let his hips fly, ramming anus with abandon. He smacked Pete's rippling cheeks with his hands and his thighs, fucking for all he was worth, flapping balls laden with boiling sperm.

"That'll do, officer," someone said, pressing a hard, cool piece of metal against Jenkins' corded red neck.

The lawman halted cold in Pete's ass, caught red-dicked.

The three boys scrambled to their feet, Pete popping off the Ranger's rod. "Wondering when you were going to show up!" Roy whooped.

"Meet the new 'fourth' member of the Banker Boys, officer," Tom said, grinning. "Wendell Washington."

Jenkins turned his head slightly, the gun muzzle creasing his skin. He looked at the young man pressing the .45 into his neck. Wendell was tall and wide, built, with kinky black hair and large brown eyes, flat nose and thick lips, velvety skin dark as night. He was as completely naked as the other three boys, his ebony cock hanging low from his pube-pebbled loins, dangerous-looking.

They wrestled Jenkins down flat on his back on the sand. Pete Banker mounted the man's cock, sticking it into his ass and then sitting down on it, letting it sink into his anus as he sank down onto the man's balls. Wendell straddled the lawman's face. He brushed his licorice-stick over the man's wet lips, the blue-black cap trailing white jizz. Then he pushed the mushroomed hood right through, fed vein-corded, noir-shaded shaft into Jenkins' mouth, as much as he could push down the lawman's throat, which, incredibly, was just about all of it.

Roy Banker dug a camera out of the bushes and snapped a couple of shots of the laid-out Ranger with a boy riding his cock, another fucking his mouth. "For the papers!" he yelped. "Maybe."

Then he dropped the camera and lined up alongside Tom, on their knees at Jenkins' head. Jenkins reached up his hands and gripped the young men's thrust-out cocks, tugged. As Pete bounced up and down on the man's dong. As Wendell stuffed cock into Jenkins' mouth and throat with powerful pumps of his hips.

It was a scene right out of a hedonistic inferno. Four naked boys, one naked man, five cocks, fucking ass, fucking face, getting jacked. The sun blazed down on the sweat-glazed bodies, grunts and groans and moans sounding more and more urgently in the still, heated air, the wet splash and fap of flesh against flesh sounding faster and faster; the frenzy of manhood reaching scorching culmination.

Roy threw an arm around Tom. The boys kissed, Frenched, long, pink, slippery tongues tumbling together. They traded and swallowed each other's cries of ecstasy, Jenkins' pulling hands jerking them past the point of no return. Roy sprayed, Tom sprayed, semen shooting out of their handled cocks and striping Jenkins' face and hair, Wendell's heaving stomach and plunging dong.

Wendell cried out, spasmed, jolted by fiery orgasm. He oiled his club in and out of Jenkins' sucking mouth, blasting sperm against the back of Jenkins' gulping throat. Just as Pete grabbed hold of his own bouncing cock and stroked, spouted. He arched, ass muscles squeezing Jenkins' dick convulsively, rope after rope of jism leaping out of his ruptured prick and splashing up against Wendell's back and all over Jenkins' chest and stomach.

The big Ranger felt his own wicked orgasm, deep-down, amidst all the shouting and shooting. He pumped out his load into Pete's clasping ass, emptying his balls and his soul, so it seemed.

The Banker Boys escaped with their stolen loot and smooth hides. Jenkins lay on the sand, basking in the blistering afterglow of all-out joy, getting his breath back. It was the third time in the past nine months he'd gotten the drop on the boys, only to see them slip out of his grasp after some hard-loving. He only hoped it could continue, before some righteous lawman got it into his thick skull to really crack down.

BUMPING OFF BRADLEY
By R. W. Clinger

Bottom line: I couldn't bump off Bradley. I was supposed to take him out with a Colt Commander pistol, had it all lined up last week, had the ammo and gun, had the spot picked out where I was going to off him, had another spot chosen where to bury him, and ...

My older brother Vito said, "Papa is going to nail you to the wall."

"Only if you tell him," I replied and stared at Jimmy Bradley in his torso-tight T-shirt and cuffed jeans inside Bradley's Cleaners on Eastman Street in downtown Chicago. Bradley was the sexiest bad boy on the East Side: auburn-colored hair slicked back with Dep, five-eleven frame of nicely built muscle, sea-green eyes with thick lashes, a dimple in the center of his right cheek. The guy was top-notch sexy as hell and totally melted me; no wonder I couldn't bump him off.

"You're thinking with your dick," Vito said in his thick Italian. He waved a finger at me and suggested, "Nino, you're smarter than this. It's bad enough you like guys, but why do you have to like Jimmy Bradley?"

"I can't answer that," I replied, and studied Bradley as he bent over to pick up a load of white sheets in his father's cleaners: bulbous ass, thin legs, perfect splay of back.

He asked, "Papa is going to take away your allowance if he finds out about this."

I shook my head and confirmed in a persistent manner, "Papa is not going to find out."

Vito sat to my right in the passenger seat of Papa's sky blue Chevrolet Bel Air convertible and gazed at me with a challenging stare. Truth was we looked like twins: black eyes and matching hair, olive-colored skin, six-two frames, Sicilian-thin, clean-shaven faces, hairless chests, and big tools between our legs; spitting images of the Tortelli men before us.

He said, "How do you plan on handling this situation?"

"I haven't thought about that yet?"

"Does Papa know you're fucking a Mick?"

"I'm not fucking him. And, don't call him a Mick."

"But, you want to fuck him, right?"

I didn't even have to think about it, and replied, "I do."

Vito rolled his dark eyes, and suggested, "The guy has a list of people to bump off. You know that, right?"

"I like the dangerous ones."

Again, Vito rolled his eyes. "Nino, get your shit together. Papa runs a business. Don't interfere with your cock."

"Any of us Tortellis on that list?'

Vito shrugged his shoulders and said, "I really don't know."

What he did know was simple: I was hard between my legs for the Irish lad and wanted my spike to be touched, licked, and played with until it sprayed a white-gooey load over Bradley's chest, face, ass, cock – wherever.

"Think about it, Nino. Keep yourself out of trouble."

"What if I don't? What if I just want to fuck around with this guy and …"

Vito slammed his fist to my chest and gawked at me with much intimidation, "Listen to me, little brother. Fuck Bradley all you want. Get it out of your system … and then bump him off. That is what Papa wants you to do."

Honestly, I was afraid of my older brothers, all six of them (Anthony, Ricardo, Luigi, Leonardo, Vinnie, and Vito). Each of them scared the Jitterbug out of me, maybe because I was the youngest, only twenty-one, and was still wet behind my ears.

1955. Papa liked the fights, helped take down J. Edgar Hoover, considered his business "The Outfit," and enjoyed listening to Buddy Holly. He liked his zombies and iconoclastic martinis, and always sported an expensive fedora. That year was kind of tense. The attorney general wanted to see Papa's books for tax evasion, and life was hell. Walt Disney's *Lady and the Tramp* opened in my hometown. *Peter Pan* was on Broadway, which I wanted to see, but Papa wouldn't front the money for my trip and …

A day after my conversation with Vito, I sat at the soda fountain bar across from Bradley's Cleaners. Sometimes a guy just wanted to get away from The Outfit and enjoy some Fats Domino on the jukebox. A root beer float with two scoops of vanilla ice cream was my favorite. Not three sucks into the float, and I had a steel barrel positioned against my spine. The familiar voice of Jimmy Bradley grumbled into my right ear, "You and I have some business to discuss, Mr. Tortelli. I suggest you step away from your float and lead me over to the cleaners without making a scene. If you cause any interruptions at all, I promise to pop lead into your back."

Bradley's breath warmed the right side of my neck and caused an instant boner to form in my slim-fitting slacks. Pre-sap fired out of my gun and glazed my balls. As instructed, I rose from my root beer float, left change on the bar for the soda fountain clerk, and escorted Bradley to his daddy's cleaners across the street.

In the middle of Eastman Street, I found the balls to ask Bradley, "I'm on your hit list, aren't I?"

"Keep walking," he said, nudging me with his hidden handgun, a Browning 380.

"My entire family is on that list, aren't we?"

Again, he nudged me with his gun. That time he said, "Don't fuck with me, Nino."

I had no doubt my uncles, brothers, papa, and cousins were all on Bradley's hit list. The Bradley family was our biggest threat on the East Side. Our families had rivaled for the past twenty years, and would continue to rival for the next twenty years.

"Don't kill me," I chanted in front of his cleaners.

"Shut the fuck up and get inside," the Irish bad boy said.

I opened the double glass doors, stepped inside his domain, and listened to his direction, "Head to the back of the place."

The cash register and waist-high counter sat at the front of the store. Behind the counter were a row of steamers, washers, dryers, and a moving S-shaped mechanical rack where clothes hung in plastic bags, all of which were labeled with client numbers and names.

Once in the back of the store, surrounded by three walls of freshly washed and pressed clothes in plastic bags, Bradley said, "Get naked."

193

I took in his handsome face and nicely constructed body, and questioned, "Get naked?"

He waved his Browning at me and replied, "Take your clothes off, Mafia guy, I want to see what kind of snack I'm about to have." Although he was Irish, Bradley sounded like East Side Chicago all the way. No one would have ever guessed he came from Knockbrock, Ireland, as a baby, an immigrant some twenty-one years before with his mother and father.

"Snack?" I asked, completely confused.

"Strip, Nino. Show me your cock. Get naked. I plan to make a snack out of your dick and balls."

A man who knows he is on a hit list never argues with his nemesis. Hurriedly, I kicked off my Jarman shoes, removed my James Dean-like jeans and dropped my Earl Pique polo shirt to the cement floor. There, I exposed my hairy balls and upright private part. All nine inches of my stem were at attention, and a bubble of ooze decorated its cap.

Bradley checked me out from head to toe. I could feel his eyes all over my body: rounded shoulders, corded neck, pumped and hairless pecs, dented navel among ripped abs, tangled pubic triangle and balls. Unexpectedly, he reached forward with his right hand, pulled the middle of my shaft towards him like a slot machine, released my stick, and snapped it against my torso. The bubble of goo at its apex flung against my stomach and stuck. "Nice," escaped the Irish mobster, and a greedy smile spread across his face that told me: I want to eat you all up.

"Bradley, what's going on here?"

He gave me a hard look, then eyed up my cock, and chanted, "Word on the street says that you have a thing for me. Is that so?"

Again: a man who knows he is on a hit list never lies to his nemesis. I nodded my head, sneered with greed, and admitted, "Bradley, I would like to bump my cock into your ass … That's how fucking hooked I am on you."

It was the first time he was quiet during our meeting. Bradley dropped to his knees, set his Browning 380 on the cement floor to his left side, held my swinging balls in his right hand, tugged down on my nine-inch shaft with his left hand, and slipped my cock into his warm mouth.

Irish men could blow, I determined rather quickly. As he continued to hold my balls, keeping a sturdy grip on their hairy orbs, his other hand positioned three fingers around the base of my pole and gently tugged down on its extra skin, which covered my tool like a cocoon. Heated passion was then discovered as he bobbed his head to and fro, enlightening both our worlds with a steady blowjob. Heavy licks and moist sucks ensued.

I moaned above him, held onto his shoulders, banged my hips forward, and slammed my stick down his throat. My motion was swift and reliable for both of our pleasures. Heedlessly, I bolted forward, pulled away, and bolted forward again.

Slurps and groans transpired from Bradley. He gagged and groaned in a sloppy and ravenous manner. Saliva dripped out of his mouth and fell to the cement floor between us. Moans of satisfaction escaped the young man: deep, guttural, and passionate. His palms discovered my bare hips and assisted in his reckless but agreeable motion.

I stood dizzy above him and trembled: perplexed, lost, windblown, and amiable under his mouth-spell. My mind twirled and raced with utter bliss. Overcome with his mouthy work, I shivered with pure delight, fully intoxicated by his hunger and man-with-man desire. A sweep of energy rushed throughout my torso, and I felt an unstoppable orgasm rise between my legs. Hastily, I applied an exuberant amount of force to the bad boy's shoulders and pushed him away. In a matter of seconds, my right palm jacked the upright shaft between my legs and doused Bradley's left check with my sticky load. Among the plastic-protected clothes, limited light caused my pearl-white ooze to gleam on his flesh: three globs of man-residue, my explosion.

Papa would not approve. That was the thought that seeped into my mind as I found my jeans on the cement floor, stepped into them, and pushed my nine-incher and balls away.

Bradley used my Earl Pique polo to wipe the splat off his face. Afterwards, he beamed his adorable smile, finally rose from his knees, dropped the shirt to the floor, and collected me in his Irish arms. Our lips gently brushed together as our eyes intimately connected. Before kissing me, he whispered in a heated rush, "You're number nine on my list."

"I knew that. Our families hate each other."

"You rather like me, though. Don't you, Nino?"

I couldn't lie. I wouldn't, if I knew what was best for me. "I do." A sigh of delight escaped my mouth as woozy fondness was fully discovered.

He kissed me then: with tongue and closed eyes, with a forcefulness that I found gratifying, with his bad boy manner that seemed untamable and free-willed. Bradley's palms clamped around my torso and provided a hearty squeeze. His swollen middle met my still-swollen middle and …

Abruptly, the kiss ended, and he pushed me away. Heated breath escaped his mouth. Anger shifted into his sea-green eyes. He gawked at me with translucent fire, reached down for his Browning, found it with his left hand, pointed its small barrel at my chest, waved it to his right in quick movement, and demanded, "Get out of here, Nino. Run for your life before I fall for you."

Two days later, Papa wanted to see me, which was never good. My father was far too busy with cheating drug dealers, illegal gambling, tax evasion, laundering money, offing his enemies, and other crimes. His office was all mahogany with very little light; a place where the Omerta was as holy as the Bible. Papa sat behind his titanic desk with his fingers woven together. A smile surfaced on his aged, handsome face, and he said, "Nino, please sit," referring to the high-back chair across from his desk.

I sat; any good son would.

Papa poured himself two fingers of Bollinger vodka without ice, chugged it down, and placed the tumbler on the right side of his desk. His intriguing eyes met mine, held there for the longest of minutes, and then he said, "You know why you're in here, don't you?"

I nodded my head and replied, "Jimmy Bradley." Truth was I shivered in my father's presence, terrified of the man and his power. One wrong move, and I could have easily become his next victim. But, I was his youngest son and my father's pride and joy.

"Exactly, my son," my father chanted in a calm and collected manner.

I was then lectured on *La Cosa Nostra* (this thing of ours), the meaning of my Sicilian family's existence. Papa mentioned betraying the family, and cousin Acilio, who was sent to Sicily to live after he failed to bump off one of our family's enemies. He talked about the administration again, the Commission (our ruling body), and rats (men who violated our family's practices). He rose from his massive chair and moved around his desk. He stood beside me and clamped his palms against my cheeks, kissed my forehead, pulled away, and said, "My son, my blood. Be careful."

Our meeting then ended. Minutes later, I found my balls, my Colt Commander pistol, and went in search of Jimmy Bradley to bump him off.

The Starlite drive-in was playing *The Night of the Hunter* starring Robert Mitchum and Shelley Winters. The place was packed with teenie boppers, young adults, and various mobsters. Bradley and three of his Irish cronies were in a black Dodge Coronet with a flathead straight six cylinder engine and a single barrel Stromberg carburetor. The vehicle was almost as sleek as Bradley.

I waited patiently in the nearby woods for Bradley to exit his Coronet and head for the crapper. My Colt Commander was tucked inside my jeans and pressed against my tight torso. Once Bradley entered the men's crapper, I followed behind.

Positioned behind him at the urinal, I placed the Commander to the back of his head, and whispered, "Bradley, we meet again."

He didn't move. In fact, he didn't even take a piss. The bad boy stood with his arms down at his sides and asked, "You finally found the balls to bump me off, didn't you, Nino?"

"A man's got to do what a man's got to do."

"Are you really a man, Nino?"

Pissed, I nudged the pistol against the back of his skull and rattled off, "Come with me. I have plans for you in the woods."

The scene that unfolded within the next few seconds was rather top-notch action-packed. Bradley zipped up his goods, abruptly swung his right arm out and backwards, and flung it into my ribs. Pain surfaced, but Mafia sons could always handle it. Within seconds, he bolted out of the crapper, veered left and right through cars, and headed to the woods, exactly where I wanted him to go.

I followed behind. Our action was so quick that no one even spotted us, or seemed to care, especially since Robert was wooing Shelley on the big screen. Bradley vanished into the thick woods to the left. Approximately thirty feet inside the hulking timber, I leashed my right palm over his right shoulder and took him down with some brutish force. Bradley thumped to the mossy earth, face down. I pounced overtop him, flipped him onto his back and ...

Our chests collided together and offered a heated moment between young men in lust. His eyes connected to mine and sexual fire was birthed between us. We breathed heavily, huffing and puffing for oxygen. His sea-green eyes reflected in the thin moonlight that found its way through the cumbersome foliage. Our middles met, rubbed together, and grew firm.

"You can't kill me," he wheezed, completely out of breath, "because you're attracted to my dick."

I didn't respond and kept him pinned to the earth. My Colt was positioned at his forehead, and ... I stared at him with infatuation, bliss, something that Papa would have certainly not approved of. As my pulse raced, more blood gushed through the tool between my legs and grew harder. There, I became lost in Bradley's eyes, captivated by his stare and handsomeness, his power and hunger, his innocence and charm.

Again, he whispered, "You can't kill me."

His Pour Monsieur cologne and sweaty aroma was alluring to my senses. Truth was I wanted to bury my nose against his neck and lick the swollen cords that lined there. I wanted to rip his clothes off his nicely built body and have my way with his mobster skin. I wanted to ...

"Did you miss me?" he panted.

Obviously, he felt the flag between my legs: stiff-hard, perfectly veined, vibrating.

"Kiss me or kill me, Nino ... It's your call."

With that said, I removed the pistol from his skull, leaned over his lips, and provided a hearty kiss to my enemy.

I was blown away: lost, consumed by his mouth, in a state of windswept ecstasy between bad boys. Again, Papa would not have approved.

The beef between my legs fully hardened and pressed against his own engorged timber. Moisture collected within my jeans; pre-sap erupted with such ease and coated my cotton.

Beneath me, Bradley continued to pant. His chest heaved for breath. The solid pick between his legs thumped under my weight, ready for action with my hands, mouth, or ass – whatever he wanted from me.

I reached between our connected middles with my empty hand and found the cement-hard tool under his denim. A hearty squeeze followed, as well as a light moan from my target/prey. With heated fury I moved my palm north and south, massaging his weapon.

Bradley moaned beneath my hand- and mouth-hex, trapped under my tender care. He surfaced a few seconds later, though, breathed heavily, and instructed, "Not here, Nino. Meet me at the cleaners in a half hour ... You can finish me off there."

It was a trap; it had to be. A set-up to have me offed. The Bradley family reeled me in by Jimmy's charm and handsome looks, and arranged for me to enter their cleaners at night to "take care" of me. It was my death warrant, an invitation to my sudden demise; a murderous tragedy that they wanted to look like an accident.

That wasn't the case. Bradley really liked me: my torso and lips, my rounded shoulders and pumped thighs, the instrument between my legs that he wanted to eat up whole and toy with for the next few hours. There was a note on the front, glass door of the cleaners in Bradley's script:

GO TO THE OFFICE IN THE BACK. ENTER THE OFFICE. TAKE THE INTERIOR DOOR TO THE RIGHT. ENTER A SHORT HALLWAY. WALK IT. ENTER A STAIRWELL TO THE RIGHT. TAKE IT. ENTER THE DOOR TO THE LEFT. I'M THERE.

He was there. Without his goons. Without his cronies. Without his henchmen. Without his guns. The windowless room was a hideout of sorts; an underground apartment that no one knew about. Bradley lay on a full-sized bed in the buff and sported eight inches of dick in his right hand. Candles were lit and offered a romantic zeal to the room, and his body: cut chest with just the right amount of muscle, strawberry-colored nipples, hairy navel, and adorable face.

As I stripped out of my clothes and dropped them to the Tom Adams carpet, I said, "This isn't a set-up, is it?"

Bradley stroked his meat up and down two times, winked at me, and said, "I was hoping you'd plug me with your Italian cock."

"Let's see what happens, guy," I replied, sauntered over to the bed, and dove between his muscular legs with an opened mouth.

There, overtop him on my knees, I licked and lapped at his pecker, and sent him into a flurry of enjoyment. My head bobbed north and south as I plugged the back of my throat with all eight inches of his steel-hard muscle. I gagged and groaned in a brutal manner, but seemed to enjoy our bond at the same time. Hypnotically, my motion was swift and deliberate. The up and down movement on his dog was unrelenting, and caused my nemesis to grasp the back of my skull while he carried out ludicrous murmurs of pure elation.

That was the monumental point in time to bump me off if Jimmy Bradley wanted to. He could have easily positioned his Browning 380 against my left temple and blew my brains out, ending my mobster life and becoming a hero in his family. That didn't happen, though. Instead, he ground his hips upwards, choked me with his eight inches, garbled my name, and begged me to get him off.

I was a tease by nature. Like a squirrel to a dog, I did nothing more than taunt him on that full-size bed with my licks, laps, and sucks. My tongue twirled around his shaft's rounded head, pulled away, and twirled again. Eventually, I gasped for air, found some oxygen, and decided to further our sexual street-game. I flipped the man over and spread his bulbous and hairless ass with my probing fingers.

Tongue and fingers delved inside his system in a hyper game of thug-lust. Heedlessly, I dabbed my tongue at his Irish center, replaced the tongue with two fingertips, pushed the tips inside him, provided him with a counter-clockwise twist of excitement, and hastily pulled out of him. Again, I continued that racy but pleasurable act: a dab with my outstretched tongue, a two-fingertips packing, a counter-clockwise twist by my fingertips, and a swift pull-out. Again ... again ... and again, I carried those plays out, and sent my naked companion/nemesis/killer in writhing delight.

I knew spew shot out of his gun and splashed the sheets where he lay. Cream exited his shaft as he ground his hips against the sheets and mattress, accidentally fucking the bed's cotton. An exploding gasp exited Bradley's mouth with a blatant groan, and he gurgled, "I blew, Nino ... You made me come."

Honestly, I felt selfish and didn't really give a crack about his needs. Hungrily, I wanted my torso to bang into his torso with my nine inches of upright cock.

"Bump it into me, Nino," the hit man on the bed whined. He spread his legs for my entrance and his pink-tight hole squinted at me.

I pushed four of my nine inches into his core, pulled out, and spanked his bottom. Then, I pressed all of my nine inches into his hub with elaborate zeal. There, I left the slab of meat to cuddle his insides, twisted my pole from left to right, and eventually released the meat out of him. Rashly, I held onto his hips, directed my banger into his bottom again, throttled all of it into his slender opening, shifted three inches out, careened all of it inside again, and processed that motion for the next seven ... nine ... eleven minutes.

Jimmy Bradley murmured foibles beneath me. His head was buried in the feather pillow and unintelligible sounds were heard: garbles, gurgles, and grunts.

I bumped into Bradley again ... again ... and again. Sweat flung off of my forehead and stung his back. I trembled behind him in pure satisfaction as our bodies combined and fell apart. My meeting with his man-crevice was everything I expected it to be: warm, tight, and with much friction. My fingertips dug into his hips as I lunged my weight forward, backed out, and charged forward again.

Self-elation was discovered within the next few seconds. I grumbled his name, pumped my cock into his throbbing hole, pulled out, and found my vertical beef with both palms. Hands worked in feisty motion as I jacked myself off. Perspiration-covered hips jolted to and fro. My breathing was intensified to the nth degree. Two ... five ... and eight handy strokes with both fists caused a surge of guy-energy to burst throughout my core and ...

White ooze spiraled out of my timber and glazed his back. Puddles formed against the nape of the goon's spine and hips. Dribbles of the gunk collected against his shoulder blades and the base of his neck. Some of the gooey man-blow splattered Bradley's auburn hair.

After my sex-act with his bottom, I spanked him, told him he was a good fuck, and rolled him over, onto his back. Having my torso lined with his sticky ooze-covered torso, post-sexed and fully spent, we breathed with ferocious bursts of energy, tangled within the bed's heated sheets. With our mouths only inches apart, I whispered, "Our fathers will kill us."

"I don't think so."

"Mine will. I'll be deported and have to live in Sicily."

"I'll hide you out here."

"You do like me, don't you?" I inquired, and rubbed his chin with fingertips.

"What can I say? I like the bad boy in you," he chanted, dove his lips to mine, and sealed us together, again.

The following morning, my older brother, Vito, warned me that Papa knew about my tryst with Jimmy Bradley in the underground apartment. Vito said, "He's going to murder you, chum."

"It was nice knowing you, Vito," I replied.

Papa then called me into his office. I expected my one-way ticket to Sicily where I would live in shame with my Italian family and those who were jettisoned from our Chicago family.

My father told me to close his office door behind me and to have a seat; I listened. He then poured two tumblers of Bollinger vodka, keeping one for himself. After passing me a tumbler, he shared, "You're a very bad boy, Nino."

"I'm sorry, Papa," I whispered, ashamed. "I couldn't rub Bradley out. It's not in me."

Papa smiled, nodded his head, and shared, "It's commendable. You're a man now … One with honor and dignity. I'm very proud of you."

My father had murdered men in that room. Was I next? Did he have the potential to bump off his own son after my insidious betrayal?

"Nino," Papa continued, "I have come to amends."

"Amends?" I questioned, baffled.

Papa raised his tumbler and said, "To families of similar nature. To your kindness and respect. It takes a very strong and brave man to disobey me." He took a sip of his vodka, sat back in his chair, and relaxed.

"What about Bradley?" I inquired, concerned that maybe one of my brothers or uncles would bump the man off and carry out the job I failed to accomplish.

"I have bigger interests," Papa confirmed.

"What about his family?" I asked, fearing that my father, the man who raised and loved me, would hurt Bradley by knocking off his relatives one by one.

"I promise never to hurt the Bradley family again. We are similar."

"Amends," I whispered, smiled, and took a sip of my vodka.

Papa stood from his seat, walked around his desk, kissed me on my forehead, cupped my chin and forced me to look him in the eyes. Alone, just the two of us inside his office, he chanted, "You're different, Nino. I know that. I get that about you. There's no reason to send you off to Sicily when you are my son."

A warm rush of acceptance in my family shifted through my core. Change in my life was discovered. Warmness coated my insides and caused me to smile as I whispered, "*La cosa nostra*, Papa."

"*La cosa nostra*," he chanted, and kissed me on my forehead again, forever my protector.

TWIN IGNITION
By Milton Stern

My mother was not happy, but with so many bills looming over our heads, I had no choice. The year was 1934, and after my father killed himself, I was left at the age of nineteen to support my mother and me. In the 1920s, he had been a successful businessman, owning his own car dealership, but with the Great Depression came the hard times, and he gave up. He thought his life insurance would take care of us, but for a smart businessman, he sure was stupid to think they would pay on a suicide.

I had to quit school and find a job, but no jobs were to be had outside the PWA and CCA, and those would barely pay enough to allow my mother to stay in a one-room apartment let alone our house. Losing my father was enough, but losing the house would be unbearable. After all, it had been in her family since before the Civil War. We lived in Maryland, near what is present day Rockville, but more north, on a an acre that had once been over 100, but had been sold off acre by acre until we only had our surrounding property to our name. My father's Nash dealership was located right outside Washington, DC, but after selling our car, there was no evidence we were ever in the automobile business.

To make matters worse, I quit school, and my mother was distraught. That was when Morty Cohen called. Morty was an old acquaintance of my father's, and he was checking in on us. He was not a favorite of my mother's because of his rum-running days during Prohibition, and although he could legally sell alcohol now, we weren't quite sure what he did, but we felt it was best not to ask too many questions.

After finding out I left school and was looking for a job, he offered me one. My mother said no, but what he was willing to pay would keep us in the house and allow me to go back to school part-time. "What if you end up in jail?" she would ask. "What if he asks you to do something illegal?" she would go on.

I explained I was only being hired to drive a car, be a chauffeur for his son, Marc. "What could be illegal about that?"

I took the job.

Marc was about ten years older than I, but he didn't like driving a car. In those days, driving a car required skill and mechanical know-how. Depending on the car, you had to know how to double-clutch, control the spark advance, drive with mechanical brakes, no power anything, and if the car broke down, know what to do to get it running again. I knew all of those things, and I liked to drive.

Morty had a car delivered to our house for me to use when driving Marc around, and because he liked my dad so much, he said I could have the car for personal use as if it were mine, provided I took care of it mechanically and kept it clean – Marc did not like a dirty car. I agreed, and when they delivered a 1934 Nash Ambassador Twin Ignition Eight, I was thrilled. That was one of my father's favorite cars to sell, and this one was beautiful, with a dark green exterior and dark green wool interior, as well as all the latest options, including a synchromesh transmission.

I dressed in my best suit and drove down to Marc's home to pick him up. I had not seen him in a few years, but from what I remembered he was around five-ten, with dark brown wavy hair and olive skin. I knew he played football in College, and he had the build for it. To look at him and me, we looked as if we were twins separated at birth by a decade – same hair, coloring, build and even prominent features. However, his eyes were brown and mine, green.

For almost a month, I drove him around all day to this office and that office, and to various restaurants. I started work at 8:00 am and finished around 6:00 pm. Twice a week, I would drive to school for my night classes. The job worked out perfectly, and my mother had calmed down.

On a few occasions, he asked me to drive over to a house in the Cleveland Park section of Washington, DC, not that far of a drive in those days before all the traffic they have now. When we went there, I would wait downstairs, while he would go upstairs and do whatever he was doing for an hour, come back down, and we would be on our way. The owner of the house was an older woman, who wore a bit too much make-up and was larger than I preferred. I am no idiot, so I figured this was a high class brothel, and Marc was screwing some girl. Of course, at his age, most men were married, and with his looks, I couldn't imagine why he paid for it. But I was not there to make inquiries. My job was to wait until he needed to go somewhere else. I usually brought my school books with me, so I could study whenever he had an appointment or a lunch engagement.

Marc was not much of a talker. I would look at him in the rear-view mirror, and he had no expression at all and always looked out the window as we drove along. He never asked me any questions, nor I, him. It was a pleasant arrangement, and I settled in easily.

Driving that Nash Ambassador Twin Ignition Eight was a pleasure. Every night I would pull into the garage and clean it as soon as I arrived home. I would also check all the fluids and make sure any mechanical issues were addressed.

Surprisingly, Marc gave me weekends off. I was sure he would need a driver for social engagements, but those were accompanied with his family in their car.

One afternoon, he asked me to take him to the house in Cleveland Park, and as usual, I waited in the parlor while he went upstairs. Usually, I did not ask to use a bathroom in someone's home, but I had to take a leak. So, I asked the overly painted owner, and she directed me upstairs.

I walked past a row of rooms and found the washroom at the end of the hall. After relieving myself and washing my hands, I walked back, but I noticed one of the doors was slightly ajar. I am usually not a nosy person, but something told me to look inside, and my God, I did not expect what I discovered.

A young man around my age was on his hands and knees moaning while he was being fucked in the ass by another man. The young guy looked at me and winked, and I just backed up and scurried down the hallway, downstairs and back to my seat in the parlor.

The madam came over to me and asked, "Are you OK? You look as if you've seen a ghost."

"I'm fine," I answered.

She then poured me a shot of whiskey and handed it to me. I am not a drinker, but she motioned for me to drink it, and I did in one gulp. Then I handed her the glass.

"Another?"

"I better not. I'm driving."

"I can guess what you saw," she said. "The first time you see something like that it is a shock, but don't let that bother you, it happens to chauffeurs in here all the time."

"Chauffeurs?"

"Oh sure. You young men have to wait down here while your bosses go upstairs and have a little pleasure with some young man, and it never fails that someone leaves a door open. I think they leave the doors open on purpose just to shock their drivers." She winked.

"They are all boys up there?" I asked.

"We are all boys, my dear," she answered and winked again before leaving the parlor.

All boys? I thought. But for some reason, I wasn't disgusted, just shocked. I had heard about stuff like this the short time I was in school, but I never thought I would see it. So Mark was into boys. This explained his being a bachelor at twenty-eight.

I never mentioned to Marc what I saw, and he never hinted I even knew what he was doing in that house. For the next couple of months, I did my job, stayed out of his business, and did my homework in the parlor of the brothel without giving any thought to what was going on upstairs.

Then one afternoon, while I was studying biology – ironically – the madam came over to me and asked, "Would you go upstairs and get your boss? His father is on the phone."

I nodded, then thought: His father is on the phone? He knows? Then I wondered why the madam didn't go upstairs and get him herself. But I was a good employee, so I went to the room she indicated.

I knocked on the door, and Marc told me to come in. I didn't look up; I just uttered to the rug, "Your father is on the phone, sir."

"The hell he is," Marc said, "Now get out of your clothes and shove your cock into this boy's mouth."

I looked up, and the boy was no boy; he was a man, older than I by at least five years with a mustache, black hair and a heavily muscled body. Marc was fucking him in the ass and sweating so much his athletic body was shining.

"I said get out of those clothes and feed him your cock!" he demanded.

Ever the dutiful employee, I did as I was told, and my cock sprang up as soon as I was naked.

"Close the door!"

I turned and closed the door then positioned myself in front of the handsome 'boy,' shoving my hard cock into this mouth. My head about exploded. Did I mention I was a virgin? No one had even touched my dick before, and this was amazing.

We were like twin ignitions – a spark plug on each side of the block.

Marc kept pounding from the rear, so I pounded from the front, and he was looking at me and smiling. That was the most emotion he ever displayed since I started working for him. Then Mark leaned forward and motioned for me to do the same. He grabbed the back of my head and kissed me, opening my mouth and shoving his tongue in it.

Well, that was it. I came with a roar, and Marc did the same. I guess he had been at it for a while. We filled that 'boy' to the brim.

Everyone dressed, and we went back to the car after Marc paid the madam.

He didn't say a word for the rest of the afternoon until it was time to drop him off at home.

"From now on, you come upstairs with me. I'll teach you all you need to know," he said in a matter-of-fact tone.

He then exited the car, and I drove home.

I worked for Marc until the war. Although over forty, he enlisted. So did I.

He was killed in action in Italy and is buried in a military cemetery in Palermo.

I returned, and a day has not gone by during my long life when I don't think about Marc and those afternoons at the house in Cleveland Park.

WASTE NOT, WANT NOT
By Mark Apoapsis

"Dino?" I asked into the dark.

There was a sleepy sigh, and the rasp of stubble against a pillowcase. "What now?"

"How many guys have you rubbed out?"

"None."

"None? But you're supposed to be the best. That's why Uncle Clem wanted you to show me the ropes."

"I'm the best because I get it done without having to waste anyone. Although we do use ropes. Now shut up and go to sleep, Falito."

"You mean we didn't fly into San Francisco so you could kill someone?"

Again, I heard the sound of his heavy stubble against the smooth satin of his pillowcase. "Don't make me come over there."

With a delicious shiver, I drew the covers over my bare shoulders. Eventually, despite my excitement about what I'd get to witness tomorrow, the soft sound of my cousin's slow, deep breathing lulled me to sleep.

# # # # #

When the alarm went off, I wanted to rip its little striker off to keep it from making that annoying jangling sound, but that would require moving. Several seconds passed, during which I seriously considered smashing it, but Dino got to it first and expertly silenced it without damaging it.

"Rise and shine, *cucinu*. Up and at 'em. Big day today." He sounded entirely too cheerful. Mornings were the only time I wondered if we were really related. I groaned and buried my head in the pillow.

"Get up! You want to spend your whole life in the dry-cleaning business?" He waited two seconds, then, without further warning, he yanked the covers off me, grabbed my undershirt with one hand and my bare shoulder with the other, and rolled me off the bed and onto the floor. Lying at his feet, I gamely grabbed his bare ankle and managed to force him off balance. We wrestled in our underwear in the narrow space between our hotel beds. I held my own pretty well, and he was sweating and breathing hard by the time he was finally straddling me with my wrists pinned above my head.

"Wow, that was harder than I expected," he admitted. "You've really put on a lot of muscle these last few years."

"Well, I'm not a teenager anymore," I pointed out, submitting to his squeezing of my biceps, shoulders, and – with a hand sliding into the arm opening of my undershirt – chest muscles.

"You'll make a good enforcer. But having you in this undignified position reminds me of the first thing I wanted to tell you: You don't work over anyone yourself, not until he's tied up and helpless, and usually not even then. It's undignified. Let your boys do it. We've got guys that are even bigger and stronger than us; that's what they're there for. Besides, I find that by the time a man's tied up and helpless, there's usually no need to work him over to get what I want."

"Are you going to show me some examples today?" I asked eagerly.

"You bet. That's what we're here for. But we have a little time before we have to get ready, so ..." With that, he lowered himself onto me and trapped the top of my head in the crook of his elbow, positioning his armpit over my face. Immediately I said, "I give up!"

"Say 'uncle,'" he demanded.

According him that powerful word would be the ultimate submission. We'd grown up knowing that our Uncle Clemencio was one of the most powerful men in New York City, able to have anything done to anyone with a wave of his hand. So I refused to say 'uncle.' Instead, I struggled uselessly with my nose buried in his armpit hair and my shoulder trapped under his abrasive cheek until he finally decided it was time to take our showers and get dressed.

# # # # #

"Why these two cops?" I asked. We were watching from an upper story of the warehouse as the pair of cops drew their weapons and one of them cautiously approached the building.

"They're the only ones in vice who wouldn't accept our payoffs. They've raided two of our bars, and they've been staking out some of the others and scaring off the clients."

"Do their wives not know they're out drinking?"

He stared at me. "Don't you know what our business in San Francisco involves?"

"I figured bookies and whores, like back home."

"I thought you knew. We own a bunch of discreet little bars where homosexuals gather. A lot of the cops think it's not all that much worse than gambling or prostitution, and are willing to look the other way if we grease their palms. These two – ahh. Watch this. That younger cop has realized his partner's in trouble and is trying to call for backup. But he's just going to get a lot of static. We've got a radio engineer in the next room with a jamming device. That's mostly so every cop in the city doesn't witness him calling for backup; his dispatcher is working for us and has a sudden temporary hearing loss."

"You don't leave anything to chance."

"That's right. Notice how you didn't hear any guns firing? You won't. We also had someone on the inside who unloaded their guns this morning just before they were called here."

"Jeez, how many cops are we paying?"

"A lot of them we don't need to pay, we just blackmail them."

"With what?"

"Think about it. I told you about our business."

"You're not telling me that some cops are homosexuals!"

"More than you'd think," he said, still looking out the window. "Although most of the clientele tends to be ex-Navy men who got discharged here when the War was finally winding down and couldn't face going back to their hometowns with everyone knowing why they got a dishonorable discharge. It's a growth industry, and Uncle Clem got us in on the ground floor."

That didn't jibe at all with the image I'd always had of homosexual bars filled with debauched old men and obvious *finocchios*. Big tough cops holding hands with manly sailors? That would be something to see!

The young cop was peering around the car as if he heard something going on, maybe sounds of a struggle. "You said you never kill people. So how are you going to get rid of these guys?"

"With gentle persuasion. You'll see. Always remember, you gotta be gentle with cops. They're like a family themselves, and if we kill one of their brothers, or even break a few bones, it would start a war. At the very least, they'd crack down on us and shut down all our businesses in their jurisdiction."

At that point, the young cop bravely approached the warehouse with his useless gun drawn, and our boys swarmed around him.

"C'm'ere." Dino adjusted my collar and straightened my tie. "Ready for your first lesson?"

I followed my cousin downstairs.

# # # # #

Our boys had efficiently bound both cops, hand and foot, to wooden chairs by the time we reached the main room of the warehouse. The first thing Dino did was to remove the hats of the helpless cops and toss them aside. The older one was an Irishman with thick brown hair and a hairline just beginning to recede; the younger guy, a blond Pole, was at most a year or two older than I was.

"You won't get away with this," the older cop blustered. "If you kill us, every ..."

"Yeah, yeah, I know all that. I just explained it to my cousin here, who I'm training. That's why we brought rubber hoses."

Both cops' eyes widened.

"That's right. They don't leave a mark if used carefully, and they hurt like hell. As you well know, if your department works like they do back home in New York."

"What do you want?"

"If you were a little older, I'd suggest you take a desk job, but it would be a shame to waste all that muscle." He felt the cop's arms and chest, much as he'd done to me, but this time it was meant to be insulting in its familiarity, even though it was two layers of clothing less intimate.

"Go to hell."

212

"So we've arranged a job offer for you in homicide. Much more exciting and prestigious than vice; everyone knows that. You'll get a pay increase, of course."

"Are you trying to bribe me, you scum bag?"

"Fine. I tried to be a gentleman about it, but you're making me do it the hard way." He glanced at his boys. "Take off his shirt!"

They had to untie one arm at a time in order to strip him to the waist, but we had far too many men for the cop's struggles to do him any good.

"You didn't think I was going to beat you through all those layers of clothing, did you?" he said to the cop when he was once again tied securely, slumped in defeat with his muscular, hairy chest heaving with exertion, or suppressed sobs. "It stings a lot more this way." As a cynical jab, he added, "Don't you find?"

The cop gulped. With his throat bare, I could see his Adam's apple bob. But with a visible effort, he met my cousin's eyes. "Do your worst."

"OK. We'll start with your partner. Take off his shirt, too."

The younger cop turned out to have impressive abdominal and arm muscles, although his chest muscles didn't compare well to his partner's or to what I knew Dino had under his suit. The hair on his chest and forearms was invisible except when the shafts of light slanting down through the dirty windows hit it just right, as he squirmed, and turned it golden.

The dark-haired cop had watched in horror as his partner was stripped to the waist. Now, as Dino picked up a rubber hose and made a show of examining it, he said, "Leave him alone! Maybe we can make a deal."

"The deal is that you take the transfer, and your rookie partner here starts over in LA."

"What? That won't be good for the kid's career."

"Maybe he needs a new career." He looked over the young bare-chested cop critically. "You know, our taverns just give the patrons a place to drink, and to meet, and what they do afterwards is their concern. But we do business with a family that has some establishments that provide, shall we say, on-site entertainment to depraved appetites."

"Even you wouldn't go that far," the older cop whispered. His partner seemed too terrified to speak.

"They have businesses in several major cities." He gripped the young cop's muscular shoulder; his skin looked almost creamy in contrast with the Mediterranean complexion of my cousin's hand. "He'll be just another chained and naked prisoner in the worst part of a strange city. No one will believe him when he says he used to be a cop." He paused, but both cops were too stunned to speak. "Let's get an idea of how high a price we could get for him. Strip him naked."

# # # # #

As we left the warehouse, with our boys busy loosening the bonds of the prisoners just enough to let them free themselves eventually and put their shirts and hats back on, Dino said smugly, "See how it's done? I didn't need to even beat either of them. Always remember, blood is expensive. If you murder a man, his friends or family or the police will come after you. If you humiliate him instead, he'll be ashamed to tell anyone. And the more powerful he is, the less he can afford to admit what you did to him."

"Is it true, what you said about having business associates who would buy him?"

"Of course not. But people will believe we're capable of anything. And they'll believe homosexuals are capable of anything. It occurred to me if I put those two together, I'd have a really scary bluff."

"Wow. Do you stay up nights thinking up these things?"

"None of your business what I stay up nights thinking of," he laughed. "Nah, I just made that up on the spot when he didn't cave in quite fast enough, and I thought I was going to have to actually have his partner beaten. That hose would have left a red mark for a few minutes, and I thought about what a shame it would be to see that creamy skin messed up. Then I started thinking about how a homosexual would see it, and that gave me the idea. And it worked pretty well, didn't it?"

"Really well. I really believed you were going to have that cop stripped naked." The boys had gotten no further than unbuckling the blond's belt before his partner agreed to our demands.

"This might be a way to handle to something else I promised to do on this trip. Come on."

# # # # #

"What did they do?" I asked as we sat in the car and watched the boys tossing around three guys on the street, about my age or a year or so

214

younger. They had caught them while they were playing stickball with three of their neighbors. Their opponents were now watching the beating uncertainly, along with a growing crowd.

"They ruined the daughter of a local businessman who's a friend of our family. He asked Uncle Clem to have them killed, but we thought that was a little harsh. It's not like they murdered anyone. But still, a beating didn't seem to be enough. They took her for the weekend against her father's wishes. That calls for serious punishment. It may even be a crime, depending on whether she went with them willingly, but the police would never take it seriously; they would say she led them on. If they did, she would have to appear in court and publicly admit what happened, which would ruin her reputation even further. So the law is even less help than usual. That's where we come in."

"It looks like the boys are holding back. I don't see any blood. Look, that one's just lying on the ground, and our guy isn't kicking him in the head or even the ribs."

"Yeah, I really hate to order a serious beating that takes weeks to heal. And it would be a shame to permanently scar three handsome young guys for life. This is just to soften them up, with a little public humiliation in the bargain. Did you see how tough they were acting when we pulled up?"

They didn't look so tough now, as they were dragged by the armpits into our boy's cars with their feet scrabbling behind them and their shirts pulled halfway up, exposing their bellies.

They looked even less tough when all their clothes – the latest street-punk fashions – were roughly removed and they were strung up by the wrists. I was surprised Dino would do that, even after his bluff with the cop, but his men followed his orders without batting an eye. Three leanly built young punks. Probably Anglo-Saxon; they had the whitest butts I'd ever seen, especially the blond one.

Dino introduced himself to the bound and gagged prisoners, explained why they were here, and gave them the same story about sexual slavery as he'd spun for the captured cops. He claimed that some business associates would be arriving soon to bid on them.

While we were waiting, he inspected our catch closely. "Have you ever seen one of these, Falito?" Dino asked as casually as if he were fingering an interesting variety of sausage at the meat stand.

"Is he a Jew? I always wondered what a Jew looked like naked."

"I doubt it, since I see his chums aren't. I'm seeing this more and more in guys your age I deal with. But yeah, this is what they look like."

Over the next twenty minutes, one by one, several well-dressed men showed up. I knew who most of them really were because Dino had let me cram into the phone booth with him when he called them, so I could hear. One was just our glassware supplier, one worked at our bank, one was our local attorney, and one was our travel agent. All in legitimate businesses, nothing to do with homosexuals. The fifth was an enforcer for a local family we had close ties to. Finally, there were two Orientals, dressed in expensive tailored suits, same as the rest.

The banker inspected the blond man closely. "I'll give you a hundred fifty for this one."

The glassware wholesaler walked around the prisoners, inspecting them front and back. "I'll give you three hundred for the whole set," he said. "I can chain them together on their knees and let my customers take their pick."

The Orientals looked over a smooth-chested dark-haired guy, squeezing him in various places as if gauging his ripeness. They argued with each other in an odd up-and-down language, and finally one said "two hun'red dorlar." They had even me convinced that they planned to ship the poor guy across the Pacific.

"Four hundred for all three," the enforcer bid. "I can put them on a stage and train them to ... you know ... perform together for my clientele."

"I've already got a combined bid for three fifty," Dino pointed out. "Can anyone offer me more than fifty for this one?"

"He's not worth that much." the glass merchant said. "Look at all that hair on his chest. Too manly looking. No one wants a hairy, muscular guy kneeling at his feet."

I could tell from his voice that he was making this up as he went along, and had never met a homosexual in his life. Dino rolled his eyes but played along: "Remember, you can always shave him as smooth as you want. And those muscles won't last long if you starve him."

"My establishment only has room for one," the banker claimed. "My final offer is two hundred for this one."

"I know you've only got one barrel to chain him to," Dino said, walking behind the blond, "but after ten or twelve customers take turns at him, don't you think he'll be worn out?" He slapped the merchandise on the rump. "Buy two or three, and you can toss him in a corner to watch one of his pals take his place."

By this time, the gagged men were wide-eyed with terror.

The Orientals took a look at the hairy-chested prisoner, argued among themselves, and finally said "One hun'red dorlar."

"You see? They think he's worth a hundred dollars, and they have to cover shipping and handling on top of that."

"Half a grand for all three," the enforcer said.

No one else was willing to raise their bids. The punks exchanged glances, looking pathetically grateful, when they realized that at least they wouldn't be separated.

After the street punks were carried outside – securely trussed up and with a single sheet wrapped around their naked bodies and the whole bundle wrapped up with rope – one of the Orientals said in perfect American English with California accent, "How'd we do, Mr. Divito?"

"You guys were great!" Dino squeezed the man's shoulder as if he were an old friend. "Those suits look good on you; you can keep them as my gift."

"Really? Wow! Thanks!"

"How's your father?"

"Very well, thanks. Still excited about owning his own restaurant. Although we're still struggling. That's why we're a few months behind on the payments."

"I understand. I'm sure business will pick up later this year, and you'll pay us back … with interest."

"Thanks for your patience," said the other Oriental. "I'm not sure the bank would have been so understanding. Even if we'd found one that would give us the loan."

"Don't look so surprised, cousin," Dino told me in Sicilian. We'd both picked it up from our parents, though we rarely used it with each other. "They were born here, just like us, so they're as American as you or I. And they have the same dreams and loves as any man. And fears. Understand?"

In English, he said, "This is my brother Rafael. Falito, this is Mike Yee and his brother John." We shook hands like Americans, neither

217

bowing nor kissing. They were younger than I'd thought, now that I looked closely. And they did have an obvious family resemblance; I'd just overlooked it because I'd always been told that Orientals all look alike.

"By the way," John Yee asked Dino, "what did those guys do, anyway, to deserve to be stripped naked and terrified out of their minds?"

"Defaulted on a loan," Dino said casually. "Thanks again for your help."

The high bidder came back in. "All loaded up and ready to go."

"Remember," Dino told him, "make them really believe they're about to be taken to some kind of homosexual club next weekend and put on display. Or worse! Don't give them any clothes until Saturday night when you try to transport them to the 'club,' and then let them escape. Naturally, we'll reimburse you for expenses, but it shouldn't be much: bread and water, and maybe a bare mattress for the three of them to share."

"I've got some men I can spare for guard duty. Any special instructions? Should my boys have any fun with them?"

"Don't rough them up, if that's what you mean. Unless they disobey, of course. They've already been lightly worked over once. But anything that reinforces the illusion that they're destined to be turned into sex slaves would be appreciated."

# # # # #

The shrill bell of the phone woke me up at an ungodly hour the next morning. I drifted back to sleep as Dino took the call. The next thing I knew, he was whipping the covers off me. We must have been on a tight schedule, though, because instead of rolling me onto the floor and instigating a tussle, he just grabbed my legs and swung them off the bed, and headed to the bathroom.

"We only have one or two more jobs to do," he called from the shower as I shaved, "and our flight isn't until tomorrow morning, so we should have some time to enjoy San Francisco this afternoon and tonight. What do you feel like doing? They've got a good selection of shows with live girls, what with all the sailors."

"Aren't we going to inspect any of our properties?"

"What, are you nuts? You know we avoid direct association with our criminal operations as much as possible. Besides, it scares off the clientele."

"Oh. Well, I've been hearing about that new bridge since I was a kid. Can we go see that?"

"The Golden Gate? Actually, we'll get a good view of that this morning while we're working." He turned off the water and stepped out, drying his hair.

"I'm really learning a lot. Thanks for bringing me."

"Any questions so far?"

"Do you always strip the guys you lean on?"

He laughed. "Not always. Today we're going back to basics. My boys have had the O'Neill brothers all night, and they still haven't agreed to do business with us. So we're going to give them concrete boots. Is that traditional enough for you?"

"You mean they're going to sleep with the fishes?"

"Hopefully it won't come to that, but we'll make them think so. They're rum runners, and they're too self-righteous to sell to our bars. Hypocrites!" He finished drying his back and started on his chest. "So we have to buy from other channels. It's cutting into our profits, having to pay liquor tax." Bending toward me, he dried his legs.

"So you when you stripped the cops to the waist, it was just to make them think you were really going to beat them with the hose?"

"Yeah, that, and give them more time to think about it. But also, stripping a man makes him feel vulnerable." He began drying his arms, and added with a grin, "Even when you're not holding a rubber hose. Now get in the shower. We don't want to keep the O'Neill brothers waiting."

I grinned back and eagerly pulled off my undershirt, then my briefs.

# # # # #

Dino hadn't mentioned that we were going out on a boat. That was a real treat, and a chance to see the Bay. The O'Neill brothers, who had Irish features and looked to be roughly our respective ages, were tied to wooden chairs near the stern, with their hands behind their backs and their legs unfettered. Both men were hatless, revealing reddish-brown hair. They were wearing shirts and dress slacks but no jackets. Their neckties had been loosened, and their collars unbuttoned to expose their unshaven throats, and a few stray chest hairs curled over each brother's undershirt. I wondered if there was any family resemblance in the patterns of hair across their chests, and whether my curiosity on that point would be satisfied.

"Have they changed their minds?" Dino asked.

"No."

"Start mixing the cement."

The oldest of his boys, a man with steel-gray hair, drew some water while a sturdy young guy brought over a sack on his shoulder and began pouring the powder in for the older one to mix.

Dino put his hand on the older-looking brother's shoulder. "Logan, Logan. How did it come to this? It would save me so much trouble if you'd just agree to deal with us."

"Never! Our family has been providing booze to hard-working, God-fearing men for a generation. We started during Prohibition, you know. I'll not be helping this city descend into degeneracy."

"And yet you sell to brothels and card rooms. Surely the Church doesn't approve of those either."

"A man's got to draw the line somewhere," the younger-looking brother put in.

"But, Liam," Dino said reasonably, "Are your principles really worth your lives?"

"The cement's ready, Mr. Divito."

"Pour it into buckets." He said quietly to me, "Do you want to take this one? I think you're ready."

I nodded, trying not to show how thrilled I was in my cousin's confidence in me.

The boys had wheeled over the wheel barrel filled with cement and were preparing to force Logan's feet into an empty bucket. "Wait!" I said. I bent down to look at Logan's shoes. "These are Italian leather. It would be a shame to destroy them. We can sell them." I unlaced a shoe and tugged it off. Purely on impulse, I also peeled off his black sock, just to feel his bare foot squirming helplessly in my hands.

Liam's shoes were similar. When I had both men barefoot, Dino told the boys, "Give us a minute," and took me by the arm and led me to the opposite end of the boat, where he spoke to me softly enough that they wouldn't be able to hear us over the engine noise.

"That was a brilliant idea! You're really cut out for this."

"Thanks," I said, feeling a warm glow spread through my body at this praise.

"Can you tell me why it's such a good idea?"

I had acted mostly on instinct, but now I thought it through. "Um, because bare feet feel more vulnerable?"

"Good. Anything else?"

"Because it lets them feel the cement squishing between their toes?"

"Very good! It's important to make them feel the reality of the their impending doom, so they believe it. Now, can you tell me the one thing you did wrong?"

"I did something wrong?"

"Don't worry; it's your first time. But never kneel at a man's feet. Always have your boys do the work of tying his ankles, or in this case, removing his shoes. It's the symbolism. On some level, it makes him feel like you're submitting to him, no matter how helpless he is."

"Right. Symbolism. I guess that's another reason bare feet are better – in shoes, they can slide around just a little, which gives them an illusion of freedom. But for a man to not even be able to wiggle his toes ..."

"*Cucinu*! I can't believe we've wasted you in the laundering business this long. You belong in this line of work. All right, you have about five minutes before the cement gets too hard, so be sure to order their feet encased by then."

"We're really doing that?"

"If necessary. We'll even let it harden around their feet, if that's what it takes. We've got hammers and chisels."

We went back. I'd have enjoyed forcing those bare feet into the bucket with my own hands, but I knew I'd have to have the boys do it. Not that I wanted to murder them; I knew we'd let them go in the end. I just felt sorry for their dry cleaner; the cuffs of those nice dress pants would get caked in cement, and it would never come out. That thought gave me an idea. "Were they wearing jackets?" I asked the boys. "Do you still have them?"

They had them onboard, and one of the boys, the old guy who'd been mixing the cement, fetched them for me. I made a show of inspecting them. "These are worth a lot. But only with the matching pants. Get their pants off."

The rest of Dino's boys obeyed me without hesitation. It was my first taste of this kind of power. Back home, the orders I gave generally resulted in pants being hemmed or mended or cleaned and pressed, not being stripped off two rich and powerful men. I physically felt the rush of power, and it got even better when my cousin laid his hand on my shoulder and gave me an approving nod.

It was fun to watch Logan's face as his younger brother was stripped of his pants and he was unable to do anything about it. It was even more fun to watch Liam's face as his older brother, who had probably once seemed invincible to him, was rendered half naked.

Logan struggled harder as his bare feet were raised and placed in the bucket. His hairy legs trembled as they were held in place by strong hands while the concrete was poured. Then it was Liam's turn, and Logan forgot all about himself as he watched his brother's feet encased in cement.

"I don't suppose you'll change your minds at this point?" I asked as we waited for the cement to harden. I tried to sound casual, but actually my heart was pounding as hard as theirs probably were as the minutes dragged by and the concrete hardened. They remained silent, but I could see their resolve wavering.

I had someone check the cement periodically. When it was hard enough, I waited a few minutes more and finally gave the order. The boys prepared to untie both men from the chairs. The brothers exchanged a despairing look. I've always considered myself an empathetic man, and suddenly I thought about how I would feel if Dino and I were in their position: helpless, and taking one last look at each other in what we thought were our final moments on Earth. "Stop," I said.

Dino's boys looked at me expectantly.

"Not both at once. Him first." I pointed to Logan, the one Dino's age. They untied him and, grabbing him by his upper arms, began dragging him backward, the bucket scraping along the deck.

"Logan!" his younger brother shouted.

"I'll see you soon, Liam," he said tearfully. One of the boys grabbed his legs just above the cement while another held his arms, and at my signal, they started to lift him.

"Nooooo!" Liam cried.

"Are you ready to do business with us?" I asked, trying not to sound indifferent.

Liam's head sank to his chest, and he sobbed. I stepped over to him and lifted his chin, forcing him to look me in the eye. His blue eyes were filled with tears. It was the first time I'd made a grown man cry. Two of them.

"Turn his chair, so he has a good view," I ordered.

"Wait! We'll agree to whatever you want."

I gestured to the boys, who gratefully laid their heavy, struggling burden on the deck, face up. I went to stand over Logan, doing my best to loom. "Will you go along with this?" I asked, nudging his bare thigh with my toe.

"Yes," the terrified man said. "Just promise to let us go."

# # # # #

"Terrific job! I am so proud of you, *cucinu!*" Dino told me as his driver took us down Market Street. He knocked my hat off and tousled my hair. "C'm'ere." He hooked a hand around my neck, grabbed my cheek and roughly drew me close, planting a kiss on my other cheek. "Ordering them killed one at a time was exactly the right thing to do."

"I'm glad they backed down at the last minute. I don't know what I would have done otherwise."

"You could have pretended to change your mind about which one to kill first, and bought more time. Speaking of which, Logan is the older brother."

"I know."

"So you chose to threaten the older one first and pressure the younger one? I would have done it the other way around."

"Huh. It never occurred to me to do it any different."

"Well, it worked anyway, and you did everything else perfectly. Now, just one more stop, and we've got the rest of the day free."

Our last stop turned out to be a whore house, where someone who owed the family money back East had made an appointment. It was owned by another local family ours often exchanged favors with. Dino took me and one of the boys in and arranged with the madam to have the girl leave the client alone in the room.

"Don't worry, pal," Dino told the startled man in the bed as we barged in. The guy was about halfway between our ages. He was well-built, but defenseless. At least, his arms, shoulders and chest were well-built; the rest of was covered by a blanket. "I just want to talk to you." The man nervously drew the blanket further up as my cousin sat down on the edge of the bed, but Dino took it gently from his hands and slowly pulled it back down, even further than it had been, revealing a ridged abdomen. His torso was tanned to nearly the same shade of brown as my brother's hand passing along its length, much darker than my own chest. I noticed the clothes and hat lying on the dresser and realized the guy was a sailor, and probably worked with his shirt off in the casualness of an all-male environment at sea.

"My name is Dino Divito." The sailor's eyes widened in recognition, and he drew the blanket up toward his chin. It seemed to be an unconscious reflex.

"I'm told you wracked up quite a gambling debt last time you were in New York. I happened to be in town, so I thought I would drop in and give you a friendly reminder." Casually, Dino drew the blanket down again, this time stopping just soon enough to leave the guy's private parts covered. Where his tan ended, a few inches of amazingly pale Anglo-Saxon skin, never exposed to the light of day, were visible. It contrasted sharply with the wispy black hairs that trailed from his belly button downward and met thicker, curlier hairs peeking out above the edge of the blanket.

"My wallet's in my pants," he said with a soft accent that sounded Southern to my untrained ear. He pointed across the room. I noticed he had a tattoo on his biceps.

I got it out to hand to my cousin, and while I was at it, I tried on his sailor's hat.

Dino fished through the wallet. "You do realize this isn't nearly enough, don't you?"

"That's all I have, sir, I swear."

"Take it easy, pal," Dino said, laying his hand on the muscular suntanned shoulder. "Tell you what. I'll take half of what you've got here as interest. You can pay us back the next time you're in New York. How does that sound?"

"That would be terrific. Thanks, Mr. Divito!"

"We'll send the girl back in. Have fun." He squeezed his shoulder, stashed the cash inside his jacket, and gave him a parting pat, just above the edge of the blanket.

On my way out, I placed the sailor hat on the naked man's head.

"Nice touch, playing with his hat," Dino said in the hallway. "As long as we're here, kid, see anything you like? My treat."

"Uh, no. Isn't there more business we can do? I'm learning a lot."

"We're done. Time to relax and have some fun, *cucinu*." He reached over and loosened the knot of my tie, then let the tie slide through his fingers before releasing it.

"You go ahead, if you want."

"Are you kidding? My brother-in-law would kill me if he found out."

"Why would Drago care if you screwed a whore?"

"Not Drago, stupid! I'd kill him if he cheated on Bonfilia. I mean Severina's brother, of course. Anyway, we've got some time on our hands. We could ride a cable car. See a show. You sure you won't change your mind about those live nude girls? Okay, then, how about Robert Douglas? There's a new movie playing at the Fox called *Homicide*. Crime dramas are always good for a laugh."

# # # # #

My shop on Canal Street had a sign that said "We don't just dry clean. We also launder." Our little joke.

I was in my office in back, catching up on the books – I'd fallen behind during my trip to San Francisco the month before; it's a headache when you have two sets of them to maintain – when my cousin Primeiro burst in. "Come with me, Falito. I need you."

I dropped what I was doing and followed him out of the store – not as willingly as I'd have followed his younger brother Dino, but in my family, when someone says he needs you for something, you don't ask questions.

"Do I finally get to lean on someone?" I asked eagerly as his driver sped off with us.

"No, nothing like that. Well, in a way: my brother."

"What?!"

"He just broke into our sister's house and dragged Drago out. His boys told me they drove them to an abandoned slaughterhouse in Jersey." Primeiro seemed upset. I knew he liked Drago a lot. I myself thought he was a little too arrogant and hotheaded.

"What did Drago do?"

"Bonfilia claims he slapped her around. She started a fight when she supposedly found out he was having an affair. Dino was at my house when she called. I've never seen him so mad. I think he's going to kill the poor guy. I tried to stop him."

"But if he hit your sister ..."

"Oh, Drago deserves to be taught a lesson, I guess. But not to be beaten to death."

"Would Dino do that? He said he's never killed anyone."

"That's business. With family involved, there's no telling what he'd do."

"So what do you want me to do?"

"Talk some sense into him. Unless he's already killed the poor bastard, in which case we help him dispose of the body; he's not used to that, and he may not be thinking straight."

"How am I supposed to talk sense into him if he won't listen to his older brother?"

"Just your being there may make him think twice. I know I never would have killed anyone in front of him, even back when I was in that end of the business. Not with him watching me with those puppy dog eyes. You, you're like the younger brother he never had."

The thought that Dino might want my approval almost as much as I wanted his was a world-shattering revelation right up there with the concept of cops kissing sailors, an image that still haunted my nights, trying to picture it, ever since San Francisco.

When we arrived, Drago was still unharmed, more or less, but Dino had him chained by the wrists to a meat hook dangling by a chain from the ceiling. Drago's nose was bleeding, although it didn't look broken, and his face was slightly swollen, as if he'd been punched a few times. It could have been a lot worse; a lot of guys I knew would have beaten their sister's husband to a pulp for what he'd done. Drago was lucky he wasn't in the hospital or the morgue before I could get here. But my cousin looked angrier than I'd ever seen him. I suspected he was keeping himself under just enough control that he could take it slowly and enjoy it.

Three buttons of Drago's expensive silk shirt were undone, revealing his hairy chest, but that was how he normally wore it. It worried me, knowing how Dino worked, that he hadn't had his boys remove any of Drago's clothes, or stripped him with his own hands. It might mean he wasn't planning to merely humiliate him.

"Why did you bring Falito? I don't want him to see this."

"Exactly," Primeiro said.

I gave it a try. "You can't kill your own brother-in-law, Dino! Do you want to make your sister a widow? Her baby grow up without a father?"

Dino buried his face in his hands, clearly torn by conflicting emotions. I walked up to him and put my arm around his neck, pressing our foreheads together. After a moment, I put my arm around his broad shoulders and led him away from Drago. Primeiro took a step toward their injured brother-in-law, but Dino grabbed his arm and said, "No!"

We both put our hands on Dino, leaning close in a sort of three-man huddle, until he calmed down. Finally he said, "Let me at least teach him a lesson he'll never forget. If I swear not to kill him or maim him, will you trust me and not interfere?"

His brother started to object, but he ignored him and turned to me. "*Cucinu*, you know how I work. Will you play along while I scare the hell out of him?"

This was more like the man I knew. "Of course, Dino."

Dino walked back to his helpless brother-in-law and took a pair of brass knuckles out of his pocket. I heard Primeiro curse under his breath, and laid a restraining hand on his chest.

"I was going to save these for later, but I think I need to speed things up before they change their minds," Dino said.

"Please, Dino," Drago begged. "I told you I was sorry, that I'll never do it again."

Dino ripped Drago's shirt open, buttons flying everywhere. He tucked half of it into the back of Drago's belt, leaving his bare flank exposed. "One good rap from this can crack every single one of your ribs, one by one," he said, gently tapping it on the bottom of his brother-in-law's rib cage as he spoke.

"*Cognatu!*" Drago whispered pleadingly.

"Don't call me that! Since, apparently, my sister's not good enough for you." He worked his way up Drago's left flank, one rib at a time. He was obviously not hitting him hard yet; there was no sign of pain on Drago's face, just stark terror. Then Dino rubbed his hand over the bared part of his hairy upper chest, eliciting a sudden gasp. I realized the brass knuckles must be cold. He held his hand frozen in that position a moment while his brother-in-law squirmed. I noticed that Drago owned about ninety percent of the chest hair in the room, unless Primeiro was twice as hairy as his brother.

Dino gave him a push at the center of that hairy chest, setting him swinging. "I think you make a better punching bag than brother-in-law." With his left hand, the one with bare knuckles, he jabbed him in his exposed belly each time he swung close, but this seemed timed more to keep him swinging than to inflict much pain. Finally, he halted the swing by digging his fingers into Drago's trousers and grasping his belt. He then unfastened both, and pulled his brother-in-law's trousers and underwear down to his knees. Primeiro gasped; I don't think he'd ever seen his little brother in action before. With his shirt now hanging freely, Drago's chest was now mostly covered, but his private parts were exposed, framed by their black nest of hair.

Dino knelt and reached between his brother-in-law's naked legs. Drago's panicked eyes searched the room, seeking any possible ally. His eyes met mine in a silent plea. I'd been so busy admiring Dino's work that I'd forgotten I was supposed to argue. I said, "Dino, this man is the future of your side of the family!" That was an exaggeration, but Primeiro had three daughters, and his wife was running out of time to produce any sons, and for some reason Dino's wife Severina had still not gotten pregnant. I walked over and stood beside him. "You hear me?"

"It's true. Scary to think how easily I could crush the best hope of another grandson for Pop." He was gently cradling his brother-in-law's testicles in the palm of his hand. I heard Drago whimper, either in fear that the fist was about to close, or merely from the cold of the brass touching his nut sack. He looked about as defeated as a man could get. I should know, after that intensive weekend of on-the-job training in San Francisco.

"Don't throw away the future, Dino! When you're an old man and Uncle Clem is gone, you'll probably be head of the family. Which would you rather have, a bunch of big strong nephews enforcing your interests someday, or revenge today over a little domestic quarrel?" Following an instinct, I pushed Drago's shirt aside and ran my fingers through his chest hair to emphasize my point. "You could be wiping out three or four strong, hairy-chested nephews in one second."

Still on his knees, Dino looked up at me with an unreadable mix of emotions in his glistening eyes. But he didn't let go of Drago. I knelt beside him and gently took him by the shoulders. When he didn't try to shake me off, I reached between Drago's trembling hairy thighs and gently pried Dino's hand loose, trying unsuccessfully not to touch Drago's family jewels myself in the process. Then I slipped the brass knuckles off his hand and put them in my pocket, and helped him up.

"You did good, kid," Dino whispered to me as I led him out of earshot, after I had untied Drago's wrists and eased him into Primeiro's arms. Primeiro was now speaking softly to his brother-in-law, and fastening his pants because his hands were trembling too much for him to do it himself.

Shortly afterward, two of my boys arrived with a car to take me back. I'd called them from the phone booth outside and let Primeiro take Drago home in his.

"Want a ride?" I asked Dino.

"Thanks, but my boys will pick me up. They're supposed to call the phone booth every half hour to see if I'm done, and it's almost time."

"You've got blood on your cuff," I observed.

"It's only Drago's."

"Let me take that back to the shop. I can probably get it out if it doesn't sit too long."

"Nah, I've got work I was supposed to do today. I don't have time to go home and get another shirt."

"You can borrow mine." I began unbuttoning my jacket.

"That's all right." He moved to walk out the door. I reached out with some half-formed idea of stopping him, and to my surprise, my boys caught my intention and moved to block his way, looking to me for instructions. They were two of my youngest men, only a little older than I, and very strong. This was the first time I'd ever found myself in a situation where I had muscle with me and Dino didn't.

Dino turned back to me with a look that said, 'there seems to be a misunderstanding with your boys; will you please call them off.'

Suppressing a grin, I said, "Grab him and take off his shirt."

229

The look on Dino's face as my boys grabbed his arms and reached for the buttons was priceless: astonishment, humiliation, and more than a little pride. I savored the sight of him stripped to his undershirt, his muscular arms still in the grip of my boys, for a long moment before I took off my own shirt and draped it over his shoulder. Until that day, I'd never seen my cousin not in total control of what happened to him.

All the way back, alone in the back seat of my car, I held that memory in my head, and when I was sure no one was watching, I pressed Dino's shirt to my face and breathed in his familiar scent, fondly remembering all those times he'd trounced me.

# # # # #

More weeks went by with no indication I was going to be assigned a job. At this rate I'd still be running this dry-cleaning shop when I was 30, even 40. I'd never felt so alive as that weekend in San Francisco, standing by my cousin's side with two shirtless cops at our mercy. Why'd Uncle Clem bother to send me for training if he wasn't going to use me? I'd be happy just to work as Dino's assistant, but I hadn't even seen my busy cousin since he took me to a play to thank me for talking him out of what he almost did to his brother-in-law. Knowing my interest in Broadway musicals, he'd used his connections to acquire a pair of almost impossible-to-get tickets to a new show everyone was talking about, *South Pacific*. Great seats, too. The first act had featured a bunch of sailors lamenting the lack of women on their island, and with my newfound knowledge of sailors, I'd wondered if a few of them were a lot less frustrated than they pretended. And the provocative story line about racial intolerance had made me think of the Yee brothers. I couldn't discuss business with Dino in public, of course, but I'd privately resolved that if I were ever called upon to lean on them to get their father to make good on his loan payments, I would treat them exactly the same as any other men. I could just picture it.

My thoughts were interrupted when a customer came in. That happens once in awhile; last year we'd actually grossed enough to cover the income taxes on the money that keeps rolling in from nowhere. This customer had a small bag, big enough to hold maybe one set of clothes. He was Sicilian – unremarkable in this Italian neighborhood – but not a member of my family and not a regular customer.

"I'll come back on Thursday to arrange payment."

"Depending on what this is, sir, we'll probably have it done by then, but if you'll leave a phone number ..." But he was already out the door.

I looked to see what was in the bag, hoping Thursday was realistic. The first thing I pulled out was a nice jacket. It would need repair, I saw. The sleeves had been ripped halfway off at the seams. Next was a shirt, which would need new buttons; every single one was missing. A sock had gotten mixed in – no, two. And a pair of shoelaces. Who the hell sends shoelaces to the dry cleaners? The pants matched the jacket ... wait a minute. They looked familiar. This material looked and felt exactly like Dino's suit. I checked the labels. Both were his size exactly. Then why hadn't I recognized the man who delivered it? I knew all of Dino's boys. I looked again at the jacket sleeves. Usually that kind of rip happens when someone grabs a guy from behind and he struggles desperately to get free.

A cold shiver went down my spine. I unfolded the pants with hands that were already trembling. The knees were filthy, as if the wearer had been forced to kneel in an alley. Stuck to them was a tie, the same color as Dino's favorite tie. And at the bottom of the bag was a man's undershirt. I held it to my nose and confirmed my worst fear. I detected the lingering scent of one of the few men I'd wrestled with enough to recognize unmistakably by his smell.

My hand was shaking so much I almost couldn't dial the phone. Halfway through the number, I realized I couldn't trust my voice. I couldn't risk breaking down and crying like a *finocchio* while talking to my uncle. I hurled the phone against the wall, and three of my boys came running in from the back at the loud jangling crash. Swell, I thought. Now I've destroyed the property of the phone company, possibly the largest and most powerful organization we do business with.

# # # # #

I was still staggered by the weight of the responsibility Uncle Clemencio had placed on my shoulders. I'd always thought my first job would be something little. Something that, if I screwed up, would cost us a minor business opportunity. Not cost us my cousin's life. But Uncle Clem had said that all of his other enforcers were too heavy-handed; they'd go in with guns blazing and start a war between the families. Dino had been the only one he had trusted to handle delicate situations like this, and Dino had trained me. Apparently, Dino had given him a glowing report about me from our San Francisco trip. Also, Drago had credited me with saving his life. My uncle was confident I'd have just as good a chance of getting Dino out alive as anyone and do it without repercussions. He'd promised to give me all the men I wanted. I asked for all of Dino's boys and a few of his own.

On Thursday, the same guy who'd dropped off the package showed up as promised. I called two of my boys in from the back – though I could probably have handled him myself; he was of medium build and looked a few years older than Dino – then asked him, "Who are you?"

"I represent the Greco family."

"What's your name?"

"That's not important. All you need to know is that I'm here on behalf of the Grecos, to deliver a message."

I caught my boys' eyes and jerked my head, and one of them grabbed each arm.

"Maybe you don't understand how this works. If I don't report back in an hour, they'll kill your cousin," he said with much more calm than I could have managed if I were flanked by two large hostile men.

"A lot can happen in an hour," I said darkly, but gestured for the boys to release him. "What is it the Grecos want from us?"

"They're interested in purchasing the new tavern your family opened on Christopher Street."

I'd heard of that. The ones in San Francisco were so profitable that we'd decided to get into the business locally. "Because it threatens their monopoly on homosexual hangouts," I said flatly.

"You're a sharp kid. Now, Fausto Greco wants to meet with Clemencio Divito or his designated representative. Alone."

Nice of them to realize Uncle Clem was much too important to put himself in another family's hands like that. "My uncle has already designated me to handle this situation," I said, my voice sounding steady despite the pounding of my heart.

"You'll need to bring a signed and notarized power of attorney with you. A car will pick you up tomorrow morning at noon outside the Woolworth's on John Street. Make sure you're alone." He turned to go, but I gestured for my boys to grab him by the arms again.

He sighed. "How many times do I have to tell you, kid? They know I'm here, and they have your cousin."

"I just want to give you a tour of our facility here, since you were nice enough to drop by. Here, let me take your hat, since you'll be staying awhile."

"Look, I'm just a messenger," he said, sounding noticeably less calm as we marched him toward the back room. "I don't know where they're holding him."

"Here, have a seat. This is our steam press. It's a lot quicker than ironing, because it's big enough to do a whole leg or arm at once. Normally, we don't steam-press a guy's clothes while the guy's still inside them, but I'm kind of in a hurry today."

"You don't scare me, you young punk."

He was calling my bluff. And even if I wanted to torture him, I wasn't at all sure the boys could hold him in the awkward position it would take to get his arm or leg in the press, and it wouldn't open wide enough for his torso. So next I tried what I figured Dino would try if the initial threat didn't work. "I can't help but notice that your pants don't have a proper crease in them. Let us give you a complementary pressing."

He looked alarmed as two of my boys knelt at his feet and removed his shoes, then his pants.

"Hand me his wallet when you empty out the pockets. Now stretch the leg out good and tight. Make sure it can't slip away." This was all for show; normally it doesn't take two men to press clothes. I had my largest boy lean on the press with all his considerable weight, more like we'd use if we were flattening the man's leg instead of his pants leg.

"After you finish the pants, do his jacket. You got it wrinkled when you grabbed his arms. I'll be back in a minute."

I found a driver's license in the wallet. It said his name was Fazio Messina. With the new phone in front, I called my uncle's underboss. "I know him," he told me. "In fact, I was at his house just last year for his oldest son's eighteenth birthday party."

"Terrific. Here's what I want you to do ..."

When I came back, Fazio's pants, jacket, shirt, and T-shirt were hanging neatly on a rack, looking very crisp. His chair was close enough to the steam press that his chest and legs were flushed from the heat. I would have guessed he wasn't much older than Dino, if I hadn't just found out he had a son just a couple of years younger than I. On a sudden inspiration, I picked up an iron on my way over to him.

"Please! I swear I don't know where they're holding him."

I pulled up a chair to face him and patted his bare knee. "Take it easy. I believe you. Just tell me if they're really planning to take me to a meeting to negotiate my cousin's release, or if it's a trick. Am I going to wind up in chains in a basement somewhere?"

"The meeting's legit, I swear! Mr. Greco will treat you good. It's in a swanky hotel. I reserved the suite myself."

"Get him a pen and paper, so he can write down the address and room number." To Fazio I said, "How much muscle will he have with him?"

"Just three who'll escort you up from the car. But one of them will be armed, and the other two are huge. And he'll probably have his bodyguard." He accepted the pen and paper and scribbled down a hotel name and room number.

"Good. You've been very helpful." I patted his cheek. Always wanted to do that to someone.

"Does that mean you'll let me go?" he asked forlornly.

"Absolutely. But it's very important that you act like nothing happened, and not tell anyone that we know where the meeting's going to be."

"I swear on my children's life!" he said, placing his hand on his bare chest.

"Everybody hear that? Good. Give him back his clothes and let him get dressed."

On his way out, he passed his first-born son being muscled into the shop by two of my uncle's boys. He was a handsome guy, almost my own age. All we needed to do was hold him overnight. So why was it that all I could think about was how wrinkled his shirt was?

# # # # #

I arrived at the designated corner right on schedule, and they didn't keep me waiting. No sooner was my car out of sight than a car pulled up and two men got out. They took my briefcase away, then frisked me very thoroughly, unbuttoning my jacket and feeling my armpits, the small of my back, even my crotch. This wasn't something I'd ever had to put up with, and what made it even more humiliating than having it done on a public street, in front of the crowd of businessmen heading for lunch, was knowing that some of Dino's boys, now answering to me, were watching from a car parked nearby.

They shoved me into the back seat, one getting in after me and the other sitting beside the driver, and quickly headed in the direction of the East River. I resisted glancing back to make sure my boys were tailing us. Even if Fazio was keeping his mouth shut, there was always a risk that he'd betrayed something in his behavior or that they'd noticed his son was missing. They might have changed the meeting place as a precaution. Or he might have been lying from the beginning. Maybe they didn't want to meet with me at all, but to eliminate me, or at least kidnap me like my cousin.

When the car suddenly swerved into an alley, knocking me into the shoulder of the guy in my left, I was sure Fazio had spilled the beans, if the hotel story hadn't been a lie to begin with.

A man was waiting for us in the alley, opening the car door with one hand and pointing a pistol at me with the other, as the man who had frisked me got out behind me. I half expected to be forced to my knees and shot on the spot. Instead, they hustled me up a waiting fire escape as the car drove away. I hoped I'd at least get to see my cousin one more time, even if they were going to kill us both. Then again, it would be even worse if they made me watch him die. They marched me quickly through the building, down some stairs, and out a back door where another car was waiting, with a driver and two big men in the back seat. The space left between them looked too small for me. "Get in and lie down across their laps," the gunman said, prodding me in the back with the pistol.

I sprawled across four legs that felt as thick and solid as tree trunks. "Don't try anything funny," said the one behind the driver, grabbing my thighs. "We turned the tables on your smart, tough cousin, and we'll have no trouble dealing with a young punk like you."

"Yeah, he bawled like a baby," said the one whose lap my face was in. He knocked my hat onto the floor and forced my head down. "I'm going to miss him when ..."

Then the passenger door opened in the front, shutting him up, and the gunman got in. I spent the ride with one thug casually resting his hand on my butt, as if it just happened to be a convenient armrest. The other thug snuck three thick fingers under my collar and started massaging my neck in a way that was both painful and disturbingly pleasurable, and gave me the impression he was strong enough to crush my spine under his thumb if

I resisted. I forced myself to relax and let him do what he wanted, praying we were really heading to the hotel Fazio had claimed we'd be. The boys I'd assigned to tail us had surely lost us when we'd switched cars; they had no way of knowing I was in this one even if it passed right by them.

Finally, we stopped, the door that had been propping up my shins opened, and I was dragged out by the ankles. "On your feet." I tried to hide my relief when I turned around and saw the hotel Fazio had written down. As we entered, I was flanked by the huge thugs from the back seat, and as soon as we were in the elevator their huge hands closed painfully around my biceps. It was just as well; my nerves were so frazzled that I probably would have led the way right to the suite, forgetting that I wasn't supposed to know the number.

I was greeted by a short, well-dressed man about Dino's age. "Thank you for coming, Mr. Divito. I'm Fausto Greco. I hope my boys didn't get too enthusiastic about escorting you here." He signaled them to release my arms.

"They took my briefcase," I said plaintively. Although I was new at this, I knew I should try to calm down if I didn't want them to think I was weak. "It had uncle's p-power of attorney document."

"I've got your briefcase right here," said the gunman from behind me.

"You sound a little worked up, Mr. Divito. Come and have a brandy. My boys will wait out here." He added to his large bodyguard, "You, too, Eabroni."

"He's already been frisked," the gunman assured Eabroni when the big goon reached inside my jacket and started feeling through my shirt.

Fausto put his arm around my shoulders and led me into the adjoining room, which had a table with a bottle of brandy, two glasses, and a golden pen sitting conspicuously in the middle of the dark polished wood. The neatly made bed was against the far wall.

"I'm my father's authorized agent for real estate matters," he said after I had taken the brandy with trembling hands and downed it too fast. He poured me another. "We can sign everything right here."

"How do I know that you'll release my cousin unharmed?" I made no attempt to keep my voice from quavering as I added, "How do I know he's even alive?"

He stood and walked over to a phone on a small desk, and dialed a number. "How soon can you have him ready to go?" He smirked. "Well, that will save time. Drop him off and call me back from a phone booth ... At the hotel, you dope! Where do you think?"

Hanging up, he said, "They're dropping him off at his brother's house."

"Just like that?"

"A gesture of good faith."

And I suppose they considered me a substitute hostage of comparable worth, however much I disagreed.

"It should only take fifteen minutes, and then you can verify it over the phone."

I was relieved, but at the same time, almost disappointed. I'd vaguely pictured myself being led to wherever they'd been holding Dino and allowed to heroically sling his half-conscious and half-naked form over my shoulder and carry him away personally. But the important thing was that he was safe.

After his boys called back, I was allowed to dial Primeiro's house. "I don't know how you did it, cousin, but they just dropped him off safe and sound," he said.

"Can I talk to him?"

"Sure. He wants to talk to you, too."

"Falito? Where are you? I just got here. How'd you hear so fast?"

"Dino! It's good to hear your voice." My own voice was breaking, and I fought the instinct to turn my face away from Fausto. Let him see my tears. I could sense that he was enjoying watching a man in his power break down. I knew the feeling.

"Are you all right?" I asked. "Did they hurt you?"

"I'm fine, *cucinu*."

I heard muffled female voices. Dino held the phone away from his mouth and said, "Damn it, Freddie! Keep that door shut." In the background, I heard his brother sending someone to his bedroom for some of his own clothes to lend him.

On my side, I heard some faint sounds from the outer room filtering through the solid oak door. "What was that, Dino?" I asked loudly. "I can't hear you."

"I was talking to Primeiro. The women are outside the study, wanting to fuss over me."

"Are you sure you're all right?" I asked, still in a raised voice.

"Just a little sore. And tired; they didn't let me get much sleep. I can hear you just fine, by the way."

"What are you sore from?" I asked loudly.

"I'd rather not talk about it. But don't worry, I'm okay. Listen, *cucinu*, I gotta go. Are you somewhere safe?"

"Yeah," I said, trying to sound like I believed it.

"Good. When can you come over? I thought about you a lot, while they were ... holding me."

"I have some work to finish up, but in an hour or two, with any luck." We said goodbye reluctantly, and I hung up. Turning to Fausto, I said, "You didn't give him any clothes when you let him go?"

He shrugged. "That isn't the way I would have done it, but my brother had some kind of grudge against him. He wouldn't tell me why. But you and I, we can deal with this like gentlemen, right?"

"Of course. Show me the contract you want me to sign."

"As you can see ..." there was a muffled sound of laughter from the next room. Fausto glanced at the door, looking annoyed, then continued, "this is a simple title transfer of your Christopher Street property, for a consideration of five thousand dollars."

"Five grand for a profitable business?"

"Under the circumstances – what the hell are they doing out there?" he muttered as deep male laughter reached us again, this time from at least two men. "Excuse me, please."

He strode over to the door and opened it. I couldn't resist following. As I stood behind him, I only wished I could see his face.

The outer room was crowded with men. All but three of them mine.

The thug who'd rested his hand so casually on my butt was stretched out on the carpet floor, his shirt unbuttoned, being straddled by an almost equally large man with another one pinning his arms above his head. His chest muscles bulged under his tight undershirt, which had been pushed up to his belly button, just enough to expose his naturally tan belly with a trail

238

of hair down the center, and he writhed and pleaded as his exposed flesh was tickled mercilessly.

The erstwhile gunman, who had wispy black armpit hair and pathetically skinny arms and legs for someone in his line of work, was standing with his wrists pinned behind his head. It had taken only a single one of my boys to immobilize him while two more tormented him. The gunman's trousers were around his ankles, his shirt and jacket were gone, and one man was tickling his left armpit while another had inserted a pistol – possibly the one taken from him – into the right arm opening of his undershirt and was probing his chest with it. Judging by the way he was reacting, the muzzle was cold, and had found some sensitive flesh.

The remaining thug, the one whose heavy-handed massage had left my neck aching, was lying on his back on the coffee table with his head toward me. His hairy legs were raised in the air, each huge bare foot held captive in the hands of another of our boys, who were tickling the soles. They had him down to his boxer shorts, and his muscular chest, covered in whorls of hair, heaved as he laughed helplessly. His desperate attempts to get away were thwarted by two more of my boys, who slapped his meaty shoulders back down on the polished wood every time he tried to rise.

Eabroni, Fausto's personal bodyguard, was still being strip-searched. One of my boys was pointing a gun at him as the big man stood there meekly with his arms raised, revealing bushy armpits. A holster and a knife lay at his bare feet. As I watched, the man searching him removed a small pistol he'd found tucked into the waistband of his pants. Opening the pants, he discovered a garroting rope that had been tucked in, too, but concealed beneath his undershirt. He yanked up the undershirt, revealing a well-muscled abdomen, and pulled it off the unresisting bodyguard's hairy chest and upraised arms. Tossing it aside, he reached again for his pants.

All in all, the boys Uncle Clem had lent me were doing a terrific job of following my general instructions. But behind Fausto's back, I silently pointed at the one on the floor and made a quick unzipping gesture near my fly and mimed spanking myself. My boys immediately rolled the thug over and were pulling down his pants and briefs when I closed the door.

"Looks like it's just you and me," I told Fausto casually. And I had four inches and at least twenty pounds of muscle over him. I put my arm around his narrow shoulders and guided him back into the negotiating room, giving his biceps a squeeze through his suit to see how much meat he had on his bones. Make that thirty pounds, I thought. "Let's get back to business," I said brightly. "I'm sure we can find a reasonable price for us to buy all your holdings. How's four thousand per property sound?"

LUCK BE A LOUIE TONIGHT
By R. W. Clinger

Louie Vocello was on the hunt for me, I knew. I owed him forty thousand grand because I had a gambling problem. The mobster was nice enough to lend me the dough, which I had six months to pay back. That time was long gone, and I still didn't have the goon's cash, which prompted his chase.

1948 in Las Vegas was … intense and considered the desert playground. The post-War days still had Tommy Hull running the El Ranchos Vegas Hotel-Casino and gangsters, Benjamin "Bugsy" Siegel and Meyer Lansky, were widely responsible as the organizers and prime movers behind early development of crime. The largest employer in the valley was tourism and entertainment, mostly strippers and dancers. The Flamingo Hotel had been open for two years; a place where all the thugs stayed and carried out their raunchy business.

Other events that transpired during that same year included: the Cold War started, NATO was just being formed, Gandhi was murdered, and a gallon of milk was eleven cents. Hollywood was glitzy with Bob Hope, Gary Cooper, and James Cagney. The majority of the country listened to the rhythm and blues. The first transistor was developed and …

I admit I had problems with cards. Poker was not my friend. Blackjack had kicked my bulbous ass. And, slot machines raked me over the coals. My debt increased by the day, hundreds after hundreds, which eventually grew into thousands.

How did I know the goon, Louie Vocello? By a friend of friend, of course. Louie liked me upon our first meeting and loaned me the forty K. His beautiful brown eyes gleamed with his adorable smile, and he said, "If you don't pay me back, I'll have to kill you. Just so you know that."

I knew a few things about Louie. He worked for the Godfather, Vincent Vocello, who just so happened to be related to Bugsy. Vincent was a notorious bad boy behind seven recent deaths in Las Vegas; all trials were still pending. He was the Don's nephew with Sicilian blood, good Italian looks, and not conscious when it came to knocking off someone

241

with an outstanding debt. If a certain somebody fucked with him, he fucked back. Doing his family wrong was a very bad situation, and death was the resolution with no questions asked according to the Vocello code.

To my surprise, he caught up with me at a private club called Dullkemper's: maroon-colored draperies lined the walls, gold and crystal chandeliers hung from the ceiling, jazz singers performed on a small stage, and smart looking waitresses/prostitutes waited on the card tables. All the high stake gamblers nested at the club: Billy Bob Hill, Shaker Wilson, Walter "Motley" Madison, and Taylor "One Eye" Kundra. All of us sat around a poker table and played Five-Card Stud. Three hands into the card gig, and Louie busted through the front door of the club. Two Sicilian cohorts had his back: Leo "Arm Bar" Casanetti and Nino Mallonni. All three of the gangsters were dressed in solid navy knitted waist coats, matching ties, pressed dress shirts, and carried Marlin shotguns.

Louie trotted up to me, put the barrel of his Marlin to the back of my skull, and said, "Gentlemen, I'm very sorry to barge in on your game like this, but I am forced to collect a payment from this rat."

The four gamblers dressed in gray and black zoot suits around me watched as I was pulled away from the table by the back of my neck. He rushed me into one of the club's private rooms and locked us inside.

The small back room was accented with maroon satin seats that lined each wall. Reflective mirrors reached from the seats to the ceiling. Light jazz flooded into the room.

Louie tossed me against one of the satin-covered seats and blared, "Petey Locke, you owe me!"

I swear, the goon took in my curly blond hair, emerald-green eyes, and five-ten frame when I stood up. He licked his lips, waved his Marlin at me, and inquired, "What do you have to say for yourself?"

I said the first thing that came to mind: "I'll pay the forty K off."

"How do you plan to do that?"

I shrugged a shoulder and replied, "Whatever you want from me … I'll do it. Just don't off me."

"I should off you, though."

"Tell me what to do for you. I'm sure we can work this out."

The bad boy shared a hearty laugh, waved the Marlin from my toes to my forehead, and instructed, "Strip out of your clothes. I want to see your skin."

Truth was, I found his request rather peculiar. Guys like Louie and the other Vocello boys had wives and numerous girlfriends on the side. Perhaps he was different and liked the company of a twenty-two-year-old blond male such as myself; one that just happened to be in debt up to his ears. Obviously, the thug preferred cock opposed to …

"Strip," he coached, mesmerized with my golden boy smile, and maybe hungry for my pale skin and lightweight build.

I listened; otherwise he would have murdered me right there in Dullkemper's. Without trepidation, I pealed my Carisa shirt off, Wrangler jeans, and sandals, all of which were dropped to the room's floor. Then, I stood, completely naked in front of the gangster who had my life in his hands.

The man took in my bony shoulders, strawberry-colored nipples, no-fat stomach, triangle of blond curls above my four inches of limp cock, and my hairless and droopy balls.

"Turn around," the goon instructed.

I obeyed him, since my life was on the line, spun around, wiggled my bare ass for his strange pleasure, and asked over my right shoulder, "Two grand and you can have it, Louie. What do you say?"

"One grand, with the option for more use, but only if I like it."

"Deal," I said, working off my debt, providing my ass for payment, and for his horny pleasure.

Within seconds he placed the Marlin on the satin-covered seat behind him but didn't unload the weapon. Then, I watched him in one of the mirrors as he unbuttoned his slacks and pulled out his goods.

What was underneath the material was rather a shock to me: nine solid inches of uncut tool with droplets of ooze against its rounded tip. Below his shaft was more equipment: two swinging balls decorated in tangles of Sicilian-black hair.

Without another word spoken between us, two events transpired: I grew bone-hard between my legs, and he shuffled quickly towards my bottom, hungry to pop his dog between my bulbous bottom-cheeks.

What transpired next was a blur for me. He shoved his swollen beef between my legs and started to dry-hump my ass. His plump lips found the length of my smooth neck above my right shoulder, and he began to swab it with his wet tongue. The gangster's left hand wrapped around my side and grappled my left pec. His right hand reached around my sweat-covered torso and discovered the firm seven inches between my legs. The man's synchronized motion ensued: swabs to my neck, humps to my bottom, and his right hand busy at work on my cock.

"Louie, what are you doing back there?" I inquired.

His lips pulled away from my neck and he chanted, "Getting my money's worth."

Forty thousand dollars was a lot of cash, and a lot of hand jobs, but I was willing to pay my dues, particularly since he was so handsome, rough, and the type of badass guy I wanted to mess around with. I allowed him to continue his game with my skin and moaned in front of him as his right hand started to jack my gun up and down in quick motion. Perspiration clung to my forehead and shoulders as I shifted my hips forward, pumping his warm fist.

Behind me, he continued to dry hump me. His cock rolled between my rump-cheeks, but didn't enter my narrow hole. The dude was actually getting off by our combination, potent and skilled with his labor. He was quite overjoyed that I had become his full interest, easy meat that he could taste, ride, and accomplish whatever else he wanted to carry out with me, since I owed him a shitload of cash.

I was into that gig with the hit man. His extension of hard shaft felt exhilarating between my legs, and his hand job that occurred at my front was just as intoxicating. He was feisty with his hands and built up a fine rhythm on my tool, and with my bottom. Again and again, he applied kisses and licks to the length of my neck above my right shoulder. His left hand was firm on my pec, and he purposely pressed its nipple between two of his fingers.

A masculine grunt escaped my mouth as I jolted my weight forward, into his palm, and then backed into his nine-inch tool. Two more thrusts ensued, one after the next, and a sweeping flood of elation careened through my core.

His pumps to my ass and cock were relentless and passionate. His moaning was a total aphrodisiac for me; a long and obtrusive noise that caused my body to swell with heated bliss. Within a matter of seconds, the brute's combined motion became erratic and out of control. His breathing intensified, and sweat from his pelvis decorated my bottom.

Truth was his jostling palm in front of me was too much to handle. The steady up and down motion spun me into orgasm. Dizziness was found, and a deep murmur was trapped behind my teeth. White goo spiraled out of my hose and splashed against the private room's floor. A vat of the gluey substance twirled out of my pole, which left me spent and almost unable to stand.

Behind me, he informed, "Spin around. Watch me blow." The mobster released his junk from between my legs and stepped one foot back.

I listened, trying to catch my breath. Still dizzy, I turned around and admired his upright cock between his hairy thighs. The shaft was obnoxious in size, a pool stick with veins and excess skin, delectable looking.

The thug spread his feet apart and started to jack his beef up and down with a spirited strategy. Dozens of hip-thrusts into his two palms ensued. The man's delicious looking Sicilian face turned an auburn red, which was laced with deep satisfaction. His movement was hyper and unstoppable. The man began to growl, turned an even darker shade of red, and eventually fired his cargo on the floor. Long strings of his pent juice flew to the maroon-colored carpet, one after the next, and almost decorated my sandals. The look in the handsome man's eyes was remarkable: alluring, mystified, and numbed. After he came and tucked his cock away, he moved up to me, drew me towards him, and connected our faces together. The kiss with him was hallucinogenic and rich with emotion. Following that mouth-to-mouth kiss, he pushed me away in a forceful manner, and said, "You now owe me thirty-nine thousand dollars."

I winked at him, licked my lips in a sexually devious manner, and shared, "You can fuck it out of me if you want it."

Again, the gangster connected his lips with mine, pushed me away, and escaped the room in a flurry, vanishing from my side and heading off to his next state of business.

I had to leave Las Vegas; that was my current thought process. The sooner the better, of course. Louie Vocello was going to hunt me down and … probably kill me with his Marlin or bare hands. You didn't fuck with the Mafia, I knew, and certainly not the Vocello family.

I packed a bag with my belongings and planned to hitch a ride west to Malibu. My uncle lived in a small stucco house with a yappy dog. He wrote short stories about the Depression and his two years spent in Germany, fighting the Nazis. My plan was to spend a month with him, gain some cash, and then maybe head to Hollywood. I had the look for films, and an acting ability. I could make movies and discover a new life for myself. A change like that was needed. Hollywood called for me, which I felt in my soul.

On the way out of Las Vegas, one of Louie's men picked me up in his Buick Roadmaster while I hitched on Las Vegas Boulevard. The guy was gorgeous, in my opinion: thick brown hair, puppy dog eyes, twenty-eight years old, muscular build, dimples in his cheeks, thick neck, and a tiny scar above his right eyebrow. Rumor had it that he was a heavyweight fighter and broke a lot of backs. He also was one of the Vocello family's best hit men. Mr. Handsome aimed a K-38 Target Masterpiece at me and told me in a blunt manner, "Get in."

I tossed my single bag into the backseat and climbed inside, just as he had instructed.

"Louie wants to see you."

I expected nothing less, of course.

Fighter pulled the Roadmaster over, blindfolded me, and said, "You don't need to know where we're heading."

"Got it," I replied and settled into my seat for the short drive ahead.

I believe fifteen minutes had passed in the interim. I was then pulled out of the Roadmaster, pushed up a flight of stairs, walked down a long hallway (I believe), and entered a room where our heels echoed on a cement floor. I smelled oil and gasoline around me. Behind me, Louie's firm voice said, "Leave us alone."

Fighter walked out of that unseen place.

I was pressed over a vehicle's hood; my shirt lifted, and I felt cool metal against my stomach. I asked in a hushed manner, "Are you going to kill me?"

"On the contrary, Petey. You're my newest favorite thing." He reached around my front, unzipped my jeans, pulled them down to my ankles, and asked, "Do you want to leave the blindfold on, or should I take it off?"

"On," I replied, and glowed with a smile over the vehicle's hood, knowing exactly what was coming next.

Behind me, he got busy on his knees. My ass cheeks were spread apart, and his tongue dragged across my rump's hole. One slap to my right buttocks was felt: a light sting that was quick and steady. His tongue dove into my hole where it licked and lapped at my core, hungry for my taste, and infatuated with my skin. He panted and slurped behind me, into his play, and eventually pulled off and away for oxygen.

My palms rested on the car's hood. I begged him, "More, Louie ... Don't hold back."

The man did not have to be told twice and went to work on my ass again with his fingers and mouth. He slurped and ground his face into my hub. He moaned with deep satisfaction and found pleasure in spanking me a second time. His force caused the blindfold to slide above my right eye and ...

I took in my surroundings: Coca-Cola machine, pin-up girl Rita Hayworth on a calendar, three Chevrolets, a Cadillac, and a Model T Ford that needed repairs, tools everywhere, greasy rags, oil cans, and a radio, which was off. The place was familiar to me: J. P. Russet's Garage on East Tropicana Avenue in downtown Las Vegas. I only knew the place because I passed it on my way to The Flamingo almost every day.

He said behind me, "I have more plans for you, pal."

Such as: A bullet to my head? Lacerations? Catching me on fire? Beating the hell out of me? The choices were limitless, of course. My body could be buried in the desert within just a matter of minutes. Or, cement seemed to work fine for hiding corpses, didn't it?

My rump was slapped again, and its cheeks were pulled open. During a single grunt on my part, I felt his nine inches of steel-like pole enter my bottom with missile speed. All of his protein wedged itself inside my tunnel, and he began banging me in a nonstop fashion.

I let out an obnoxious roar and jumped off the hood of the car with pain. Pleasure was soon discovered, though, and I fell back on the black Delahaye 148L's hood, dragged my clipped fingernails over its paint, and gritted my teeth.

His ride was repugnant and rough, but I loved every minute of it. Influential and swift thumps occurred to my backside and caused me to go numb. His cock rammed into me with speed, pulled out, and rammed inside again. Truth was I fell under his dick-spell, collapsed against the metal hood, anesthetized by his drastic motion. Moans of pure elation exited my semi-parted mouth. My torso shivered on the metal, bliss-filled and overcharged with euphoria.

The oddity of that event between the two of us inside the garage was nothing less than a spectacle for any viewer. Although there wasn't a voyeur in sight, I felt as if I were being watched by a Vocello brother, cousin, or the godfather himself. That feeling passed so quickly, though, since I felt a release shift through my torso, and an explosion between my legs.

I confess, some decades later, my tool rubbed against the hood of the Delahaye and built up a comfortable friction. The underside of my hose rolled to and fro against the black steel, which was a full-blown turn-on for me. Bottom line: I pleasurably fucked the car as he continued to fuck me.

No longer was it possible for me to keep my load stored inside my body. Following a jilt to my system, that unexplainable vibration when a man reaches his orgasm, sticky spurt leaked out of my dog and decorated the Delahaye's hood and my tight belly. An awkward sound that was somewhat muffled was released from my throat at the same moment. Feeling surfaced again within my body and proclaimed that I was spent, empty of my Petey-cargo, and ready for food, a nap, or perhaps cuddling with the bad boy behind me.

Louie was primed to blow his own load, I quickly learned. One thump to my ass followed by two more rapid thumps. He let out a gasp, exhaled carbon dioxide from his lungs, and announced in a roar, "Firing, squirt!"

Within seconds, his pick was pulled free from my hub, and he jacked the stick with all his might. I heard a second gasp escape him, another warning, and then his churn flew onto my back and sizzled against my spine and shoulder blades.

I was then spun around, hooked by his right hand and drawn to his lips. Our mouths connected yet again: with much passion, chins touched, and saliva was shared in a heated manner. He pushed me away, into the hood of the Delahaye. My ass was then lathered in my own wet and sticky spent. A harsh slap to my left cheek sent my head spinning, and he smiled down at me in his boisterous and sexy manner, "I like you too much. You're dangerous for me. I can't keep away from your skin. I'm addicted to your ass."

"I'm leaving town," was the only thing I could say, even if I found his rushed compliments as music to my ears.

"Remember, you can run from me, but you can't hide. I'll find you wherever you are, Petey. Your ass is mine, and I always keep what I own."

He was serious, in mobster mode. The grin on his adorable face told me not fuck around with him. He had killed many men because they refused to subject themselves to his needs. I didn't want to be one of those men. Besides, I liked him: his roughness, sex appeal, and his chaotic sex. He leaned over me, brushed fingers against one of my cheeks in a caring manner, and whispered, "You're toxic to me ... I shouldn't like you."

Before he pulled away, I replied, "You do like me, though."

The thug shared an empowering wink with me, a last kiss for the day, and left my side. Within seconds, he vanished from J. P. Russet's Garage and eventually returned to the El Ranchos Vegas Hotel-Casino to meet up with his Mafia family, leaving me alone.

Two days later, Louie found me in The Flamingo gambling the morning away. He pulled me away from a slot machine by the scruff of my neck, and scolded me for gambling money away; money that I just happened to owe him. He drove me across town, deep into the desert and ...

It was over for me. I was done ... finished. He was going to pop a bullet in my skull and bury me somewhere in the desert. I was being offed by the Mafia. Petey Locke's days were finalized.

He parked his blue Ford Deluxe in the middle of nowhere: cactus everywhere, long-tailed lizards, Juniper and Joshua trees, cottontail rabbits, elf owls, rosy boas, and hummingbirds. The temperature was moderate for a change, and soothing. A light wind blew across the arid plain. He and I walked between two massive boulders and into what looked like a salt basin. He turned around, faced me, and said, "We needed a little privacy away from the city." The guy started to undress and drop his Zoot suit and fedora to the desert floor. His hairy chest gleamed in the morning sun. His nipples were hard points, and his nine inches of tool was already standing upright between his legs, ready for use. The thug used his right hand and pulled his engorged shaft down like a one-arm bandit, released it, and the stick slapped against his tight stomach. A burst of horny laughter and smile escaped him, and then he said, "Show me a good time, Petey. Get on your knees and suck me off."

I was hungry for his plump lips, furry chest, inflated tool, and bulbous ass … whatever he wanted to share with me. Within seconds, I faced him, locked my lips to his, and shoved my tongue down the back of his canal-like throat. My fingers found his firm nipples and squeezed their swollen apexes. My face pulled away from his moist lips and fell southward, against his corded neck, over his plated chest, and ended up at the tip of his uncut stick. I extended my tongue and toyed with the excess skin that covered his rod. Left-hand fingers pulled down on his furry-warm balls and caused the man to grunt with pleasure. Above me, he demanded, "Lose your clothes and blow me," in a gruff manner; a demand I desired to hear.

As requested, I undressed and started to blow him in the desert sand. Morning heat connected us together as he stood still in the brilliant, red-orange light. A traipsing wind found its way between the hulking boulders and teased our flesh like straying fingers in a queer bar. Limitless groans and grunts echoed in our secluded area. My head bobbed up and down on his meat. I gagged once … twice … three times, overcome by his prick's size. Saliva dripped out of the corners of my mouth and glazed his furred balls.

"Enough," he said, and pushed me away. "I want you to rim my ass, pal." He found his suit on the sand, picked up the material, and smoothed the fabric, piece by piece, over a hip-high sandstone with a flat surface. Next, he bent over the stone, locked his arms, pressed his palms flat against its surface, spread his legs as if he were being searched by a cop, and coached over his left shoulder, "I don't have all day, Petey. Get to work on my ass."

I stood, closed the ten-foot gap between us, positioned myself behind him, lapped at his spine with my extended tongue, fell to my knees again, lathered his two-orbed ass with an open mouth, and lightly moaned with satisfaction. I then decided to tease him with my right index finger, which gently grazed his compact hole, but didn't push inside. Swift finger-touches transpired on his pink and hairy core; tantalizing pleasure that caused the bad boy to murmur unrecognizable jargon in front of me.

One slap to the mobster's ass jarred him forward. A hearty laugh escaped him, overwhelmed by my unexpected hand gesture. Next, a string of slurred sounds escaped his semi-parted mouth as I drew my tongue, not inside or over his compressed man-hole, rather, around its furred center.

He was ecstatic on the rock, horny as hell for our connection in the climbing heat, and begged, "Lick me, Petey … Wedge your face in there."

Why not? I had a debt to pay and … his ass was looking mighty tasty for my needs. Forcefully, I spread his hole apart with all my fingertips and planted my lips against his heated center. One lick transpired into the next lick rather quickly, which were then followed by a succession of ass-probing laps, swirls, and brisk darts with my protruding tongue.

Unstoppable whimpers erupted from the gangster on the rock, which ensued for the next few minutes. Then, lost in his sexual indulgence, under the care of my physical desire, he shared a firm demand, "Cock … use your cock on me. I want you to bang me."

"I'll fuck you for three thousand green off my debt," I interjected, dealing with the man.

"One thousand he moaned."

"Two thousand … and that's my bottom line," I said between his legs, breathing on his droopy balls.

"Deal," he replied and caused the both of us to smirk with selfish glee.

He stood, turned around, and sunbathed in the soothing light on the piano-size sandstone. On his back with his eyes closed, glistening in the sun's radiant beams, he placed his palms behind his head as a pillow, spread his legs for my easy access, and was ready for whatever could happen between two naked men secluded in a Nevada desert.

Upright and positioned between his legs, with accuracy, the tip of my firm extension rubbed against his constricted opening. A soft mumble was heard from him, which was then followed by a devilish chuckle.

Granted, I was only seven inches long, but knew exactly what to accomplish with my equipment. In truth, I was much better at fucking men than I was at gambling; a handful of once-naked gentleman/poker players would have agreed with me. My skills had certainly not changed: I was an expert at breaking a man's bottom, but not a casino's bank account.

One inch of my throbbing pole entered his guy-chute with caution. Two slid comfortably inside the man with such ease. Three … four … five inches caused him to whimper with delight on the stone. Six and seven inches lay inside his warm and tight slot until I was ready to ram him with an unyielding and rigid current.

My thumps to his hole were ferocious and steadfast, but exactly what the goon lusted for. I rushed into him with hyper motion, extracted my beef, and banged him yet again: eighteen times … twenty-three times …

thirty-four times, until I saw tears surface in the corners of his cocoa-butter brown eyes.

"Harder," escaped his mouth; such a minor request on his part, since I was surely willing to hurt him with my cock.

What transpired after a hefty sequence of butt-bolts was rather a shock to me. He went into a hectic and horny rage, and yelled up at me, "Fuck me! … Shove your cock deep inside me! … Faster, motherfucker … and harder!"

They were words that I had never heard him speak before, requests that I had found as motivation for a pleasing jaunt inside his rump.

Again, he yelped on the rock as my beef continued to break his ass apart and add wanted pain to his epicenter. His rough boy face grew flush, and his beautiful eyes seemed dull and fall into the rear of his skull. The goon was in more pleasure than I ever anticipated.

Bolt after continuous bolt with my metal-like tool caused him the greatest elation. Both of us knew my movement was brisk and rough, but he craved nothing less. Instead of complaints, he instructed, "Stroke me, Petey … Get me off."

Swift motion on his dick with my right hand sent the mobster into a spin of abrupt satisfaction. Awkward grunts lifted out of his mouth while he attempted to shift his hips upwards, but couldn't, because of my meaty slab of cock inside him.

After three immediate tugs on his rod, he burst a gallon of cream against my chest. Flaxen-white strings of his male-glue glistened on my plated abs, hung from my pyramid-shaped nipples, and clogged my dented navel.

Honestly, the man became limp on the rock, possibly dizzy and airless because of my ass-nailing and hand job. Soon to follow was his greedy smile, which told me he enjoyed my humps, and announced, "Your turn, guy. Spray your gunk all over my hairy chest. I'm ready to wear it."

I yanked my junk out of his cozy hub, spread my legs a little, and began to add steady north and south jolts to my pecker. Humps and groans were added to that rippling effect, a woof! two woofs! and then a soft murmur.

What shifted through my middle was nothing less than a vibration of naughty fulfillment, which only caused my palms to become more erratic on my post and shift wildly up and down.

I called down to the thug, "Spraying, Louie," and exploded my pent juice all over his still-erect shaft and droopy bear-balls. The goo garnished the gangster and caused a spirited smile to form on both of our faces.

After my eruption, I backed away from the bad boy, found my white T-shirt to clean up the mess on my chest, tossed it into the desert, and said, "You driving me back to the city, or do I have to walk?"

Louie laughed at me, sat up, climbed off the rock, and grabbed his own tee for a quick clean-up. While his spew-removal session was carried out, he said, "Petey, I don't know what I'm going to do with you."

"How about you keep me for a while?" I questioned and slipped into my Wranglers.

"You'd like that, wouldn't you? All the money and fucking you needed. A Ford Anglia to drive. Debt-free. Hell, I would want that."

"You think about it, mobster. I'll be around if you want me."

"It's always a possibility," he replied, scooped a kiss away from me, and led me through the desert again, back to his Delaraye, and we returned to the city.

I could run, but I couldn't hide … kept rushing through my mind. Louie's words, and his promise. If he didn't find me, one of his henchmen would. Perhaps his theory regarding my whereabouts was correct. Malibu wasn't far from Las Vegas. Nor was Hollywood. I would be found, and easily. Even if I had decided to leave the city/state/country, the Vocello family would eventually discover me, and take what was theirs.

A day had passed in Las Vegas, two days, three days. Eventually, I had finally decided where to go and what to do with my life. I carried my bag to the El Ranchos Vegas Hotel-Casino and found myself in Louie's suite. His lush pad overlooked the heart of the gambling city. The view reached across the desert and caused me to fall in love with the place.

I found him in bed alone, sleeping. The man didn't stir awake at my unannounced arrival. He snored lightly and possibly dreamed of having an entourage of young men to fulfill his every sexual wish.

A shower called for me; I hadn't bathed in two days. I undressed, dropped my jeans and white T-shirt to the floor, kicked off my sandals, and found the bathroom. Inside, I stood under the hot spray for the next ten minutes, washed all of my parts, and …

A gun was fired and a bullet whizzed through the shower curtain and nearly grazed my forehead. The shooter outside the shower popped off a second shot, which almost nailed me in my right thigh. As fear buzzed through my system, I called out Louie's name.

"Petey, is that you?" he questioned from the doorway, soft spoken and out of gangster mode. Then, a playful laugh echoed inside the bathroom.

"It's me!" I exclaimed, knowing he was playing a game with me.

"What are you doing here?" he laughed.

"I'm your boyfriend now," I pulled back the shower curtain and showed off my goods: wet chest, cock at full mast, soap clinging to my balls.

The guy was into me in every way: my good looks, my charm, and sweet personality. So, I had a gambling problem, but that didn't mean I couldn't be liked.

"What are you talking about?" One of those irresistible and soulful grins spread over his handsome face.

"I have a debt to you and ... I'm here to pay it off. It doesn't get any simpler than that."

"What else are you here for?" He adjusted the mound of meat inside his cotton boxers.

"To be your boyfriend," I admitted and waved a finger at him, coaxing him into the shower with me.

"My assistant," he corrected, keeping his relationship with me under wraps.

"Yes, your assistant."

Again, a greedy grin spread across his chiseled face. In a matter of seconds, he lost his white boxers by pushing them down to his ankles. He stepped out of the fabric and entered the shower. In doing so, he said, "Where did I leave off with your skin, pal?"

"I think you can figure that out."

He turned around and rubbed his bottom against my still-erect shaft. The man looked over his right shoulder, and begged, "Ride me."

I didn't object, and wouldn't for the next two years, now a part of Las Vegas, and the Vocello mob.

About the Authors

Derrick Della Giorgia was born in Italy and currently lives between Manhattan and Rome. His work has been published in several anthologies and literary magazines. Visit him at www.derrickdellagiorgia.com.

DesertMac lives with his husband of 30 years (just married in '08 of course) in Palm Springs, Ca. He's had two short stories and a novella published by STARbooks Press and has the serial novel on several story sites.   http://groups.yahoo.com/group/DesertMac_Forum/   email: desertmac2000@yahoo.com.

J.S. Cook resides in St. John's, NL, with her husband of 25 years, Paul, and their two spoiled rotten dog-children Lola and Sheppy. She is the author of numerous novels, and her work has been widely anthologized. http://joannesopercook.com.

Landon Dixon's stories have been published in numerous magazines and anthologies.

Logan Zachary (loganzachary2002@yahoo.com) is an author of mysteries, short stories, and over forty erotica stories, living in Minneapolis, MN, with his partner, Paul, and his dog, Ripley, who runs the house. www.loganzacharydicklit.com.

Michael Bracken, author of 11 books and almost 900 short stories, is a freelance editor and writer living in Texas.

Milton Stern is an author of biographies, novels, screenplays, and dozens of short stories, living in Maryland with Esmeralda, his rescue beagle. www.miltonstern.com.

N. A. Hayes resides in Chicago, IL, with his partner and their cats. His published work includes fiction, poetry and cultural criticism.

R. W. Clinger writes for and has three novels published by STARBooks Press. He is currently at work on a new novel.

Rob Rosen, Lambda Literary Award nominated author, has been published in more than 125 anthologies. Please visit him at www.therobrosen.com.

Rob Saldarini is a college professor and inclusion training facilitator. His creative fiction includes a novel and short stories. <u>MyBrothers@optonline.net</u>.

About the Editor

Eric Summers resides in West Palm Beach, Fla., and he has a special place in his heart for good fellas ... and bad ones.

earing any underwear. "Excuse me," I said, having a hard time look

linded by that bulge in his crotch, "but don't I know you?" "Maybe

ind of t   bout

with Ray   God,

t loser?   in?" h

aid. "Lik   stron

ce body   e on C

lly, he l   I eve

u up to t   any id

istaking   e sam

a, I coul   ery lo

ood raci   ne sw

ing with   e in st

we go   behin

ill see   in pu

ed?" he   vent to

rivacy.   grabb

-hard. I

k, traci   t, so f

ed it, ha

with my   bing

bbing, I   n coch

he sound of unzipping filled the small space. I don't know who's h

, but before I knew it, I had his rod in my hand, and mine was in hi

nt to do?" he asked, his tone challenging. I knew exactly, and sank